A GRISLY MURDER
HOMICIDE DETECTIV
INTO HIS MOST CHALLENGING CASE YET,
AND VERY QUICKLY IT'S GOING TO GET
VERY PERSONAL...

M000220457

Praise for James L. Thane's New Novel SOUTH OF THE DEUCE

"An expertly-plotted page turner that kept me on tenterhooks until the pulse-pounding finale, *South of the Deuce* sizzles like an Arizona summer—without sacrificing the chills—as Phoenix homicide cop Sean Richardson hunts down a sadistic killer.... James L. Thane has a masterful hand with a thriller." – *Owen Laukkanen, author of Deception Cove*

"Thane reads like Michael Connelly and his Phoenix is detailed."—*Paul French, CrimeReads*

Praise for the Novels of James L. Thane

"*Crossroads* is a deep dive into the kind of deadly conflict that a vast and beautiful landscape can produce. There's treachery in Thane's Big Sky country, and battle-worn lawyer Dave Matthews is determined to peel back the layers to reveal the always-elusive truth. An engrossing read!"— *Gerry Boyle, author of Strawman and the Jack McMorrow mysteries.*

i

SOUTH OF THE DEUCE

James L. Thane

Moonshine Cove Publishing, LLC
Abbeville, South Carolina U.S.A.
First Moonshine Cove edition November 2020

ISBN: 978-1-945181-849
Library of Congress PCN: 2020907854
© Copyright 2020 by James L. Thane

Cover photograph by the author; cover and interior design by Moonshine Cove staff

James L. Thane was born and raised in western Montana. He has worked as a janitor, a dry cleaner, an auto parts salesman, a sawyer, an ambulance driver, and a college professor. Always an avid reader, Thane was introduced to the world of crime fiction at a tender age by his father and mother who were fans of Erle Stanley Gardner and Agatha Christie, respectively. He began his own writing career by contributing articles on intramural basketball games to his high school newspaper. He is the author of

 three earlier novels featuring Phoenix homicide detective Sean Richardson: No Place to Die, Until Death, and Fatal Blow. He has also written a stand-alone mystery novel, Crossroads, which is set in the Flathead Valley of northwestern Montana. Jim is active on Goodreads, and you may also find him on Facebook, Twitter and at www.jameslthane.com. He divides his time between Scottsdale, Arizona and Lakeside, Montana.

www.jameslthane.com

Other Works

The Sean Richardson Series

No Place to Die

Until Death

Fatal Blow

South of the Deuce

The Flathead Valley Series

Crossroads

Nonfiction

A Governor's Wife on the Mining Frontier

Again, for Victoria

SOUTH OF THE DEUCE

Part One

1

Stripped naked, Allie Martin weighed not quite a hundred pounds, and the man who thought of himself as Chris Nelson lifted her limp body from the tub almost effortlessly. He turned and gently laid the body on a large piece of heavy-duty plastic sheeting, which the folks at Home Depot described as "Husky." Nelson had no idea how the marketing geniuses might have come up with that label, but whatever the case, the stuff was certainly sufficient for the task at hand.

He positioned Allie face down on top of the handbag that he'd centered on the plastic sheet. Then he laid the edges of the sheeting over her body lengthwise and taped them off. Moving from her head to her toes, he neatly folded the two ends of the package and sealed them as well. Then he picked up the body, slid it face up into the back of his van, and quietly closed the doors.

Nelson hated to say goodbye this quickly. Allie had proved to be an excellent playmate, and the thrill of finally running her to ground had been exquisite. Clearly, she had not enjoyed their time together nearly as much as he, but through no fault of her own, a destiny that had been forged years before she was even born had placed her in his path. She might have had a life; she might have had hopes and dreams that were yet unfulfilled, but in the larger scheme of things, all of that meant nothing. The only thing that mattered was the mission, and although she would never understand why, Allie Martin was the most critical key to its success. However sad her fate, it was simply inevitable.

Nelson made one last trip up the stairs to ensure that his equipment was put away and that everything else was in order. As he did, the digital clock on the table next to the bed flipped over to two-forty-seven a.m. He sighed heavily at the thought of how little sleep he was going to get before his own bedside clock roused him into the new morning. He knew, though, that he was still so jacked from the events of the long evening that he'd probably never get to sleep tonight anyhow. Tomorrow would be a very long day.

Looking at the bed, he decided that it would probably be a good idea to spring for a new set of sheets, and he made a mental note to swing by Bed Bath & Beyond sometime in the next couple of days. Otherwise satisfied, he snapped off the lights in the loft and made his way back down to the garage. Standing by the door, he listened carefully in the unlikely event that anyone would be passing by at this hour of the morning. Hearing nothing out of the ordinary, he hit the light switch, plunging the garage into darkness. Then he slowly rolled back the large garage door, which moved silently on its well-lubricated track.

Just before three o'clock on a morning in early June, the temperature in Phoenix was still in the low eighties. It had rained briefly around midnight and the air was heavy with humidity and with the pungent smell created when the rain mixed with the oils on the Creosote bushes that populated so much of the area. The clouds had now passed out of the Valley and a half moon hung in the early morning sky, weakly illuminating the world outside of the garage. Somewhere down the street a dog barked twice, but otherwise the night was eerily quiet.

The door hit the bumper at the end of the track and shuddered briefly. Moving quickly with only the moonlight to guide him, Nelson got into the van, cranked the engine, and slowly backed out of the garage. Once clear, he threw the transmission into park, got out, and closed and locked the garage door behind him. Returning to the van and watching carefully, he backed out into the street and headed west.

Not surprisingly, traffic was relatively light and, driving exactly at the speed limit, it took him only about ten minutes to get from the garage to the intersection of Lincoln and First Street downtown, just south of the Talking Stick Resort Arena where the Suns had flailed their way through another losing season before missing the NBA playoffs yet again. He turned South on First and drove another few blocks through the darkened neighborhood, which was a mixture of warehouses, older homes, and weedy vacant lots.

This was the second-trickiest part of the whole endeavor, and as he drove along First Street, Nelson watched closely for any sign of life. Faint light appeared around the edges of closed blinds in the windows of a couple of homes, but otherwise the houses along the street were dark and quiet, the residents seemingly still hunkered down until morning. He saw no one walking along the sidewalks, and his was the only vehicle moving in either direction along the street. At the intersection of First Street and East Hadley, Nelson hung a left and drove another block to the corner of Hadley and Second Street. Then he braked to a stop at the northeast corner of Central Park and cut the headlights.

This was far from the best part of town, and thus the park was protected by a high chain link fence. All the gates were secured with chains and padlocks. After one last look to ensure that he was alone, Nelson jumped out of the van, leaving the door cracked open and the engine idling. From behind the seat, he grabbed a set of heavy-duty bolt cutters, then ran over to the fence and snipped the chain on the gate closest to the corner. Nelson pulled the gate open and jogged back to the van. At the back of the vehicle, he opened the double doors, set the bolt cutters inside, and gathered Allie Martin into his arms for one last time. His heart pounding, he stepped through the gate, went down on one knee, and laid the package containing the body face up on the grass just inside the fence.

From somewhere on the other side of the park, a couple of cactus wrens chattered back and forth. Nelson turned toward the sound for a moment and then turned back. Still crouching near the body, he briefly touched a finger to Allie's lips through the plastic sheet. Then he trotted back to the van, closed the rear doors, and jumped into the driver's seat. Less than a minute and a half after pulling to the side of the street, Nelson was rolling once again, and Allie Martin had already disappeared from his rearview mirrors.

2

I was lost in a deep, dreamless sleep when the buzzer went off a little after six on Tuesday morning. I batted at the damned alarm clock a couple of times before realizing that it was my phone and not the clock that was so rudely intruding into my morning. When I finally managed to connect to the call, a voice at the other end complained, "Jesus Christ, Richardson, what took you so long to pick up? You think I've got all day here?"

"Good morning to you too, Sergeant. What can I do for you?"

"You can get your lazy ass out of bed and on the job. We've got a woman lying dead in Central Park. She's wrapped up in a plastic sheet like a mummy or some damned thing, and your team is next up. I'm calling McClinton now. Assuming it doesn't take me another half an hour to wake *her* up, she should be joining you shortly. Pierce and Chickris will be along as well."

With that he disconnected, presumably to call out my partner. I sat up in bed and took a long look at the woman who was lying next to me, naked and still dead to the world. Thirty seconds later, her phone began ringing and she finally stirred back to life. Shaking my head at the thought of a missed opportunity, I crawled out of bed and quickly shaved, showered, and dressed. Twenty minutes after getting the call, I grabbed a banana on the way out the door and headed downtown.

***

The scene was a small park that took up a single city block in one of the oldest sections of town. Most of the activity seemed to be taking place in the northeastern corner of the park, but patrolmen had strung crime scene tape around the entire block and had closed off the city streets immediately adjacent to it. Several squads were parked haphazardly around the park, their mars lights flashing against the early morning light. Three members of the Crime Scene Response Unit were already at work, processing the scene.

I reached the point where Second Street was closed to traffic and a patrolman moved the barricade long enough for me to pull my department-issued Impala through. I joined the other city vehicles that were now lined up along the street and killed the engine. Scooping up my cell phone, I got out of the car and stood for a moment, bracing myself and surveying the larger scene. Then I flipped open my detective's shield, slipped it over the pocket of my suit coat, and headed toward the park.

It had rained overnight, raising the humidity considerably. Under a bright, sunny sky, the temperature was already in the low nineties, and clearly, we were in for another very uncomfortable day. A patrolman was standing at the perimeter, maintaining the log, and he was already sweating visibly in his dark uniform. I signed in and asked him to bring me up to speed. Wiping his brow with the back of his hand, he nodded in the direction of the activity and said, "At five thirty-five this morning, an unidentified male called 9-1-1, saying that there was a girl's body lying in the park wrapped up in a plastic bag.

"I responded to the call, confirmed that there was a body lying there, called for backup, and then began securing the area. The other squads got here over the space of fifteen minutes or so and the crime scene guys got here about twenty minutes ahead of you. Except for the techs, no one else has gone anywhere near the body, at least not since I've been here. Fortunately, it's still early enough, especially in this part of town, that hardly anybody's up and about yet."

I nodded my understanding and walked over to greet Gary Barnett, the leader of the CSRU team. Now in his early forties, he was still rail thin and looked like he could be blown away by the first stiff breeze to come along. Working hard on the gum that substituted for his Marlboros when he was on the job, he wished me a good morning and walked me inside the fence that protected the park. Lying on the grass, positioned about five feet inside the fence, was the body of a young woman which had been neatly wrapped in a large piece of thick plastic sheeting.

Hunching down to get a closer look, I could see that she was, or had been, an attractive young blond, about five feet, one or two inches tall and weighing perhaps a hundred pounds, with wavy, shoulder-length hair. She'd been wrapped naked with her arms at her sides. Her dark blue eyes were open, staring blankly through the plastic, oblivious to me and, fortunately, to all the other final indignities that would now be visited upon her. Her wrists and ankles were badly bruised, suggesting that before her death she'd been very tightly restrained. The rawest of the abrasions, and doubtless the most recent, was the one around her neck where she had finally been strangled to death. Positioned carefully over her pubic area was what appeared to be an expensive handbag bearing the monogram of Louis Vitton.

I'd come into the department in my early twenties, and fourteen years on the force, including seven as a detective in the Homicide Unit, still had not inured me to scenes like this. The violence that some human beings were capable of inflicting on others continued to stun me, especially when the victim was as young and apparently vulnerable as this one. She'd been someone's daughter, maybe someone's sister, someone's wife or lover, perhaps even someone's mother. She'd been savagely ripped away from all those relationships and denied all the prospects that life might have held for her. And, as inadequate a response as it certainly was, all I could do was silently promise that I'd do everything in my power to bring down the son of a bitch who had deprived her of all that.

Shaking my head, I rose to my feet and turned to see my partner, Maggie McClinton, signing into the log. I noticed that she was wearing the same white skirt that she'd had on yesterday, although this morning she'd found a dark blue shirt to go with it which nicely complimented her toffee colored skin.

Her thick dark hair was cut in a relatively short style that suited her well and which was easy to brush into place on mornings like this when she was forced to race out of the house first thing. She'd taken time enough to apply the minimal makeup that she usually wore, and a pair of sunglasses shielded her bright hazel eyes against the early morning sun. I moved over to meet her as she walked through the tape and said, "Good morning, Detective McClinton. Nice of you to join us."

She shot me a look and said, "Don't even start with me this morning, Richardson. I got way too little sleep last night."

My turn to shoot her a look, but she ignored it and said, "So what do we have?"

I caught her up to date and we walked over to look at the body together. After taking a close look at the victim for herself, she rose to her feet and said, "I take it we have no idea who she might have been?"

"None," I said. "I'm hoping that there might be some ID in the purse, but we're all on hold until the M.E. gets here and officially pronounces her."

Maggie turned back to look at the scene in the street behind us. "And where in the hell do you suppose she might be?"

"No idea, but I'm sure she'll show up soon."

As the words left my mouth, I saw a tan Toyota 4Runner pulling through the barricade. The SUV was tricked out with an off-road package and looked like it had spent about the last six months being driven hard through the desert without ever seeing the inside of a car wash. It came to an abrupt stop and a couple of seconds later, Sara Morgan, the county M.E., stepped out of the driver's side, grabbed her bag from the back seat and hurried in our direction.

At thirty-four, she'd had the job for the last year. A tall attractive brunette, she was a huge improvement, both professionally and aesthetically, over the guy who'd held the job before her. Ignoring me, she walked up to Maggie and said, "Sorry I'm late to the party."

"No problem; I just got here myself," Maggie replied, her tone suggesting that nothing of any importance could have possibly taken place before her arrival.

Once inside the fence, Sara hunched down and examined the body through the plastic sheeting, slowly shaking her head. Then she pulled on a pair of latex gloves and used a small knife to slit open the plastic wrapping at the victim's throat. She reached through the opening, touched her index and middle fingers to the carotid artery, and officially pronounced the result that had been evident all along.

I looked over to Gary Barnett and said, "Is it okay with you if we cut another opening and remove the purse rather than waiting for Sara to do it in the morgue? It would be nice to have a head start on a possible identification."

"No problem. We'll want to take the purse, of course, but it won't hurt to take a look now."

I turned to Sara. "Will you do the honors, Doc, as long as you have your instrument handy?"

She nodded and moved down to the victim's abdomen. Looking through the plastic, she said, "For what it's worth, this looks like a fairly classic bag. I don't think Vitton has made this particular purse for quite a while now."

"Well, if anyone would know…" Maggie said, smiling.

"Right," the doctor replied. Using the knife again, she cut three lines in the plastic around the purse, creating a flap. Then she reached her gloved hand through the flap, removed the purse, and handed it in my direction. I gloved up, took the bag from Sara, and carefully opened it. At first glance, it appeared to be completely empty.

I looked from Sara to Maggie and they both shook their heads. Then I noticed a small zippered compartment inside the bag, and inside the compartment was a driver's license. I removed the license and handed the bag to Gary who stepped away to log it in as evidence. Then I showed the license to Maggie and Sara. It had been issued by the state of Arizona and belonged to a woman named Ellen Friedman.

The photo on the license showed the face of an attractive, dark haired woman who, if the license could be believed, was forty-two years old at the time it was issued. The license noted that Friedman was five feet seven inches tall and weighed a hundred and twenty-seven pounds.

And it had expired on September 17, 1977.

3.

Maggie was the first to react. Looking over my shoulder at the license, she said, "What the fuck? How in the hell does Ellen Friedman's DL wind up in a purse on this girl's body?"

Still staring at the license in disbelief myself, I said, "I haven't the foggiest idea, Maggie, but the thing sure looks genuine to me."

I turned to Sara. "You said you thought you recognized that purse as a classic. How old do you suppose it might be?"

She shook her head. "Assuming that it's not a very good fake, pretty old; I've never seen one exactly like it."

"Could it possibly be from the 1970s?"

"I suppose, but I don't understand. Who's Ellen Friedman?"

"She was the first victim in what would become one of the most famous cold cases in Phoenix history. In 1975, she was kidnapped, sexually assaulted over a period of several days and then dumped right here in this park. During the next year and a half, three other women were abducted, murdered, and then left in this general neighborhood. It seemed certain that the same killer was responsible for all four crimes, but after the fourth victim, he stopped—at least he stopped killing women in Phoenix—and he was never identified or captured. Even after all this time, every recruit coming through the academy still hears the story."

Maggie handed me an evidence bag. I dropped the license into the bag, then sealed, signed, and dated it. Looking up, I saw the other two members of our unit, Greg Chickris and Elaine Pierce, walking over to join us. Turning to Maggie and Sara, I whispered, "Not a word about this ID, not even to Pierce and Chickris. This goes no farther than the three of us until I have a chance to brief the Sergeant."

The two women nodded their agreement and I slipped the license into my jacket pocket just as Pierce and Chickris reached us. They took a quick look at the body, then Elaine turned to me and said, "Any idea who she is?"

"None, unfortunately."

Looking to Sara, I said, "How long before you can get her on the table and at least get us some fingerprints?"

Nodding toward the street, she said, "The bus is here and unless you guys need to have us wait, we'll load her up and get her over to the morgue right now. Once we're there, I'll open the package, get a set of prints, and send them to you immediately."

I used my phone to take a picture of the victim's face. Even through the plastic sheet, the result was good enough to use for comparisons with the photos in Missing Persons Reports. I gathered Maggie, Elaine and Greg together and said, "The 9-1-1 call came in just after five thirty from an anonymous male. We need to do a canvass of the neighborhood to see if anyone heard or saw anything unusual overnight.

"Elaine and Greg, why don't you guys grab a few of these patrolmen and organize the canvas. Check with Dispatch and see if they were able to trace the number of the caller. Maggie and I will head back to 620 and brief the Sergeant. Then we'll start going through the MISPERS reports looking for someone who might match up with the victim."

***

As I headed back to my car, I saw that a Channel 2 news van had pulled up just outside the barricade blocking Second Street. Reporter Ellie Davis and a cameraman were standing by the barrier and she waved at me when I looked in their direction. Before long, this would almost certainly be the biggest news story in the city, but for the moment at least, for the sake of the investigation, I wanted it contained as much as possible.

I stepped over to the barrier and Ellie said, "Good morning, Sean. What's the scoop?"

The cameraman made ready to record the conversation, but I waved him off and said, "No public comment for the moment, Ellie, although Media Relations will probably have something later. Off the record for now, as a source close to the investigation, I can tell you that we have the body of a young woman who has been murdered, probably elsewhere, and then left in the park. We have no idea who she is.

"The Medical Examiner is just now removing the body, and other officers are about to begin a canvass of the area to see what, if anything, they can learn. I'm going back to Headquarters and look through missing persons reports to see if I can make an ID, and now you know virtually as much as I do about the situation."

"Thanks, Sean. Okay if I call you later for a follow up?"

"You can call me, Ellie, but I don't know when or if I might have anything to tell you."

"Fair enough. Talk to you later."

4.

While Pierce and Chickris began organizing the canvass, Maggie and I extracted our cars from the gridlock that had formed around the park and drove over to the Police Headquarters building, which was located at 620 West Washington Street, only a couple of blocks away from the site where, in 1873, my great-great grandfather had established one of the first retail stores in the Salt River Valley.

At the time, the Phoenix population had consisted of about five hundred hardy people who were somehow surviving without air conditioning in and around a townsite of three hundred and twenty acres, and my great-great grandfather had begun the foundation of the family fortune by selling supplies to the early settlers and to the U.S. Army at nearby Fort McDowell. I was fairly confident that, as an enterprising businessman, he would have welcomed the opportunity to serve the needs of the much larger customer base, but I often wondered what he would have thought of the rest of the changes that had so transformed the valley in the intervening years.

We climbed the stairs to the Homicide Unit on the third floor, and I made a brief stop in my office. Then we walked on down to the office of our sergeant, Mike Callahan, who'd been promoted into the position five months earlier after ten years as a homicide detective himself. Everyone in the division had been extremely happy about the prospect of working with him, rather than someone who might have come in from the outside. He knew the job; he knew the people, and he'd turned out to be an excellent boss. He looked up from the report he was reading and waved us into chairs in front of his desk. Gesturing in my direction with his reading glasses he said, "So, what've we got?"

"A mystery of the first magnitude, I'm afraid. On the surface, we've got a young, unidentified woman who was almost certainly killed somewhere else, then wrapped up in plastic sheeting and left in Central Park."

"And below the surface?"

"Sealed inside the plastic along with the body was a Louis Vitton purse which the M.E. suggests could date from the 1970s. This was inside the purse."

I handed him the evidence bag containing the driver's license and watched the shock register on his face. "What the Fuck?"

"Exactly our reaction," Maggie said.

"It gets worse," I added. "I stopped by my office on the way down the hall and checked the computer. Today is the anniversary. Ellen Friedman's body was discovered on exactly the same spot in Central Park forty-three years ago this morning."

He took a long minute assimilating the information then said, "You're not suggesting that some psycho killed Friedman and the other women forty years ago and then disappeared; that he held on to Friedman's purse and DL for all that time, and then came back to kill someone else now?"

"Anything's possible, I suppose, although it seems a stretch. Even assuming that the guy was only in his early twenties when he did Friedman, he'd be at least in his sixties by now. And where in the hell would he have been all this time?"

"But if it's not the same guy," Maggie said, "How does a new killer get hold of Friedman's purse and ID? And why would he decide to kill another woman and dump her body in the exact same place on the anniversary of the Friedman case?"

The sergeant and I both shook our heads and he handed the DL back to me. "Who else knows about this?"

"Only the three of us and the M.E. She identified the handbag as a classic and was looking over my shoulder when I took the DL out. She knows not to say anything about it to anyone. I thought it best to tell you first; we didn't even tell Elaine and Greg."

"OK," he said, "the first thing we need to do is make sure that damned license is genuine. While I brief the lieutenant, you get over to the lab and hand-deliver it to a tech who can get on it right now. Emphasize that he or she reports back to you and says absolutely nothing to anyone else. Then get to work on getting an ID on the victim and keep me posted the second you come up with anything. For the moment at least, the Friedman connection stays with us; the second the media get ahold of this we'll have a fuckin' circus around here."

**

I walked across the street to the crime lab and left the license with one of the document techs, emphasizing the sergeant's instructions. Then, back in my office, Maggie and I began checking missing persons reports. Barely five minutes into the search, Maggie said, "I think I've got her." Reading from the screen on her laptop, she said, "Allison Martin, twenty-nine, blonde/blue, five-one, ninety-seven pounds. Divorced, lives alone, reported missing Saturday by her mother, Kathy Martin."

"The description sounds right," I said.

I pulled up the picture I'd taken with my phone and held it next to the monitor, erasing any doubt. Checking the form for the mother's contact information, I made a note of the address and then printed out a copy of the report she'd filed. Ten minutes later, we were on the road.

**

Greater Phoenix is a huge metropolitan area that includes a couple dozen smaller cities and towns in addition to Phoenix itself. Maggie and I were headed to Scottsdale, which adjoins Phoenix on the east. The community of about two hundred and twenty-five thousand people is the wealthiest in the metro area, hosting the most expensive homes and the most exclusive golf clubs as well as the toniest shops, resorts, and restaurants.

People living in the Valley's other cities occasionally refer to the town as "Snottsdale," capturing the contempt that some feel for the town's residents and their perceived values. But I've found that large numbers of people living in Scottsdale don't fit the stereotype, and

I've also encountered enough vain, self-centered, and generally unpleasant people in other parts of the Valley to believe that they shouldn't be so quick to pass judgment on others.

Fortunately, traffic was moving at a smooth pace, and twenty-five minutes after leaving the headquarters building, we pulled through the gates of a luxury condominium development off 76th Street in north Scottsdale. The complex had been designed using what I guessed was a Tuscan theme with lots of stonework and tiled roofs. The streets were wide and inviting and the developer had left a surprising amount of open space populated with ponds and water features. All in all, it looked like it would be a very pleasant—and no doubt expensive—place to live. I found Martin's building with no trouble and we parked in a spot reserved for guests opposite the front door.

Maggie and I climbed the stairs to Martin's second-floor unit, and I paused for a moment in front of the door. This was, without question, the hardest part of the job, and I knew that no one ever got used to it. Certainly, I never would. I looked to Maggie, who nodded that she was ready, then I took a deep breath and rang the bell.

Less than a minute passed before the door was opened by a striking woman whose hands suggested that she was somewhere in her late fifties or early sixties. Otherwise, I would have guessed her to be in her early fifties at the outside. Her dark hair was expertly cut; the tee shirt and shorts she was wearing showed a shapely and athletic figure, and her face suggested that she'd either been very blessed genetically or, in the alternative, that she'd received the attention of one of Scottsdale's many excellent plastic surgeons.

"Ms. Martin?" I asked. "I'm Detective Sean Richardson of the Phoenix P.D. This is Detective Maggie McClinton."

Martin took a quick glance at our IDs and shields, then said, "Is this about Allie?"

"Yes, Ma'am, it is," Maggie said. "May we come in?"

Martin stepped away from the door and gestured us into the small entryway. We followed her into a tastefully furnished living room that looked out over a grassy common area, and Martin settled lightly into a leather club chair. Maggie and I took seats on the sofa opposite the chair. In a halting voice, Martin said, "Two detectives coming here in person and unannounced—this is bad news, isn't it?"

"Yes, Ma'am," I replied, "I'm very sorry, but I'm afraid it is."

Before I could say anything more, Martin crumpled into herself and began shaking her head and weeping softly. I got up, pressed my handkerchief into her hands and said, "We're very sorry, Ms. Martin."

I returned to the couch and Maggie and I sat quietly for a few minutes as Martin worked through the initial stages of her grief. Finally, she wiped her eyes and looked up at me. "Tell me," she said in a quiet voice.

"I'm afraid that there's not much to tell yet, Ma'am," I replied. "Early this morning, officers discovered the body of a young woman who had been left in Central Park in downtown Phoenix. The woman's identification was not left with her, but in checking the reports of missing persons, we tentatively identified the woman as your daughter."

"How did she die?"

"We don't know for certain yet, Ms. Martin, but it appears that she was strangled to death."

Suddenly, Martin looked up. Wide-eyed, she turned to me and said, "Where did you say she was found?"

"In Central Park. It's just south of the Talking Stick Arena downtown."

"No, no," she said, shaking her head violently and crying again with a renewed urgency. "This can't be."

Maggie stepped over, crouched down, and touched her arm to Martin's. "What is it, Ma'am?"

Martin struggled to bring herself back under control. Finally, she looked up to Maggie and said, "Forty-three years ago, my mother— Allie's grandmother—was found murdered in Central Park."

5.

I stared at Kathy Martin, dumbfounded. "Ms. Martin, you're telling us that Ellen Friedman was your mother?"

"Yes. She was murdered when I was twenty-one. I was away at college at the time. But how did you know her name?"

I looked to Maggie, then turned back to Martin. "I'm very sorry, Ms. Martin, and I know that this is going to be an additional shock, but a vintage Louis Vitton handbag was found with your daughter's body this morning, and your mother's driver's license was in the bag."

The woman was clearly as stunned as I had been by the revelation. She stared at me for a long moment as if she couldn't believe what I'd said. Finally, she sobbed, "How in the name of God could that be possible?"

"We don't have any idea, Ma'am," Maggie said. "Our technicians will be checking the license to make sure that it's legitimate—that someone didn't fake it for some purpose—but we're fairly certain that it is your mother's license. Do you remember; did your mother own a Vitton bag?"

"Yes, at least one. She had a collection of expensive handbags. I still have a couple that belonged to her, but if I ever knew, I don't remember which bag she might have been carrying when she was abducted."

She hesitated for a moment, apparently still trying to process the information, then said through her tears, "What can this possibly mean?"

"We don't know, Ms. Martin," I replied. "To be completely honest, we're just as baffled as you are. Your mother's murder investigation is still discussed in the Police Academy training courses and so Detective McClinton and I were aware of her name. And of course, we were shocked to discover her license this morning

28

and then to further learn that today was the anniversary of the day your mother's body was found. Now to discover that the victim we found this morning in that exact same spot was Ellen Friedman's granddaughter… Honestly, Ma'am we don't know what to think, but clearly the two crimes are linked in some way.

"Obviously, we'll be trying to determine what that connection might be but, for the moment, do you know if your daughter was having problems with anyone who might have wanted to harm her?

"No, no one. Allie was a very gentle soul; she had no enemies at all."

"Was she involved with anyone?"

Martin shook her head. "No. She was divorced eight months ago. Her heart was broken, and she was determined not to begin dating again for a good long time."

Maggie opened her notebook. "What's the ex-husband's name?"

"Dan Marlowe. Allie went back to using her maiden name after the divorce."

"How long were they married?"

"A little over three years."

"Any problems there, do you think?"

"No. I hate the bastard for leaving Allie, but the divorce was his idea. He became infatuated with someone else and wanted out. The ink was barely dry on the divorce decree when he married the bimbo. They then moved to Portland and Allie hadn't had any contact with him since, at least as far as I know."

"And no problems with anyone else that you know of?"

"No."

"Where did Allie work?" I asked.

"She was a travel agent. She worked in an office downtown."

I made a note of the agency's name and the name of Allie Martin's boss. "Where did Allison live, Ms. Martin?"

"She and her husband had a condo in north Phoenix. She got it in the divorce and was still living there."

"And you've been there since you reported her missing?"

"Yes. She wasn't scheduled to work on Saturday, and we had plans to go to the farmers' market. I went to pick her up at around ten o'clock, but she didn't answer her door. I let myself in, but she wasn't there. I checked and found her car in the garage, and so I assumed that she might have just run to the mailbox or something. I waited about fifteen minutes and when she hadn't returned, I called her cell. But all I got was her voicemail. I left a message asking her to call and then waited in the condo, assuming that she'd call me right back. But she never did."

With that, she began sobbing again. After a minute or so, she blew her nose and said, "I'm sorry, but I just can't manage this. Allie was my only child..."

"Please don't apologize," Maggie said. We can't begin to imagine how difficult this must be, especially under the circumstances."

I gave her another moment, then said, "I gather that when you were in the condo, nothing looked disturbed?"

"No."

"You noticed nothing missing or out of place?"

"No. I looked on the counter to see if she'd left me a note, but she hadn't. Then I walked through the condo and everything seemed in perfect order. But that's what I would have expected; Allie is ...was compulsively neat."

"Could you tell, had she slept in her bed Friday night?"

"No. The bed was neatly made, but I have no way of knowing whether that was from Friday morning or Saturday."

"And you talked to the people at her office, of course?"

"Yes. Her boss told me that Allie had worked until five o'clock on Friday afternoon and that they left the office together. She said that Allie was planning to have dinner and drinks with a couple of her girlfriends. I called one of the women and she said that they had dinner at the Greene House in Kierland Commons and that they then had drinks in the lounge at Eddie V's in the Quarter. She told me that they finished up a little after ten and that Allie said she was going straight home. I've talked to several of Allie's other friends and that was the last any of them saw or heard from her. Several of them told me that they'd tried to call or text her but that they didn't get any response."

"So, it would appear that Allie made it safely home sometime after ten, that she parked in her garage and was then abducted sometime during the twelve hours between then and the time she was to meet you on Saturday morning."

Martin nodded, and I said, "OK. Ms. Martin. Thank you for your help. I'm sure that we'll have other questions for you later, but if you can't think of anything else that might bear on the matter, we'll leave you for now. Would you like us to call anyone to come and be with you?"

"No, thank you. I think I'd really rather be alone for now." Looking up, she said, "What will happen next?"

"Sometime this afternoon, we'll need you to come in and make a formal identification of the body. There will be an autopsy and at some point after that, your daughter's body will be released to you and you can make the funeral arrangements. In the meantime, we'll be pressing forward with the investigation. But please be assured that we will do everything in our power to find the person who did this, and again, we're very sorry for your loss."

6.

At noon, the small bar just off Second Street was crowded with people who had emptied out of shops and offices downtown in search of a lunch that might perhaps be accompanied by a drink or two. After sitting in his own office for much of the morning, being totally unproductive, Chris Nelson fought the midday traffic and drove downtown specifically for the sake of eating here and even more specifically for the purpose of scoping out the young redheaded barmaid who worked the lunch shift on Tuesdays.

Forty years ago, the block on which the bar was located had been among the last remaining portions of the fabled Deuce, Phoenix's long-time skid row district, which ran along Second Street from Van Buren south to the railroad tracks and extended a block or two east and west of Second along the way.

For much of the city's history, its vice had been centered here. Intermixed among the more legitimate business establishments were whorehouses, bars, gambling dens, pawn shops and flop houses, along with the population that these institutions served and employed. Less than a block away from the spot where Nelson was now enjoying a burger and a beer for lunch, was the site of the La Amapola Bar where, early in 1976, Ernesto Miranda—he of the famous Supreme Court decision—had been knifed to death, apparently without the courtesy of any warning, Miranda or otherwise.

Two and a half months before Miranda's unfortunate demise, a young waitress from the La Amapola named Laura Garcia had been abducted, apparently as she was leaving work. Four days later, her naked body was found in a vacant lot, a couple blocks south of the Deuce. Garcia had been the second victim of the killer who was stalking the city back then, and the man who had raped and killed her was never identified or brought to justice.

In the four decades since the murder of Laura Garcia, the several city blocks that constituted the Deuce had all been razed in the name of urban renewal. The bars, SRO hotels and other establishments that had dotted the area back then had been bulldozed and replaced by Symphony Hall, a theater for the performing arts, a Hyatt Regency hotel, and the Talking Stick Resort Arena. In and around them were offices, restaurants, and retail establishments, including the bar where Nelson was currently lunching.

The redhead who'd captured Nelson's attention was a vivacious and very attractive twenty-four-year-old woman named Corrine Ray. Ray lived with a female roommate a little more than a mile north of the bar in an older apartment building that had recently been rehabbed and which was popular with the young students, hipsters and others who were now flocking into downtown Phoenix.

By paying close attention to the conversations that swirled around him, Nelson had learned that the young woman was working to pay her own way through college. Given her work schedule and her budget, she could only afford to take two or three classes a semester, but she'd carefully mapped out a six-year plan that she hoped would lead to a nursing degree. He'd heard Ray tell another customer that her long-term goal was to work as an eldercare nurse, and that she'd been inspired to do so by a nurse who had attended to her grandmother in the latter stages of her grandmother's life.

Counting today, Nelson had only ever seen the young woman up close four times and had been very careful never to engage her in conversation beyond the minimum necessary to order his food and drinks. He always paid cash and, while in the bar, dressed and comported himself in a manner so as not to stand out in any way at all. Having settled his aim on the young woman, it was vitally important that no one ever remember seeing him anywhere near the place.

Looking over the lunchtime crowd, he noted that, as the city fathers and mothers might have hoped, the area along Second Street now attracted a much more upscale clientele than it had forty years ago. But sitting at the bar, watching Corrine Ray banter with the other customers while he ran Laura Garcia's rosary through his fingers, Chris Nelson smiled and thought to himself that in a great many respects, the world really hadn't changed that much at all.

7.

Maggie and I left Kathy Martin to her grief and returned to the office. While Maggie filled out the paperwork necessary to secure the warrants for the search of Allie Martin's home and automobile, I called the detective bureau in the Portland P.D. and explained our situation. They agreed to send someone out to interview Dan Marlowe and determine his whereabouts over the past weekend. Kathy Martin had indicated that there were no problems between our victim and her ex, but I needed to be sure that he couldn't have been in Phoenix when his ex-wife had been abducted.

An hour later, Maggie and I picked up the warrants and drove over to the victim's condo, which was in a gated complex in northeast Phoenix. The community was maybe ten or fifteen years old and consisted of perhaps twenty two-story buildings. While it was not nearly as upscale as the complex in which Allie's mother lived, the buildings and the grounds were of an interesting modern design and appeared to be very well maintained.

Martin's unit was on the second floor and we decided to work our way through the unit and then move on to the garage. The front door opened directly into the living room with the dining area and kitchen to the left of the living room. A hallway behind the kitchen led to two bedrooms and two baths. Most of the furniture looked like it had come from a middle of the line chain store in which a customer could buy a room full of pieces that were designed to be sold as a set, the sort of "starter" furniture that a young couple might buy when they were first setting up housekeeping together. As Kathy Martin had suggested, everything in her daughter's home seemed in perfect order, and we saw nothing that suggested that anything untoward might have befallen her there.

The smaller bedroom had been set up as a den/office with a couch and a small desk. On the desk was an Apple MacBook, which we gathered up so that the techs could go through it, but we found no address book and no phone. Maggie found several purses in the master closet, but they were all empty, and the purse that the victim might have been carrying the night she was abducted was nowhere to be found.

We locked up the unit and moved down the stairs to the door that led into the small, single-car garage. Inside was a red Mini-Cooper that appeared to have been freshly washed. A few boxes were stacked on a row of shelves at the front of the garage but, as had been the case upstairs, everything appeared to be in good order. We went through the car but saw nothing to suggest that anything out of order might have happened in it. Unhappily, neither the victim's phone nor her purse was in the car either.

The garage was stiflingly hot and once finished, Maggie and I locked the door behind us and retreated to the shade of a nearby Palo Verde tree. Maggie looked to me and said, "Ideas?"

"It looks to me like she must have been grabbed just as she got home Friday night. It's possible that someone got into her car, but if so, why would they force her to drive here and park in her own garage? More likely the guy was waiting for her here.

"Judging by the fixtures I'm seeing, it doesn't look like there would be very much light around here at night. I'm guessing that the guy was hiding in the shadows and grabbed her when she came out the garage door and started up the steps."

"Yeah, that sounds plausible to me. The guest parking area is only a few feet away. If the guy has a vehicle waiting there, it would be pretty simple to grab her as she's going up the stairs, incapacitate her in some way, dump her in the vehicle and drive off. Of course, he'd have to get lucky and hope that no one else was out and about at the moment Martin got home, but I'll bet there's not a lot of activity around here at that time of night."

"Probably not," I agreed. "Let's go knock on some doors."

***

We spent the rest of the afternoon interviewing neighbors in Martin's building and in the surrounding buildings that had a view of the front of Martin's. By six o'clock, we'd managed to talk to people in about half of the units that we'd targeted, but no one had noticed anything out of the ordinary on the night that Martin had been abducted. None of them had seen any strangers lurking about suspiciously, and when we asked about unfamiliar vehicles, most people just shrugged and observed that there were always several unfamiliar cars, trucks and SUVs in the parking places allotted to visitors. But no one had seen any vehicle that seemed to stand out in any particular way.

Maggie and I had driven to the complex separately, not knowing where the case might take us from there. Having completed our initial pass at the units nearest Martin's, we agreed that I'd go back to the office and begin completing the paperwork that would have to be done before the end of the day. Maggie would stay and try to talk to residents in other units who didn't have a direct view of Martin's building but who might have been out for a walk or something on Friday night and might possibly have seen something off norm. It was a pretty thin reed to hang our hopes on, but at the moment, it was all we had.

Back at the headquarters building, I secured Allie Martin's laptop in an evidence locker then called Technical Services, gave them the number for Martin's cell phone, and asked them to see if they could find its current location. I opened my own computer and found an e-mail from a detective in the Portland P.D. The detective said that they had interviewed Dan Marlowe, Allie Martin's ex-husband, who insisted that he had been at home in Portland all weekend long. Marlowe's wife and three other witnesses confirmed the story, which seemed to eliminate even the tiniest possibility that Marlowe had returned to Phoenix and murdered his ex-wife.

I dashed off a quick message, thanking the detective for her help and then spent a couple of hours beginning the case book that would inevitably extend to scores of pages before the investigation was concluded.

By eight-thirty, I'd been on the case for fourteen hours straight and had done all I reasonably could do for the day. I shuffled the papers into a neat pile then grabbed my phone, tapped the "Messages" icon and typed:

Enough for tonight. In 30 min I'll be in the bar at Tutti. Dinner & drinks?

***

A couple minutes after nine, I settled onto my usual stool at the bar in Tutti Santi. The restaurant was still fairly busy for that time of night and for this time of year, when anyone with the means and the good sense to do so had already fled the Valley for cooler climes. At the tables and in the booths behind me in the dimly lit room, several couples and a few foursomes were lingering over dinner and drinks, and as always, the place served as a welcome refuge from the heat and the troubles of the world outside. Dan, the bartender, set a rocks glass in front of me and grabbed a bottle of Jameson 18-Year-Old Limited Reserve from the shelf behind him. He turned back, looked at me and raised his eyebrows. "Oh, yeah," I said.

He poured me a healthy dose, neat, with a glass of water back. I picked up the glass and saluted the guy who was staring back at me from the mirror behind the bar and who seemed to look more like my father with every passing day. I'd long been a dedicated runner and so was significantly thinner than my father had been, but at six-two, we would have been virtually the same height. I'd inherited his thick black hair, though I wore mine longer than he, and as had been his fate once he reached his middle thirties, the first hints of gray were creeping into my temples. My eyes were a bit deeper blue and, I'd been told, appeared colder and less trusting than his.

The most notable difference between our faces was the fact that my nose had once been broken, back when I was still working Vice and wound up in a fight trying to take down a pimp who was running twelve and thirteen-year-old girls. It had healed over time, and now only someone looking closely would see that it was just slightly out of alignment. The pimp, on the other hand, had spent a month in the hospital before being transferred to the county jail and ultimately to prison. I was not sorry to hear that he was still gimping around with a pronounced limp.

Four months after I arrested the pimp, my father, then two months shy of his sixtieth birthday, was shot to death in a liquor store holdup. He'd stopped on his way home from his office to pick up a bottle of Scotch and was standing at the checkout counter when two robbers, wearing ski masks and brandishing pistols, charged into the store and demanded that the clerk empty the register.

In the grainy, black and white recording from the store's lone security camera, the young woman trembles nervously as she opens the register drawer. As she does, one of the robbers turns to my father and apparently demands his watch and wallet. My father sets the bottle of whisky on the counter and raises his hands, signaling that he's going to comply.

With this left hand, he slowly reaches into the inside pocket of his suitcoat and removes his wallet. He sets the wallet on the counter, removes his watch, and lays it alongside the wallet. Then he backs away a couple of steps. Meanwhile, the clerk, who is now crying, has finished emptying the contents of the register into a brown paper bag. She too takes a step back, raising her hands in supplication and apparently pleading with the robbers not to hurt her.

The smaller of the robbers grabs my father's watch and wallet, drops them into the bag with the cash, and then steps away from the counter. The larger of the two has yet to take his eyes off my father who is still standing there with his hands raised, saying nothing. Then, for no apparent reason, the man raises his gun and shoots my father in the chest. My father clutches at the wound and begins to fall toward the floor. As he does, the shooter steps forward and fires another bullet into my father's forehead. Even before my father has finished falling, the man turns and fires two more shots, killing the young clerk instantly.

Less than three minutes after they entered the store, the two men back slowly out through the door and drive away in a stolen Chevy Camaro. They have never been identified, captured, or punished. Three months after the most traumatic day of my life, I transferred from Vice to the Homicide Squad and would spend the next seven years of my life in an effort find justice, if not for my father, then for as many other innocent victims as I possibly could.

As the mental video faded to black for about the thousandth time, I shook my head and took a long first sip of the Jameson, still thinking about my dad. Five minutes later, I looked up to see the County Medical Examiner walking through the door in a pair of what I assumed were Jimmy Choo heels along with a blouse and skirt that were probably even more expensive than the shoes. A number of eyes followed her across the floor as she took the stool next to mine and gave me a peck on the cheek.

Without even having to ask, Dan set a glass in front of her and poured a Matua Sauvignon Blanc. We touched glasses, and each took a sip. Then Sara touched my hand and said, "Long day."

"Yup. And I know we need to talk about it, but for the moment let's stay off duty and talk about something else until after dinner."

"Fine by me. What would you like to talk about?"

"Anything except the case. You pick."

She leaned closer and said, "Well, we could start by talking about the opportunity we missed this morning when both of our phones went off at that god-awful hour."

"That *was* unfortunate, and believe me, even with everything that's been going on today, I haven't stopped thinking about it."

"Nor have I, so let's not linger too long over dinner."

***

An hour and a half later, we were sitting on the couch in my living room, each of us with a fresh drink in hand. I took a sip, set the glass on the coffee table, and turned to Sara. "OK, let's get the business out of the way. I don't need the full report now; just give me the CliffsNotes."

She set her own glass on the table. "Pretty much what you'd expect, based on what you saw this morning. The poor woman had been used very badly over the last few days and in the end, was strangled to death with a narrow wire of some sort. So far, there's no sign of any drugs or alcohol in her system, but it will be a few days before we can say that definitively. Her last meal was a pizza with sausage and green peppers on it and she ate it about three hours before she was killed. She'd been dead for around five or six hours before we found her in the park. And you?"

"Shaping up to be the most confusing damn case I've ever seen. Forty-three years practically to the hour, after Ellen Friedman's body was found in that park, we find a young woman's body in the same exact spot, wrapped up with Friedman's purse and driver's license. And then it turns out that today's victim, Allie Martin, was Ellen Friedman's granddaughter."

"What?"

"I know. You can imagine the reaction that Maggie and I had when Martin's mother told us that she was Ellen Friedman's daughter. I have no idea what in the hell could be going on here, but it looks like someone is playing a very sick game. Was there anything on the body that's going to help us—hair, fibers, DNA, anything?"

"No, nothing, I'm sorry to say. The body was thoroughly scrubbed from head to toe before being wrapped in the plastic sheeting. There's no semen, hair, fibers, or anything else that's going to help you identify the guy who did this, unless the crime scene guys develop something off the plastic she was wrapped in. But I wouldn't hold out a lot of hope. This is obviously an asshole who's watched a lot of 'CSI Missoula,' or wherever the hell they're setting that show now."

I nodded then said, "OK, enough of that for tonight."

I took the wine glass from her hand, set it on the table beside me, then pressed her back into the couch and gave her a long, deep kiss. She pulled me close then finally broke the kiss and whispered, "About damned time."

We'd been seeing each other for a little over five months now. Of course, we'd known each other practically ever since she took the job as M.E., but we'd worked especially closely together on a case I'd closed about six months ago, and when it was over, I asked her out to dinner for the first time. It was clear long before then that we had a lot of interests in common, and while I'd been attracted to her ever since I'd met her, I wasn't going to presume that she had the same interest in me. But once I took the plunge and asked her out, it was clear that she did, and it wasn't long before we were spending three or four nights a week together, either at my place or at hers.

Sara was a couple of years younger than I, an extremely attractive woman who loved the outdoors and who, at the same time, was also a major clothes horse. In less than forty minutes, she could be out of her hiking boots, showered, made up, and dressed to kill in a pair of Manolo Blahniks, and looking spectacular either way.

Neither of us had any idea where this relationship might be headed. I was in love with Sara, but I was also extremely gun shy when it came to relationships. I'd previously been married for a little over six years and had now been widowed for a little more than two. A year after Julie's death, I finally began a relationship with a woman named Stephanie whom I'd met at Tutti Santi where she was tending bar. We'd cared for each other a great deal and might possibly have had a future together, but a few months after we'd begun seeing each other, her mother had fallen ill back in Ohio, and Stephanie had returned home to care for her. When it became apparent that she would not be able to leave her mother for some considerable time, we reluctantly agreed to go our separate ways.

Once Stephanie and I parted ways, I'd had a couple of other, very brief relationships before meeting Sara, but neither of them held the promise of anything long term. Sadly, the life of a homicide detective is often death on marriages and other such entanglements. The hours can be brutal, especially when you're on a fresh case, and, of necessity, the job very often has to take precedence over family plans and schedules, no matter how important or how long planned an event might be. If you're dedicated to the job, as a practical matter you're married to it, and only the most tolerant and understanding of spouses or significant others can make the adjustments and sacrifices necessary to preserve a relationship with a homicide detective.

Given her role as the county M.E., Sara understood the pressures of my job and the importance of doing it as well as I could. She insisted that she loved me at least in part because of my dedication to the task and to the victims for whom I was often the last remaining advocate. Perhaps the fact that her own job was demanding and often unpredictable made her more sympathetic to my situation, and happily, thus far at least, neither of our careers had put any significant pressure on the relationship we were building. For the moment, then, we were both content to take things slowly and preserve a considerable amount of our respective independence, and I counted myself very lucky that we had found our way into each other's lives.

8.

On Wednesday morning, Sara and I dragged ourselves out of bed a little after five, determined to get in a run while it was still "only" in the high eighties. We managed five miles and by the time we were done, we were both so thoroughly exhausted that we could have taken a long, cold shower and crawled right back into bed. Sadly, that was not an option, and by seven o'clock, we were both out of the house and headed to our respective offices.

Mine is on the third floor of the Police Department's headquarters building, which was constructed in the early 1970s. It's a sterile, butt-ugly, three-story concrete fortress that takes up most of a downtown city block. In truth, it looks like a structure that would have been more at home in East Berlin in the early 1970s as opposed to a booming American city, and if anything, it gives off a vibe that repels rather than welcomes visitors. Seeing it for the first time can be a hugely depressing experience and walking into the building even after all this time, I still wonder what the city's leaders must have been smoking when they approved the plans for the place.

Once inside, I detoured by the cubicles on the second floor where the Cold Case Detectives work and saw John Hammond already on the job. Hammond had been my first partner in Homicide and had spent a couple of years showing me the ropes before he transferred into the Cold Case Unit. We spent a couple of minutes catching up and then I asked him to check the Ellen Friedman investigation in the Case Management files.

"Jesus, there's a blast from the past," he said. "What's up?"

I explained the connection of the Friedman case to the one that my team had caught yesterday, and Hammond simply shook his head in disbelief. He called up the case, briefly scanned the file, then said, "Nobody's looked at this one in years—no new leads and no new evidence since the original investigation stalled out. The Murder

Book and supplementals will be on micro fiche over in R & I. Be sure to let us know if you guys turn up anything that would give us a way back into this one."

I promised John that I'd keep him posted, then walked over to the Records and Information Bureau. I gave the Departmental Report Number of the Friedman case to the clerk and told her I'd like to take a quick look at the material on a viewer. She set me up at a machine and I skimmed the files just deeply enough to jot down the names of the four detectives who had worked most closely on the case. I then filled out a request to have the entire file printed out and tried to impress upon the clerk the importance of getting the file ASAP.

Back upstairs at my own desk, I called the HR department and discovered that two of the four detectives who had originally worked the case had died. Another was living in Florida, but the records indicated that the lead detective on the case, Jack Oliva, was now seventy-eight years old, still collecting his PD pension, and living in the Willo District in downtown Phoenix, not all that far from where he had once worked the Friedman case.

HR provided the phone number and my call was answered by a man who sounded pretty sharp for a retired guy of seventy-eight. I chided myself for having expectations that a sensitive seventy-eight-year-old person might have branded as ageist, then identified myself and asked if I might come out to discuss one of his old cases. Without asking what case I might have been interested in, he told me that would be fine and that thirty minutes from now would work for him.

Oliva's house turned out to be a small brick bungalow on Edgemont Avenue in a neighborhood that probably dated back to the 1930s when Phoenix was still a small town and Willo was a suburb. Like many of the other homes in the historic area, Oliva's had been lovingly restored, and the front yard was attractively landscaped with several shrubs and mature trees. The guy who greeted me at the door was a rangy six feet or so, with a full head of silver hair and light grey eyes. He was wearing a black tee shirt over a pair of dark blue jeans and appeared to be in very good shape, even for a man who might have been significantly younger than seventy-eight. It struck me that I should be so lucky to age that well.

I introduced myself and he said, "Come on back to the kitchen. I was just finishing breakfast. Would you like a glass of juice or some coffee?"

I replied that a glass of juice would be great, and Oliva led me past the living room into a small, but efficiently designed eat-in kitchen. He offered me a chair at the table, poured me a glass of orange juice, and sat down opposite me. "I must say, Detective, you've aroused my curiosity. Which of my old cases is coming back to haunt me?"

"Sean, please. Did you see or read accounts of the young woman whose body was found in Central Park yesterday morning?"

He nodded, and I continued. "As I'm sure you'll understand, we're trying to keep this very close to the vest, but the victim was bundled up in plastic sheeting. Wrapped in the plastic with her was a vintage handbag, and inside the handbag was the driver's license belonging to Ellen Friedman."

Oliva's eyes widened. "What the fuck?"

"Well, that's the unanimous reaction. And to add to the confusion, yesterday was the forty-third anniversary of the day Friedman's body was discovered, and our victim was Friedman's twenty-nine-year-old granddaughter."

Oliva looked away, shaking his head for a moment, then turned back. "Holy Jesus Christ."

"Exactly. Not surprisingly, we have absolutely no clue as to what might be going on here. Our victim, whose name was Allison Martin, was clearly targeted by someone who was not only familiar with your case but who was also able to get his hands on Friedman's purse and DL. Like Friedman, Martin was abducted, sexually assaulted for several days and then dumped in the park."

Again, he shook his head. "More than any other case I ever worked, that's the one that's haunted me the most. Some asshole killed those four women and I never got a whiff of him. So, what can I do to help?"

"I'm really hoping I can pick your brain to see if, between the two of us, we can figure out what in the hell might be going on here."

"You think it could possibly be the same guy?"

"That seems a stretch, but if it isn't how does my guy come up with the purse and DL? And what makes him target Friedman's granddaughter on the anniversary?"

"You been in the file?"

"No. I took a quick look at the microfiche this morning and they're printing me a copy. But before I started digging into it, I thought I'd see if you could give me a general overview and share your insights. It would be a huge help once I get into the file. For starters, did you have anybody you thought looked really good for it?"

"No, I'm sorry to say. We took a hard look at the husband, of course. The guy was in some financial straits and the wife came from a very wealthy family, so he inherited a pile of dough at a very convenient time. But the guy never felt right to me for it. He seemed to be genuinely devastated and he had a pretty solid alibi. He could have hired it out, of course, but you just get that feeling in your gut, you know?"

I nodded and he continued. "Then, of course, the other women were killed, and he had no ties to any of them that we could find and no motive that we could figure. He also had pretty good alibis for the times of at least two of the other killings, so we pretty much counted him out.

"The first three victims all had ties of one sort or another to the Deuce. Friedman was a housewife who volunteered at a soup kitchen down there. The second was a waitress who worked in one of the bars, and the third was a hooker who freelanced in the area. The last was a TV news reporter who was making something of a name for herself covering the killings.

"One of the other guys we looked at was the pastor who ran the soup kitchen where Friedman volunteered. The bastard was pretty full of himself and could have broken his wrist from patting himself on the back for all the good works he was doing. One of the other women who volunteered down there at the time told us that he considered himself something of a ladies' man and that he had his eye on Friedman, who was a pretty sexy number.

"The woman told us that Friedman had shut him down cold and was thinking about quitting the volunteer job. But then she got killed shortly after Pastor Goodworks put the move on her. We wondered, naturally, if he was a guy who didn't take rejection well and who might have gone after her. Also, of course, this was a guy who was frequently down in the Deuce; he knew the neighborhood and would have had access to the other victims. But we found absolutely no evidence against him, and then when the other women were killed, he alibied out in the second and third cases. As I recall, he was out of town at a convention in the one case and leading a weekend retreat in the other."

"Nobody else?"

"Some minor characters, and you'll see their names in the file. In each of the four cases, we had guys who might have been good for one or more of the killings, but we never had any solid evidence against any of them. Beyond that, it seemed certain that none of them would been able to do all four of the women, and we were dead certain that it *was* the same guy all four times.

"I tell you, Sean, it was the most frustrating goddamn case I ever worked. We put in thousands of man-hours without getting a hint of a viable doer."

"You said that your possibles might have done one or more of the killings but apparently couldn't have done all four. I'm sure you must have considered the possibility that two guys might have been working together, allowing one of them to have an alibi each time one of the women was grabbed?"

"Of course, we thought about that, although it's pretty rare for a sick bastard like this to be working with a partner. But we never developed any relationship among the guys we were looking at to suggest that they even knew each other, let alone that they might have been working together."

"Any idea why he might have suddenly stopped?"

He shrugged. "Nothing that hasn't already occurred to you, I'm sure. Normally, once a guy like that gets started, he doesn't stop until he's caught. So, perhaps he moved to another city and took up there. The computer networks weren't nearly as sophisticated back then as they are now, so it's possible that he killed other women somewhere else and the detectives there never made the connection to our cases.

"The other possibility, of course, is that he got caught and convicted for something else entirely and was sent to the can. If there's a chance that it is the same guy, I guess you need to be looking for some mope who's now sixty-five to seventy years old and just got released after a forty-year stretch."

"Well, for sure we'll run the names from your file through the computer and see if we get a match. It would be great if we did, but I can't imagine we'll get that lucky."

"Well, we sure as hell never did."

"Do you have any idea if the two main guys you looked at are still alive?"

"I don't know about the pastor; he'd be in his middle eighties by now. Friedman's husband died about five years ago. He stayed in touch and called me periodically, wondering if we had any new leads, then I saw his obit and knew he wouldn't be calling anymore. Poor son of a bitch went to his grave not knowing what happened to his wife and it looks like I will too, unless you can pull a rabbit out of a hat here."

"I'll do my best, but I could really use your help, Mr. Oliva."

"Jack, please. And if there's anything at all, don't hesitate. If my killer is still out there and I can still do something to help bring the bastard down, I could die a happy man."

49

9.

I left Oliva, noting that I'd doubtless have a lot of other questions once I got into the file. Again, he assured me that his time was mine and made me promise that I'd keep him posted.

Back in the office, I found a message from Technical Services saying that they had been unable to locate Allie Martin's cell phone. The logical assumption was that the killer had destroyed the phone, perhaps removing or damaging the battery and the SIM card, thus making it impossible to trace the phone. A warrant had been served on the service provider who would turn over the phone's records within the next day or two. I also found an email from Gary Barnett, confirming that the driver's license found in the handbag with Martin's body was genuine and that there were no fingerprints or anything else on either the license or the bag itself to suggest who might have wrapped it up with the body.

I stepped across the hall to catch up with Maggie, only to discover that she'd turned up no one at Martin's apartment complex who could shed any light on what might have happened to her. "However, in the good news department," she said, "the condo complex has video cameras on the gates, recording all of the vehicles going in or out. I've got a warrant coming that will allow us to pull the discs or whatever the homeowners' association is using to capture the video. If the bastard did grab her outside her condo, we ought to have him coming out through the gate as he was leaving."

I agreed that was very good news and described my meeting with Jack Oliva. Then together we caught the sergeant up to date. "R & I is running a copy of the Friedman file," I told him. "I figured that we'd try to get a feel for the people who surfaced one way or another in the Friedman case and see if we can find any sort of connection between any of them and the people in Martin's life. In particular, we obviously want to know if there was a new man who might have worked his way into her life who has ties to someone from her grandmother's case."

"That sounds like the most logical approach," he said. "Give me a status report of some kind early this afternoon."

10.

The company that managed the HOA for Allie Martin's complex had offices in a building on Raintree Drive in Scottsdale. Just after two o'clock, Maggie and I presented our warrant to the receptionist at the front desk. She passed us off to Michael Lee, the property manager for the complex and he, in turn, handed me a thumb drive in exchange for the warrant.

"As you may have noticed when you were at the property," he said, "only one gate allows drivers to enter or exit the complex. All residents entering through the gate have a remote or a code they can punch into the keypad to open the gate. Visitors who don't have a code can use the call box to phone a resident who can then buzz them in. As you'll see, though, the gate rolls back and forth very slowly and so it's easy for a second or even a third car to roll right into the complex behind someone who's used a remote or punched in a code to open the gate. But irrespective of that, all vehicles passing through the gate are recorded by two cameras.

"As you requested, we've given you the video of every vehicle that either entered or left the complex from noon on Friday to noon on Saturday. You'll see that one camera shows the license plate of the vehicle as it enters the complex and the second shows the left side of vehicles entering and the right side of vehicles exiting."

I dropped the thumb drive into an evidence bag and Maggie asked, "How many people have remotes and codes that will let them through the gate, Mr. Lee?"

"To be honest, hundreds. Every resident gets a remote and also makes up a four-digit code that they alone are supposed to know. But, although we ask them not to, most residents freely give their codes to visitors and delivery people rather than making them call up. And often they simply pick a progression of numbers like 5-6-7-8 or a set of numbers like 9-9-9-9. Given how long the system's been in place, the truth is that you can punch in about any four numbers you can think of and it won't take long to find a combination that works."

***

Back in my office, Maggie pulled up a chair alongside my desk and I plugged the thumb drive into my computer. Once the video began rolling, I fast-forwarded to ten o'clock the night that Allie Martin went missing. Assuming that the kidnapper had been waiting for Martin and had grabbed her as soon as she got home from her night out with her girlfriends, we would first watch for her Mini-Cooper to come through the gate. We'd then begin watching for vehicles that left the complex within the next few minutes.

Once the video hit ten o'clock, I slowed the speed to medium and after a couple of minutes, a red Mini approached the gate. I reversed the video a few frames and then Maggie and I watched at regular speed as Martin's car reached the gate at ten thirty-seven. One window on the computer screen gave us a clear view of Martin's license plate and the second window showed the left side of the car and a clear view of Martin herself as she pointed a small remote at the gate and then waited for the gate to roll open before passing through.

We watched the gate close slowly behind her and continued watching the video at regular speed. Five minutes after Martin drove into the complex, a Lexus sedan pulled out. We made a note of the plate number, and the second camera, which was now looking through the passengers' side window, showed a female with long, blonde hair at the wheel.

Over the next four minutes, a Honda sedan and a BMW SUV followed the Lexus out of the gate. Then, at ten fifty-two, a Ford Econoline van that was either black or dark blue, pulled up to the gate and waited to exit. The second camera showed a magnetic sign advertising a plumbing service on the right side of the vehicle. The passenger's side window was so heavily tinted that the driver inside remained invisible.

I wound the video back to eight o'clock and then began fast-forwarding again, looking for the van's arrival. It flashed by after only a few seconds, and I backed up a bit. Then Maggie and I watched in real time as the van followed a vintage Chevy Corvette up to the gate at eight thirty-two. The guy in the Vette used a remote to open the gate and, once it rolled open the van simply followed the Corvette into the complex.

Maggie jotted down the license plate number, and I reversed the video again, pausing at the moment when the camera provided the closest view of the driver's side of the vehicle. Through the windshield, we could vaguely see that the driver was almost certainly a male, but that was about it. He was wearing a hooded sweatshirt tied tightly around his face, and a pair of large dark glasses obscured much of the rest of his face. He appeared to have a large bushy mustache, but there would be no hope of identifying the guy from this picture.

I ran the plate number, and according to the computer, it belonged on a three-year-old Toyota Corolla registered to a woman in Glendale. I called the number listed on the registration and found the woman at work. "As far as I know, my license plate is right where it belongs on the back of my car," she said.

I waited for several minutes while she walked her cell phone out to the parking lot to double check. "Well, shit," she said, apparently standing at the back of her car. "The damned plate is gone. I suppose I'll lose an entire afternoon at the friggin' MVD trying to get this mess straightened out."

A call to the manager of the plumbing company whose number was on the side of the van confirmed that they used inexpensive magnetic signs on the side of their vehicles. The manager assured me that they had no black or dark blue vehicles in their fleet. Nonetheless, he checked the records and confirmed that the firm had not answered any service calls from Allie Martin's complex on the night she went missing. I ended the call, turned to Maggie, and said, "Looks like we've got a winner."

We spent the next several minutes rechecking every view we had of the vehicle, freezing the images, and straining to see any damage or other markings that might help to identify it, but we found nothing. Of course, given the fact that both the license plate and the magnetic signs on the van had been stolen, there was a good possibility that the van itself had been stolen. Still, we'd turn the video over to the magicians in Technical Services in the hope that by isolating and magnifying the images, they might find something that we were not seeing. For the time being, though, it appeared that our suspect van, stolen or not, would most likely remain safely concealed in the sea of such vehicles that traveled the metro area's congested roadways on a daily basis.

11.

For the moment at least, Chris Nelson's van was hidden away in his rented garage, safely off the Valley's roadways, congested or otherwise. He'd purchased the van for cash from a private seller two weeks before abducting Allie Martin and had immediately driven it to the garage without bothering to register and license it in his own name. For the most part, he'd be taking it out of the garage only on special occasions and always on those occasions with borrowed license plates. For the purpose of grabbing Martin, he had also liberated two magnetic signs from a truck belonging to a plumbing company, and he'd later dropped both the signs and the license plates into a dumpster, miles away from the garage.

Forty years after Ellen Friedman's death, the *Arizona Republic* had thoughtfully run a long article commemorating the anniversary. The article had also described the three murders that had occurred in the wake of Friedman's and summarized the investigations that had followed. The reporter had interviewed a couple of the detectives who had been involved in the investigations and they reluctantly agreed that the chances of finding and convicting the women's killer or killers at this late date were basically slim to none. Nelson stumbled across the article just shy of three years later, along with a number of other relevant items, and had thus been inspired to set his own plan into motion.

The reporter who wrote the *Republic* article had interviewed Friedman's daughter, Kathy Martin, and had mentioned Allie Martin, the victim's granddaughter. But the article did not contain a photo of either woman, and thus Nelson had no way of knowing what the granddaughter might look like. But a little time spent on the Internet had produced Kathy Martin's address and phone number, and when Nelson called the woman, pretending to be a high school classmate looking to contact Allie about an upcoming reunion, Martin had cheerfully provided the name and the phone number of the travel agency where Allie worked.

Two days later, Nelson walked into the travel agency and, after quickly surveying the nameplates on the desks of the respective agents, he stepped over to Allie Martin. Acting on an impulse, he introduced himself as Chris Nelson and told her that he was thinking about taking a vacation to Tuscany. Twenty minutes later, "Chris Nelson" walked back out the door with a handful of pamphlets, Allie Martin's business card, and a series of images roiling through his mind of what he might do with the sexy young woman, if and when he could get a hold of her. And thus, a legend was born.

Three days after that, Nelson was waiting outside the travel agency just after five o'clock and watched as Martin left the office and walked to her car. He had no trouble following her to the gate of her condo complex. Taking no chances, he broke off at that point and went home. But he returned the next afternoon, trailed an elderly woman in a Cadillac through the gate, and parked in a visitor's spot with a good view of the entrance.

At twenty minutes after five, Allie Martin's Mini-Cooper drove through the gate. Nelson waited until the Mini had passed behind him. Then he pulled out of the parking space and trailed Martin to the front of her building. He paused for a moment as she pulled into her garage and then watched as she walked out of the garage and headed up the stairs, before driving back to his own home.

From that point on, it took all the will power Nelson could summon to force himself to wait until the forty-third anniversary of the day that Ellen Friedman had been abducted. But at long last the day finally arrived, and late that afternoon, Nelson parked across the street from the travel agency. He watched as Martin and another woman came out of the office and locked the door behind them. The two said goodbye and Martin walked to her car. Nelson followed her to the Kierland Commons shopping mall and watched as she slipped the Mini into a narrow parking space across the street from the Greene House.

Martin walked over to the restaurant and greeted a woman who was sitting out on the patio. Satisfied that Martin would be occupied for at least an hour or so, Nelson drove to his rented garage and exchanged his regular vehicle for the van. He'd earlier attached the stolen license plates and magnetic signs to the van, and leaving the garage, he drove very slowly and carefully to Martin's condo complex.

Nelson knew that many such communities recorded the vehicles entering and leaving their grounds, and so before leaving the garage, he had put a sheet of cheap, do-it-yourself plastic window tint on each of the van's side and rear windows. A block from the condo complex, he pulled to the side of the street and carefully pasted a large fake mustache above his lips. Then he pulled up the hood of his sweatshirt and tied it tightly around his face.

Even though night had fallen, he put on his largest pair of sunglasses and, after checking himself in the mirror, he focused his attention on the gate leading into Martin's complex. Only a couple of minutes later, An older Corvette drove up to the gate. Martin pulled up behind the Vette and followed it into the complex. He drove directly to Allie Martin's building and parked in a visitor's slot only a few feet from the stairs leading up to her unit. Then he moved back into the rear of the van and settled in to wait.

A little over two hours later, the red Mini-Cooper appeared, coming slowly around the corner. Nelson applied a generous amount of chloroform to the rag he was holding in his right hand and checked to ensure that there was no one else about. He then slipped out of the van and moved around to the side of the vehicle where Martin's headlights would not illuminate him.

The night was almost completely quiet, save for the purr of the Mini-Cooper as it approached the garage. Dressed all in black and pressed up against the dark van, Nelson was virtually invisible.

Lights were showing in only a few of the windows in the neighboring units and, fortunately for his purposes, no one was out and about.

The Mini paused momentarily in front of the garage as the door rose slowly. Then Martin pulled the car into the garage and the door rolled slowly down again. As it did, Nelson raced over to the entryway and pressed himself flat against the wall next to the door leading from the garage to the stairs. The stairway was not that well illuminated, and Nelson hoped that anyone who might happen to look out a window in that direction would see only a dark shadow against the wall.

A moment later, the door to the garage opened and Allie Martin stepped out onto the concrete pad that fronted the stairs leading up to her condo. She barely had an instant to register what was happening before Nelson spun her around, pinned her arms to her sides, and slapped the rag over her mouth. Allie struggled ferociously but lasted for only a few seconds before succumbing to the chemical. Then Nelson gathered her up along with her purse, slipped her into the back of the van, and headed home to the garage, the level of his anticipation building to a nearly impossible high.

***

A day after he left Allie Martin's body in the park, Nelson squeezed his regular ride into a parking space on North First Street, about a block and a half from the Roosevelt/Central Light Rail Station and about three blocks from Corrine Ray's apartment building.

Ray was a nursing student at ASU, who went to classes in the mornings before reporting to work at the bar where Nelson had spotted her. In addition to a couple of lunch shifts, she worked four evenings a week, clocking in at four o'clock in the afternoon and usually leaving a little after midnight. Her apartment was only a mile from the bar and she almost always walked to work. Leaving the bar late at night, though, she always walked the couple of blocks from her job to the Washington/Central Light Rail Station. There she hopped on the northbound train and rode to the Roosevelt/Central

Station where she got off and walked the block and a half to her apartment building.

Watching her carefully on several occasions now, Nelson realized that the young redhead was always very cautious going to and from the train at night. She walked at a brisk pace and always seemed alert to her surroundings. Three times Nelson had watched as she passed a male on a street that was otherwise largely deserted, and as she did, Ray had dropped her right hand into her open handbag, grabbing a can of pepper spray, perhaps—or even worse—a small gun?

Nelson realized that there was no chance of safely grabbing the woman off the street on her way to work. There was simply too much traffic and there were too many other people around at that time of day. Likewise, he concluded that attempting to take her as she walked from the bar to the train station after work would also be way too risky. The safest opportunity would come as she left the Roosevelt/Central station and headed home. She was occasionally the only person who left the train at that point who walked west in the direction of her apartment. The streets were much darker here at that time of night and there were far fewer people around. On two separate occasions, Nelson had watched Ray walk from the station to her home without passing anyone else on the street.

After walking the woman's route again in the middle of the afternoon, Nelson finally settled on a spot that he thought would work best. He understood that he might have to lie in wait on three or four different nights before the conditions would be absolutely perfect, but unlike the case with Allie Martin, the exact dates really didn't matter. Forty-three years ago, the original killings had taken place over a period of a year and a half, and Nelson had no intention of being that patient. It was important, he felt, to announce his arrival by matching the dates of Allie Martin's abduction and murder to the anniversaries of the abduction and murder of her grandmother. From now on, though, events would be moving much more rapidly.

12.

On Thursday morning, we received the records for Allie Martin's cell phone. We also got a preliminary report from Rick Muhlstein, the head of the investigative staff in the computer lab, regarding Martin's computer. Thus far, the techs had found nothing on the computer that looked like it would be of much help.

Martin had not kept a diary—at least not on the computer—which might have suggested, for example, that some new man had recently appeared in her life. She had a Facebook account that she used sparingly, but otherwise she devoted little time to social media. The techs provided us with a copy of the calendar that Martin kept on the computer and which was apparently linked to her phone. They also sent over a copy of her Facebook postings for the previous four months.

Muhlstein noted that the text messages that had been sent to and from Martin's phone had been mirrored on her MacBook. He included a copy of the texts sent and received for the three weeks prior to Martin's abduction and promised a final report on the computer within the week.

I quickly scanned the text messages and Facebook posts but saw nothing that jumped out at me. The texts seemed to be routine exchanges between Martin and a number of friends, all of whom appeared to be female. The last several texts all referenced Martin's plans to get together with her girlfriends for dinner and drinks on the night she was abducted, and she had neither sent nor received any messages after arriving at the Greene House that evening.

The Facebook postings appeared equally innocuous. As Rick had noted in his report, Martin had only a handful of friends on the site and had only occasionally posted pictures or other updates regarding her activity. Her most recent post was a picture of herself and two other women out for drinks in the bar at Mastro's Ocean Club a week and a half before she was killed. As Muhlstein suggested, it didn't appear that we were going to get any helpful leads from either the computer or her phone.

At ten o'clock, Maggie and I met in the conference room with Chickris and Pierce to line out a plan of attack. Elaine was in her mid-forties, a tough bottle blonde whose two divorces were mute testimony to the toll that working homicide could take on a relationship. But, like many another detective, when given the choice, she'd picked the job over the relationship both times out.

Chickris, on the other hand, was still happily married, at least for the moment, and he and his wife had just had their second child. He was a gifted natural athlete, but the job and the two small children were both doing serious damage to what had once been a scratch golf game.

After kicking things around a bit, we decided that Maggie would go through the cell phone records, looking for anything there that might point us in a helpful direction and interviewing the people in Martin's contact list. Elaine would chase down the Facebook friends, after eliminating the ones who were also in Martin's phone contacts. Greg would interview the other staff members at the travel agency and begin widening the circle from there, depending on what he discovered.

***

While Maggie, Gregg and Elaine were busy chasing down the details of our victim's recent past, my job was to get into the files of the Friedman case in the hope of finding some clue that would link Martin's murder to that of her grandmother and that might somehow explain how the killer had come up with Ellen Friedman's driver's license and handbag.

The Records and Information Bureau had sent up a printed copy of the Friedman Murder Book, and I grabbed a Mexican Coke out of the small refrigerator in my office and settled in at my desk. Just as I flipped open the cover of the file, my cell phone buzzed, and the screen indicated that Ellie Davis was calling. I connected to the call and we exchanged the usual pleasantries. With that out of the way, Ellie said, "I'm calling for two reasons, Sean. First of all, I'm wondering if you can give me a progress report on the Martin investigation."

"You know that's not my job, Ellie. We have a Media Relations Unit and you should be calling them for the official news."

"I've already done that, of course. But I'm wondering if there's anything you can add to the official report, off the record and just for old times' sake."

"Old times" had involved a brief but intense relationship a few months earlier when Ellie and I had both been otherwise uninvolved. We'd remained friends and occasionally had dinner or drinks together, and while she never seriously attempted to take advantage of our relationship to get information otherwise unavailable to the press, she was not above making the occasional light-hearted effort when the story was especially significant.

I smiled at the memory and said, "As lovely as those old times were, Ellie, there's really nothing I can tell you that you didn't already get from Media Relations."

"Well, here's the thing, Sean, and this is the second reason why I'm calling. I was digging into Allie Martin's background and discovered that she was the granddaughter of a woman who was murdered and left at the same spot in Central Park forty years ago. I'm assuming that you know that, of course; I'm just wondering why no one over there has thought to mention it to the press."

I took a deep breath and said, "Actually, forty-three years ago, Ellie, and of course we know that. But we have a very good reason for not mentioning it and I can't tell you what it is, even off the record—at least not yet."

"You're putting me in a difficult spot here, Sean. I assumed that you must have a reason for not making the connection public, which is why I'm calling. I don't want to do anything that will complicate matters for you, but this puts an interesting twist on the killing and, at least as far as I know, I'm the first reporter to make the connection.

But I certainly won't be the only one to do so, and if I don't run with this now, someone else will beat me to the punch. The news will still be out there, and I will have lost the scoop."

"I understand that and I realize that other people are bound to make the connection. I was really just hoping that it would be later rather than sooner. I understand the position you're in relative to the competition, and I'm certainly not going to ask you to hold the story. But I'm also not going to comment on it, even privately. I do appreciate the heads up, though."

"You're welcome, and I'm sorry. I hope I'm not screwing up your investigation, but I've really got no choice here. Why don't you let me make it up to you by buying you a drink one of these nights?"

"Believe me when I say that you may owe me a lot more than one drink for this one, Ellie."

"Whatever." She laughed. "See you soon."

***

Before digging into the Friedman file, I walked down to the sergeant's office to give him the bad news. "Realistically," I said, "someone was bound to make the connection fairly quickly. If nothing else, Kathy Martin's friends will be commenting about the fact that both her mother and her daughter were abducted and killed in the same manner and left in the same spot. But neither they nor the press will know that the killer left Friedman's DL and handbag at the scene of Martin's murder. I asked Kathy Martin not to tell anyone about it and that's really the critical piece of information that we need to be keeping to ourselves."

Leaning back from the stacks of files that covered most of the desktop, he put his feet up on the remaining vacant square foot. "I know that," he said, "but even this is going to complicate matters and draw attention to the case that we could do without. Did Davis say when she'd be doing the story?"

"I assume that she probably posted a report to the station's website as soon as she got off the phone with me and that she'll be reporting on the air live at six and ten."

"Well, shit," he said, shaking his head. "Do me a huge favor and catch this bastard before then, will you?"

13.

Back in my office, I started by reviewing the list of people that Oliva and his team had interviewed during the Friedman investigation. As is always the case of course, most of the interviews were with the victim's family, friends, and acquaintances in the hope of gathering information that would lead the detectives to a viable suspect. Beyond that there were interviews with several men who had been suspected of possible involvement in the crime.

As Oliva had told me, they'd looked hard at the pastor who was running the soup kitchen where Friedman volunteered. The notes indicated that at least two witnesses had suggested that the pastor, whose name was Joseph Turner, had demonstrated a strong interest in Friedman. One of the two told the detectives that Friedman had rejected Turner's advances in no uncertain terms and had tried to keep her distance from him in the time that followed.

The file indicated that Turner did have what amounted to iron-clad alibis for the times of two of the other killings, but nevertheless, I punched his name into a couple of databases only to discover that he had died two months before Allie Martin was abducted and that he thus apparently had a pretty good alibi this time around as well.

During the course of the investigation, the team had also interviewed a number of men who had been "clients" of the soup kitchen where Friedman had volunteered. They'd also talked to several other men who'd been in and around the Deuce at the time of the crime. But most of these men had long disappeared from the public records, which was hardly surprising. This was a very unstable, transient population consisting mostly of men who were living on the margins of society, surviving from day to day and moving from city to city. If and when they did work, it would have most often been at menial jobs where they were most likely paid in cash, and most of them would have seldom, if ever, appeared in the public records of the day to begin with.

Oliva's team had ultimately dismissed virtually all these men as possible suspects and we were almost certainly never going to find any of them to re-interview at this late date. But it was hard to imagine that any of them could have been involved in the Allie Martin case anyway. Certainly, one of them might have killed Martin's grandmother, but it seemed highly improbable that one of them might have been stable and organized enough to have killed Ellen Friedman, carefully saved her purse and driver's license, and then resurfaced forty-three years later to track down Allie Martin and abduct and kill her in such a highly-disciplined manner.

Reading through the notes, I found that Oliva's team had turned up four other men that they considered viable suspects in the Friedman case, at least for a time. However, there wasn't sufficient evidence to make a compelling case against any one of the four, and the team had never been able to find a link between any of these men and the three subsequent killings.

I ran the four names through a variety of databases, checking to see if any of the men had ever been sentenced to prison and recently released, but I was not especially surprised when I got no hits. I then checked a variety of other records to see how many of the four were still alive at this point, how old they would be, and where they might be living. I discovered that two of the four had died. The records indicated that the remaining two were still living in the greater Phoenix metro area.

The first, William Needham, was now eighty-three and living in Sun City West. Back in 1975, Needham and his wife had belonged to the same country club as Ellen and Brian Friedman. A couple of other members of the club told Oliva's team that Ellen Friedman and Needham had been involved in a brief affair a year or so before Friedman's murder. The two members, who belonged to a ladies' golf league with Friedman, indicated that Friedman had terminated the relationship and that Needham's marriage had broken up shortly thereafter. The women said that, following his divorce, Needham had attempted to rekindle his relationship with Friedman but that she had refused to become involved with him again. Friedman's husband had apparently remained clueless through the entire sequence of events.

Other members suggested that Needham apparently had a reputation around the golf club as being something of an asshole who didn't like losing, whether in business, on the golf course, or perhaps in his love life. At the time of Friedman's death, Needham was single and living alone in the home he had shared with his wife before the divorce. He was on vacation that week and told the investigators that he had spent the time alone at home, just resting and relaxing.

Curiously, for a guy who almost always played golf at least three times a week, Needham had not played a single round during the four days over which Friedman was missing. In the wake of his divorce, Needham's social life seemed to revolve around the men's card room and grill at his club. But a check of the club's records indicated that he had spent no time in the card room and had eaten only one meal in the grill over that four-day span. When asked to explain this deviation from his normal pattern of conduct, Needham said that he simply hadn't felt like going out.

According to Oliva's notes, the team had interviewed Needham several times. In one of the later interviews, Needham suddenly remembered that he'd been sick a couple of days while being off that week, which he now offered as one of the reasons he hadn't gone by the club. When pressed about the matter, Needham said that he had no proof of the claim because he hadn't gone to the doctor and had treated himself by taking over-the-counter medicine. But the team turned up nothing to contradict his story and they had no evidence that would allow them to pursue him as a suspect.

The other remaining possibility was a drapery installer named Bruce Robinson. Two months before her death, Ellen Friedman had ordered new living room drapes from a local decorator and the decorator, in turn, had contracted with Robinson to do the installation.

Robinson had first come out to the house one afternoon to size up the project. Friedman had felt very uneasy in his presence and on the day that Robinson was to return to install the drapes, she invited a girlfriend to come over to spend the afternoon with her so that she would not have to be alone in the installer's company.

The friend in question was Louise Hampton, a neighbor. Hampton told the detectives that Robinson was a "total creep," and that she could certainly understand why Friedman would not have wanted to be left alone with him. "I don't know a woman who would have," she said.

Hampton indicated that Freidman was reluctant to leave Robinson alone in the living room for fear that he might steal something, and so the two women had remained in the living room for the two hours it had taken Robinson to complete the installation. "It clearly shouldn't have taken much more than an hour," Hampton recalled. But she said that Robinson worked very slowly and spent as much time trying to make conversation with Friedman as he did installing the drapes.

"The guy apparently thought he was James Dean or something," she told Oliva. "He showed up in jeans, boots and a white tee-shirt that was molded to his upper torso, even though his body was nothing to rave about—anything but, in fact. He had long, greasy hair, styled something on the lines of the younger Elvis, and he acted like he was God's gift to women. He was practically drooling over Ellen and clearly, he was not at all happy that I was there. I'm sure he was dragging things out, hoping that I would have to leave so that he could be alone with her.

"When he realized that I wasn't going to leave, he finally finished up, and he seemed apparently oblivious to the fact that Ellen clearly did not want to converse with him. She wrote him a check and as he took it from her, he basically invaded her personal space and stood very close to her. He thanked her for the work and told her that he was always available to do any sort of odd jobs around the house. He gave her a card with his number on it and, in what I assume was supposed to be his 'sexy' voice, he told Ellen to call anytime that there was anything he could do for her—as if she was suddenly going to call him up and ask him to come over and jump into bed with her.

"The whole thing was beyond disgusting and after he left, Ellen called the decorator and told her how unhappy she was that the decorator had contracted the job to that slob. The decorator insisted that she too was shocked, and she assured Ellen that she'd never use the guy again."

The file indicated that the detectives had interviewed the decorator who told them that she *had* called Robinson, told him that she was very unhappy with his conduct, and informed him that she would not be using him again. Oliva personally interviewed Robinson who betrayed no apparent distress at being contacted by the police. He showed no surprise and expressed no regret on being informed of Friedman's death. He told Oliva that the victim was "a stuck-up bitch," and laughed off the idea that he might have been attracted to her in any way, let alone sexually. "She was old enough to be my mother," Robinson said. "She'd be lucky to get any man under sixty into the sack. I certainly had no interest in fucking her."

Like William Needham, Robinson basically had no alibi for much of the time that Friedman was missing. He claimed to have been at a bar, shooting pool on one of the evenings in question, and detectives found a couple of witnesses to verify the claim. He'd had one job installing draperies—for a different decorator—on the day after Friedman was abducted, but otherwise could not account for his whereabouts.

At the time, Robinson was living alone in a cheap rental house in south Phoenix. He willingly allowed the investigators to search both the house and the panel truck that he used for work. But they found no evidence to suggest that Ellen Friedman had ever been in either the house or the truck or that Robinson might otherwise have been involved in her abduction and murder.

I made a note of Robinson's current address, along with Needham's, then picked up my phone and called Jack Oliva. "Sure,

I remember both of those assholes," he said. "Robinson, in particular, was a total shitbag. But unfortunately, even back then just being a jerkoff wasn't a hanging offence in Arizona. To be honest, I would have liked either one of them for doing Friedman, but as hard as we tried, we found no concrete evidence linking either one of them to the crime or to any of the others."

"Would you like to come out of retirement long enough to talk to them with me?"

"I'd love to if you think it would be of any help, but I don't want to get in your way."

"Not at all. I think it might be very interesting to see how they'd react if you were sitting in on the interviews."

"You don't have to ask me twice. When and where?"

"I thought I'd try to track them down this afternoon if that works for you. Could I swing by and pick you up in an hour or so?"

***

Oliva indicated that an hour would be fine, and when I pulled into his driveway he was waiting at the door, dressed in a pair of grey slacks and a blue blazer over a white shirt that was open at the collar. The clothes were fashionable and appeared relatively new as opposed to something that an old retired guy might have worn to work fifteen years ago and then kept hanging in the closet for special occasions. Oliva wore the clothes well and it occurred to me that he'd still be a pretty big hit with the ladies, not all of whom would have to be even close to his own age. He settled into the passenger seat, belted himself in, and said. "Nice ride. The city must be paying a lot better these days."

"Not so you'd notice." I laughed.

"Well, there weren't a lot of detectives driving Bimmers back when I was on the job."

"And there still aren't. I was just lucky enough to be born into a little money. My department ride is in the shop today and since there's not much chance that we'll be arresting anybody this afternoon, I thought I'd drive my personal car rather than going through the hassle of checking out another department vehicle, especially given the fact that most of them were probably already in service back when you were still on the job."

"I'm certainly not complaining. Maybe you'll let me borrow it sometime."

"No problem," I said, pulling away from the curb. "As long as you help me get one of these clowns to confess to killing both Friedman and her granddaughter."

"You think there's any real chance?"

"Who knows? Needham is now eighty-three and living out with the old folks in Sun City West, so he's probably not a strong possibility. Robinson's sixty-six and is probably the better candidate of the two. What I keep coming back to, of course is the issue of Ellen Friedman's handbag and DL. Obviously, someone with a connection to your case had to have kept them as souvenirs. They then had to wrap them up with Allie Martin's body or pass them on to the person who did. Needham and Robinson are the only two guys that you looked at for Friedman who are still alive."

Oliva smiled and said, "Be careful about that 'old folks' shit, Junior."

I laughed and brought him up to date with the progress of the investigation thus far. He listened carefully and shook his head. "I find it hard to imagine that even a sixty-six-year-old guy could have overwhelmed Martin and dragged her into that van, let alone someone who's eighty-three. I suppose he could have forced her at gunpoint, but still—"

"I know, but if nothing else, we need to eliminate them from consideration."

***

Twenty minutes later, I pulled up in front of Needham's house on West Sky Hawk Drive in Sun City West, an "active adult retirement community," northwest of the city proper, which was open to anyone who might be at least fifty-five years old or "better." Needham's residence was a small stucco home, maybe fifteen hundred square feet, with a two-car garage and a tan tile roof, in a development that appeared to date from the early nineteen-nineties. The other houses in the neighborhood were of similar construction, located on small lots that were perhaps a fifth of an acre in size. It appeared that the developer had offered three or four basic floor plans, and Needham's yard, like all the others, was desertscaped with a couple of Palo Verde trees, three small cacti, and a couple of landscaping boulders planted in a base of crushed granite pebbles.

Oliva and I walked through the tiny courtyard that fronted the house and I rang the bell. A minute or so later, the door was opened by a petite woman wearing white shorts and a blue tee shirt who looked to be in her middle seventies and whose face was buried under about a pound and a half of makeup. I showed her my badge and I.D., introduced Oliva and myself as detectives from the Phoenix P.D., and asked if Needham was in.

Her eyes widened, and she made no effort to move away from the door and invite us in. "Whatever in the world would you want with Bill?"

"We just have a couple of questions, Ma'am; we're hoping that he might be able to assist us in an investigation."

"Well, I doubt that very much," she said, stepping back into the room, "but I suppose it can't hurt to ask."

She led us into a small living room that was light and inviting. A few pictures hung on the off-white walls; a white couch, a matching loveseat and a couple of tables were arranged on a tan Berber carpet, and white plantation shutters fronted the picture window that looked out onto the yard. Without asking us to take a seat, the woman said, "Wait here and I'll go get him."

While we waited, Oliva instinctively reverted to detective mode and we both surveyed the room, looking for clues about the man who might inhabit it. But there wasn't much to learn. Save for a couple of photos sitting on the tables that might have been of children and grandchildren, the room was curiously devoid of personal touches. It didn't look like a room where a man of Needham's generation would spend a lot of time, and I speculated that the woman of the house had probably been responsible for decorating this room, at least.

A couple of minutes later, the woman reappeared, pushing a very elderly looking man in a wheelchair. While he might have once been a terror on the golf course and in the card room, William Needham had shrunk almost completely into himself and now weighed probably no more than a hundred and thirty pounds. To all appearances, he'd been confined to that chair for a good long time.

The woman, whom I assumed was his wife, steered the chair to a spot next to the couch, then sat on the loveseat off to the side, obviously curious as to why two detectives would want to talk to her husband. Although he appeared physically weakened, Needham's brown eyes were bright, and he gave the appearance of being mentally sharp. Before I could even make an introduction, he looked at Oliva and said, "I remember you."

"It's been a while, Mr. Needham. How are you?"

"How the hell do I look—and who's your new partner?"

I offered my hand and said, "Sean Richardson, Mr. Needham."

He lifted an arm and shook my hand weakly, looking as though he wasn't sure whether he wanted to or not. Then he looked back to Oliva. "I would have thought you'd have been long retired by now."

"Actually, I am, Mr. Needham. I'm simply assisting Detective Richardson with this investigation."

"And which investigation is this?" he asked, turning to me. "I assume that you're not still trying to figure out who killed Ellen Friedman, and if you are, it still wasn't me."

"Actually," I said, "we *are* still trying to determine who killed Mrs. Friedman, but as you may have seen on the news, Mrs. Friedman's granddaughter was murdered over the weekend and we're now attempting to determine who killed her as well."

Needham raised his chin and shifted a bit in the chair. Looking from me to Oliva, he said, "I don't watch the news and I didn't kill anyone. Not this weekend or any other." Nodding in the direction of the woman, he said, "As my wife will tell you, except to go to bed, I

74

haven't been out of this chair in a year and a half, and I haven't been out of this house in the last two weeks."

Unprompted, the woman said, "That's correct, officers, and I'll testify to it if you need me to."

"That probably won't be necessary, Mrs. Needham," Oliva replied. Turning back to Needham, he said, "With forty years to think about it Bill, have you come up with any more thoughts about who might have killed Ellen Friedman?"

The man seemed to disappear for a moment back into the fog of long-distant memories, then he snapped back to the present and shook his head. In a soft voice, he said, "No, Detective, I haven't. And I haven't stopped thinking about it either. Nodding in the direction of his wife, he said, "All that was obviously long before I met Marjorie of course, and whether you believed it or not, I did love Ellen. And that didn't change for a long time, even though she rejected me. No matter what you thought back then and no matter what you think now, I never could have harmed her."

Oliva looked to me and I said, "Okay, thank you for your time, Mr. Needham. Sorry to have interrupted your afternoon."

14.

Needham's wife showed us to the door, and we thanked her for giving us the time. Back in the car, Oliva said, "I think you can safely strike him from your list."

"Yeah, it was certainly a long shot, but long shots are all we've got at the moment."

"Well, for sure that was all I ever had on this damned case. Maybe we'll have better luck with Robinson."

Robinson's address was in south-central Glendale, about sixteen miles from Needham's. We fought our way through stop and go traffic on Grand Avenue and arrived there about thirty minutes after leaving Sun City West.

While the homes and yards in Needham's development had been scrupulously maintained through the years, no doubt under the firm hand of an active HOA, most of those in Robinson's neighborhood were in a sad state of disrepair and neglect. It was an older area that looked to have been built in the early seventies and whose glory days were clearly behind it—the kind of a neighborhood where you could park a couple of junked cars in the yard and be fairly confident that no one was ever going to complain about it. The houses had been poorly maintained and most of the yards barely attended to at all. A few of the homes were separated by wooden fences, many of which were leaning badly and looking like they could simply surrender and fall over at any moment. Driving down the street, I guessed that it had been a good number of years since any of these places had been featured in the Parade of Homes.

Robinson's house looked tiny, probably somewhere short of eleven hundred square feet, with a roof that was missing several of its asphalt shingles. The front yard was small a patch of dirt, populated by a few hardy weeds and a tree of indeterminate lineage that obviously hadn't been trimmed in years. The roof over the carport was sagging a bit, and in the carport, a man wearing only jeans and a pair of boots was fiddling around at the back of an aging panel van with a yellow paint job that had been bleached out by the sun.

The guy looked to be in his mid-sixties and in reasonably good shape, albeit with something of a gut that was hanging out over the top of his Levi's. He'd lost most of his hair and what remained had grown out and was gathered together in a short ponytail. He was darkly tanned and looked like someone who spent a lot of time outdoors.

As he saw Oliva and I approaching, he pushed the doors closed, blocking our view of the interior of the van. Then he turned, gave us a look, and said, "What?"

"Mr. Robinson?" I asked.

"Who wants to know?"

I flashed him my badge and I.D. and said, "I'm Detective Sean Richardson; this is Jack Oliva."

Looking at Oliva, Robinson smirked and shook his head. "I remember you, and whatever it is now, I didn't do it."

Oliva smiled. "Exactly what it is that you didn't do this time, Bruce?"

"Whatever you're thinking of trying to pin on me. You didn't have any luck last time and you won't do any better this time."

"Well," I said, "Would you mind if we went inside out of the heat and talked for a couple of minutes, Mr. Robinson?"

"Yeah, I would mind. Anything you have to say to me, we can do it right here."

"Fine by us," I replied, even though I'd been hoping to get a look at the inside of the house. "As you obviously recall, Detective Oliva interviewed you a long time ago about the death of a woman named Ellen Friedman. Are you aware that Ms. Friedman's granddaughter, Allison Martin, was murdered over the weekend?"

Robinson's face gave away absolutely nothing. "What of it?"

"Is there any chance that you might have been acquainted with Ms. Martin?"

"Not hardly."

"You're sure?" Oliva asked. "You were quite taken with her grandmother just before she was killed."

"Says you."

"Actually, as you'll recall, a number of people told us that. You had high hopes in that department and Friedman shut you down cold. I remember that it didn't sit very well with you."

"You remember shit, Detective. Do you have a touch of the Alzheimer's now in your old age?"

Before Oliva could respond I said, "Could you tell us how you spent last weekend, Mr. Robinson, starting with Friday night?"

"I could, but it's none of your damned business."

I stepped in a bit closer and said, "Well, Mr. Robinson, we're going to make it our business and it would be a lot easier for all of us if you'd just tell us. If you haven't done anything wrong, there's no reason for you not to answer our questions. But if you don't, we're going to be digging into your life and we'll be all over your ass until we find out. And believe me we *will* find out in the end, so you might just as well tell us now."

Robinson backed away a bit, hesitated for a few seconds, then spit into the driveway and turned back to me. "Friday night I was home. I watched a DVD, drank a few beers, and went to bed about ten thirty. And even before you ask, no; there wasn't anybody here with me who could vouch for me. I can't prove I was here, but you sure as hell can't prove that I wasn't.

"Saturday morning, I helped a buddy install a washer and dryer and we took his old ones to the dump in my van. Saturday afternoon and evening, I was here, alone again. Sunday, I had a huge hangover and slept in until eleven, and so, yeah, I missed church again. That afternoon I watched golf on TV, then ordered in a pizza for dinner. I watched a little TV while I ate the pizza and went to bed early."

"What kind of pizza, if you don't mind my asking?"

"Meat Lovers, with extra green pepper. Is that a crime now?"

"Not as far as we're concerned," I said. "But you might get an argument from some people."

***

We spent another ten minutes or so, dancing around the issue of how Robinson had spent his weekend, but the guy didn't budge from his story and we weren't able to catch him in any obvious inconsistencies as we probed and asked him to repeat parts of the story. I thanked him for his time, and Oliva and I left him to his business. Back in the car, Oliva said, "Does that look to you like a guy who'd spend a lot of time watching golf on TV?"

"Not really. But I suppose if he was sufficiently hung over, he might have just laid on the couch and watched anything that happened to be in front of his eyes. More interesting was his answer to my question about the pizza. The Medical Examiner said that Allie Martin's last meal was a pizza with sausage and green pepper."

"That *is* interesting. But I'd imagine that Papa John and the rest of his cronies probably delivered about a million pizzas around the Valley Sunday night that had sausage and green pepper on them."

"True, and I really would have liked it a lot better if his damn van had been dark blue instead of piss yellow, but I'm still going to be looking hard at the guy. He's obviously still capable of having abducted and killed Martin. He's living alone; he could have held her in that crappy house over the weekend, and his alibi sucks. More important, of course, at the moment I haven't got a single other lead."

Oliva nodded his agreement and I said, "On another topic, did you or your team ever talk to Joseph Turner's brother, Frederick? I didn't see his name in the file."

Oliva spent a minute or so searching his memory bank, then shook his head. "I don't think so, at least not that I remember. But then, of course, maybe I *do* have a touch of the Alzheimer's. Why do you ask?"

"Not to worry, there's probably no reason that you would have talked to him, let alone remember him. He's eight years younger than

79

his brother and probably didn't enter into your case at all. But I checked the good pastor's obit, and other than the pastor's son, who would only have been a kid back in the Seventies, it appears that the brother is his closest surviving relative. I thought I might talk to him on the one in a million chance that at some point along the line the pastor talked to him about the case and maybe told him something useful that he hadn't thought to tell you."

"Well, it certainly sounds like another 'I' to dot or 'T' to cross or whatever. I can only hope to hell that he's more help to you than I've been."

15.

By the time I dropped Oliva off and got back to my office, it was twenty after five. The team had agreed to meet at five thirty to discuss the day's developments, and so I grabbed a Coke and headed down to the conference room. I found Maggie and Elaine already there, and promptly on the half hour, Greg appeared, bearing a bag of chips and a jar of salsa. "Good man," Elaine said. "I don't suppose you thought to also bring a pitcher of margaritas?"

"If only," Maggie sighed, reaching for the chips.

I summarized the events of my day and ended by suggesting that we'd want to take a closer look at Bruce Robinson. "It's admittedly a thin straw to be grasping at, but he was a viable suspect in the Friedman case and he's still certainly capable enough that he could have done Martin. Tomorrow let's get into the records and see what we can find. Then we can branch out from there, talking to his neighbors and whatever friends we can find to see what makes the guy tick and what he really might have been up to this weekend."

"Well, it may be thin, but it's a helluva lot more than I got," Elaine said. I talked to most of Martin's Facebook friends and left private messages for the others. There weren't that many, mostly family and close friends. Only a handful of those were males and none of them had become friends recently.

"They all appeared to be on the up and up. Martin hadn't given any indication on the site itself that she was worried or nervous about anything, and all the people I talked to said that she'd not indicated anything like that privately. They all insisted that there was no new man who'd recently appeared in her life; nobody was stalking her, and she wasn't getting any strange messages or phone calls."

"Ditto for the people who appeared on the phone bill," Maggie said. "And the bill itself doesn't indicate any brief calls where some asshat might have been calling and breathing into the phone or whatever. Nobody I talked to had any helpful information."

"Same here," Greg said. "I interviewed everyone Martin worked with at the travel agency. It's a small staff; they'd all been together for at least a couple of years, and they all know each other pretty well. They all told me that Martin did not seem to be troubled about anything, that she seemed to be finally getting over the whole divorce business, and that lately she seemed genuinely happy most of the time.

"The manager and I went through her client list, looking to see if some strange guy might have recently appeared in Martin's life as a client rather than a social acquaintance. But virtually all the people she'd worked with in the last couple of months were repeat clients or couples. She didn't book any trips for single men, save for a few businessmen who had been clients for a long time.

"That's certainly not to say that one of those men might have become obsessed with her and finally decided to act on it, but there's no evidence pointing in that direction. Besides that, if there was such a guy, how would he have come up with the purse and the DL?"

No one had a good answer for that, and I said, "Okay. For the moment at least, there appears to be no logical entry into the case via the people in Allie Martin's life. Obviously, she was targeted by someone because of her relationship to Ellen Friedman. Somewhere, somehow, our doer came into possession of the handbag and DL and decided to replicate the crime that had been committed against Martin's grandmother. Martin may have never even seen the guy before the moment he grabbed her.

"Our best prospect right now is Robinson. He's the only viable suspect from the Friedman case who's still alive and in good enough shape to have gone after Martin. God forbid that there's another guy who's roughly Robinson's age who did Friedman and the others but slid totally under the radar in the investigation forty years ago. If that's the case, I don't know how we're ever gonna get this fucker."

16.

I spent a little over an hour doing paperwork at my desk and then decided to call it a day. Sara had said that she was in the mood to cook something at home and generally just veg out for the evening. It sounded like a great plan to me, and I got to her place a little after eight, having run by my own home long enough to change into a pair of jeans and a tee shirt. She gave me a long kiss at the door, and I handed her a bottle of wine. "I didn't know what you might be making, but I grabbed a bottle of Topel Zin on the way out the door."

"Perfect," she said, taking the bottle. "I've made a Bolognese sauce to serve over pappardelle. This will be great with it."

Back in the kitchen, she planted me on a stool at the breakfast bar and opened the bottle. It's an excellent wine and we probably should have given it at least a little time to breathe, but this was a weekday evening after a long day at work, and so Sara poured us each a glass and we attacked it like a bottle of Two Buck Chuck.

Sara is as precise in her kitchen as she is at work, and I learned very early on that she preferred to work without interference, no matter how well intended the offer of help. I have absolutely no problem with this and was happy to sit out of the way, enjoying the wine, watching her work, and catching up on the events of the day. Over the next thirty minutes, she finished putting together a salad while the Bolognese simmered slowly on the cooktop. Then she boiled a pot of water, cooked the pasta, and removed it from the water about thirty seconds before it hit al dente. She mixed some sauce into the noodles; I poured us each another glass of wine, and we settled in at the table.

Dinner was excellent, as I knew it would be, and we lingered in the kitchen for an hour or so, finishing the wine and relaxing in each other's company. It was just short of ten o'clock when she took my hand and said, "I'm going to leave these dishes until the morning in favor of doing something much more enjoyable now."

"An excellent idea. Do you mind if we stop briefly in the living room along the way? A reporter is breaking a story about our case tonight and I didn't get a chance to see it at six. I'd like to have some idea what I can expect out of it when the morning rolls around."

"Why don't *you* stop briefly in the living room and watch your story while I get into something much more comfortable and enticing. I'll wait for you in the bedroom, but please don't be long."

She gave me a kiss that definitely whetted my appetite and headed off to the bedroom. I collapsed onto the couch, picked up the remote, and tuned the television to Channel 2. The news was just beginning and, after a report about a six-vehicle pile-up on the Pima Freeway, the anchor segued to Ellie's report.

From somewhere, Ellie had managed to come up with photos of both Ellen Friedman and Allie Martin. As the pictures were displayed behind her, Ellie began by saying that, "The mystery surrounding the tragic assault and murder of twenty-nine-year-old Allison Martin deepened today when this reporter learned that Ms. Martin was the granddaughter of Ellen Friedman, the first victim of a serial killer who haunted Phoenix back in the nineteen-seventies and who was never captured and brought to justice.

"Like her granddaughter, Friedman was abducted and held for a period of several days before her body was left on the same spot downtown where her granddaughter's body was discovered this past Tuesday morning. Adding to the mystery is the fact that Allie Martin's body was left in the park on the forty-third anniversary of the day that her grandmother's body was discovered there.

"When questioned, Phoenix police indicated that they were aware of the connection between the two cases, but they refused to speculate about why someone might have targeted Ms. Martin on the anniversary of her grandmother's abduction and murder. When asked about their progress, a police spokesman would only say that the investigation was proceeding, that detectives were exploring several leads, and that they hoped to bring the case to a swift resolution. Stay tuned to Channel 2 for further developments."

With that, Ellie passed the baton back to the anchor and I snapped off the set, only wishing that we had several leads to follow. And personally, I wasn't betting on anything close to a swift resolution of the case.

I assumed that Ellie's report would not do us any real harm and I hoped that the business of the handbag and driver's license would not somehow leak and become public knowledge. Our killer had to realize that we were coming after him and he was almost certainly attempting to taunt us by wrapping up the handbag and DL with Allie Martin's body. The disclosure of the fact that Friedman and Martin were related would certainly ramp up public interest in the case, but I wasn't anxious to have it turn into an all-out circus.

Watching Ellie on television, or seeing her in person for that matter, always brought back conflicting memories. She was a very attractive woman—smart, funny, and very sexy. The brief time we'd spent together had been extremely intense and even though we'd both agreed that we really weren't very well suited to each other much beyond the bedroom, I couldn't help but wonder from time to time what might have happened if we'd each tried a bit harder to make it work.

I'd never been keen on the idea of exchanging stories with a new lover about my past adventures and entanglements. I knew, of course that Sara had a history before she met me but figured that was none of my business. In that department, I've always assumed that what's past is past, and the only thing that really matters is how you move forward together. Accordingly, I hadn't ever told Sara that Ellie and I had once been involved. If the subject ever came up, I'd have to deal with it then. For the moment, though, I sat on the couch for another minute or so, getting my mind right, and then headed off to the bedroom.

17.

A little before ten o'clock, Chris Nelson turned on the television set in his family room and switched to Channel 2. They'd had the most complete coverage of the Allie Martin case thus far, and so he had taken to watching their newscast live. So as not to miss anything important, though, he was also recording the newscasts on channels 5 and 12 and would fast-forward through them later.

Watching the coverage gave him a rush greater than he had anticipated and intensified his need to grab Corrine Ray, the sexy young bartender, sooner rather than later. He loved watching the police spokesman promise an early resolution of the case while tap dancing around the fact that they didn't have jack shit in the evidence department.

Nelson was also enjoying very much watching the reporter who was leading the coverage for Channel 2. He guessed that she was somewhere in her early thirties with medium-blondish hair, brown eyes, great cheekbones and, of course, the perfect set of teeth that was a prerequisite for a job in television news these days. The woman had a body that was even better than the face, and even though she didn't dress all that provocatively, she really didn't need to in order to get his motor running.

Nelson speculated that thousands of men around the Valley were now watching Ellie Davis report the connection between Ellen Friedman and Allie Martin while fantasizing about what they might like to do with the reporter if they could only get her alone for an hour or two. They were all a bunch of gutless mopes, he thought, who would never have the nerve to go beyond the simple fantasy. But Chris Nelson figured that he was anything but another of those clueless chickenshits. And when it came to Ellie Davis, he was already beyond the fantasy stage and was actively planning for the time they'd be spending together later.

The third victim in the original killing spree had been a hooker who worked in the Deuce and the fourth had been a young TV reporter who had been desperately attempting to build her rep by reporting breathlessly on the first three killings. She hadn't been nearly as smart or as attractive as Davis, but her own abduction and murder had won her a level of attention and fame she would probably would have given anything to achieve, if only she hadn't had to die to get it.

Nelson assumed from the start that his fourth target would have to be a television reporter and he prayed that it would be someone worthy of his attention. He'd gotten his wish and then some when Channel 2 assigned Davis to cover the Martin case. On Channel 5, a male was doing most of the reporting on the case, and so naturally, he was automatically DQ'd. On Channel 12, two different reporters had covered the case thus far, one male and one female. But the female was not nearly as hot or as otherwise interesting as Davis, so Nelson's choice was a simple one, and as he turned off the newscast following her report, he wondered if she could possibly be as much of a treat in bed as he hoped she would be.

***

Following the news, Nelson left the house at ten thirty, an hour and a half before Corrine Ray would normally leave work and begin making her way home. By eleven, he was in his rented garage, screwing down the new license plate that he'd "borrowed" for the purpose of abducting the young woman and otherwise completing the preparations for her arrival in the loft above the garage. At eleven thirty, he was parked across the street from the bar, crunched down in the driver's seat and watching the front door of the place. He'd left the cheap plastic tint in the windows on either side of the front of the van and was confident of the fact that unless someone stepped right up to the van and looked carefully through one of the windows, no one would notice he was there.

In the best of all possible worlds, Nelson would grab the bartender on a Friday night so that he would have the entire weekend to enjoy her company without having to waste any time going in to work. But, of course, he couldn't absolutely guarantee that he would be able to get at her on a Friday night. Thursday was his fallback position. If possible, he would take her tonight, just to be on the safe side, even though it meant that he would have to spend an excruciatingly long day at work on Friday, unable to get at her. And if tonight didn't work, there was always tomorrow night.

As Nelson waited in the van, growing increasingly impatient, a small number of people passed by on the sidewalk in front of the bar. Finally, a couple of minutes before midnight, the door of the bar swung open and Corrine Ray stepped out onto the sidewalk. As always, she'd worn jeans and a tee shirt to work, and both the jeans and the shirt were a bit on the snug side—perhaps, Nelson thought, to encourage tips.

Just the sight of the woman got his pulse racing, and Nelson watched as she stood for a moment in front of the bar, looking up and down the street. Then she turned and began walking alone in the direction of the train station.

Nelson waited until she was around the corner and out of sight. Then he fired up the van and rolled north up the street. He jogged over to Central, and at Portland Street, he turned west and immediately pulled over to the curb. He turned off the ignition, made his preparations and moved over into the passenger seat, which was closer to the sidewalk where Ray would pass. He saw no one out on the street, and over the next several minutes only a handful of cars passed by.

Not quite twenty minutes after Nelson pulled to the curb, he saw Ray approaching his position, and his heart sank when he saw that she was walking with a man who had apparently gotten off the train at the same stop. The two appeared to be acquainted and were laughing about something as they neared the back of the van. Obviously, he couldn't make his move now, but this was, after all, why he'd developed the Thursday night contingency plan in the first place. And as he watched the couple pass by, he was already planning to be back in place twenty-four hours later.

18.

Joseph Turner's brother, Frederick, lived on East Highland Avenue, just south of the Biltmore Fashion Park. I'd made an appointment to see him on Friday morning and at ten twenty-five, Maggie and I pulled to a stop in front of his house.

The neighborhood dated from the nineteen-fifties, but the homes and yards had all been very well maintained. As was common in communities of this vintage, the homes all still had lawns rather than desert landscaping, and Turner's house was a one-story brick affair with an asphalt shingle roof and a carport on the east side of the house. A concrete walkway led from the carport to the front door, and a small ramp was built over the threshold in front of the door. I rang the bell and in less than a minute, the door was opened by a man in a wheelchair—my second in two days.

I knew that Turner would now be seventy-three, and the man in the chair looked right for the part. He appeared healthy enough for a man of that age, save for the fact that he was missing most of his left leg. Maggie and I introduced ourselves, and Turner rolled his chair back across the laminate flooring and invited us into a living room with a large sectional done up in a dark brown fabric of some sort.

Maggie and I sat on the sectional while Turner maneuvered the chair into a spot across from us. A pair of crutches leaned up against the wall behind the chair and Turner opened the conversation by apologizing for being in the chair and not standing to greet us. "Most of the time, I'm fine with the crutches and my prosthesis," he said. "But occasionally the damned thing still really bothers me, and so I have to spend a couple of days in the chair."

"Don't worry about it at all," Maggie replied. "If you don't mind my asking, how did you lose your leg?"

"Car wreck, coming home from a bar. As fate would have it, I was stone-cold sober, being the responsible designated driver, even though the term hadn't even come into fashion back then. But some clown who was not nearly as responsible as me and who was behind the wheel, drunk as the proverbial skunk, T-boned my car, cost me the leg, and ruined a good portion of the rest of my life."

"I can imagine," I said. "I take it that you were still fairly young, then?"

"In my late thirties. I was in sales at the time, and I'd always been very active—a very physical guy with a three handicap on the golf course and a pretty decent tennis player as well. So, needless to say, things changed pretty dramatically. I had to find a new job that didn't require me to be so mobile; I haven't been on a golf course or a tennis court since, and I don't mind telling you that I still miss it every damned day. But enough of my sorry whining; why did you want to see me?"

"Well, Mr. Turner," I said, "we're investigating the death of Allison Martin. I'm sure you've read or heard about the case."

He nodded. "I wondered if that might be it. I couldn't imagine why else a couple of detectives would want to talk to me."

"Sir?"

"I've seen the news and so I'm aware of the relationship between the girl and her grandmother. As you certainly know, the police questioned my elder brother in the case of the grandmother, so what else could you be here for? What I don't understand is what you think I might know about any of this business."

"Maybe nothing, of course," I said. "And we'll ask you please not to share this with anyone else, but the connection between the two crimes goes well beyond the simple fact that the two victims were related. Two items that belonged to the grandmother, Ellen Friedman, and which have been missing since her death, were discovered with the body of her granddaughter."

Turner appeared genuinely shocked by the news. "Good Lord," he said. "What were they?"

"We're keeping that a secret, Mr. Turner," Maggie replied. "But obviously, someone with knowledge of the crime against Ms. Friedman is involved in the murder of Ms. Martin."

Turner nodded slowly. "But I still don't understand why you might want to talk to me about it."

"Well, sir," I said, "Given the connection between the two crimes, we're going back and talking to as many people as we can who were interviewed in the original case. We know that your brother recently passed away, and so we can't talk to him. As small as the chance might be, we were hoping that you might be able to shed some light on the situation. We know, of course, that your brother was an important witness in the Friedman case. Did he ever talk to you about it?"

"A witness?" Turner snorted. "You don't have to sugarcoat it, Detective Richardson. For a while there, my brother was the leading suspect in the case. Do you think I don't know that?"

"No, sir; I'm sure you do. But the detectives did clear your brother of any involvement in the killing and so in the end, he was important to the case as a witness rather than a suspect."

"Perhaps that's the case, but it doesn't mean that my brother wasn't seriously affected by the whole thing."

"What do you remember about the case?" Maggie asked.

"Not all that much, really. I was eight years younger than Joe, and much to his consternation, back then I spent most of my Sundays on the golf course rather than in church. Still, he did occasionally badger me into helping out with his various charitable endeavors."

"Did that include the soup kitchen that he ran downtown?" Maggie asked.

"Yeah, that was his principal charity at the time. I don't think he really expected to make a lot of converts down there, but he honestly believed in the notion that we were all God's children and that each of us had an obligation to assist those less fortunate than ourselves, even if they were drunks, hookers, and the like. I gave him a hand there from time to time, although not as often as he probably would have wished."

"Did you ever meet Ellen Friedman?" I asked.

"I've wondered that for the last forty-three years, and the truth is that I don't remember. There were several women who volunteered there—mostly society women of the day who weren't working themselves and who thus could afford the time. I met some of them, but I don't specifically remember ever meeting Friedman. Her picture was in the paper when she was killed, and naturally I learned that she had been one of the volunteers. She looked vaguely familiar, but I had no recollection of ever having been introduced to her.

"To be honest, though, I only volunteered at the kitchen a handful of times. When I did, I simply stood in line, handing people plates, or ladling soup into bowls, or whatever else they asked me to do. And once my time was up, I was in my car immediately, headed home or back to the office or whatever. I was really pretty clueless about what was going on even in the soup kitchen, let alone the larger neighborhood."

"What was your brother's reaction to the murder?" I asked.

"He was horrified, of course, and to some extent he blamed himself."

"How so?"

"Well, as you know, of course, three other women were later killed by the same person who murdered Mrs. Friedman. All of them had some connection to the neighborhood where Joe's soup kitchen was located, and so it seemed likely that the killer was someone who frequented the area. Joe assumed that if he'd never invited Mrs. Friedman to work at the soup kitchen she wouldn't have been killed. I tried to tell him that it was ridiculous for him to be blaming himself, but to be honest, I think that the thought haunted him for the rest of his life and I'm sure he was still praying over it until the day he died."

"In talking to you, did he ever suggest a possible suspect—someone who occurred to him maybe even years later as a person who might have committed the crimes?"

"Not to me. And believe me, if any such thought had occurred to him, he would have been on the phone to you guys the moment that it did."

Maggie made a note and looked up to Turner. "Did any such person ever occur to you, independent of your brother's recollection?"

Turner paused for a moment, then folded his hands in his lap. Looking up at Maggie, he said, "Yeah, in fact there *was* a guy; one of the deacons in Joe's church. Steve something—Shelby? Shelton? Something like that. He volunteered down there a lot more regularly than I did and, on those occasions when we worked there together, it struck me that he had a very strong interest in the women who frequented the place—not the other volunteers like Mrs. Friedman, but the 'clients,' as my brother called them.

"I always thought that the guy was kind of strange. He never tried to engage the women in any way, but he had a way of looking at them that seemed pretty creepy, like he was mentally undressing them, you know? When the police questioned Joe about the murder, I asked him if he thought that this Steve guy could have possibly been involved. But Joe dismissed the idea out of hand and insisted that Steve was too upstanding—a pillar of the church, a married man, a father, blah, blah, blah. Joe wouldn't even consider the idea, let alone mention it to the investigators."

"Did you ever mention the thought to the detectives?" I asked.

He shook his head. "I was never interviewed in the case and so never had the opportunity."

"Do you know what might have become of the guy?" Maggie asked.

"No idea. I barely knew him at all, not even well enough to remember his last name for sure. If I'm remembering right, he moved away from Phoenix not too long after all this happened."

"You said he was a deacon in your brother's church," I said. "Would the church records still go back that far?"

"I don't know. My brother's church was a non-denominational affair that he began himself. When he finally retired, he recruited another minister to take over, but the new guy didn't have nearly the charisma or the organizational skills that Joe had, and the church only survived for another couple of years after Joe stepped down. I would imagine that whatever records still exist would be among my brother's personal things."

"And who would have possession of those?" I asked. "I noticed in the obituary that your brother was a widower."

"His son, Jason, inherited everything. If there were any surviving records, he'd have them, assuming he hasn't already disposed of them."

Turner had nothing else to offer and so Maggie and I rose to our feet. Handing him a card, I said, "If on the off chance anything should occur to you…"

"Of course," he said, sticking the card in the pocket of his shirt.

Turner escorted us back to the door, shook our hands and apologized for not having been more help.

"Not a problem," I replied. "Thank you for your time."

***

It was coming up on noon when we finished the Turner interview, and since we were almost right across the street from the Biltmore Fashion Park, I convinced Maggie that it would be an excellent idea to swing by Zinburger for lunch. We scored a table outside, and even though the temperature was somewhere in the middle nineties, we were perfectly comfortable under the misters that cooled the patio. Even at Zinburger, Maggie ordered a salad, which seemed blatantly sacrilegious. But given that she'd agreed to come, I held my tongue and decided not to give her any grief about it.

While we waited for our food to be served, we rehashed what we'd learned from Turner. Maggie took a sip of her iced tea and said, "Do you suppose there's even a tiny chance that this Steve person could have been the original killer?"

"I don't know, Maggie. What's most interesting is the fact that he apparently moved out of town at roughly the same time the killings stopped. That could explain why the fourth victim was the last, at least here in Phoenix. I sure as hell hope that there is some record of the guy in Joseph Turner's papers and that the son hasn't already incinerated them or some damned thing. But we'd better make talking to the son our next order of business."

The waitress interrupted our conversation at that point to serve our food, and as she did, I looked up to see two women, a blonde and a brunette, approaching the table from behind Maggie's chair. Each of the women was weighted down with shopping bags from Saks and from some of the smaller boutique stores that populated the Fashion Park. Both were in their late thirties and very well-tended—tall, sexy, and dressed to kill.

Now wishing desperately that we'd gone practically anywhere else for lunch, I stood as the blonde stepped around Maggie, lifted a hand to my shoulder and attempted to kiss me on the lips. I turned, giving her a cheek instead. Smiling in a particularly mischievous way, the blonde turned to her friend and said, "Beth, this is my son, Sean."

I shook my head. "Amanda, as you know very well, I am *not* your son, something which would be especially miraculous in any event, given that you're four months younger than I am."

Unfazed, she slipped her arm around my waist, leaned into me and said, "Well, step-son then, if you want to be so formal about it. And, as I've told you before, I really do wish you'd call me 'Mom.'"

"To be honest, I doubt that my mother would like that very much."

"Well, I would. I'm very proud to have a boy as smart and as handsome as you."

She finally released me and introduced her friend. I nodded and introduced Maggie. Struggling valiantly to keep a reasonably straight face, Maggie extended her hand to Amanda. "Sean's told me so many wonderful things about you, Mrs. Richardson. It's very nice to finally meet you."

I shot Maggie a look, but Amanda positively beamed. Her friend, Beth, seemed totally clueless, and stood watching the exchange as if it were the most normal conversation in the world. We made small talk for a couple of minutes, then Amanda announced that they were running late for a luncheon appointment with a couple of friends and would have to "scoot along." She leaned into me and kissed my cheek again. "Call me sometime soon, Sean. It's been way too long, and we really should catch up. Besides, I worry about you spending so much time alone and probably eating nothing but junk food. I want to take you out for a nice, healthy dinner, maybe at True Food or Kale and Clover, or someplace like that."

Without waiting for a response, the two said their goodbyes, assuring Maggie that it had been "great" meeting her. We watched them make their way down the sidewalk, then Maggie turned back with a huge shit-eating grin on her face. She snagged one of my fries, popped it into her mouth, and said, "Your mamma's hot for you, Sean."

"Bite me."

"I'm serious. And you never even mentioned that your stepmother was such a Major Babe. I always imagined that she was some poor little old lady living alone in a dingy apartment with only a herd of cats and your father's memory to sustain her."

I laughed. "Not hardly. More like a luxury condo in north Scottsdale and only my father's money to sustain her—or at least a pretty decent share of it."

"And where's your share again?"

"I don't get it until I'm forty, at least not unless I quit the department and finally go into the family business."

"Come again?"

"All the time I was growing up, my father dreamed that I'd someday join him in the company, the two of us working side by side, as he had with his father and as my grandfather had done with my great grandfather."

"So, what happened to that?"

"I don't know, Maggie. The truth is that, as much as I wanted to please him, I just had no interest at all in being a real estate developer. When I decided on a pre-law major rather than business, he told me that he respected my decision and that he would still pay for my undergraduate degree. But if I wanted to go to law school rather than come into the business, I would be on my own from that point on."

"He disowned you?"

"Financially, perhaps, but certainly not emotionally. I was still his son and he loved me as much as he always had. I think it was simply his way of telling me that if I wanted to be my own man, I should go all the way and not be dependent on him for financial support any longer.

"The result was, when I finished the B.A. I had to delay going to law school until I could put some money aside. So, I took the exam to join the department, thinking I could save a little money, maybe take some night school courses, and ultimately get the law degree. I'm sure my dad thought it was just a passing fancy—that I'd get tired of being a cop pretty quickly, that I'd lose my enthusiasm for being a lawyer as well, and that I'd ultimately come to work in the business. And he revised his will with that thought in mind."

"How so?"

"Well, my dad and Uncle Phil each owned fifty percent of the business. Then when Dad was killed, under the terms of the divorce, his will left ten percent of his share to my mom in lieu of the alimony she would have collected had he continued to live. Ten percent went to Amanda and his remaining thirty percent went to me with the stipulation that I didn't get it until I either turned forty or came to work in the company. In the meantime, Uncle Phil is the trustee and votes my share of the stock."

"And what does the lovely Amanda think about that?"

"She has no problem with it at all. Any real interest that she had in the company ended the moment my dad promoted her out of the secretarial pool and into the matrimonial bed. Uncle Phil's doing a great job; the company's making piles of money, and so Amanda is free to spend her days lunching and shopping without having to do any work at all."

We finished lunch, split the check, and headed back to the department. As we stepped out the door of the restaurant, Maggie gave me another huge grin and said, "Your step-mom does have a thing for you, Sean, and I think it's kind of cute in a kinky sort of way."

19.

Jason Turner owned an insurance agency with an office in small strip mall on Bell Road. A little after two o'clock, Maggie and I stepped through the door and asked to see him. The receptionist, a trim young brunette, buzzed Turner, and he told her to show us in.

Turner's office was relatively large, with a good grade of furniture, a computer sitting on an exceptionally clean desktop, and three upholstered clients' chairs arranged in front of the desk. The man himself was as immaculate as the office, trimmed out in an expensive blue suit, a crisp white shirt, and a blue tie with a small check pattern. He appeared to be somewhere in his middle forties, about five-ten, with a full head of light brown hair and eyes so dark that they almost looked fake. He was obviously a guy who put in his time at the gym and looked to be in very good physical condition.

Maggie and I went through the motions of showing him our badges and IDs and Turner invited us to sit. We took two of the chairs in front of the desk and Turner came around the desk and took the third, moving it around a bit so that he was facing the two of us. I explained that we were investigating the death of Allison Martin and that in the process of doing so we were also talking to people about the related killing of Martin's grandmother. Turner gave me a perplexed look. "I'm not sure how I can help you, Detective. Naturally, I've seen the reports on the news, but I was only three years old when Mrs. Friedman was killed, and I know nothing about her grand-daughter."

"We understand that, of course, Mr. Turner," I said. "But we were talking with your uncle this morning and he suggested that you might still have the records left from your father's church. Based on what your uncle told us, we're hoping there might be a lead in those records that would be of help."

Looking even more confused, Turner said, "I don't understand; why would you be talking to my uncle about this? And why would you think that there'd be anything in my father's old papers that would help?"

"The first victim, Ellen Friedman, volunteered at a soup kitchen that your father ran downtown at the time of the killings," Maggie said. "We were talking to your uncle in the hope that your father might have shared with him any thoughts about someone at the kitchen who might have showed an interest in Mrs. Friedman. Your uncle suggested that there was a deacon in the church who volunteered down there and who might fit the bill. We were hoping that we might find some record of this guy in your father's papers."

"Well, Detective McClinton, this is all news to me. I really don't know what sort of records my father might have kept, although I know that there are some. Almost everything he left is still at his home and I've been slowly working my way through it, trying to clean out the house so that I can put it on the market. But I've been so busy otherwise that I've barely made a dent in it. I know that there are some file boxes stored in the garage, but I haven't looked through them. If there are any surviving records from the church, they'd be in those boxes."

"What we're hoping to find," Maggie said, "are employment records or any other sort of information about a man who was a deacon in your father's church back in the late seventies. Your uncle said the man's first name was Steve, and he thought that the last name might be something like Shelton or Shelby. Does that ring a bell?"

Turner shook his head. "How long did Uncle Fred say that this guy had worked with Dad?"

"He didn't say for sure," I replied, "but he suggested that the man had left Phoenix maybe in early 1977 or so."

Turner shrugged. "I have absolutely no memory of anyone like that, but I was still a small child in 1977."

"We understand that, sir," Maggie said. "And that's why we're hoping that there might be some record of the man in your father's papers."

"Well, you're certainly welcome to look if you'd like; I don't know when I'm going to have a chance to get through them myself."

"When would be a convenient time for you?" I asked.

Shaking his head, Turner said, "To be honest, Detective, there isn't going to be a convenient time. As I said, I've been so busy lately that I haven't had a chance to make a serious start on going through Dad's things. I've been pecking away at it as I can squeeze out the time, but that's about it."

The silence hung in the air for a few seconds, then Turner said, "Do you really need me to be there when you're going through the papers?"

"Well, probably not, if you don't mind us going through them without you being present."

"That's not a problem at all. There are about nine or ten file boxes in the garage and I'm assuming that, if there are any church records, they would have to be in those boxes. I'd be happy to give you the key to Dad's garage. If you guys want to go over there and dig through that stuff, it's perfectly fine with me."

"You're sure you don't mind?"

"Not at all. In fact, you'd be doing me a favor. If you wouldn't mind leaving me a note for each of the boxes you open, indicating what's in the box, then maybe I won't have to go through them myself." Smiling, he looked at me and said, "That looks like a pretty nice suit you're wearing, though, and I certainly wouldn't think you'd want to wear it into Dad's garage. Your oldest pair of jeans and a ratty old tee shirt would be much more appropriate."

"Point taken," I said. "Thanks for the offer and for the advice. If it's okay with you, we'll probably try to get at it tomorrow morning."

"Fine with me, and the earlier in the morning the better. That garage can get pretty warm once the sun starts beating down on it."

Turner walked back around the desk, took a seat, and wrote down the address of his father's home. He then opened a drawer and came out with a ring of keys. He slipped a key off the ring and passed the address and the key over to me. "Go over anytime you'd like. This key is a duplicate. When you're finished, you can just leave it on the workbench in the garage and pull the door closed behind you."

21.

At seven thirty the next morning, I pulled into the driveway that fronted Joseph Turner's garage and parked next to a Buick sedan that was sitting in the driveway. I used the key that Turner's son had provided to unlock the side door to the building and found myself in a two-car garage, half of which had been given over to storage. There was the usual assortment of lawn and garden tools that one might expect to find in a garage, along with a couple of pieces of furniture and a freezer that had been left unplugged with the cord draped over the lid. Nine banker's boxes were stacked in the middle of the space that had been reserved for parking a car, and on top of one of the boxes was a note from Jason Turner addressed to Maggie and me.

"Detectives Richardson and McClinton: I swung by last night and separated these boxes from the rest of the junk in here. Any church records should be in them. I've pulled Dad's car out to give you room to work, and I left the key on the workbench. When you're finished, will you please set the boxes out of the way and pull the car back in? You can just leave the key in the ignition. Thanks—and I hope you find what you're looking for."

The note was signed, "J.T.," and I folded it in half and stuck it in my pocket. Maggie and I had taken the precaution of securing a warrant to search the garage and even though she had not yet arrived with the paperwork, I popped the top on the first box and set in to work.

A fairly large number of files had been squeezed into the box, and according to the labels, the files all contained material relating to Joseph Turner's tax returns for the last eleven years. The second box held the tax records for the ten years preceding that, and I jotted a note describing the contents, taped it to the top of the first box, and set the two boxes aside for Turner's son.

I'd just opened a third box when Maggie stepped into the garage. Like me, she'd opted for jeans and a tee-shirt. But while I was wearing a standard Eddie Bauer black tee that had set me back all of about fourteen ninety-five, Maggie's shirt was a brilliant white number that looked like it was fresh off some designer's shelf and had obviously cost something far north of fifteen bucks. "Nice shirt," I said. "I can hardly wait to see how clean it looks by the time we get through mucking around in all of this dust."

"Thanks. I wore it so I'd have a good excuse to make you do all the heavy lifting. But in exchange, I did bring breakfast."

With that, she passed over a bag containing a couple of maple-frosted donuts and two cups of black coffee. I pulled a couple of the file boxes away from the pile, made a pass at wiping the dust off them, and then Maggie and I sat down on the boxes and spent a few minutes working on the coffee and donuts.

With breakfast out of the way, we went back to work on the boxes. We were able to dispose of five of the nine pretty quickly, given that they obviously contained no records relating to Turner's church activities. Two other boxes contained church records from years well after the period in which we were interested, leaving us two boxes of church records dating from the early nineteen seventies to the early eighties.

Those two boxes contained tightly packed files that related to a variety of the church's activities, including committee meetings, fundraising efforts, charitable activities and so forth. We had no idea where our Deacon Steve might show up, assuming he was in there at all, and so we had no choice other than to go painstakingly through each of the files hoping that he might appear in some capacity.

We assumed that a deacon would almost certainly be involved in a variety of church activities and so the most obvious place to start was the records of the church committees. Over the next couple of hours, we skimmed through the minutes of the meetings of several committees. We found four committee members with the first name of Steve, but none of them had last names that began with an S or that sounded even vaguely like Shelby or Shelton. And none of the four was identified as a deacon.

We found seven men who *were* identified as deacons in the committee records, but none of them was named Steve, and branching out, we found no one with a name even remotely close to the one we were looking for in any of the other church records. Since Fred Turner had been certain that the man he wondered about *had* been a deacon, I kept a list of the names of all the deacons we found in the records, but otherwise we came up empty-handed. A little after noon, I dropped the top back on the last box, pushed it out of the way and said, "Well, shit."

Maggie looked around the garage as if hoping a piece of useful evidence might suddenly pop out of the debris that surrounded us. "I second the motion. Do you suppose Turner misremembered the name or the role the guy played in the church? Maybe he wasn't a deacon."

"I have no idea, Maggie. But in either case, I don't know how we identify him with what we've got here. It would have helped if the pastor had at least kept a record of the people who volunteered at the soup kitchen. But from what these records indicate, and based on what his brother told us yesterday, it was a pretty loose operation, staffing-wise. There's just no way to know which of the people in these records might have volunteered down there, let alone other members of the church who don't even appear here. It looks like we've spent a long, hot, dusty morning for nothing."

As Jason Turner had warned us, the garage had warmed dramatically as the morning progressed, even though I'd opened both of the doors to let some air circulate through. Maggie wiped the sweat from her brow and said, "Dusty is right. And you were also right about the tee shirt; I sure as hell hope that the cleaners can save it. So, what's our next step?"

"Christ, I don't know, Maggie. Maybe we need to consult the fuckin' Psychic Hotline. The best remaining lead we have, thin as it might be, is Bruce Robinson, the ex-drapery installer. He's now the only person left from the Friedman case who might possibly be the link between that case and ours, at least that we can find. And again, that assumes that Friedman's killer even crossed the radar of the original investigation. I just hope that by the time we get to the office on Monday, Pierce and Chickris will be able to give us a good idea of what the guy's been up to for the last forty years."

***

I spent the rest of Saturday afternoon in the office, catching up on paperwork related to the case, and that night I took Sara to Eddie V's. I reserved a table in the lounge, and we listened to the Judy Roberts trio with Greg Warner on drums and Greg Fishman on Sax while we ate dinner and nursed a bottle of wine, taking time out to dance several times. We then spent the night at my house, but we both had laundry, house cleaning and other assorted chores to do the following day and so spent Sunday night apart in our own homes. And thus I was sleeping alone at five forty-five on Monday morning when the sergeant woke me with the news that another young woman had been found strangled, wrapped in plastic, and abandoned in a vacant lot a couple of blocks south of the old Deuce.

21.

The scene was a vacant lot at the corner of Second and Tonto, right across the street from the park where the body of Allie Martin had been left. The lot had been graded to a flat tan surface, with a few weeds poking out of it, and a realtor's sign that advertised the property for sale.

I arrived about six forty-five and parked behind Maggie who was just getting out of her car. Together we walked over and greeted Gary Barnett who was already on the job, along with two other members of the Crime Scene Response Team. He shook his head and said, "Looks like you guys have a really sick bastard on your hands."

A concrete block wall, about six and a half feet high and running east and west, separated the lot from the neighboring property to the north. Two-thirds of the way along the length of the property, the wall turned ninety degrees. From there it ran about six feet north before turning east again and running to the narrow gravel alley at the back of the property. The package containing the body had been left in the inside corner of the wall, which would have made it virtually impossible to see in the darkness.

The package was wrapped exactly like the one we'd found only six days earlier. In this case, the victim was a redhead, a bit taller than Allison Martin and perhaps a few pounds heavier, but certainly just as attractive. Like Martin, this victim had been packaged naked, with her eyes wide open. But in this case the young woman's hands were folded in front of her, laying across her stomach. And looped through her fingers was a Catholic rosary with a white tag tied just above the crucifix.

We stood quietly for several minutes, assimilating the scene, then Gary broke the silence. "I'm sorry to say that it looks like your guy didn't leave us any more evidence here than he did in the park— which is to say, none at all, except for whatever the M.E. might find once she opens the package. But I'm guessing we're going to come up with zip again."

Less than five minutes later, Sara pulled to a stop in the street and got out of her 4Runner, carrying her bag, and dressed in jeans with a blazer over a white tee shirt. She walked over, looked down at the body and, apparently without even thinking, gripped my arm and said, "Ah, fuck."

After a couple of seconds, she composed herself and released my arm. Appearing somewhat chagrinned, she said, "Sorry about that."

She too took a moment to assess the situation, then knelt next to the body, retrieved a small knife from her bag and slit a hole in the plastic near the victim's throat. She officially pronounced the woman dead and I asked her to cut another small hole so that I could remove the rosary. She nodded, moved down to the victim's abdomen, and then cut another small opening.

I gloved up, gently removed the rosary from the young woman's fingers and dropped it into an evidence bag. I then reached into the bag and turned over the tag that had been attached to the crucifix. The name on the tag had been printed with what looked to be a blue ballpoint pen. The lettering had faded, and the ink had almost disappeared in a couple of places, but still I could easily make out the name "Laura Garcia."

I showed the tag to Maggie who simply shook her head sadly and said, "Oh Christ, Sean."

I signed, sealed, and dated the bag, then handed it off to Gary. "We'll need whatever you can get off this ASAP. In particular, we need to know when the name was printed on that tag. Was it fairly recent, or could it have been written forty years ago? And can you tell us how old the rosary might be?"

Gary promised that he'd do his best, and over the next forty minutes, Sara took the body off to the morgue and Barnett and his team finished their preliminary assessment of the scene. Greg and Elaine arrived and began organizing a canvass of the neighborhood, although none of us was holding out any real hope that it would produce any more results than had the one a week earlier. Maggie and I would go back to headquarters to update the sergeant and to begin looking through the missing persons reports.

This morning's activity had attracted a larger group of reporters, and as I headed back to my car, several of them shouted questions at me. I detoured over to the space where they were contained behind the crime scene barricades and gave them the standard spiel about not having any information for them now and referring them to Media Relations, who would have a briefing later in the day.

From their vantage point, the reporters had been able to clearly see the body and a couple of the TV cameramen had filmed the attendants loading it into the M. E.'s van. A reporter from Channel 5 shoved a microphone in my direction and said, "This body was wrapped in plastic just like the one in Central Park last week. Is it the same killer, Detective?"

"I'm sorry," I said, "but it's way too early to know anything like that at this point and I won't be making any comment here."

The Channel 2 cameraman filmed the exchange, and while the other reporters continued to shout questions as I turned and walked away, Ellie Davis simply nodded at me, turned to her cameraman, and began filing her report.

***

After briefing the sergeant, Maggie and I got into the missing persons' reports and again found our victim almost immediately. A young bartender/cocktail waitress named Corrine Ray had been reported missing by her roommate when the victim failed to return home from work on Friday night. In this case, we had no photo of the missing woman filed with the report, but the physical description matched perfectly.

The victim's apartment was in a building downtown on West Portland, less than two miles from the spot where her body had been discarded. Her roommate was Jennifer Hansen, a stocky brunette who was somewhere in her middle twenties and clearly distraught. "We were going to a party at a friend's here in the building after

Corrine got off from work Friday," Hansen told us. "She texted me a little before midnight to say that she was leaving work. I expected her to be here no later than twelve-thirty, and when she didn't show up, I texted her back but got no answer. I waited thirty minutes or so and then tried to call her, but it went straight to voicemail. When I didn't hear anything by morning, I called the police."

Hansen's eyes were rimmed red. She wiped away another tear and turned to Maggie. "Is it my fault? Did I wait too long to call you guys?"

"No, of course not," Maggie said. "I'm sorry to say this, but by the time you realized that Corrine was late getting home, it was probably already too late to save her. There was nothing you could have done."

Hansen shook her head, like she wasn't sure she believed it, and I said, "You told us that she always took the train home when she worked late at night. Are you sure she would have done that on Friday?"

"Yes. In her text, she told me that she was headed to the train."

"So, she would have walked only a couple of blocks from the place where she worked to catch the train and only another couple of blocks once she left the station to get home?"

Hansen nodded.

"Do you know if she'd been having problems with anyone—a boyfriend, perhaps, or maybe some guy who was hassling her at work?"

The young woman wiped her eyes again and shook her head. "No, she wasn't dating anyone exclusively right now. Of course, guys hit on her all the time, especially at work. But she was used to that. She was very outgoing and took it all in stride. She never mentioned having a problem with anyone that way, and I know that she would have."

"Ms. Hansen, does the name Laura Garcia mean anything to you?" I asked.

111

She thought about it for a moment, then said, "No, I don't know her. Who is she?"

"No one important. I was just wondering if Ms. Ray might have ever mentioned the name."

"What about her family?" Maggie asked.

"They're still in Eugene, Oregon—that's where Corrine was from. She has a mother, a father, and a younger brother still up there."

"And have you heard from them?" I asked.

"I called them on Saturday to tell them that Corrine was missing. And I talked to them again yesterday to tell them that she still hadn't come home. But I haven't called them since I heard this morning." Beginning to sob again, she said, "I just couldn't. I'm sorry."

"Not to worry," Maggie said. "That's really our job anyhow."

"Ms. Hansen," I said, "Was Corrine a Catholic?"

"No. I think she was raised a Lutheran, but she wasn't religious at all anymore."

"Do you know if she had a rosary and if she might have normally carried it with her?"

"A rosary—you mean one of those prayer bead things?"

I nodded, and Hansen said, "No. Corrine never prayed. What would she be doing with one of those?"

***

Hansen had virtually nothing else to contribute. She told us that Corrine Ray had relied exclusively on her iPhone for e-mail and other online activities and that she had no computer or tablet. She always carried the phone in a pocket or in her bag, but of course we hadn't found either the bag or her clothes. She had Facebook and Snapchat accounts but, according to her roommate, she was not very big on social media.

Hansen gave us the contact information for Ray's parents in Oregon, and back in the car, Maggie made the call that no cop ever wants to make. Ray's mother answered the phone and was obviously devastated by the news, even though she admitted that she and her husband had been fearing the worst. She told Maggie that she and her husband would be flying to Phoenix as soon as possible and would contact us when they had arrived. She told Maggie that the name Laura Garcia meant absolutely nothing to her and that she was sure that the family was not related to anyone by that name.

Maggie concluded the call and relayed the conversation to me. "So, in this case," I said, "it would appear, at least for now, that there's no connection between Garcia and Ray, save for the fact that they both tended bar in the same neighborhood roughly forty years apart. And our killer, who somehow has what appears to be Laura Garcia's rosary, leaves it with Ray's body and tags it so that we'll be sure to make the connection."

"That's what it looks like to me," Maggie agreed. "I wonder what Bruce Robinson was up to over the weekend."

22.

Back at 620, we found that Pierce and Chickris had returned from doing the canvass and that their interviews had produced no useful information. "The body was obviously left there sometime overnight," Elaine said, "but we have no idea when. No one that we talked to saw or heard anything unusual until a little after five this morning when a man leaving for work saw the body and called it in."

Maggie and I brought them up to date with regard to what we had—and hadn't—found on Friday and Saturday and asked what they'd come up with on Bruce Robinson. "According to the MVD, he's sixty-six years old," Elaine said. "He's apparently spent the bulk of his adult life doing the equivalent of odd jobs and working mostly for cash off the books. He's not registered to vote and has never served on a jury. He rents the place in Glendale and has apparently never owned any real estate. He has only one vehicle registered in his name, a ten-year-old panel van that he bought used."

"Two arrests," Greg added, "both for drunk and disorderly. The second time was fifteen years ago, but he got no jail time in either case. Other than that, he's accumulated a handful of speeding and parking tickets, all of which he paid. There's nothing in his file suggesting anything in the area of sexual assault or any other sort of violence.

"The neighbors say that he keeps mostly to himself, but then it's that sort of neighborhood. Nobody reports having any sort of trouble with him and the people we talked to claimed to have no idea what Robinson might have been doing the weekend that Martin was being held somewhere. None of them seemed very happy to talk to us and, if they did know what the guy was up to, we got the general impression that they wouldn't have been particularly willing to share the information with a couple of cops anyway."

***

We agreed that Elaine and Gregg would begin interviewing Corrine Ray's neighbors and fellow employees in an effort to understand what was going on in the young woman's life and who, if anyone, might have posed a threat to her. We were fairly confident that we were just going through the motions in that regard, but still, it had to be done. Maggie would secure the video from the security cameras in the Washington/Central and Roosevelt/Central stations and from the light rail train itself for late Friday night into early Saturday morning and check the recordings to see if anyone had been paying particularly close attention to the victim or if anyone might have followed her off the train.

My assignment was to brief the sergeant and then go have another talk with Bruce Robinson. "Obviously, we're looking for someone with a tie to the original killings," I told the sergeant. "Someone who committed the crimes and kept souvenirs, then went underground for forty years and has now resurfaced to start all over again. Either that or someone who found the cache of souvenirs and decided to replicate the crimes himself.

"Now that we know that the Martin killing was not just an isolated incident, I'd like to ask Jack Oliva to come in and help me go through the records of the old cases. There has to be a link in there somewhere that ties the original cases to ours. Oliva knows those records better than anyone, and he's a lot more likely to find the connection than we are."

"I have no problem with that if he's willing to do it. Of course, I can't pay him."

"I don't think that'll be a problem, but I'll let you know what he says."

***

Back at my desk I called Oliva and explained that our killer had struck again. "This time he killed a young cocktail waitress and instead of a DL, he left us a rosary with Laura Garcia's name tagged to it."

115

"Aw, crap," Oliva said. "Garcia was a cocktail waitress, of course. She was also illegal and, as far as we could tell, had no DL or any other form of official ID. Still, she was attractive enough that she could get the job at La Amapola and get paid under the table. Forty years ago, of course, people in Arizona didn't get as bent out of shape about that sort of thing as they do now."

"Did she have any family here?"

"Not that we found. Her friends told us that she came north with an older brother, but he'd moved on to someplace in California by the time she was killed, and we were never able to contact him."

"So, in this case we have no family tie; the guy just picked a waitress who worked near the spot of the old La Amapola."

"And the bastard sure didn't waste any time, did he? My guy waited four months from Friedman to Garcia. Yours only waited a week."

"Which scares the hell out of me. If this asshole plans to replicate your guy's entire pattern, he could be scoping out his next victim right now."

"Assuming it's not the same guy."

"Correct. I'm about to go talk to your buddy, Bruce Robinson again; want to go along?"

"Love to," he replied.

23.

We got to Robinson's place a little after noon, only to discover that he wasn't at home. The carport was empty, and his van was nowhere in sight. Standing under the carport by the front door to the house, Oliva looked around at the fences that separated Robinson from his neighbors on three sides and said, "Given as well as this spot is shielded from view, it'd be a piece of cake to back a van up to the door here and unload someone into the house, especially after midnight."

"No question," I said.

We walked around the perimeter of the house, pausing to peek through windows that looked like they hadn't been washed since sometime during the Carter administration. From what we could see, Robinson was about as carless with the interior maintenance of the house as he was with the exterior. Dirty dishes were stacked in the kitchen sink; several beer cans and a carryout pizza box had been left on the coffee table in the living room. But sadly, there were no chains, ropes, handcuffs, or anything else that might have been used to restrain a kidnap victim lying around in plain sight.

A blackout shade had been affixed tightly around the inside of the frame of the window we assumed to be the bedroom and it was impossible to get even a sliver of a view into the room. "The guy must be very sensitive to light," Oliva said.

"Yeah, either that or he really likes his privacy in that room."

We ended our tour back under the carport, trying to stay out from under the blazing sun. Just off the edge of the concrete drive was the standard garbage bin issued by the city of Phoenix. I lifted the lid and saw that the bin was about half full. Two standard-sized black plastic garbage bags had been dumped into the bin and jammed into the bin on top of them was a piece of clear plastic sheeting. The exposed edge of the sheet showed a somewhat jagged line, indicating clearly that the piece had been cut from another. Lying on top of the sheeting was an empty roll of packing tape in a red plastic disposable dispenser.

Oliva studied the contents of the bin, then turned away for a moment. Turning back, he looked me straight in the eye. "If the lid on that bin had been closed when we first saw it, we'd have had no legal grounds to open it and look in. But since it was standing open like that, so that anybody walking by could see into it, we'd be perfectly within our rights to take a closer look at that tape dispenser and piece of plastic sheeting. Or you would, I guess, since you're the one with the badge."

I waited a moment myself, then said, "I guess this is our lucky day."

I pulled a pair of latex gloves from my pocket, slipped them on, and then picked the tape dispenser out of the bin. It was, or had been, a roll of two-inch-wide Scotch Mailing and Storage Tape. I carefully set the dispenser back into the bin, leaving it as I had found it. Then I pulled out my phone and dialed Gary Barnett. When he answered, I said, "Two Questions, Gary. First, can you identify the type of tape that was used to seal the package that Corrine Ray was wrapped in?"

"Probably not, I'm afraid. All I can tell you is that the tape was two inches wide and that it probably came from a standard roll that you could buy in any hardware, office supply or grocery store in town."

"Okay, then second, was the plastic sheeting that she was wrapped in cut from a larger piece, or does it appear that the killer used a whole sheet of plastic?"

"No, he didn't. The piece he used was cut from another piece. The line on one edge is not exactly straight."

"So, if I showed you a piece of plastic sheeting that's obviously been cut from another, you could lay them side by side and see if they matched up?"

"Sure," he replied. "Please tell me you've got the other piece."

"Keep your fingers crossed. I'm going after a warrant now."

I relayed the conversation to Oliva and then phoned the sergeant and explained the situation. "Obviously, we need to get permission to seize the contents of this garbage bin and we need to try to make the warrant broad enough to cover Robinson's house and van."

"On the basis of what you've found, getting into the house and van might be a little tricky, but I'll do the best I can."

"Okay, I'm going to sit on this until someone gets here with a warrant; I don't want Robinson coming home and disposing of it."

"Understood," he said.

I disconnected from the call and slipped the phone back into my pocket. Just as I did, Robinson's van rounded the corner and pulled into the drive. Oliva and I stepped aside, and Robinson braked the van to a stop under the carport. Jumping out, he slammed the door and said, "What do you assholes want now, and what the fuck are you doing rooting around in my garbage?"

"Well, Bruce," Oliva said, "If you didn't want people looking into your bin, you should leave the lid down."

"The hell. It *was* down."

Oliva simply shrugged. "Not when we got here."

Turning to me, Robinson said, "What the hell is up with you cocksuckers? Why have you been out riling up my neighbors and telling them that I might be the guy who killed Friedman's fuckin' granddaughter last week?"

"No one's told your neighbors any such thing," I said. "Detective Oliva and I warned you that we'd be poking into your business if you didn't cooperate with us. But instead you gave us some bullshit story about how you spent your weekend, with no one to corroborate it. We had no choice but to try to verify your whereabouts."

Refusing to back down, Robinson turned from me to Oliva and said, "You had no goddamned right to do that. I haven't done anything. You got no cause to be hassling me."

"Maybe, maybe not," Oliva said. "Where were you Friday night, Bruce?"

"None of your fuckin' business."

I closed the gap between us and stepped well into Robinson's personal space. Jabbing a finger into his chest, I said, "The hell it isn't. And if you don't have a good answer right now, you'll be on your way downtown."

Robinson took a step back. In a voice that suddenly sounded a lot less assured, he said, "You can't do that."

"We can, and we will. Where were you on Friday night, Mr. Robinson?"

"Here. All night."

"Alone?"

"Yes."

"And Saturday?"

"Shit, I don't know. Out and around. I had some errands to run and other crap to do."

"Anybody to vouch for you?"

"No. I had lunch at the McDonald's on Grand. The receipt is in the garbage inside. I got gas later and that receipt is in there too."

"How long were you out running these errands?" Oliva asked.

"Hell, I don't know. A couple of hours, maybe."

"And Saturday night?" I asked.

"At my sister's in Surprise. I had dinner with her and her old man. I got home about eleven."

"What about Sunday?"

He shook his head. "I slept in, had some breakfast, and changed the oil in my van. I did my laundry in the afternoon then ordered in a pizza and watched TV until I went to bed around ten."

"What's the plastic sheeting and the tape for?" I asked.

Robinson looked into the bin and hesitated for a moment. Still staring into the bin rather than looking at me, he said, "I moved some furniture into storage on Friday. I wrapped it up in plastic to protect it."

"Where'd you get the plastic?" Oliva asked.

"At the Home Depot, and what the fuck does it matter to you guys anyway?"

"Does it come in a roll or do you just buy a package of it?"

Now looking totally flustered, Robinson said, "On a roll, a hundred feet long and twenty wide. You unroll what you need and then unfold it out."

"Jesus, Bruce, you must have had a lot of furniture to wrap," Oliva said.

Robinson shook his head. "Only a couple of pieces; I use it to wrap other stuff too and when I'm painting a room or some shit like that."

Nodding in the direction of the bin, I said, "Looks like you had a little left over."

"I screwed up and cut a piece that was too small. I had to cut another, and so I just threw that one away."

With that, Robinson stepped over to the bin and slammed the lid down. "Any other questions?" he asked.

Before either Oliva or I could answer, Robinson stepped behind the bin, tilted it back on its wheels and began rolling it toward the rear of his van. I grabbed his arm and said, "Sorry, Bruce, but you need to leave that bin right where it was."

"Like hell I do."

"Like hell you don't. We have a warrant on the way to seize that bin and until it gets here, the bin stays right where it was."

"Bullshit."

Spinning out of my grasp, he again began wheeling the bin toward the van. Again, I grabbed his arm and this time he turned around, grabbed me by the shoulders and pushed me away. Oliva moved in immediately, pulled Robinson off me and shoved him face first into the wall of the house. "Bad move, Bruce," he said. "Assaulting an officer is never a good idea."

As Robinson swore at us and attempted to break out of Oliva's grip, I gave him another shove up against the wall and told him to assume the position. Apparently coming to his senses, Robinson quit struggling and said, "Shit, I haven't done anything. Why are you doing this to me?"

***

I cuffed Robinson, read him is rights, and then Oliva and I walked him to my Impala and stuffed him into the back seat, with Robinson cursing the two of us and all of our ancestors. I rolled down the window to give him some air and then called the lieutenant to report the news and to check on the status of our warrant.

An hour later, Elaine Pierce arrived with a warrant that allowed us to seize the contents of Robinson's garbage bin and to search his home and vehicle. I introduced Elaine to Oliva and while Oliva brought her up to speed with respect to what had transpired, I walked the warrant over to the car and showed it to Robinson. "You goddamned son of a bitch," he said, "you've got no fucking right to treat me like this."

"The paper says I do, Bruce. Now, do you want to give me your keys or do you want us just to kick the door in?"

His response was to draw his knees up to his chest and slam his feet into the front seat of the Impala. Then, almost in a whisper, he said, "Please, don't do this. I haven't done anything."

"Are you going to let me have the keys?"

He waited, fuming for another few seconds and then said in a defeated voice, "They're in the van."

I gloved up again, walked over to the van and opened the rear doors. The cargo area was empty, but I noted four rings that had been bolted to the floor, one in each corner of the cargo area, which might have been used to tie down a load or, perhaps, for some other purpose all together.

I checked the pocket in the passenger's door and took a quick look in the glove compartment but saw nothing that aroused any suspicion. The same was true of the pocket in the driver's side door, which contained only a few tattered street maps and an open pack of Marlboros. I grabbed the key ring from the ignition and closed up the truck, leaving it for the techs to go through once they'd towed it into the garage at the crime lab.

I handed Oliva a pair of gloves and Elaine came up with a set of her own. "Let's do an initial walkthrough to see if anything jumps out at us that would justify having the techs tear this place apart."

I sorted through the keys on Robinson's ring and found one that worked on the door leading into the house from the carport. I opened the door and the three of us stepped into the disaster that was Robinson's kitchen. Dirty dishes were stacked haphazardly, overflowing the kitchen sink. The counters and the tabletop were filthy, and it looked like the floor hadn't been mopped in years.

A short hallway led from the living room to a bathroom that mirrored the condition of the rest of the place, and to a small bedroom where Oliva and I had observed the blackout shade while surveying the house from outside. I snapped on a light which illuminated a double bed that had been left unmade, with rumpled sheets that clearly hadn't been washed and ironed in a while. A Dell computer sat on a small desk under the window and a flat-screen television was positioned on a table at the foot of the bed, facing the headboard. A single nightstand with two drawers sat next to the bed, and a lamp, a small bottle of lube and a box of tissues were sitting on top of the nightstand.

A tripod with a small video camera attached stood next to the desk, aimed in the general direction of the bed. I stepped behind the camera and pressed the power button. Three icons, apparently representing three different videos, appeared on the camera's screen. The first button was highlighted and when I pressed the "play" button, I found myself looking at two children, maybe ten or eleven years old, engaged in a disgusting sexual act on Robinson's bed. Shaking my head, I turned to Elaine and Jack, both of whom were still standing in the hallway. "The two of you need to come in and witness this, but be careful not to touch anything. Then we'll lock up this pigsty and leave it for the techs."

I moved aside, leaving room for Elaine and Jack to step in and look at the screen. On seeing the video, Oliva just closed his eyes for a moment and shook his head. Elaine then stepped in to look and said, "That lousy motherfucker."

I stopped the video and powered down the camera. Then I carefully removed it from the tripod, dropped it into an evidence bag and signed, sealed, and dated the bag. Back outside, we each took a deep breath of fresh air and I then called Gary Barnett and told him to get a crew to the house. "Be sure to grab the computer, of course, and then take this dump down to the studs. We want to be sure that we find everything this bastard is hiding in there."

Gary indicated that he'd already sent a flatbed to load up Robinson's van and take it back to the lab and that he'd have a crew ready to go through the house in just under an hour. I told him that Elaine would stay to guard the place until the techs arrived and that I'd be taking Robinson in to be processed into the system.

Oliva and I walked back to my car and as we settled into the front seats, Robinson again began to protest. I turned, looked over the seat and said, "Bad luck, you disgusting piece of shit. We found your videos and you're going down hard. One more word out of you and I'll come back there and beat the living crap out of you. Then we'll both say that you tried to come over the seat and get at me and that I had no choice but to defend myself."

Robinson spit on the floor. "Fuck you," was all he had the chance to say before Oliva turned slightly and threw his left elbow into Robinson's face. Robinson's nose cracked loudly, and he screamed in agony. Oliva turned back, looked over to me and said, "You can charge me with assault if you want."

"Fat fuckin' chance," I replied.

***

Robinson remained quiet for the rest of the ride with his broken nose dripping a little blood, but not as much as I would have expected. I dropped Oliva at his house and as he got out of the car he said, "Good working with you, Sean. I hope we can do this again."

"I'd enjoy it. I'll stay in touch."

I got Robinson back to the stationhouse without further incident and herded him into booking. "The preliminary charge is producing child pornography," I told the booking officer. I'll be coming up with a lot of other things to add on later."

Upstairs, I reported in to the sergeant, telling him that we almost certainly had Robinson dead to rights on the child pornography. "It's clearly his bed in the video and I'm sure his fingerprints will be all over the camera."

"Anything to tie him to the Ray or Martin killings?"

"Nothing that appeared to the naked eye, save for the plastic sheeting and the empty roll of packing tape. I'm hoping that the lab can match up the two pieces of sheeting and that the techs will find additional evidence in the van or in the house that will link him to Martin and Ray. But for the moment all we've got for sure is the kiddie porn, and that will certainly be enough to hold him until the other tests are in."

"Okay. Keep me in the loop."

***

I walked the camera across the street to the lab, then returned to the headquarters building and hunted Maggie down in her office. I described my afternoon, and she said, "Well, I sincerely hope he turns out to be our guy. Unfortunately, Pierce and Chickris got nothing worthwhile from Ray's neighbors. I spent most of the afternoon watching video from the light rail people, but I didn't come up with much of anything either.

"We have a young guy wearing a backpack who boarded the train at the Washington station right after Ray. The guy sat in the same car as she did, but he seemed to be paying no attention to her at all. He then got off at the Roosevelt station, but he did so ahead of Ray, rather than waiting for her to get off and then following her. It's possible, I suppose, that he'd been scouting her and knew that she'd get off there and so got off first and was waiting down the street to stuff her into a vehicle of some sort as she was walking by. But if

125

that's the case, the guy is very good. He had his earbuds in and seemed to be totally lost in his own little world."

"Does the video show which way he went once he got off the train?"

"Unfortunately, not."

"And there's nothing else on the video of any interest?"

"If there is, I sure as hell didn't see it."

"Well, it's probably a long shot, but why don't we print the guy's picture and then get a couple of reserves posted in each of the train stations for a couple of nights? If the guy's a regular on the train at that time, maybe we can get a line on him and interview him just to rule him out."

***

Maggie agreed to get the pictures printed and to talk to the commander of the Reserve Division. In the meantime, I chained myself to my desk for a couple of hours, doing the day's paperwork and catching up on some miscellaneous crap. Afterwards, Sara and I met for dinner at Tutti Santi. I was not surprised to learn that the autopsy report on Corrine Ray would be of no more help than the one on Allison Martin had been. "As with Martin," Sara said, "the body had been carefully washed before being wrapped in the plastic. We got nothing from it."

"Well," I said, "On the bright side, we did see a bathtub in Robinson's house. But the guy's such a filthy slob that it's hard to imagine he would have been able to clean the tub so completely as to leave no trace at all. I reminded Gary to thoroughly check the tub drain, of course. Maybe something will turn up there."

We decided to spend the night at my place and once there, we plopped down on the couch to watch an episode of the Danish TV series, "The Bridge." Sara was particularly taken with the performance of Sofia Helin as Swedish police detective Saga Noren. We'd binged our way through the first season pretty quickly, or at least as quickly as our schedules would allow, and were now just starting the second. Sara had stretched out on the couch, lying with her head on my lap, and about halfway through the episode she looked up and said, "You know, if you had Saga on your team, you'd probably already have the cuffs on this guy."

"The hell, she'd need at least another three episodes, minimum. Besides," I said, cupping her breast, "you just like her because she's got such a strong sex drive and because she's so direct about it."

Sara nestled a bit more comfortably into my lap, put her hand over mine, and began squeezing it so that I was lightly massaging her breast. "That's certainly one of her most attractive qualities," she admitted. "So why don't you just keep doing what you're doing for another twenty minutes or so until this episode is finished, and then I'll give you an even better example of a strong sex drive."

24.

At mid-morning on Tuesday, I was sitting in my office when Gary Barnett walked through the door and dropped into my visitor's chair. "Let me guess," I said, "you didn't come all the way across the street and up two flights of stairs in this fuckin' heat just to give me good news."

"Afraid not," he replied. "We found enough disgusting kiddie porn in Robinson's house to put him away for a good long time. And he's clearly not just a consumer; he was producing the shit in his bedroom. The people in vice and child welfare are going to have their hands full for quite a while with this one, so you did a really good thing getting this bastard off the streets."

"And the bad news?"

"The section of plastic sheeting that you gave us does not match up to either of the pieces that Martin and Ray were wrapped in and we found absolutely nothing in the van or anywhere in the house to tie this creep either to either of them. In particular, we cleaned out the bathtub drain practically all the way out to the city sewer line. There wasn't a single hair in there that belonged to either victim. I'm sorry, Sean, but based on what we've got, he's not your guy."

"I'm sorry too, Gary. So, what you're telling me is that we're basically back at square one. We don't have a single piece of physical evidence from either case to point us in the direction of the killer."

"I'm afraid not. We do have the two plastic sheets, and each of them was cut from another. If you can bring us a piece that matches either of them, we'll be in business. Also, I can tell you with some certainty that the rosary you found with Ray's body is probably at least forty years old. It's been handled a lot; somebody obviously said a lot of Our Fathers and Hail Marys with it.

"It's impossible to date the writing on the tag with anything close to pinpoint accuracy, but it's naturally faded over a long period of time. The way in which the tag was stored would obviously have influenced that, but all in all, I'd say that there's an excellent chance that the rosary could have belonged to Laura Garcia and that her name could have been written on the tag back when she was murdered. Otherwise, at least for the moment, I'm sorry to say that we've got next to nothing."

***

I collected Maggie and walked down the hall to relay the news to the sergeant. "So, what you're telling me is that we're basically nowhere," he said.

"I'm afraid so," I said, "unless by some miracle we find the guy that Maggie noticed on the video from the train and he turns out to be our killer. But I'm guessing the odds of that are about as good as our chances of hitting the Powerball."

"We've interviewed a pretty wide circle of people around both victims," Maggie said. "But we've come up with zilch. Neither woman told anyone that she had concerns about a possible threat and it seems clear that both were chosen, not because the killer knew them but because they fit the pattern of the original crimes, Martin in particular, of course. Almost certainly, neither of them knew the killer and neither saw it coming until the moment it happened."

"There is another issue we need to consider," I added. "It seems pretty clear at this point that this asshole is determined to replicate the original killings. Which means that he'd be targeting a hooker next, and a TV reporter after that. At least in the first two cases, he's moving much more quickly than the original guy, assuming the killers are not one and the same. We should probably be warning women in the sex trades and TV people to be extra careful."

The sergeant nodded. "Media Relations will be doing a briefing this afternoon. I'll recommend that they emphasize that. In the meantime, you guys need to get back into those files and figure out how our killer came up with the souvenirs from the original killings. Even if they're not the same guy, there's got to be some connection."

***

Back in my office, I grabbed my phone and called Ellie Davis. She answered immediately, and I said, "Hey, Ellie, it's coming up on noon. Can I buy you lunch somewhere?"

"Would this be a business lunch or something more personal?"

"A little of both, actually."

"Well, with that combination, how could I possibly resist? Where did you have in mind?"

"How about the Arrogant Butcher at noon? That's good and reasonably convenient for both of us."

"Works for me. I'll see you then."

I called over to reserve a table and then, given that the sun was beating down and the temperature was already in the high nineties, opted to drive to the restaurant, even though it was only about three-quarters of a mile away. I parked in a public garage near the restaurant and walked through the door a few minutes before noon to find Ellie waiting at the hostess station.

She was wearing heels and a blue sleeveless dress. As had almost always happened during the brief period when we were dating and were out in public together, she had attracted the attention of several other diners, in some cases, of course, because they recognized her from the news, but mostly because she always looked even more spectacular in person than she did on television. I slipped the hostess a ten-dollar bill and requested a quiet table off in a corner somewhere. Once we were seated, Ellie leaned across the table, covered the top of my hand with hers, and said with a smile, "Now, you've definitely got my attention; it's been a while since we've done this."

"It has," I said, returning the smile. "And I wish it were for a happier reason."

The server interrupted at that point to take our drink orders and then we spent a couple of minutes looking at the menu. In the end, Ellie settled for the soup of the day and a small salad while I ordered a BLT. The server pronounced the choices "excellent" and retreated in the direction of the kitchen. Ellie gave her a moment to get out of range, then leaned across the table and said, "Have you ever, even once, had a server take your order and say, "Jesus, that dish totally sucks. I'd never order it?"

"Not even once," I laughed, "especially not in a place like this."

She toyed with her water glass for a moment, then said, "So why did you call this meeting, especially since you just indicated that it wasn't for a particularly happy reason?"

Shaking my head, I said, "Media Relations will be giving an update on our case this afternoon. Before they do that, I wanted to talk to you in person."

Ellie leaned forward a bit and arched her eyebrows. "As you know," I said, "this bastard we're hunting has now killed two women, duplicating very closely the first two killings in the series from the middle Seventies. And, irrespective of what Media Relations might say, we're not even close to identifying him, let alone catching him. That's for your personal information, by the way and not for attribution."

She nodded, and I continued. "We're assuming that the killer is going to be targeting a prostitute next, since that what the original killer did. Media Relations will be warning women working in the sex trades to be especially vigilant. And they'll also be warning female television reporters, since the fourth original victim was a TV newswoman."

I reached across the table and took her hand. "I wanted to talk to you personally, Ellie, rather than just let you hear the generic warning from the briefing. As I'm sure you already know, the TV reporter who was the fourth original victim was making a name for herself with her coverage of the killings, and I'm sure she was targeted specifically for that reason. Beyond that, as I'm sure you also know, the victim worked for your station."

"I know."

Squeezing her hand, I said, "Ellie, you've been front and center on this story since the morning we found the first body. Of all the TV people who have been covering the investigation, no one has done it more prominently than you. I have to think that this guy has almost certainly got you in his sights already."

She drew her hand back and said, "So what do you want me to do—are you asking me to drop the story?"

"No, of course not. I would never presume to tell you what to do. I know this is a big story for you and that you already have a lot invested in it. I don't expect you to give it up, and frankly, as much reporting as you've done on the story already, I'm not sure that it would do that much good anyway."

"So, what then?"

"I guess what I'd *really* prefer is that you quit your job this afternoon, move up to Alaska, and take a job on a fishing boat or some damned thing until we have this bastard in chains. Failing that, I hope you'll be extremely careful. I still care about you a lot, Ellie, and it would kill me if this guy got his hands on you."

She reached over and took my hand again. "Thank you for that, Sean. It means more to me than you know. But specifically, what do I do, especially since I know nothing about commercial fishing and have no intention of moving to Alaska?"

"At a minimum, you need to get your bosses to assign you some security, especially when you're going to and from work and when you're out of the station on assignment. So far, the killer has grabbed his victims at night, near their homes. The original TV victim, Karen Rasmusen, was taken from the parking lot at her apartment at six o'clock in the morning as she was leaving for work.

"You're probably safe enough while you're at the station and when you're locked inside your apartment. But don't be going out to meet any sources alone, especially if you've never met them before. And for god's sake, don't open your door at home to anyone that you don't know, including delivery guys who insist that they absolutely have to have a signature."

Ellie swallowed hard. "I know what you're saying only makes good sense, but still…"

Squeezing her hand, I said, "'But still,' my ass, Ellie. This guy is very, very good, and I'm sure that neither of the first two victims ever saw him coming. I've seen the things he did to those poor women. You've got to promise me that you're going to be beyond careful."

"I'm having trouble imagining that the station is going to be willing to pony up money for any bodyguards."

"You make it very clear to those cheap bastards that this recommendation is coming directly from the P.D. and that I will personally crucify them if they refuse and something happens to you. If you want, I'll be happy to call your boss myself."

"That probably won't be necessary, at least for now. But I'll let you know if and when it is."

I paid the check and walked Ellie to her car, which was parked one level above mine in the garage. At the door, she opened the locks then turned, put her arms around me and pulled me close. In a quiet voice, she said, "Thanks for the warning, Sean, and thanks especially for still caring so much. It occurs to me that I should have been a much better girlfriend."

Before I could say anything in response, she gave me a quick kiss, got into her car, and headed back to work.

25.

Growing up as the child of two rigid and essentially humorless parents, Chris Nelson knew very little joy as a youth. He was expected to study hard, to apply himself diligently to the household tasks that were assigned him, and basically to be seen but not heard. Even his "free" time was closely circumscribed, and he was allowed very little opportunity to watch television, to play video games, or to be otherwise "unproductive." Rather he was supposed to read and study, and otherwise make the best use of his time so that he might one day graduate from a good college and ultimately become an upstanding member of society.

His parents spoke little more to each other than they did to him, and mealtimes often passed with very little conversation. In later years, Nelson would often wonder how his parents had ever managed the coupling that had ultimately produced him. Not surprisingly, sex was never discussed at the dinner table or anywhere else in the house where he grew up, until one afternoon when he was eleven and his mother sat him down in the family room for "The Talk."

It was a very brief discussion in which his mother explained that babies resulted when a man put his penis somewhere into a woman's body, although Nelson was left a bit unsure as to exactly where that "somewhere" might be. His mother stressed the fact that sex was a sacred act, ordained by God for the purpose of procreation, and that it was never, ever to be contemplated outside the bonds of marriage.

Regrettably, she told her son, "bad" boys and girls sometimes engaged in sexual activities outside of marriage, and the results were always catastrophic: People contracted horrible, often fatal, diseases. Girls got pregnant. Boys became fathers much too early and ruined the rest of their lives. People went to Hell.

At some point, his mother explained, Chris would meet a nice girl. They would get married and settle down, and then, at an appropriate time, they would begin to have children. Until then, Chris should never even think about sex. He should never look at girls in "That Way," and he should definitely keep his hands off of his private parts save for bathing and going to the bathroom.

Young Chris was not quite sure what to make of the whole idea. Naturally, by this time he'd heard other boys discussing sex, but he hadn't really understood the complexity of it all. Then a couple of months after he and his mother had discussed the issue, he watched a man kiss a woman in a movie in a way that seemed particularly intense, and for the first time he experienced a vague sexual stirring that left him confused and ill at ease. It felt sort of nice, but he knew that it was wrong, and he had no idea what to make of it.

A week or so later, he woke up out of a dream with the first erection of his life. Confused, he reached down and touched himself, and that was the ball game. After that, he masturbated every once in a while, when he simply could not resist the pressure. He knew it was wrong, of course, but he simply couldn't help himself, and in church on Sundays and Wednesdays, he prayed for God to give him the strength to be better. For whatever reason, though, God chose not to do so, and Nelson's obsession mounted.

At that age, most of Nelson's male friends were naturally experiencing the same sort of confusion about their budding sexuality. Most of them were less inhibited about it, however, and few of them felt the guilt that bore so heavily on Nelson. They traded stories at school and elsewhere, and occasionally passed around a magazine that had been liberated from a father or an older brother, and which cleared up at least some of the confusion surrounding anatomical matters.

One afternoon when Chris was twelve, he was hanging out with a couple of friends at the house of one of the boys whose parents were gone for the afternoon. The boy insisted that he had something "great" to show his two friends and led them into his father's home office which was supposed to be off limits. From the back of a cabinet, the boy came up with a commercially produced videotape.

On the front of the box was a naked woman staring provocatively into the camera. On the back of the box were several photos of the woman, bound and gagged.

In the family room, the boy inserted the tape into the VCR and the three of them watched as four men led the woman into a room, laid her across a table, and tied her wrists and ankles to the legs of the table. They then proceeded to have sex with the woman in ways that the young Chris Nelson could never have imagined. Initially, the woman seemed terrified and attempted to resist, but before long, she appeared to get turned on by the action and by the end of the scene, she was begging the men to continue.

Chris assumed that the woman was acting, at least at some point, but was it at the beginning of the scene, or was it later? Either way, the action was extremely stimulating and when the tape was over, he made an excuse to leave and raced home. Once there, he locked himself in the bathroom and brought himself to a mammoth climax. Looking at himself in the mirror once he was finished, he knew for certain that he was going to Hell. But he was no longer so sure that it might not be worth it.

***

After that experience, Nelson masturbated increasingly more often while worrying less and less about the consequences. As a junior in high school, he began dating and had his first very tentative sexual experiences with a girl. As a sophomore in college, he finally lost his virginity to a girl who was known to be "easy" and who'd had way too much to drink at a party.

The girl let Nelson lead her upstairs and lay her down across a bed in a guest bedroom. He pulled off her clothes and she guided him into her. He'd been fantasizing about this moment for years, and once inside the young woman, he moved slowly at first, but then grabbed her wrists and pinned her to the bed while he pounded into her as hard as he could until he exploded into the condom he'd had brains enough to carry with him.

In the years that followed, Nelson graduated from college, found a good job, and went through a succession of relationships. In each case, he tired of plain vanilla sex fairly quickly and encouraged his girlfriends to become more adventurous. Some were more willing than others, and a couple of them had allowed him to tie them up in bed. Ultimately, though, they all bailed on him, refusing to push the sexual envelope as far as he would have liked.

Eventually, he found a couple of prostitutes who were willing to play games with him—for a hefty fee, of course—but even that eventually proved to be insufficient because he knew, naturally, that the women were only acting. And ultimately then, it was only when he found himself looking at Allie Martin, tied down on the bed in the loft of his rented garage and terrified beyond belief, that he finally reached the moment he'd been aiming at since that afternoon so long ago when he was only twelve years old.

26

Sara had a book club meeting Tuesday night and so I was on my own for the evening. I got home about 6:30 and changed into a pair of jeans and a tee shirt. I cued up a Brian Chartrand playlist on my phone and set it to play through the house audio system. As Chartrand began singing, "Miss You Now," I made myself a generous Tanqueray and tonic and then went rummaging through the refrigerator in search of something that might constitute dinner. I'd just settled on some leftover Rigatoni Pipitone from Tutti Santi when the doorbell rang.

I slipped the pasta back into the refrigerator and went to the front door. Looking through the sidelight, I saw my father's widow standing there in a pair of crisp new blue jeans and a red sweater. Wearing hardly any makeup, she looked several years younger than she had any right to claim and was carrying a bag bearing the logo of Mastro's Steak House.

I opened the door and she stepped into the foyer. Smiling, she said, "I know I should have called, but I did this on an impulse. Are you busy, and have you had dinner?

Returning her smile, I shook my head and said, "No, and no. I was just pulling some leftovers out of the refrigerator when you rang the bell."

"Great." She gave me a peck on the cheek and said, "I got you the Bone-In Kansas City Strip and I had them cook it rare. Let me pop this stuff into the oven for a few minutes to warm it up, and that should be enough to bring the steak up to medium-rare, okay?"

"Perfect. What would you like to drink?"

"I got the Chilean Sea Bass for myself; do you have a Chardonnay?"

"Of course."

While Amanda set the dinners into the oven to warm up, I pulled a bottle of Rombauer Chardonnay from the wine storage unit and poured her a glass. She took a first sip and said, "Excellent."

She looked down at the glass for a moment and then back up to meet my eyes. "So, tell me, did I embarrass you to death the other day and are you really, really mad at me?"

"Maybe not quite to death," I said, smiling. "And no."

"Good. And I'm sorry, but I saw you sitting there as Beth and I were on our way to lunch and I couldn't resist. I suppose your partner must think I'm a complete ditz."

"I don't know about that, but she has been giving me an endless amount of crap about you ever since."

Leaning back against the kitchen counter, she took a sip of wine, then smiled shyly and said, "Does she think my interest in you might be more than simply maternal?"

I grinned and shook my head. "If so, that's on you and not me."

She nodded, and the smile gave way to something more wistful. After a long moment, she touched my arm and said, "Well, you know, if I hadn't been married to your father…"

There was nothing I could say to that and so we stood there for the next few minutes, working quietly on our drinks, each with our own thoughts, until the buzzer went off, indicating that our dinners were ready. I quickly set the dining room table and opened an Argentine Malbec to go with my steak. Over the next hour and a half or so, we made our way through an excellent dinner and another couple of glasses of wine. As always when we were together, we talked mostly about our respective memories of my father. We also discussed her work at the local women's shelter where she volunteered, and I described a little about the case that Maggie and I were working, while tap-dancing around the gorier details.

Spearing a last piece of asparagus, Amanda said, "I've noticed that when we've talked about Maggie before, you neglected to mention how attractive she was."

I swirled a bit of wine in my glass and said, "Well, to be honest, I never really noticed that."

Amanda burst out laughing. "You are such a liar. I can't imagine how you said that with a straight face. There's got to be some chemistry there, right?"

"A little maybe, but neither of us has ever acknowledged it. Maggie is smart, tough, and a great detective. We work way too well together to screw up our partnership by doing something really retarded like getting involved with each other. And besides, I'm perfectly happy at the moment with Sara."

She reached over and covered my hand with hers. "I'm glad to hear that's still going well. She seems like a very nice woman and I like her a lot. I don't want to seem presumptuous, but I think that your father would have liked her too."

I squeezed her hand and said, "I wouldn't be at all surprised, Amanda. He would have seen a lot of the same qualities in her that he saw in you."

***

All in all, it was a very comfortable evening, and once dinner was over, I stacked the dishes in the washer while Amanda finished her last glass of wine. Then I walked her to the door where she turned, put her arms around me, and pulled me close. I hugged her for a long minute until finally she lifted her head from my shoulder and looked up at me. "Thanks for being here. I still just miss him so much, you know?"

Nodding, I said, "I know that, Amanda, and so do I. You were probably the best thing that ever happened to him, and I know how happy he was all the time that you two were together. But I also know in my heart that as much as he loved you, he would want you to move on. Most of all, he would want you to be happy again."

She shook her head sadly. "I know, Sean, but the guys I meet…. It's not a cliché to say that, all the decent, smart, attractive men are either gay, married, or otherwise taken. Either that, or they're my damned stepson. What's a girl supposed to do?"

I smiled and pulled her close for another second or two. And then, saying nothing more, she gave me a quick kiss and was gone.

27.

I forced myself out of bed early Wednesday and managed a nice long run before I headed off to work. I got to my desk at about eight thirty and found an envelope from the crime lab. I opened it to find several photos of the van we'd found on the security video from Allie Martin's condo complex and which we were certain had been used to abduct the woman.

Given the quality of the video, the photos left a great deal to be desired and showed only a fairly generic, dark-colored, 2010 Ford E150 cargo van. The only windows on the vehicle were those in the driver's and passenger's doors and in the two doors at the back of the van. The techs had included a couple of enlargements focusing in on a small dent near the rear wheel well on the passenger's side that Maggie and I hadn't noticed when looking at the raw video. Otherwise, the van looked to be in pretty good shape for a commercial vehicle of that age.

I was sorting through the photos when Maggie walked through the door with a cup of coffee in her hand and wished me a good morning. She sat down in my visitor's chair and we went through the pictures together. But neither of us saw anything that would set the van apart from a thousand others, save for the one small dent.

Maggie slipped the pictures back into the envelope and I said, "We speculated for a while that the van, like the license plates and the plumber's signs that the guy used when he grabbed Martin, might have been stolen. But I checked again yesterday, and we still have no report of a van like this on the list."

"So, you're thinking the guy had it all along?"

"Or maybe not. Let's assume you've found the box of souvenirs and decided to go into the abduction business. What are the odds that you already own the perfect vehicle for such a spree?"

"Small, I would think."

"Me too. So, if you're not going to steal the perfect vehicle, you need to buy it. You could go to a used car lot, but you really don't want to leave a paper trail leading directly to you. So, most likely you're going to buy from a private seller, pay cash, and probably neglect to do the paperwork."

"That's certainly what I'd do."

I grabbed my phone, called Rick Muhlstein over in the computer lab, and explained the situation. "What I'd like you to do," I said, "is have one of your guys do a search through Craig's List and whatever other classifieds you can think of, say from April 1 to June 1 for openers, looking for somebody selling a 2010 E150, either black or dark blue. There can't be all that many of them in that short a timeframe; maybe we'll get lucky."

"Not a problem," he said. "I'll put Jeff on it right now and get back to you as soon as I know if he's found anything or not."

***

While I waited to hear back from Rick Muhlstein, I walked over to the Records & Information Bureau and competed requests to have them print hard copies of the files from both the Petrovitch and Rasmussen cases. Then I called Jack Oliva and told him that Maggie and I planned to begin going back through the files from the Friedman and Garcia cases while we waited for the other two. Forty minutes later, he walked into the conference room, with his visitor's badge hanging over a dark, lightweight sweater, stonewashed jeans, and a pair of vintage Stan Smiths. The three of us had just settled in to work when my phone rang with the screen indicating that Rick Muhlstein was at the other end of the call.

I connected to the call and Muhlstein said, "I've got three possibilities for you, all from Craig's List. I'm e-mailing them to you as we speak."

I opened my iPad and called up my e-mail. The three ads had all been placed in the first two weeks of May and advertised 2010 E150 cargo vans. Two of the three were dark blue; the other was black. The prices ranged from $5500.00 to $7250.00. The ad for the vehicle in the middle of the range indicated that there was a "slight amount" of damage to the left front fender, so I eliminated that one from the mix since it didn't match the photos that we had.

The van at the high end had been offered for sale by a seller in south Phoenix. I called the number and the phone was answered by a woman who told me that, yes, she had advertised a van for sale, but she had not gotten what she thought were any reasonable offers and so had decided to keep it.

I dialed the number in the third ad and got a guy who sounded like he might be closing in on middle age. I identified myself and he told me his name was Hank McKinley. I asked if he'd sold the van he had advertised, and he said, "Sure did. On the second day I posted the ad, which makes me think I probably sold too cheap."

"Can you tell me about the buyer?" I asked.

"Well, he was a white guy. Middle forties, I'd guess. Offered me $4,800 in cash. I'd been hoping to get at least five, but staring at all that money, I decided to go for the bird in the hand."

"What kind of shape was the van in, Mr. McKinley? In particular, was there any damage to the body?"

"Not really. It had a lot of miles on it, and the driver's seat showed a lot of wear and tear, but the body was very good. Only one tiny dent that hardly anyone would notice. The guy who bought it didn't even mention it."

"Where was the dent?"

"Near the rear wheel well on the passenger's side. I have no idea how the damned thing got there. I was just washing the van one day and noticed it. The van was old enough by then that it didn't seem worth it to get it fixed."

I told McKinley that I'd like to come out and talk to him. He explained that he was at work but that his boss would probably let him break away for a few minutes if it was really important. I explained that it most certainly was, and he gave me the address of the shop where he worked in Mesa.

***

There'd been an accident on the 101, and traffic had slowed to a crawl. I used my cell phone to call McKinley and tell him that I'd be somewhat delayed, then I ducked off the freeway at Indian School, hoping to loop around the accident. The detour took me past the site where my dad's real estate development company was in the process of leveling an aging apartment complex in order to make way for a new high-end shopping mall.

Whenever I happened by one of the company's projects, I always experienced a welter of conflicting emotions. Even though my father and Uncle Phil had been equal partners in the company, and even though Uncle Phil had been running the operation in the several years since my father's death, I still always thought of it as Dad's company, and I always feared that he had died disappointed in me because I had chosen not to follow in his footsteps.

He'd always insisted that this was not the case, that he loved me as much as ever and that he respected the fact that I had to follow my own path in life. But I was his only child and he had always doted on me. From the time I began walking, he had often taken me into the office and out to various job sites, proudly telling anyone within earshot that he was grooming me to one day run the company myself.

Although he never would have admitted it, I understood how pained he must have been when I chose not to do so, and I understood the regret he must have experienced as he watched my younger cousins—Uncle Phil's two sons—come into the company after college and begin working their way up the corporate ladder. But I just couldn't see doing it myself. Though a love of the business had coursed through the blood of my family for four generations now, it had, for some unfathomable reason, flowed around and not through me.

For my father's sake, and for the memory of my grandfather and great-grandfather, I was enormously grateful for the fact that the enterprise would remain in the family and would continue to live on through the efforts of my cousins. Had it come down to me; had I been the only heir of my generation, I probably could and would have somehow forced myself to shoulder the responsibility. I would have been miserable doing it and probably not very good at it at all. But knowing that did little or nothing to ameliorate the sadness and the guilt I often felt for having failed to fulfill my father's dreams.

***

Forty minutes after leaving the office, I pulled up in front of what appeared to be a small manufacturing plant and parked in a visitor's slot. In the front office, three clerks were at work and I interrupted the one closest to the door and asked to see Hank McKinley. The woman invited me to take a seat and lifted the receiver from the phone on her desk.

The April/May edition of *The Tube and Pipe Journal* magazine was sitting on the table next to me, and I spent a couple of minutes skimming a fascinating article containing tips on designing tubular parts for bending. I was just getting to the good part when a guy walked through the door and identified himself as McKinley.

He stood about six-two and probably tipped out the scales at around two-fifty. But very little of the weight ran to fat, and he looked like a guy who could hold his own in almost any kind of a dicey situation. His face, though, was totally at odds with the rest of his body. Bright green eyes and a wide smile hinted that he could get along with almost anyone. He suggested that we talk out in the parking lot where we'd have a bit more privacy and opened the conversation by asking why I was so interested in his old van.

"Well, first of all," I said, "I'd like to make sure that we're talking about the same van."

I handed him the pictures that the lab had produced, and he looked at them for only a few seconds. Pointing to the picture of the small dent behind the rear wheel well, he said, "Absolutely. That's it."

"And you sold the van on May 8?"

"Yeah, that sounds right. I'd have to look at a calendar to be a hundred percent sure, but a day or so either way of that."

"What was the buyer's name?"

"Tom."

"Just Tom?"

"Right. I had the van at my house. The guy called, said he'd seen my ad on Craig's List and asked if he could come look at it. I told him sure, and he got there about forty-five minutes later. He rang the bell and when I came to the door, he said his name was Tom and that he'd called about the van.

"He looked it over pretty carefully and then we took it for a short test drive. He pretended that he wasn't all that impressed, the way you always do when you're buying a used car or truck, and then asked me if I'd take $4800.00. I told him no, that I had to have at least $5200.00. Then he pulled forty-eight hundred-dollar bills out of his pocket and told me that was as high as he'd go. I decided, what the hell—if it was going to be that clean and simple, I'd take it.

"I signed over the title and wrote him a bill of sale. Then I took my license plate off it, cleaned a couple of things out of the glove box and gave him the key. He drove off and I took the money straight to the bank."

"How did the guy get to your house, Mr. McKinley?"

He paused for a moment, then said, "I don't know. I never even thought about it until now. He just appeared on my porch. Maybe he took a cab, or someone dropped him off, but I didn't see."

"You said he was a white man and you placed him somewhere in his middle forties. What else can you tell me about him?"

McKinley shrugged. "I don't know, just a regular guy."

"How was he dressed?"

"Jeans and a grey tee shirt. He was wearing a Cardinals hat and a pair of sunglasses."

"Could you tell the color of his eyes?"

McKinley shook his head. "Nope. He never took off the glasses."

"How tall, would you say?"

"A couple inches shorter than me, say an even six feet."

"Thin, fat?"

"Definitely not fat, but not really thin, He was in good shape; looked like a guy who lifts."

147

"What about his hair?"

"Brown, medium length."

I finished making notes, then said, "Thanks a lot, Mr. McKinley, that's been a huge help. I'm wondering, though, if you'd mind sitting down with one of our police sketch artists and seeing if you could work up a picture for us."

"You mean like on TV?"

"Yeah, like that."

"What the hell did this guy do?"

"I'm sorry; I really can't tell you that. But it would be a huge help if you could do this for us."

"Well, sure. Actually, it sounds like it could be fun."

I thanked McKinley for his time and told him that the sketch artist would give him a call before the end of the day. He assured me that he'd be happy to help, and he hoped that at some point I could tell him what it was all about and what sort of bad things the guy had done with his old van.

27.

Back at the office, I lined up a sketch artist to work with Hank McKinley, then grabbed a Coke and went down to the conference room where Maggie and Jack Oliva were working through the files from the Petrovitch case. I walked through the door and asked how things were coming. Oliva leaned back in his chair and gestured in the direction of the files on the table in front of him. "It's amazing how fresh these things feel to me, even forty years down the road," he said. "I guess it's a sign of how important these cases were and of how guilty I've always felt for never having caught this son of a bitch."

I pulled a set of interviews out of the stack and settled in alongside them. "Anything jumping out at you?" I asked.

Maggie just shook her head and Jack said, "Not really. This case was the thinnest of all. Petrovitch was a local girl who dropped out of school, got into drugs, and started running with a bad crowd, as we used to say back in my day. The family was pretty dysfunctional, which could account for some of the girl's behavior, and ultimately her parents kicked her out of the house.

"She worked at a McDonald's for a couple of months but got fired for showing up late and for sometimes missing her shifts all together. After that, she turned to hooking and was living in a crappy apartment with one of her female business associates when she got killed. According to the roommate, Petrovitch went out to work one night and never came back. This wasn't unusual because she'd occasionally agree to do an overnight with a customer who had a room somewhere. The roommate wasn't really concerned until we showed up at the door the next day to tell her that Petrovitch was dead.

"Somewhere in these files is an interview with another woman who was out working that night who told us that the last guy

Petrovitch went off with was driving a tan GMC truck. She didn't get a look at the driver, and of course didn't think to look at the license plate. We showed her some pictures and she picked out a '72 GMC Suburban. But we had no one in any of the other cases that we could tie to a truck like that, and we couldn't be sure that was actually the guy who killed Petrovitch. She could have come back from the date with the guy in the Jimmy and then been picked up by another client while our witness was off doing business of her own."

Maggie looked up from a file and said, "Did Petrovitch have a pimp?"

"Apparently not. The roommate said that she and Petrovitch were both working freelance. We asked, of course, thinking that maybe a pissed off pimp or a wannabe pimp might have killed Petrovitch to set an example for other reluctant recruits. But the roommate insisted that no one had tried to lure them into his stable and that as far as she knew, there wasn't anybody who was even slightly angry with Petrovitch.

"You told us she was doing drugs," I said. "Is it possible that she pissed off her dealer or owed somebody money that she'd borrowed for drugs and that they might have killed her?"

Oliva shook his head. "We thought of that too. The roommate gave up the name of Petrovitch's dealer and naturally, he told us that he had no beef with her at all. The roommate confirmed that. She said that Petrovitch was using only occasionally and that it was mostly just pot. Petrovitch was still very young and attractive; the streets hadn't eaten her up yet, and she was charging what amounted to premium prices for a working girl in the Deuce at that time. So, she always had enough money to make the rent and to buy dope."

Maggie set down the file she was reading and said, "And you're sure that Petrovitch *was* killed by the guy who did the other three. This wasn't some creep who had nothing to do with the other victims, preying on a hooker?"

"Well, obviously, we couldn't be a hundred percent positive that *any* two of the victims were killed by the same guy. But let's say that we were ninety-seven percent sure that they all were, including Petrovitch. Our doer wasn't as tidy as yours, what with the plastic wrapping and all, but there were enough similarities among the four crimes to make it look like the work of the same guy.

"To begin with, of course, all three of the initial victims had ties to the Deuce. They were all abducted and held for a period of two to three days. They were all sexually abused in the same way; the bastard definitely had his preferences in that regard. They'd all been restrained in the same way, and in the end, they were all strangled to death with a thin wire of some sort. And when the guy was finished with them, he dumped all four bodies within a fairly confined area south of the Deuce. Naturally, we held back a lot of that, which almost certainly eliminated the possibility that we might have had a copycat jumping into the picture."

I nodded. "And none of the first three victims knew any of the others?"

"Not as far as we could determine. Although they were all down in the Deuce, at least occasionally, they moved in different circles. Neither Garcia nor Petrovitch was destitute enough to have gone to the soup kitchen where Friedman volunteered. It's possible that Petrovitch might have occasionally patronized the bar where Garcia worked, although the roommate was sure that she hadn't ever been in the place. And it certainly wasn't the sort of spot where Friedman would have hung out after her shift at the soup kitchen to relax over a Gin Fizz before going home to her husband."

He leaned back in his chair and sighed. "Of course, I can't swear that a couple of the victims never crossed paths, but if they did, we never found any evidence of it. I tell you guys, it was as big a fuckin' mystery forty years ago as it is today."

***

By mid-afternoon, we'd exhausted the files from the Petrovitch case without finding any plausible suspect who might have been linked to more than one of the crimes we were looking at, let alone anyone who might have been involved in more than one of them and who was still alive to be questioned about it.

I took a sip of my Coke, looked across the table at Oliva and said, "Okay, it's still possible that someone might jump out at us when we get into the files from the Rasmussen case, but for now, let's assume for the sake of discussion that we've got two separate killers here, one who did your victims forty years ago, and a second guy who's doing ours now. Where have the souvenirs from the original victims been all this time, and how did our guy find them?"

Jack leaned back and clasped his hands behind his head. "Well, if that *is* the case, my guy must have left them stored someplace. Your guy stumbled across them somehow, recognized what he'd found and decided to replicate the original killings, leaving items from the original victims to taunt the police in the process."

"So, a guy buys an older house, goes up into the attic and finds a box stuck away that one of the previous owners missed when they were moving out. He figures out what he's got, gets turned on by the whole idea and decides to replicate the crimes."

"In which case, my guy would almost certainly have to be dead," Jack said. "He wouldn't sell his house and move out forgetting about *that* particular box."

"Probably not," Maggie said. "Although he could have gotten dementia or something, in which case, he *did* forget about it. His kids put him in a nursing home, sold the house and overlooked the box while they're moving his shit out."

"But in either case," I said, "he's almost certainly no use to us now."

"And neither am I," Oliva said. "I feel like hell about this. Forty years ago, I let some asswipe get away with killing four women and, as a result, some other clown comes along following in his footsteps, and I have no useful advice to give at all."

"C'mon, Jack," I said. "You know that's not true. We've all got cases we couldn't close and it's hardly like you were the only guy responsible for this one. And even if you had found him and put him away, some other jerk still might have read about the killings, begun to fantasize about them and decided to replicate them, thinking that he could do it better than the original guy."

Oliva smiled ruefully. "Intellectually, I know that's true. But that doesn't mean that my gut's not turning over about it. If you don't mind, I'd like to stick with this and go through the Rasmusen files with you. Something still might pop out at me."

"Absolutely," I said. "I was going to ask you to do it anyway and we really could use your help. You still know these files better than Maggie or I ever will. Speaking of which…"

I reached into my pocket and retrieved the list of names that I'd made while Maggie and I were going through the files in Joseph Turner's garage on Saturday. I handed the list to Jack and said, "Any of these names look familiar?"

He ran down the list of names, started to hand it back to me, then pulled it back and looked at it again. He stared off into space for a few seconds, then got up, walked across the small room, and picked up a file from the Ellen Friedman case. He set it on the table, sorted through it for a minute or so, then pulled a couple of pages from the file. Then he sat down again, and, saying nothing, handed the pages across the table to me.

They were notes from an interview that Jack and his partner had conducted with a couple named Leo R. and Nora Haig. The Haigs had been friends and neighbors of Brian and Ellen Friedman, and Leo Haig had also been a deacon in Joseph Turner's church.

I quickly scanned the notes, then looked up at Oliva.

"As you can tell," he said, "we were only looking for information about the Friedmans' marriage at a time when we still had the husband as a potential suspect. We knew that they were neighbors, that they belonged to the same church, and that they got together socially on occasion. But we never had any reason to look at Haig as a possible suspect and I don't remember anyone ever mentioning that he might have had a connection to the Deuce or to Turner's soup kitchen down there."

"But he clearly did have a connection to Ellen Friedman," I said. "And he was a deacon in Turner's church. It's certainly possible that Turner might have corralled him into 'volunteering' at the soup kitchen. He wouldn't have needed it to get next to Friedman, of course, but it might have brought him into contact with the other victims. Any idea what might have happened to him?"

Oliva shook his head and I pulled my laptop across the table. I logged into a couple of databases with no result, then got a hit on my third try. I scanned the record quickly while Maggie and Jack waited, then I looked up and said, "We have a Leo R. Haig, Jr. who was released from Lewis six weeks before Allie Martin was abducted. He did eight years on a rape conviction."

***

In Arizona, people convicted of rape are not eligible for parole, and so Haig had served his entire sentence and would not have been required to report to a parole officer upon his release. However, as a sex offender, he was required to report his address to the sheriff's office. I grabbed the phone, dialed the sheriff's department, and finally got transferred to a clerk who told me that Haig had reported, as required, two days after his release. "What's the address?" I asked.

"He's at the Molester Hotel," the clerk replied, using the nickname for a residence hotel on West Adams Street, that served as home to registered sex offenders, and which was conveniently located only a block away from the police headquarters building.

I thanked the clerk, and Maggie and I left Oliva with the files while we walked across the street under a blazing sun for a word with Leo Haig, Jr. At the hotel's desk, we badged the clerk and asked to see Haig. The clerk was somewhere in his early sixties, with a pot belly, bad breath, and a few strands of grey hair arranged, not very artfully, across a shiny bald scalp. Without even checking the records, he simply shook his head. "Mr. Haig is no longer with us."

"When did he leave?" Maggie asked.

"Five weeks ago? Somewhere around there."

I took out my notepad and pen. "His new address?"

The guy snorted. "Do I look like the fuckin' sheriff's office? He has to report a change of address to them within seventy-two hours. He doesn't have to tell me dick."

***

Back across the street, I called the sheriff's department again, only to discover that, contrary to the law, Haig had not contacted them with a new address. As far as they were concerned, he was still in the Molester Hotel. I told the clerk that Haig was in the wind and that I'd be issuing a file stop on him. In the event that Haig were to be pulled over for a traffic offense or for some other violation, the arresting officer would check his computer and discover that Haig was wanted both for violating the sex offender registration law and as a person of interest in a homicide investigation.

I then called the Department of Corrections and asked them to send me Haig's file with his current pictures, the log of those who had visited him in prison, and whatever addresses and phone numbers they might have for those visitors. The clerk promised to get me the file first thing in the morning.

By then it was nearly five o'clock, and we'd exhausted the Petrovitch files. Jack said goodbye for the day and promised to be back bright and early in the morning to get started on the Rasmussen files. Maggie and I spent a little time catching up on paperwork and then called it a night, determined to get an early start in the morning, attempting to find the elusive Leo Haig, Jr.

28.

By seven o'clock on Thursday morning, I was at my desk tracking Mr. and Mrs. Leo Haig and their somewhat-less-than-illustrious son through the public records. The elder Leo had graduated with a business degree from A.S.U. and had apparently been a pharmaceutical rep for his entire working career. Born in 1942, he would have been in his middle thirties at the time when the initial killings had occurred.

He and his wife, Brenda, had owned a home in Central Phoenix from 1969 to 1983, and had then bought a house in Surprise. They were still living there when Leo died in 2009. His wife apparently remained in the house until her death in 2014. Following Mrs. Haig's death, the house was sold.

The senior Mr. Haig apparently had something of a lead foot and had accumulated an impressive number of speeding tickets through the years, but if the computer could be believed, he'd had no other trouble with the law. The computer was completely silent with respect to Mrs. Haig, who apparently did not have even a minor criminal history.

The same could not be said for their only child, who had been born in 1977. Junior first showed up in the records as a juvenile, arrested at sixteen for joyriding in a car that didn't belong to him. In his twenties, he accumulated three D.U.I.s and one arrest for aggravated assault. That charge had been pled down and he'd served six months in the county jail. Then, in 2008, he'd been arrested on the rape charge and sentenced to eight years in the state prison system.

I was still digging through the family's history when Cathy Alexander tapped on my office door a little after nine o'clock and handed me the sketch she'd drawn while working with Hank McKinley, the guy who'd sold the van used by our killer. "I'm not sure how useful this is going to be," she said. "Your witness was good with things like clothes, height and weight, but he wasn't so good with physical features like eyes, ears, chins and noses. He was limited, of course, by the fact that the guy wore a hat and never took his sunglasses off. But I'm afraid all he could conjure up was your basic, average, everyday white guy."

Looking at the sketch she'd worked up, I could see her point. On the one hand, it very vaguely reminded me of three or four people that I knew. On the other, it didn't closely resemble anyone I knew at all. Allowing for the fact that he would have aged a bit and might have let his hair grow some since the last photo I could find, there was at least an outside chance that the guy in the sketch might have been the missing Leo Haig, Jr., but that might have been just wishful thinking on my part.

Looking up at Alexander, I said, "Thanks for the effort, Cathy. It's not as much help as I would have hoped for, but at least it's something."

"Yeah," she replied without much enthusiasm. "Part of the problem, naturally, is that McKinley was trying to remember this guy after six weeks. If it had only been a few days, we might have had more luck. But at this late date, that was the best he could do."

***

I walked the sketch over to Maggie's office and said, "Recognize this guy?"

She looked at the sketch for a minute, then said, "He sorta looks like Mr. Trent, my high school algebra teacher. God, what a creep that guy was. But then it could be any one of a dozen men I've met in the last year or two."

"Yeah, that was my reaction too. And certainly, this isn't something worth giving to the media. We'd get a thousand fuckin' calls from people claiming to recognize him. But once we get the file from Corrections, I'm thinking it wouldn't hurt to put Leo Haig's picture in a six-pack and show it to Hank McKinley."

Back in my own office, I found an email from the DOC with Leo Haig, Jr.'s file attached to it. We'd scheduled a team meeting for nine thirty, and so I unplugged my computer and walked it down to the conference room. Maggie, Elaine, and Greg were already there, and I brought them up to date with respect to the Haig family.

"It's obviously a very tenuous connection," I said, "but Leo Senior was in the right place at the right time to have been the original killer, and Leo Junior was conveniently released from Lewis just in time to be the current killer. And, after reporting in as he should have, he's dropped from sight and we have no idea where he is or what he might have been up to.

"Just to suggest an even more fragile thought, we've wondered why the first killer suddenly stopped after doing Karen Rasmusen. Her body was found at the end of November 1976, and Leo Junior. was born in May of 1977. Say for the sake of argument that Senior *was* the original guy and shortly after he does Rasmusen, he learns that his wife is pregnant. Maybe the thought of being a father causes him to quit."

"Or maybe," Greg said, "once he became a father, he didn't have the time or the opportunity to continue tracking and killing women."

Elaine nodded. "If the guy was a pharmaceutical rep, I assume that he would have had a lot of time out of the office that he didn't necessarily have to account for, when he could claim that he was out pushing pills to doctors or whatever. That would have given him the opportunity to be scouting victims and otherwise attending to the killings. Then once he's saddled with a kid, he suddenly has no spare time at all."

"Agreed," I said. "I've got someone digging into the records at MVD to see what sort of vehicles Haig Senior might have had licensed back in the middle Seventies. Jack Oliva says that Nancy Petrovitch was last seen getting into a tan '72 Suburban. All these conjectures would suddenly have a lot more meat on their bones if it should turn out that Haig happened to own one.

"Meanwhile, we've got to be digging into this family as deeply as we can, getting into the records, talking to surviving neighbors etc. We've also got to find Haig Jr. sooner rather than later. We've got a fairly recent photo in the file from corrections, and we need to get it out to all the patrols at shift change. There's already a file stop out for the guy, but we need to impress upon everyone that this isn't just a routine case of some jerk who's failed to report his address to the sheriff. We *need* this asshole."

***

We spent some time dividing up responsibilities, and my first task was to run Haig Junior's most recent photo past Hank McKinley. Just after eleven, we were once again standing out in the parking lot in front of the of the shop where he worked. I handed him the six-pack of photos I'd put together and asked if any of them resembled the man to whom he'd sold his van.

McKinley spent a couple of minutes working his way through the pictures, studying each one carefully, and then he repeated the process. All the photos were of men who vaguely resembled the sketch that McKinley had worked on with Catherine Alexander, and Haig's picture was the third one in the series. But it didn't seem to trigger any special reaction, and McKinley spent no more time studying that photo than he did any of the others.

After he'd been through the pictures for a third time, he looked up and said, "Sorry, Detective Richardson, but I'm not sure the guy is here. I'm trying to imagine these men with the cap, the hair, and the sunglasses that the guy who bought my van was wearing, and I suppose he might have been one of them. But the cap and the sunglasses covered a lot of his features, and I couldn't swear for sure that he was any one of these guys."

I assured McKinley that I appreciated his efforts and thanked him again for working with Cathy Alexander to develop our sketch. We shook hands and he told me that he'd be happy to do whatever else he could to be of assistance. Then he went back to work while I went searching for the closest In 'N' Out Burger drive-through on my way back to the headquarters building.

29.

The file that the Department of Corrections had compiled on Leo Haig showed that he'd had several regular visitors through the years. His parents had apparently been supportive throughout and had visited their son together, about once a month on average, until Leo Senior died. After that, Mrs. Haig continued to appear on about the same schedule until her own death. I wondered if they believed that their son had been unfairly convicted or if they simply loved him unconditionally. I also couldn't help but wonder whether the Senior Haig might have been so understanding of his son because he himself had gotten away with the crime of raping and killing at least four women.

Haig Junior had apparently retained the same lawyer throughout his prison stretch. The lawyer showed up fairly frequently in the first year or so of Haig's confinement; he then appeared sporadically for a few years until Haig's mother died in 2014. At that point, the lawyer showed up a couple more times, perhaps dealing with the parents' estate.

Otherwise, the list of visitors contained the names of several people who appeared to be unrelated to Haig. As is often the case, the number of visitors was higher early on in Haig's incarceration and then gradually tailed off until only his most dedicated friends and relatives were still showing up, at least occasionally, by the time he was released.

Interestingly, in the eight years during which he was confined, Junior's mother was the only female to visit him. The records indicated that Haig had never married, and I wondered if he might have had problems relating to women that would have prevented him from having a Significant Other or any female friends at all.

I made a list of the visitors, making special note of the men who had visited most often and who had continued to show up at the prison until the very end. Then I found Maggie at her desk, just finishing a take-out salad, and we headed out to begin interviewing Junior's most special friends.

***

Walking out into the headquarters' parking lot on an afternoon in the middle of June, you could only shake your head at the skeptics who believed that global warming was an unsubstantiated theory. This was the fourth day in a row that the temperature was headed in the direction of a hundred and fifteen degrees, something that in my childhood days rarely ever happened in Phoenix much before early August.

I shed my suitcoat even before we got outside, and when we popped the doors on my Chevy, I guessed that it had to be well over a hundred and thirty degrees in the car. I threw my suitcoat into the back seat and slid into the car just long enough to crank the ignition and turn the AC on to "high." Then I quickly got out and Maggie and I stood beside the car with the doors open while the air conditioner pushed some of the warmer air out of the car. Maggie was dressed more sensibly for the day in a tan skirt and a simple white blouse, but no matter what anyone might have chosen to wear, there was no escaping the fact that it was goddamned hot out. Standing there, it occurred to me that when Robert Earl Keene wrote the lyrics to "Furnace Fan," he pretty much nailed it.

After a few minutes, we decided that the car was about as cool as it was likely to get, and so we gingerly settled onto the hot seats and pulled out of the parking lot, looking to interview a guy named Walter Prescott. Prescott had visited Haig, Junior, more than anyone else, averaging a couple of visits a month through the entire stretch of Haig's confinement.

The records showed him living on South Fourth Avenue, near Buckeye in the south-central part of the city. It turned out to be a small home in one of the city's less-prestigious neighborhoods, only a half a mile away from the spot where Allie Martin's body had been dumped. A chain link fence surrounded a weed-filled yard that consisted mostly of bare ground. The house itself was badly in need of attention and, like most of the neighboring houses, had burglar bars fronting all the windows. A sign wired to the gate warned anyone passing to beware of the dog.

We pulled to the curb in front of the place and saw a balding, heavyset guy who was sporting a lot of ink, out in the driveway in the full midday sun, working on a Harley. As Maggie and I walked up the drive, the guy straightened up, grabbed a shop rag out of a bucket, and began wiping his hands. He was wearing a dirty sleeveless gray tee shirt and a pair of jeans, and both the shirt and the jeans were soaked with sweat. We showed him our badges and IDs, and I asked the guy if he was Prescott. "And if I am, what's it to you?"

"We're looking for your pal, Leo Haig," I replied. "When was the last time you saw him?"

"What business is that of yours?"

"It's our business to collect him since he's failed to report his current address to the sheriff's office," Maggie said. "Do you know where he is?"

"Nope."

"So how do you and Leo know each other?" I asked.

Prescott continued wiping his hands with the rag and said, "We worked together on a roofing crew, maybe fifteen years ago, and started hanging out together. I've known him since then."

"You must have gotten to be pretty good buds," Maggie said, "given how many times you went out to visit him in Lewis."

Prescott nodded, still working the shop rag. "We *are* good buds, and the fact that you fuckers railroaded him into the pen didn't change that."

"So, you think Leo was just another innocent victim who got screwed over by the system?" I asked.

He finally threw the rag back into the bucket and said, "You're goddamn right. Leo didn't rape that bitch and she only swore he did because she was afraid her old man would find out that she let Leo fuck her."

"The prosecutor didn't see it that way," I said.

"Yeah, well, fuck him too."

I gave him a minute to cool down a bit and then said, "I'll ask again, Mr. Prescott, when did you last see Leo?"

He shook his head. "To be honest, I really can't remember."

"That seems a bit odd. You visited him pretty regularly when he was in the can, and now that he's out, you're telling me that you've suddenly lost touch?"

Again, he simply shrugged, and I said, "Look, Mr. Prescott, your buddy is in violation of the law. The longer it takes us to find him, the harder it's going to go on him once we do. And the same goes for anyone who helps him hide out. Aiding a fugitive can get you jail time of your own."

Prescott just looked away and shook his head. "Have you seen him at all since he got out, Mr. Prescott?"

The big man waited for a moment, then turned back to me. "A couple of days after he got out, we got together for a few beers. We shot the shit for a while and I loaned him a couple hundred bucks to tide him over while he was getting settled in. I haven't seen him since."

"What were his plans?"

"He said he was looking for a place to live so that he could get out of the halfway house. He was also trying to find a job. He said he'd be back in touch once he got settled. That's the last I heard from him."

"No phone calls, no nothing?"

"No."

"And you haven't heard anything second- or third-hand from friends you might have in common?" Maggie asked.

"No, I have not."

"If you had to guess, where do you suppose he might be?"

"I wouldn't have the slightest idea."

I waited a few seconds and when it was clear that he wasn't going to offer anything else, I said, "Okay, Mr. Prescott, thanks for your time. But if you should hear from Leo, tell him that the smart thing to do is to report his address to the sheriff's office and account for his whereabouts. If he's got a good explanation for why he hasn't reported in like he was supposed to, we might still be able to straighten all this out. But if we find him before he reports in on his own, he's going straight back to Lewis, no question."

I gave Prescott my card and told him to call if he heard anything or if he had any sudden inspiration as to where we might find his buddy, but I really wasn't counting on hearing from him.

***

We'd made an appointment to meet with Leo Haig's lawyer, a guy named Malcolm Webb, and after leaving Prescott, we headed to Webb's office in downtown Phoenix. He was apparently in practice with two other attorneys, and walking into the air-conditioned reception area was a huge relief after the sweltering heat of Walter Prescott's driveway. The receptionist was an attractive brunette who was wearing minimal, if any, makeup and who, for whatever reason, had chosen to dress in a way that would understate rather than highlight her natural attributes. She offered a brief smile and then picked up the phone to announce us. After only a momentary wait, a tall, distinguished looking man with gray hair walked down the hall and introduced himself as Webb.

He appeared to be somewhere in his middle sixties, a bit overweight, but still a guy with a very commanding presence. He walked us back to a fairly large and well-appointed office, and Maggie and I each gratefully accepted a bottle of water. Webb then offered us seats on a couch in a conversation area opposite his desk. He took a chair facing us and asked how he could be of help.

"We're looking for one of your clients, Mr. Webb," Maggie said. "Leo Haig, Jr.?"

Webb shook his head. After a moment, he said, "What's he done now?"

"He failed to report his current address to the sheriff's department," I said, "which puts him in violation of the terms of his release. We're trying to track him down and get things straightened out."

Webb spent a moment, apparently assessing the situation. "You're telling me that a couple of homicide detectives have been detailed to find someone who's failed to report his change of address to the sheriff? That seems a bit hard to believe, if you don't mind my saying so."

Ignoring the comment, I said, "When was the last time you saw or heard from Leo, Mr. Webb?"

"He was here in the office three days after his release to deal with some matters relating to his mother's estate."

"Can you tell us what that involved?" Maggie asked.

Webb looked over his shoulder for a moment at the view out of his office window. Turning back, he said, "As you may already know, Leo's mother died while he was in prison. Leo inherited her estate, which amounted to the house that the family had lived in and a few small investments. When his mother died, Leo instructed me to sell the house and turn all the other investments into cash. I put the proceeds into a money market account that I administered for him until he was released. When he came in, I signed the papers turning the account over to him."

"How much money are we talking about?" I asked.

Webb shook his head. "That's privileged information, Detective. If you really need to know the answer, you'll have to get a warrant and serve it on the fund manager."

"What happened to the contents of the house when you sold it?" Maggie asked.

"Leo instructed me to sell the furniture and to donate the bedding, his parents' clothing, dishes, cookware and that sort of thing to the Goodwill. Otherwise, I was to pack up the personal items and place them into storage for him."

"And you did so?"

"Not personally, of course. We hired a firm to take care of that before we put the house on the market. They packed up the things, rented a storage unit, and moved the boxes into the unit. Mr. Haig picked up the rental agreement and the key when he was here."

"And you have no idea where your client might be now?"

"No, I don't. But for that matter, Mr. Haig is no longer my client."

"He fired you?" I asked.

Webb showed a tight smile and tented his fingers in front of his chest. "Actually, more the other way around, Detective Richardson. I'd been his parents' attorney for a long time and Leo, Sr. and I were personal friends. When Leo, Jr. was charged with the rape, I agreed to defend him, but only as a favor to his parents; otherwise I wouldn't have touched the case. I continued to represent them and then, after their deaths, Leo, Jr., until the estate was settled and Junior was released from prison. But once he came in and took care of the final business relating to the estate, I told him that I would no longer serve as his attorney."

"And he gave no indication of where he might be going or what his plans might have been?" I asked.

"No, Detective, and I didn't inquire. Frankly, I had no interest whatsoever and was more than happy to finally have Leo Haig, Jr. out of my life."

30.

Webb gave us the name and address of the firm that had boxed up the personal belongings from the Haigs' home as well as the address of the storage facility on Thunderbird Road in Phoenix where they had delivered the items they'd removed from the house. The firm's records indicated that they had packed up and delivered to the storage unit eight boxes of varying sizes with loose items from the house. They had itemized the things that went into each box and had sent the list to Malcolm Webb.

The company also delivered to the storage unit fourteen other boxes that they had discovered already packed and stored either in the attic or in the garage of the house. They had not opened and inventoried the contents of these boxes, but rather sent them to the storage unit as they had found them. Once the boxes were unloaded into the storage unit, they delivered the key to the unit to Malcolm Webb. Webb continued to pay the rent on the unit out of the Haig family account until he turned the account and the key over to Leo Haig, Jr.

A little after four o'clock, Maggie and I presented a warrant to a heavy-set bleached blonde in the office at the self-storage company. She checked the company's records, stubbed out her cigarette in an ashtray that was already overflowing, and then led us to a small unit that was maybe ten feet square. She unlocked the door with a master key and rolled the door up about halfway. Turning to me, she said, "I have to be back in the office to keep an eye on things there, so I'll leave you two to do whatever you need to in here. When you're finished, please just pull the door back down. It'll lock automatically."

We thanked the woman for her help, and I rolled the door up to its fully opened position. The small unit was sweltering inside, and even though I'd been smart enough to leave my suitcoat in the car, I realized that I was going to need a long, cold shower and at least a couple of tall, cool drinks by the time we were finished sorting through the junk in front of us.

Haig, Jr. had obviously begun going through the boxes, and several of them were sitting in the middle of the floor of the unit with their flaps open and their contents spilling out. The eight boxes that had been professionally packed were obviously newer and sturdier than the ones that the Haigs had packed themselves. Picking through them, we found that a couple of those boxes were filled with books; a couple more contained framed photos and knickknacks that looked like they might have been sitting around the living room of an elderly woman.

A couple of boxes that had obviously been packed and put into the attic or the garage by the Haigs themselves contained photo albums, report cards and other memorabilia from Leo Jr.'s childhood days. Another few contained old tax returns and other financial materials that the Haigs apparently saved in case they might have needed them for an audit or some such thing. One contained letters and other materials that had apparently once belonged to Leo Sr.'s parents and that he had kept, perhaps for sentimental reasons The remaining boxes contained the usual kind of crap that you pack up and put in the attic, only to wonder years later why in the hell you ever bothered to keep it in the first place. Standing in the middle of the small space, I surveyed the situation, then turned to Maggie and said, "Houston, we have a problem."

She looked up from the box she was going through, wiped her brow with the back of her arm, and took a swipe at some dust that had settled on her skirt. "How so?"

"The packing company indicated that they packed and sent eight boxes over here. All eight of those seem to be accounted for. They said that they also shipped another fourteen boxes that they found in the Haigs' attic or garage. But I'm counting only twelve of those. It looks like our boy took two of those boxes with him."

Looking around the small space, Maggie said, "And you're wondering if those two boxes maybe contained a Louis Vitton handbag belonging to Ellen Friedman, a rosary belonging to Laura Garcia, and perhaps a few other such things?"

"The thought did cross my mind."

31.

Seeing nothing of interest in the storage unit and speculating about what Leo Junior might have found in the missing two boxes, we rolled the door back down and walked over to the office to tell the manager that we were finished. She promised to call us if Haig should appear again, then Maggie and I got into the car, cranked the A.C. to "Max," and headed back to the barn. Once there, Maggie told me that she had a date and was checking out for the rest of the evening. I arched my eyebrows and said, "Is this somebody new or one of your old retreads?"

"Somebody potentially new," she said, with a particularly wicked smile. "My friend Rita set me up with this guy who's her personal trainer. He's a couple years younger than me, but she says he's really hot and that he can actually carry on a conversation for more than five minutes at a time. I'm meeting him tonight for drinks at the Mission, and after you dragged me through that damned storage unit, I'm going to have to go home and race through the shower if I'm going to be even fashionably late."

"Well, have a good time and don't forget to use protection."

"Very funny, Richardson. But as long as it's been, if this guy is half as hot as Rita says he is, I may just drag him home and try out my new handcuffs on him."

***

Maggie headed across the parking lot to her car and I went upstairs. I ducked into the conference room a little before six o'clock to find Jack Oliva still sorting through the old case files. "Jesus, Jack," I said, "for a guy who's not getting paid, you're sure putting in a helluva lot of hours."

"Yeah, well, finding the Haig connection yesterday energized me and made me wonder what other ones I might be overlooking, so I've been going back through these files, hoping that something else will smack me in the face."

"Anything so far?"

"Not really. Did you find any trace of Haig?"

"The short answer is no. Why don't you let me buy you a beer and I'll give you the longer version while we wait for the rush hour traffic to clear out a bit."

Oliva closed the file in front of him and got up from the chair. "You don't have to ask me twice; let's go."

Twenty minutes later, we were settled in over a couple of Budweisers in a cool, quiet bar a couple of blocks east of the headquarters building. I took a long draw on my beer, which tasted especially good after the long, hot day, and summarized the events of the afternoon. Oliva's interest was obviously piqued by the mention of the two missing boxes. "Jesus, that's almost too good—and almost too convenient—to be believed. Still, it makes more sense than anything else we've seen so far. Could it really be possible that Senior did the first four and then stopped for whatever reason, boxed up his souvenirs, and put them away in the attic, saving them until he died? Then Junior gets out of the pen, starts going through the family heirlooms and gets the surprise of his life?"

I took another long sip of the Bud. "What if it wasn't a surprise? Remember that Junior went away on a rape charge of his own when he was thirty-one. What if he's a curious young lad as a teenager? One afternoon when no one else is at home, he's up in the attic, poking through the old boxes stored up there and finds Dad's keepsakes?"

Oliva took a long swallow of his own. "Jesus, wouldn't that be a moment? Either way, though, Junior obviously has a predilection at least for the rape angle, if not for the rest. Is there no evidence of any normal relationship with a woman somewhere along the line?"

"None that surfaced immediately. There's no indication that he's ever been married and again, outside of his mother, he had no female visitors while he was in Lewis. Maybe the guy just didn't relate to women very successfully and was never able to sustain a relationship, or perhaps there was something about him that simply repelled women."

"And the woman he raped—I gather from the fact that he only got an eight-year sentence, this wasn't a case where he kidnapped someone and assaulted her over several days?"

"No, at least not in this particular case. The woman was someone he knew, at least slightly. She lived in the same apartment building that he did, and he ran into her in a bar one night while her husband was working late. Haig offered to walk the woman home and, once there, she said that he came on to her. She said no way, but Haig wasn't taking 'no' for an answer.

"She claims that Haig threw her down on the couch, pulled off her jeans and panties and raped her. He claimed that it was consensual, but the prosecutor believed her. Haig's attorney convinced him that he'd be better off pleading it out rather than letting a jury hear the story from the victim, and so Haig took the deal."

"So, it doesn't play out at all like either the original killings or the new ones?"

"No, but that isn't to say that with eight years in the can to think about it, Junior might not have decided that Dad had a better idea."

"I suppose not," Oliva said, signaling the waitress for another couple of beers. "So, what are you planning to do next?"

"Well, Maggie and I got sidetracked by our trips to the lawyer's office and to the storage place. First thing tomorrow, I want to start tracking down the rest of the guys who visited Haig at Lewis. I'm also going to dig into Haig's buddy, Walter Prescott, and see what his story is. There's clearly a bond between the two of them, and as often as Prescott showed up in the visitors' room out there, it must be a fairly strong one. I'm having a lot of trouble believing that he's only seen Haig the one time since Haig got out.

"In the meantime, what I'm really hoping, of course, is that some alert patrolman will pull a car over for some reason, recognize Haig from the file stop, and drag his sorry ass back to jail for me. Then we can find out where he's been holed up and maybe discover what was in those boxes he took from the storage unit. And if we really get lucky, maybe we'll find the plastic sheeting that matches the pieces we have in the evidence locker or some other convincing evidence that will close this case and put this asshole away for the rest of his life."

Oliva nodded his head and tapped his bottle to mine. "I'll drink to that."

32.

At seven-thirty, Sara and I met for dinner and drinks at Local Bistro. We spent an hour and a half lingering over the meal and then went back to my place for the night. She'd had a very bad day, which involved doing an autopsy on a six-year-old boy who'd been beaten to death by his mother's new boyfriend. Normally, she could take in stride pretty much anything that the job threw at her, but children were the exception, and this case had been particularly gruesome.

Understandably, she was depressed, and through the evening she struggled to make anything approaching normal conversation. She barely picked at her dinner, and as we walked into my living room, I asked her how she wanted to spend the rest of the night. Saying nothing, she came into my arms, laid her head on my shoulder, and squeezed me tight. Looking up at me, she said, "Even though it's still early, what I really want is just to climb into bed and have you hold me very close for a while. Would that be okay?"

I kissed her lightly on the forehead and said, "Of course."

Saying nothing more, we walked into the bedroom and slipped out of our clothes. I pulled back the covers and we climbed into bed. Sara came into my arms and we lay like that, saying nothing, until she finally fell asleep an hour or so later. I was still holding her when my cell phone began buzzing just after one o'clock in the morning.

Cursing silently, I slipped my arm out from under Sara, grabbed the phone from the nightstand, and went out into the living room, pulling the bedroom door closed behind me. I connected to the call and found the sergeant at the other end. "What's up?" I asked.

Wasting no time with preliminaries, he said, "Jack Oliva's just been shot."

"What the hell? Who shot him and how badly is he hurt?"

"From what we know so far, he was apparently camped out in front of Walter Prescott's house. He saw Prescott and a guy answering the description of Leo Haig, Jr. enter the house around midnight. He called it in and Dispatch sent a squad to the address. But before the squad could get there, Haig came back out of the house, heading toward a car that was parked in front of it.

"Oliva got out of his car with his weapon drawn and ordered Haig to stop. Haig pulled a gun of his own and they each got off a couple of shots. Oliva got Haig in the chest and abdomen. One of Haig's shots missed; the other got Oliva in the left shoulder. They're both in surgery now. Oliva should be okay; Haig is touch and go. So, what the hell was Oliva doing out there?"

"I have absolutely no idea, Sarge. We had a beer together after we left work and he told me he was going home. He was pretty jacked about finding the Haig connection, though. He knew that Prescott was apparently Haig's best running buddy, and so he must have decided to keep an eye on Prescott's house in case Junior showed up."

"I have to tell you, Sean, I don't like this a goddamn bit. We're going to have a major shit storm on our hands by morning."

"Well, you're the boss, of course, but Oliva *did* run down a fugitive that the rest of the department hasn't been able to find."

"Sean, for Christ's sake. He's a seventy-eight-year-old civilian shooting it out with a guy who's only suspected of involvement in this case."

"But he's got a permit for the gun; he's entitled to make a citizen's arrest, and Haig shot at him first. Under the Stand Your Ground law, he's certainly within his legal rights."

"Well, we'll sort that out in the morning. In the meantime, you get the hell over there and take control of the situation."

He hung up without further comment and I tiptoed back into the bedroom, trying not to wake Sara. But as I made my way toward the bathroom, she snapped on a light and said, "What's happened?"

I quickly explained the situation and told her to go back to sleep. Then I threw on some clothes, got into my car, and raced over to Prescott's house. On the way, I punched Ellie Davis's number into my phone and woke her out of what sounded like a pretty deep sleep. It took her a moment or two to get her bearings and then she said, "Sean, what is it?"

"I'm on my way to a shooting scene, and you might want to grab a cameraperson and meet me there as soon as you can. I guarantee you it's a good story and will get you a lot of space on the morning news."

I gave her the address and she promised to get there as quickly as she could. Before she broke the connection, I said, "One thing, Ellie."

"What?"

"You didn't hear any of this from me. You were unable to sleep and were listening to the police scanner and heard the report of the shooting. Or somebody at the station did and called you, okay?"

"Sure; it actually could have happened that way. Mike, my cameraman, spends most of his life listening to the police scanner."

"Great, Ellie. I'll see you there."

By the time I reached Walter Prescott's house, the place was ringed by squad cars and other official vehicles. I saw Prescott and a woman I didn't recognize, cuffed in the back of a squad, and standing on the front porch was Patsy Desmond, a detective from the Violent Crimes Night Detectives squad. She was wearing a jacket with "Phoenix P.D." emblazoned in bold letters across the back over a pair of jeans and talking to a man who was similarly attired and whom I didn't recognize. Desmond introduced him as Louis Wright, also from Night Detectives, and I said, "what's the story, Patsy?"

She pointed at a blue Toyota Camray that was parked up the street and said, "A retired cop named Jack Oliva was parked up there watching the house, apparently looking for a guy named Leo Haig, Jr. Just after midnight, he saw Haig enter the house and called it in, telling Dispatch that Haig was a wanted fugitive. Dispatch sent a car and when the cop rolled up, he found both Haig and Oliva down in the street. Both of 'em had been shot. Oliva was in decent shape; the other guy, not so much.

"The cop called for backup and an ambulance. Oliva told him that he was working with you and asked him to call you. Instead, the cop reported to Dispatch, and they rousted your sergeant. He just called to say that you were on the way. In the meantime," she said, nodding in the direction of the car where Prescott and the woman were being held, "those two came charging out of the house and at that point, the whole thing turned into a massive clusterfuck. The two of them had obviously been drinking quite a bit and they both got belligerent. The guy took a kick at the old man lying on the ground, and so the cop cuffed him and put him in the cruiser. Then the woman came after the cop, and so he stuck her in the car as well.

"Since the cop reported that shots had been fired, Louis and I got sent over. We went inside to secure the scene and found two bags of what appears to be coke and some smaller baggies on the kitchen table. Looks like they were parceling it out for sale. The Drug Enforcement guys are on their way."

"Sounds like we're all going to be here for a while. Let me take a look."

Desmond stepped aside and said, "Be my guest."

She followed me into a small, cluttered living room with a few spare and tattered pieces of furniture, along with the oversized flat-screen TV that seemed to be de rigueur in a place like this. Behind the living room was the kitchen. A card table and three folding chairs sat in the middle of the tiny room and on the table were the suspect bags containing white powder of some sort alongside a small digital scale.

Down a hall to the right of the living room were two bedrooms. The larger of the two was apparently being used by Prescott and the woman who was now confined in the squad car alongside him. The queen-size bed had been carelessly made and articles of both male and female clothing had been tossed onto a chair that sat in the corner of the room.

Across the hall, next to the bathroom, was a smaller bedroom with a single bed. A suitcase sat next to the bed and stacked in the corner were two medium-sized cardboard boxes, both of which looked to be fairly old. I pulled on a pair of gloves and called Patsy Desmond into the room to witness what I was doing. She stood off to the side watching as I set one of the boxes on the bed.

I hesitated for a moment, hoping against hope that the box would contain additional souvenirs from the killings forty years earlier. Then I pulled open the flaps of the box to discover several letters that had been written to Leo Haig, Jr. By the dates of the postmarks, he'd been saving them for fifteen to twenty years. Below the letters were several books, also published years earlier and aimed at an audience of young males. There were materials relating to the boy scouts and some other miscellaneous things that might have been collected by a young kid, but nothing that even remotely related to the crimes I was investigating.

Disappointed, I set the box aside and opened the second one, which was obviously from a later period in Haig Jr.'s life. This one too contained a handful of books, of a variety that was definitely not intended for a younger audience. Additionally, I counted thirteen adult DVDs. The covers of both the DVDs and the books showed illustrations of naked or nearly naked women restrained in various ways and apparently about to be ravaged by the man or men leering over them. The box also contained several sex toys, but there was nothing there to suggest that Haig had ever gone beyond fantasizing about the activities portrayed in the books and DVDs.

Shaking my head, I closed the box and turned to Desmond. "These two boxes belong to the guy I've been chasing, and so I'm going to take them with me. The rest of this, I'll leave to you and the Drug Enforcement team. We can make a case against Prescott for harboring a known fugitive, and it looks like you've got him dead to rights for dealing drugs. It's possible that you might have Haig as an accomplice in that business; time will tell, I guess. Assuming he makes it, I'll want to talk to Haig about the case I'm on; otherwise it's all yours, Patsy."

33.

I wrote Patsy a receipt for the two boxes, then picked them up and headed out to my car. As I stepped out the front door, I saw Ellie Davis and her cameraman standing off to the side and shooting video of the general scene. I dumped Haig's boxes in the trunk of my car, then walked over to greet Ellie. "So, what's the story, Sean?" she asked.

"Before I get into that, Ellie, we have to set the ground rules. You can't put me on camera, and all of this has to come from sources close to the investigation, plus whatever you can get from the other patrolmen and detectives on the scene."

"Okay."

"For the last couple of days, we've been hunting a guy named Leo Haig, Jr. He did eight years for rape and was just released from prison. He's in violation of the law that requires sex offenders to report their addresses to the sheriff's department, and he's also a person of interest in another case that I can't get into. A retired detective named Jack Oliva has been assisting us with that case.

"The guy in the patrol car over there is Walter Prescott, a friend of Haig's. Jack Oliva decided to stake out Prescott's house here to see if Haig might show up. Nobody asked him to do that; he did it on his own initiative, and his instincts turned out to be excellent.

"While Jack was watching the house, he saw Haig enter the place with Prescott a little after midnight. He called Dispatch, reported the situation, and asked them to send a squad to make the arrest, which is exactly what he should have done. But before the squad could get here, Haig left the house and headed toward a car, apparently intending to drive away.

"At that point, Oliva got out of his car and ordered Haig to halt. Oliva is licensed to carry a gun and he had it out. But instead of complying with the order, Haig drew a gun of his own and fired at

Oliva. Oliva returned fire and hit Haig twice. Haig hit Oliva once and missed with another round. The patrol car got here immediately after and called for an ambulance. Both Oliva and Haig are in the hospital now; I don't know their condition.

"Since Oliva is retired, he no longer has any authority to act as a police officer. But like anyone else, when he saw a man who he recognized as a known fugitive, he was well within his rights to make a citizen's arrest. That's what he was attempting to do, putting his own safety at risk in the process. As I said, he was licensed to carry a gun and when Haig fired at him, under Arizona's Stand Your Ground law, Oliva was well within his rights to protect himself by returning fire. And in the end, he secured the arrest of a dangerous felon that the rest of the police department hadn't been able to find yet.

"Further, there's a large amount of cocaine in the house that apparently belongs to Haig and the couple in the squad car and which they were preparing for sale. The Drug Enforcement people should be here at any minute and you should be able to get them on camera talking about the drug angle."

Ellie continued taking notes for another minute or so and then looked up at me. "You're expecting some blowback because Oliva was acting as a cop when he actually isn't one anymore?"

"I suppose that there are some bleeding hearts who will try to make a case that Oliva acted improperly, but that's bullshit, Ellie, plain and simple. Haig is no innocent victim. He's a convicted felon—a convicted *rapist*—who's currently in violation of the law and who may well have posed a serious danger to the public at large. We've been looking for him for a couple days now and haven't been able to find him. Even though he's technically a civilian now, Jack Oliva *did* find him. And he got a very bad man off the streets. The guy's a goddamn hero, Ellie, and the people of Phoenix are safer tonight because of what he did."

"He certainly sounds like one to me," Ellie said. "Can I talk to him?"

"Not at the moment; maybe later, depending on his condition. I'm on the way to the hospital now to see how badly he's hurt."

"Before you race off, can you please give me just a little something on camera, even if it's not much more than a 'no comment'?"

I thought about it for a moment, then said, "Okay. You can turn on your camera, do a setup and then ask me if I can tell you what's going on. I'll make a brief statement and then you take it back; don't ask me any follow-up questions."

"Got it."

Ellie and Mike, the cameraman, took a moment to frame the shot. With Ellie in place, and the activity at the house over her left shoulder, Mike positioned me off to her left and just out of the opening shot. Once they were ready, Mike cued Ellie. She looked into the camera and opened by saying, "This is Ellie Davis, for Channel 2 News at the scene of a home in south Phoenix. Two men, one a wanted fugitive and the other a retired police detective, have been shot here tonight and taken to a local hospital. With me is Phoenix Homicide Detective Sean Richardson. Detective Richardson, can you tell us what happened here this evening?"

Ellie moved the mike in my direction and the cameraman pulled out to include us both in the frame of the shot. "Well," I said, "as you can clearly see, the investigation is just getting under way and the detectives are only just beginning to piece it all together. What we do know is that a wanted fugitive named Leo Haig, Jr. was seen leaving the house behind us by a retired Phoenix police detective. Knowing that Haig was wanted and has been described as extremely dangerous, the former detective called for assistance and attempted to make a citizen's arrest. Mr. Haig responded by firing two shots, wounding the former detective. However, the detective was able to return fire and wounded Mr. Haig. Both men are now at the hospital and I have no information about the condition of either man."

Looking at me rather than directly into the camera, Ellie nodded and said, "I understand that Mr. Haig, the wounded fugitive, had been convicted of rape and is suspected of other crimes as well. Is that correct, Detective?"

"Yes, it is."

"So, it sounds like it's very fortunate that the retired detective was in the right place at the right time."

"Absolutely."

"I'm also given to understand that there's a drug angle to this situation?"

"I can't comment on that. I can only say that members of the Drug Enforcement squad are on their way to the scene and may have more on that for you later."

With that, Ellie expressed her thanks and turned back to face the camera. The cameraman again tightened his focus on her as she said, "Obviously, the situation here is still unfolding and we'll have much more for you in only a few hours on Arizona's Morning Show. For now, I'm Ellie Davis for Channel 2 News."

Ellie waited a moment until the cameraman gave her the all clear, and then turned back to me. "Sorry, Sean; I know you said no follow-up questions, but they seemed appropriate given the circumstances. If you want, I can lose everything after your opening statement and record a new close."

"No; that's okay Ellie. It worked out fine. Thanks."

"Thanks for the tip, Sean. I'll hang around and hope to get the drug team on camera, and by the time we get to the morning news, I'll have a coherent package put together. If there's anything else you think I need to know, just give me a call."

34.

I said goodnight to Ellie and headed over to the hospital. Both Jack and Leo Haig were still in surgery and I cornered a nurse who told me that Jack was going to be fine, but that Junior probably wasn't going to make it. I called the sergeant, this time waking him up for a change, and brought him up to date, but without mentioning the fact that I'd given an interview to Ellie Davis.

An hour later the surgeon came out of the operating room and told me that Jack was on his way to the recovery suite. "The good news is that he was hit with a fairly small-caliber bullet, a .22 would be my guess, so the damage isn't nearly as bad as it would have been had he been shot by a more powerful weapon. Also, the bullet didn't hit any major arteries, and so he didn't lose a lot of blood. But he's going to require surgery and he won't be using his left arm for much of anything for a while."

"But he is out of danger?"

"Yes. Unless something unforeseen happens, he'll survive the wound. But he's going to be in a lot of pain for a while."

"When can I see him?"

"Now, if you'd like. He may be a little loopy, but he is conscious, and he's been asking for you."

***

A nurse walked me into the recovery room where I found Jack Oliva propped up in bed, connected to several machines, and looking every bit of his seventy-eight years. He watched me approach the bed and as I reached out to touch his arm, he said, "Sorry, Sean; I fucked up."

"Yeah, Jack, you did. The first rule of law enforcement is that you never let the bad guys shoot you. Otherwise, you did great. You got that asshole when none of the rest of us could even get a sniff of him."

"I was hoping that patrol would get there before Haig came back out of the house. The last thing I wanted to do was go after him myself, but I didn't know what else to do."

"You did fine, and I'm grateful. Don't worry about it at all."

"I'll bet that's not what your sergeant is saying."

"Don't worry about that either; I'll take care of him. In a couple of hours, the TV people are going to be calling you a hero who took a dangerous fugitive off the streets. They'll be hounding you to come on camera and women all over town will be throwing their panties at you."

"Fuck that shit; I just hope I didn't screw things up for you."

"No way. You know how bad we needed to find Haig and you took a big load off the rest of us by getting the job done."

"How's he doing?"

I shook my head. "I don't know, Jack. He's still in surgery and they're not telling me anything yet. But whatever happens, he had it coming. There were a lot of drugs in the house and it looks like he and Prescott were dealing. No doubt that's why he resisted arrest. Haig, Prescott and the drugs are all off the street now, and I'd call that a very good night's work."

35.

An attractive nurse, a brunette who appeared to be somewhere in her late forties, came into the room and insisted that it was time to let her patient get some sleep. I left her fussing over Jack and went home to try to get a couple of hours myself, but I was way too wired to fall back to sleep. I lay in bed with Sara, turning the case over in my mind, until she got up a little before seven. I propped myself up on an elbow, watching her get dressed and said, "So, how are you feeling this morning?"

She came to the bed, leaned over, and gave me a long kiss. "Much better, thank you. And thanks for being so understanding last night. A quiet night with you was just what I needed."

"I'm only sorry that I couldn't have spent the whole night here with you."

"It's okay," she said, kissing me again. "I understand that a man's gotta do what a man's gotta do. Can I make you dinner at my place tonight? I promise to be much better company."

"I'd like that a lot. Call me later and let me know how your day is going?"

"I will. Love you, Sean."

"Love you too, Babe. See you tonight."

***

Fifteen minutes later, I grabbed my phone and sent a text to the other members of the team, setting a meeting for nine o'clock. Then I dragged myself out of bed and into the shower. I got into the office at eight-thirty and checked in with the sergeant. "I've already had three people tell me about Channel 2's reports on the developments at Prescott's house last night," he said. "I assume that you were responsible for that?"

"Yeah, well, it was kind of on the spur of the moment, and I didn't want to wake you up again to run it by you. But after talking to you, I was thinking that we should get out in front of this thing."

He nodded. "Understand that I'm still not happy about Oliva being out there in the middle of all this, and as of now, he's officially off this case. But it seems to be playing out reasonably well. Channel 2 has practically canonized the guy, and the rest of the media seem to be falling into line. Media Relations will do the same, which I assume is what you intended to force them to do all along."

I shrugged and said, "Given the extent of his injury, he'd doubtless be off the case either way, Sarge. But he's a good guy, and he really has been a huge help in this case. In particular, he's the one who made the Haig connection in the first place."

"So, is Haig our guy?"

"It's still possible, I suppose, but it's not looking as good as it did yesterday afternoon. He was apparently hiding out at Prescott's house, and in the room he was using there, I found what I assume are the two boxes that he took out of the storage unit. Unfortunately, neither of them contains the souvenirs from the earlier crimes that we were hoping to find. I hope we'll get a chance to talk to him and figure out what in the hell he's been doing since he dropped off the radar, but it may be that he simply decided to go into the drug business with his pal, Prescott, and that he doesn't have anything to do with our killings."

***

After briefing the sergeant, I went down to the conference room to bring Maggie, Elaine, and Greg up to date. The three of them were working on coffee and donuts while waiting for me, and I couldn't help but notice that Maggie looked particularly well-rested and refreshed. I poured a cup of coffee, grabbed a chocolate-covered donut, and sat down to join them. Before I could even open my mouth, Greg said, "I just got off the phone with the hospital. Leo Haig died at six thirty-seven this morning without ever regaining consciousness."

"Well, shit," I said.

I went over the events of the night with them and then called a detective on the Drug Enforcement squad named Judy Ulrich for an update on Walter Prescott. "Prescott has lawyered up and isn't saying a word," she told me. "On the other hand, his girlfriend is singing like the proverbial canary. She says that Prescott and Haig had worked out a scheme to smuggle drugs into Lewis, using a bent guard to get the drugs in.

"According to her, Haig has been hiding out in Prescott's house virtually ever since he got out and has only been out of the house for an hour or so at a time, usually after dark when he apparently felt safer."

"So, what you're telling me is that Haig hasn't been either alone or away from the house for any appreciable amount of time in the last six weeks or so, and that there's no way that Haig or Haig and Prescott acting together could have kidnapped a couple of women and held them hostage either in that house or somewhere else."

"I wouldn't think so, Sean, at least given what she's telling us. You're certainly welcome to talk to her yourself if you want."

"I do want, Judy. I'll give you a call later and set it up. In the meantime, thanks for the help."

"We live to serve," she said.

***

I hung up and relayed the information to the rest of the team, which left them all basically shaking their heads. "Sounds like were back to Square One," Greg said. "We don't have jack shit."

"That's about it," I agreed. "We'll want to talk to Prescott's girlfriend for ourselves just to make sure, but given what she's telling the drug guys, Junior didn't do our victims. Which means that the guy who did is still out there and probably taking aim at a sex worker, even as we speak."

Part Two

36.

A little after noon on Friday, "Chris Nelson" pulled to a stop in the driveway of his uncle's house. Nelson was pretty sure he knew why his uncle had demanded to see him, and he figured that the old guy was likely pretty pissed off. Well, fuck him if he can't take a joke, Nelson thought as he rang the bell. And besides, one way or the other, there wasn't much his uncle could do about it.

After a minute or so, his uncle appeared at the door and pointed Nelson in the direction of the living room. "Where's Aunt Martha today?" Nelson asked as he took a seat on the couch.

"I sent her out shopping," his uncle said. "I thought this was a conversation we should have in private."

"Nelson" simply nodded, and after another few seconds, his uncle said, "You've been a very bad boy, Jason."

"How so?"

"Don't give me that crap; you know exactly how so. A couple of detectives were here the other day to ask me about your father and the Ellen Friedman case. Knowing that her granddaughter had just been murdered, it didn't surprise me all that much. What did surprise me was when they told me that a couple of personal items belonging to Friedman had been found on her granddaughter's body. It was such a shock, I damned near fell out of this fuckin' chair.

"After they left, I went out to the storage shed in the back and discovered that a box I had very carefully hidden away was missing. At dinner that night, I asked your aunt who might have been out there. She told me that you'd come by a couple of days after your father died, hoping I might have some old family photos that you could use at your dad's memorial service. She says she gave you the key and told you to look in the storage shed."

"She did. And imagine *my* surprise when I pulled out a box from a shelf deep in the back of the shed and, instead of finding pictures of my dad as a little kid, I found the anniversary article from the *Republic* along with the rest of your souvenirs."

"And thought you'd just help yourself to them?"

"I was only thinking of Aunt Martha. How shocked would she have been to find that box, and what would she have done about it?"

"She knows she's never to touch the stuff on my shelves out there; she'd never have opened that box."

"Well, at least not as long as you're still alive, maybe, but then what?"

"Then I won't really give a good goddamn, will I?"

The younger Turner said nothing in response and finally his uncle said, "So you found the box and decided to go into business for yourself?"

"Absolutely. I've always been a bit restive and adventuresome in the sexual department, which is why I've never settled down and gotten married. Opening that box and suddenly realizing that *you* were responsible for taking those four women was a huge rush. My poor father was haunted by those killings, especially Friedman. He was still talking it about all the way up to the end of his life, never even dreaming that I got turned on every time he brought up the subject. The second I opened that box I knew that I wanted to follow in your illustrious footsteps."

"And plant *my* souvenirs with your victims?"

"Shit, Uncle Fred, I was just paying homage to you. I was proud to be carrying on the family tradition and then you sicced the fuckin' cops onto me."

"Not hardly. At that point, I had no idea you were involved. I was simply trying to think on my feet, and so I invented a new suspect for them—Deacon Steve—and sent them off to try to find him in Joseph's papers."

"I assume there was no Deacon Steve."

"No. Did the cops go through the files?"

"Yeah, and of course they didn't find anything. They simply apologized for the inconvenience, thanked me for my cooperation, and went on their way."

The elder Turner nodded. "So where are you holding the women?"

"I rented a garage in a neighborhood well away from my place."

"And you're apparently being very careful?"

"Absolutely. Forensics has come a long way since your day, and before dumping the women, I'm putting them in a tub and scrubbing them down thoroughly to eliminate any trace of evidence that could connect them to me, to my van or to the garage. Then I'm wrapping them up for disposal in clean plastic sheeting that I've only ever touched with gloves on. The only time I'm ever in danger of being caught is when I grab them on the front end and dump them on the back. If I don't get caught doing that, I figure I can get away with this indefinitely. Obviously, the cops don't have a clue."

Again, a long pause as the two men assessed the situation. Then Jason looked over at his uncle. "So, what now—are you planning to turn me in?"

"Not hardly."

"Then what?"

"I want in."

"You what?"

"You heard me. I assume you'll be taking a hooker next, since you're following my lead. Once you've got her, I want a piece of the action."

The younger Turner paused. "I don't know as I like that, Uncle Fred, and besides, it might be pretty difficult. The place is up in a loft; I don't know how you'd ever get up the stairs."

"You've always been a bright boy, Jason. I'm sure you can work it out."

"And if I don't?"

"I'm sure you will. Otherwise, the cops might be back to see you again with a lot more relevant information than they had the last time."

"You'd only be giving yourself up as well."

"You think I care? I'm seventy-three fuckin' years old and have nothing to live for anyway. You, on the other hand, are only forty-seven. You're in good health with a lot of your life ahead of you. Are you ready to throw it all away just because you don't want to share?"

Jason turned away for a moment, assessing the situation, then turned back. "So why did you quit after the fourth?"

"Why the hell do you think?" his uncle responded, slapping the stump of his left leg. "A month after I did the TV woman, this fuckin' catastrophe happened. It would have been impossible for me to continue with only one leg. But now that I have a young, able-bodied assistant, I figure to be back in business in a really big way."

37.

Jason Turner left the house decidedly unenthused about the prospect of sharing his future conquests with his damned uncle, and he felt more than a little nervous about the fact that the old man now had a hold over him.

The family had never been particularly close, and Uncle Fred was someone that he'd seen only rarely growing up, on the occasional holiday or at other family functions. Once he'd grown to adulthood, Jason hardly ever saw his uncle—once or twice a year at most. They had very little in common beyond the family name, and they'd never established anything remotely approaching a real relationship. Hell, the old bastard didn't even use Jason as his insurance agent.

Finding the box in the shed had been a revelation. It was sitting on a high shelf at the back of the small building and looked like it hadn't been touched in years. Jason lifted the box down from the shelf, set it on his uncle's workbench, and blew the dust off the top of it. The box was not labeled, and when Jason opened it, looking to see if it might contain the old family photos that his aunt thought might be somewhere in the shed, the first thing he found was a plain manila folder. Inside the folder was the fortieth anniversary article from the *Republic*.

Curious, Jason read the article, trying to imagine why either his aunt or uncle might have saved it. Setting the article aside, he reached back into the box and came out with a large manila envelope. In it he found several clippings that had been saved from the original newspaper coverage of the killings back in the nineteen seventies. Underneath the envelope was a plastic bag containing a Catholic rosary and a pair of flesh-colored panties. Through the plastic, he could faintly make out the name "Laura Garcia" written on a tag attached to the rosary. Returning to the anniversary article to make sure he hadn't misremembered what he'd just read, he noted the name of the killer's second victim.

And thought to himself, "Holy shit!"

Sorting through the rest of the items in the box, he found Ellen Friedman's handbag which held a set of keys and a wallet containing her driver's license and several credit cards. There was also a small bottle of Rive Gauche perfume and a few other items that one might normally expect to find in a woman's purse, along with a pair of white panties. A second purse contained similar items belonging to Karen Rasumsen, including several business cards identifying her as an employee of Channel 2 and a pair of black panties. Finally, he found a plastic bag containing a skimpy pair of purple panties and a matching bra tagged with the name of Nancy Petrovitch.

Nelson was barely three years old when the killings had begun back in 1975, and only four and a half when the spree had ended, so naturally he had no independent memories of the events. But despite what he'd told the detectives when they appeared at his office, he was fully aware of the murders. His father *had* been haunted by them, especially that of Friedman. And logical or not, his father *had* blamed himself for encouraging the woman to volunteer at the soup kitchen, believing that the connection to the Deuce had doomed her along with the other victims.

The fact that this box of souvenirs was sitting in his uncle's storage shed could mean only one thing. Turner was dumbstruck by the knowledge of what his uncle had done, and he was enormously aroused by the fact that he was holding in his hands these intimate items that had once belonged to the four murdered women.

He paused for only for a moment to collect his thoughts before taking a quick look out into the yard to see if either his aunt or—God forbid—his uncle might be on the way out to the shed. Seeing that the way was clear, he closed up the box, tucked it under his arm and made his way along the side of the house to the driveway.

He locked the box in the trunk of his car, then slipped back to the storage shed and made a quick, perfunctory search for any box that might contain some old family photos. Finding nothing, he rearranged the boxes on the top shelf in an effort to conceal the fact that one of them was now missing. Then he walked back into the house, returned the shed key to his Aunt Martha, and thanked her for her help, explaining that he hadn't found what he was looking for.

Too wound up even to eat, he spent most of that evening going through the box, reading the newspaper articles, carefully sorting through the other items he had found, and thinking about the possibilities they presented. And by the time he crawled into bed a little after eleven, his plan was already taking shape.

38.

Walter Prescott's girlfriend was a woman named Kendra Phillips. The arrest sheet indicated that she was twenty-eight, but she looked a lot closer to thirty-five. A pale, heavy-set unnatural blonde, she had stringy hair that hung to her shoulder blades and dark brown eyes that were set a bit too closely together and looked like they'd seen way too much of life. Still wearing the tee shirt and shorts in which she had been arrested, she dropped into a chair in the interview room and began chewing on a fingernail that was already bitten down pretty close to the nub.

Maggie and I took the chairs across the table and went through the motions of advising Phillips of her rights. I slid the form and a pen across the table and asked her to sign, indicating that she had been given her rights, that she was freely agreeing to talk with us, and that she was willing to do so without a lawyer present. "How many of these goddamn things do I gotta sign?" she asked.

"This is just a formality," I said. "Detective McClinton and I want to talk to you about a different aspect of the case than the detectives who talked to you last night, and the procedure requires that we get your consent again."

"Whatever."

She picked up the pen and scribbled her signature at the bottom of the page without even bothering to read it. Then she pushed the pen and the form back across the table, looked up at me and said, "Who does a girl have to blow around here to get a cigarette?"

I pointed at the sign posted on the wall and said, "Sorry, Ms. Phillips, but this is a non-smoking facility."

"That's what they've been telling me all night," she said with the hint of a smile. "but I thought it was worth a shot. The other cops also told me that if I cooperated with them it would make things a lot easier on me. Does that go for you guys too?"

"It certainly won't hurt," Maggie replied.

"Good. Because I'll tell you guys the same thing I told the others. My only mistake here was screwing the wrong guy, which, I have to tell you, is something I seem to do on a pretty regular basis. I had absolutely nothin' to do with that fuckin' dope. That was all Walt and Leo's doing. I never even helped them weigh it out, let alone sell it or smuggle it into the prison."

I nodded. "So, I gather that Walt and Leo had been at this for a while?"

"I guess. I been with Walt for a year or so, and they'd been doing it at least that long."

"How did it work at the prison?" Maggie asked.

"I don't know for sure, except that Leo knew this guard. Walter got the dope to the guard who managed to get it into the prison. He gave it to Leo and Leo sold it inside. The guard then got the money back out to Walt."

"And once Leo was out?"

"They had a plan to keep it going, using the same guard. Leo had a prisoner lined up to take his place on the inside."

"Tell us about Leo," I said.

Phillips shook her head. "Not my favorite person."

"How so?"

"Walt likes a lot of sex, but then, hell, who doesn't, right? He sometimes like to watch porn while we were doing it, and he's partial to those videos where two guys get it on with one girl, you know?"

Neither Maggie nor I replied, and Phillips continued. "I didn't mind watching it; if you want to know the truth, it sorta turned me on too. But then once Leo moved in, Walt wanted to try it out for real. I said okay, just the once, to see what it would be like. But I have to tell you, it wasn't any damn fun at all, at least not for me. But Walt kept making me do it, telling me it would only be the one more time and that his poor buddy really needed it after being locked away for so long.

197

"Last night we all had a few drinks and they insisted they wanted to do me again. I finally said no fuckin' way and the two of them got pissed off and went out to a bar. They got back about midnight and came at me again. I told Walt flat out that it wasn't gonna happen and that if they made me do it, I'd cut his nuts off once he went to sleep. Leo stormed out of the house and that's when all hell broke loose."

"When did Leo first come to stay with you?" I asked.

"Four weeks ago—maybe five, It wasn't long after he got out. He had some money waiting for him, and him and Walt used most of it to buy dope. They had some really big deal in mind, and no, I don't know what the hell it was. At any rate, once they got the dope, Leo was there almost all the time. He was talking about getting away to Mexico or some such shit once they sold the stuff.

"What did Leo do for transportation?"

"He only drove a few times. He didn't have a license and was scared of getting picked up. When he did, he used Walt's car, but that was only just to run a quick errand someplace."

I nodded and said, "Once Leo moved in, was he ever gone overnight?"

Phillips shook her head. "No, I'm sorry to say."

***

We turned Phillips back over to the Drug Squad and then brought Greg, Elaine, and the sergeant up to date, confirming that Leo Haig, Jr. could not have been responsible for the two murders we were investigating. A little after noon, I ducked over to the hospital and found Jack Oliva awake, now moved out of Recovery and into a private room. I asked him how he was feeling, and he just shook his head. "You know that Haig didn't make it?"

"Yeah, I know, Jack. but I hope you're not beating yourself up about that. Everybody knows damned good and well that you had no choice. Besides, the truth is that boy was going to come to a bad end no matter how you slice it. The fact that it happened sooner rather than later, probably saved any number of other people a lot of grief."

"That may be true, but still…"

He waited a moment, looking off into the distance, and then said, "Any chance that he's your guy on the other?"

"No, I'm afraid not. I got a look into the two boxes that he apparently took from the storage place and they had nothing to do with our victims. In addition to which, it's pretty clear that once he left the Molester Hotel, he rarely ever left the house where you found him holed up and that whatever sex he was getting was coming from Prescott's girlfriend."

"Well, shit."

"I know. For a while there I thought there was a really good chance that he was our guy. Now that we know he's not, I don't know what the hell we're going to do. I hate the thought that this asshole's got another potential victim on the line and there's not a damn thing we can do to stop him at this point."

"Sorry I wasn't more help."

"Nonsense, Jack. Even if it turns out that our killer has no direct connection to your original cases, we still had to go through all those old files. Without your help, it would have taken us twice as long to get to the point where we are now, and so in that sense we're well ahead of the game, thanks to you. I only wish I knew where to turn now."

39.

When his office phone rang in the middle of the afternoon on Tuesday, Jason Turner grabbed the receiver without even looking to see who was calling, something he immediately regretted when he discovered his Uncle Fred at the other end of the line, only four days after their original conversation. "I was thinking we should have a talk about our next project," his uncle said. Your Aunt Martha is going to a book club meeting tonight; why don't you stop by around seven thirty."

"Oh God, Uncle Fred, I can't tonight. I've already got plans."

In a somewhat sterner tone, his uncle said, "I really wasn't asking, Jason, and I'm sure you can rearrange your schedule. After all, we have vitally important business to discuss, and I don't have that many opportunities when I can be alone here in the house."

The younger Turner pinched the bridge his nose and said, "Okay, I'll see what I can do."

***

It was more like eight o'clock by the time Turner rang his uncle's doorbell. Standing on the porch, he took a deep breath and told himself just to remain calm and not make the situation any worse than it already was. After a minute or so, his uncle appeared at the door, moving slowly on his prosthesis, and led Jason into the living room. "Before you sit down," his uncle said, "why don't you grab us a couple beers from the kitchen."

Jason walked into the kitchen, opened the refrigerator, and noted that his choice was either Miller Genuine Draft in a bottle or Miller Genuine Draft in a can. Grabbing a couple of bottles, he popped the caps with an opener that was lying on the counter next to the fridge, walked back into the living room, and handed one to his uncle. His uncle, who was clearly more excited about their joint "project" than Jason was, tapped his bottle to that of his nephew and said, "Here's to our adventure."

Jason sat on the couch, took a pull on the beer, and said, "So what did you want to see me about?"

"I'm anxious to get moving here. After being out of business for more than forty years, I want some action. When had you planned on grabbing the next girl?"

"Well, not for a while yet, Uncle Fred. I figure I need to let the heat die down a bit after doing the first two so quickly."

"What the hell are you worried about? You said you'd been extra careful. Certainly, you don't think that the cops are looking your way. Why would they?"

"They wouldn't, at least as far as I know. But I *am* being careful, and I don't want to do something stupid that might cause them to look in my direction."

"Nonsense, Jason. You're obviously good at this, and with the two of us planning and working together, there's an even smaller chance of getting caught."

Saying nothing, Jason took another long pull on the beer. His uncle, who clearly *was* excited about the prospect of "getting back into business," set his beer on the table next to him without even having tasted it yet. Leaning forward, he said, "So, do you have a target in mind?"

The younger man shook his head. "I don't have any particular woman in mind yet, only a type. According to the clippings you saved, Nancy Petrovitch was a slender brunette in her mid-twenties. I'm trying to find a woman very much like that, again with the idea of following your pattern as closely as possible."

His uncle nodded. "So how do you propose to select her, and how are you planning to grab her?"

"Well, I'm not going to take her off the street, like you did with Petrovitch. In the first place, there aren't that many girls out on the streets anymore, and also, I don't want to run the risk of getting caught on a surveillance camera somewhere. So, I'm planning to find someone on the Internet. A lot of these women advertise on the Web now. Some of them work out of their homes, but occasionally they'll rent a room in a motel or someplace and work there.

"They almost always post pictures with the ads, and so I've been watching the ads, looking for someone who resembles Petrovitch. I've found a few possibilities and called them, pretending to schedule an appointment. If the woman tells me that she's in an apartment or condo complex, or someplace where you have to go through a guard gate, I eliminate her as a possibility. But if she's working in a single-family home or in a one-story motel where it looks like I can get her out of the house or the motel room and into my van without a lot of trouble, I add her to a list I'm keeping."

Clearly excited just by the discussion alone, his uncle struggled to his feet. "My computer's on my desk. I want you to show me pictures of some of them."

"Christ no, Uncle Fred! Sit the hell down and don't do something stupid."

"What do you mean? It can't be dangerous just to look at a couple of pictures."

"The hell it can't." Jason shook his head. "Look, Uncle Fred, I told you I was being super careful, and you need to be too. Every time you turn on your computer, you leave a trail—especially when you do anything on the Internet. If, for some reason, the cops decided to look at you, the first thing they'd do is grab your computer and trace your browsing history. And if they were to find that you'd been looking at ads on escort sites, and especially if they found that you just happen to have been looking at an ad posted by a hooker who got abducted and killed, they'd be all over you."

"So why is your computer safe and mine isn't?"

"Because I have a special computer that I use only for this business. I bought it for cash; there's no way that it can be traced back to me, and I never use it in my home or office. I only use it in the parking lots of restaurants or other places where there's a wi-fi connection. That way, if the cops were able to trace back the messages between the hooker and me, the trail would only take them as far as the hot spot where I used the wi-fi. I also have a special phone that I only use for this business. Again, I paid cash, and there's no way to trace it back to me."

His uncle thought about that for a moment, then sat back down in his chair and said, "So how do you plan to make the grab?"

"I'll pick a woman and make a date with her. Once I'm in the room and I'm sure she's alone, I'll decide if she's really attractive enough to be worth it. Some of these women post really old pictures of themselves and descriptions that make them sound ten times sexier than they actually are. If I get some pig who's not worth the effort, I'll simply leave and try for someone else at another time.

"But if I decide that the woman meets expectations, I'll tell her that I'd really be more comfortable back at my place and offer her extra money if she'd be willing to come with me. If she agrees, I'll simply walk her out to the van easy as pie. If she says no, I'll march her out at gunpoint. In either case, once she's in the van, she's helpless. I'll tie her up and gag her, put her in the back of the van, and take her to the garage."

"And where's this garage again?"

"In an older neighborhood, not far from where you dumped your victims. I didn't want to have to drive any farther than necessary with a body in the back of my van."

"And you're planning to grab the hooker on Friday night?"

"No, Uncle Fred. I told you I'm backing off for a little while until things cool down a bit."

"Bullshit. Don't try to stall me, son. You grabbed a woman on two Friday nights, and it's clear that you've already done your homework for the next one. You were planning to do it this coming Friday, weren't you?"

"No, Uncle Fred, I really wasn't."

"Well, I am, and I see no good reason to wait. After we do this one, we can maybe wait a bit before we do the next. But I need some action now; it's been way too long for me."

Shaking his head, Jason said, "I'll think about it, Uncle Fred. But I'm not going to get careless and do something stupid just because you've got a jones for this. You also have to understand that it may not happen the first night we plan to do it. I'm not going to compromise and drag off some skanky bitch just because you're hot to fuck somebody. I need to find the right woman and it may take a few attempts."

"Yeah, yeah, but don't be trying to stall me, Jason." He finally took a sip of his beer. "So, when can I see the garage?"

"When the woman's there waiting for you, and not before. I'm being very careful about going to and from the garage. I don't want my personal car around there any more than necessary—or yours, either, for that matter."

"I don't much like the idea of you telling me what I can and cannot do. Don't forget that I'm the guy who thought up this scheme in the first place. And I'll thank you to remember that I was careful enough to get away with it. I don't need lessons from you."

Holding up his hands, Jason said, "Look Uncle Fred, I'm not trying to boss you around and I'm not trying to make you wait any longer than necessary. I understand how anxious you must be, and believe me, I'm grateful for the inspiration you provided. But you need to appreciate the fact that it's a new world out there. It's probably a thousand times easier to get caught doing this now than it was back in the seventies. I don't want either one of us to wind up rotting away in some goddamned prison for the rest of our lives because we got careless. We'll do this together, and we'll do it right. And I promise you that the rush will be worth it."

40.

Mary Jo Jackson never cared much about sex, one way or the other. She understood the powerful hold that it exerted over so many other people, men in particular, but her own sexual impulses had always been muted and she'd never felt particularly driven by the need to have sex for its own sake. That said, from a very early age, she *had* understood the power that men's sexual urges conferred upon her.

She had blossomed early into a very attractive young woman, and in consequence, beginning in junior high, she was besieged by boys. She enjoyed the attention and she dressed and comported herself in such a way as to maximize her appeal. In the tenth grade, she first let a popular boy touch her bare breasts, and a week later, the boy convinced her to give him a hand job while he fondled her breasts again. As a junior in high school, she formally lost her virginity to a star football player, and as a senior, she went to bed with an English teacher who was panting after her, in return for a "B" in his class rather than the "F" she so richly deserved. Through it all, she never experienced anything approaching an orgasm herself, but she relished the idea that she could so easily compel a man to do virtually anything she asked of him.

Never a particularly bright or enthusiastic student, Mary Jo had no interest in attempting college. And so, after leaving high school, she found a job as a checker in a grocery store for little more than minimum wage. After a couple of years, she left the grocery store for a job as a cocktail waitress in an upscale restaurant. A month or two into the job, she began occasionally having sex with the manager, and in return he consistently assigned her to the most lucrative shifts. The job also gave her the opportunity to meet well-to-do men, some of whom asked for her number and who then took her out to dinner or dancing or some such thing. They often gave her presents, and in return for the attention they showered upon her, it was simply a given that Mary Jo would have sex with them.

Every once in a while, a man that she met in the restaurant would take her home after a date, spend some time in her bed, and then leave money on the dresser as he slipped out of the room in the middle of the night. Mary Jo never took offense at this and after eighteen months at the restaurant, it occurred to her that serving cocktails was basically a waste of time and that there were more direct and more lucrative ways to make use of the advantages with which nature had endowed her.

Beginning with some of the men who had dated her while she was still waitressing, she gradually compiled a small client book. Most of the men were married and so, of necessity, had to see Mary Jo on her home field rather than on theirs. Accordingly, she leased a small office in a complex where her clients could feel safe and comfortable. She put a desk and a couple of chairs in the reception area and had a sign painted on the door advertising "Anderson Consulting Services, by Appointment Only."

In the larger of the two rooms behind the reception area, she created a comfortable bedroom. In the other, she set up a massage table, and over time, she grew her client list with recommendations from satisfied customers. She also placed an ad in the "massage" section of Fantacieland.com, a website where Phoenix sex workers advertised their availability, posting a couple of pictures of herself in a sexy bra and panties with her face obscured. She described herself as a sexy, voluptuous, twenty-five-year-old, blue-eyed brunette named Melanie, who could "melt away the stress of your everyday life." She listed a price of $200.00 for a basic one-hour "massage," which was designed to discourage the bottom feeders who might not have the potential to ultimately spend much more than the two hundred.

The two hundred bought a client a topless hand job—basically what she'd given away for free when she was still in junior high. Almost invariably a client would ask if additional services were available. If the guy was too unattractive or if it appeared that he was straining simply to come up with the two hundred, Mary Jo would tell him no. If, on the other hand, the guy was decent-looking, if he was driving an expensive car and otherwise appeared to be fairly prosperous, she would reply that additional services "might" be available for an additional gratuity, once she and the client had gotten to know each other a bit better.

It was, ultimately, a financially rewarding but nonetheless lonely life. At least in the grocery store and at the restaurant, there were fellow employees with whom she could socialize and form friendships. There was, at least as far as she knew, no professional organization of "massage" specialists with whom she could unwind and talk shop and maybe make some friends.

She was able to lease a condominium in a nice complex, and there she met a few other women that she got to know in a casual sort of way. But virtually everyone in the complex was married or involved with someone. Most of the women there who were around her own age had small children, and Mary Jo really didn't have much in common with them. When anyone asked, she told them she was a self-employed interior designer and then immediately tried to shift the conversation in another direction.

Occasionally, one of her clients suggested that he would like to "take her away from all this," but what that almost always meant was that he wanted to give her a stipend of some sort and lock her away in an apartment someplace for his exclusive use, which would have left her even lonelier and more isolated. And so, after two years in the "massage" business, Mary Jo was beginning to regret her career choice and was thinking about returning to work as a cocktail waitress, even though it would entail a significant reduction in income. And then one of her most regular customers made her a different sort of proposition.

The client, Brad, had begun seeing Mary Jo in the wake of a very bitter divorce when he wanted some straight-forward sex without any emotional or other entanglements. He was an attractive guy in his early thirties with a good job as an investment banker. He dressed well, and he was polite and very considerate of her. They had a lot of interests in common and, after seeing her for a couple of months, Brad asked her if he could take her out for a regular date. "We don't have to have sex after," he said. "In fact, I don't want to. I just want us both to be able to relax and enjoy the evening without you expecting that you're going to have to give me sex for taking you out and without me expecting that I'm going to have to pay you for spending the evening with me."

Mary Jo accepted the offer and had a much nicer evening than she had dared to hope. She and Brad were able to talk easily; clearly, he enjoyed her company simply for its own sake, and at the end of the evening he left her at her door with a chaste kiss goodnight.

Following that evening, Brad never again appeared at the "Anderson Consulting" studio, but he did take Mary Jo out for several more dates, each more relaxed and enjoyable than the last. Finally, one night after a very nice dinner at Elements in the Sanctuary Resort, Brad kissed her goodnight at the door again and turned to leave. Taking his hand, Mary Jo pulled him back and put her arms around him. "This is silly," she said. "I know now that you're attracted to me for reasons that have nothing to do with sex, and I hope by now you know that I'm attracted to you for reasons that have nothing to do with money. So why don't we go inside and make love like two regular people who care for each other, and try to forget the circumstances under which we first had sex?"

Holding her, Brad said, "Can you do that? Can you really forget that when you first met me, I was just a guy looking to buy sex?"

She kissed him lightly and said, "Can you really forget that when you first met me, I was just a girl looking to sell it?"

"If you can. And I'd love to put that behind us and begin all over again like those two regular people. I have to say, though, that while I would never presume to tell you what to do with your life, I'm not really sure that I could ever feel comfortable having an ongoing relationship with a woman who was in your profession."

Mary Jo laid her head on his shoulder. "I understand," she said. "And the truth is that I've been thinking about giving all that up and trying to go back to a regular job, like any other normal person. If there is a chance that we might have a future together, that would be all the more reason for me to do so."

Brad lifted his head away from hers and looked into her eyes. "I'd like very much to think that we could have a future together; I've come to care for you more than you know."

Mary Jo kissed him softly, then led him into the house and ultimately into her bedroom. And while she didn't particularly enjoy the physical aspect of the sex, for the first time the intimacy of the experience brought a level of peace and comfort that she'd rarely ever experienced. Lying in Brad's arms after, she began mentally calculating the steps that she would have to take to close the studio, and how quickly she might be able to do it without leaving herself strapped financially while she looked for a new job. And then the next afternoon, she made an appointment for a massage with a new client who told her that his name was Chris Nelson.

41.

Contrary to what he'd told his uncle, Jason Turner *had* settled on his next target, a woman who called herself Melanie and who was advertising "massages" on the Internet. By the pictures she posted with the ad and the description she provided, Melanie resembled Nancy Petrovitch as closely as Turner could have possibly hoped, and in checking, he discovered that she was working out of a studio at the far corner of a small strip mall in west Phoenix. Turner had scoped out the location and discovered that the space next door to the woman's studio was vacant. By early evening, there wasn't much traffic at all around the rest of the complex, and thus he reasoned that it would be a fairly simple proposition to park directly in front of the studio and walk the woman out and into the van.

He had planned to wait another couple of weeks before taking the woman, but his uncle was making him nervous. Clearly the old man was restless and anxious to get back in the game. And despite the warning that Jason had given him, he feared that his uncle might well be poking around on the Net, leaving a trail that any reasonably competent investigator could easily follow. Thus, Jason reluctantly decided that it was time to take the bull by the horns and deal with the problem before his uncle's seventy-three-year-old raging hormones got the both of them into deep shit.

Accordingly, early Wednesday afternoon he called his uncle and told him he wanted to drop by for a minute. Half an hour later, Jason pulled into the driveway and found his uncle sitting at a table out in the yard, sipping on a beer. Jason walked over, dropped into a chair opposite his uncle, and said, "After our conversation last night, I've decided to go ahead and make a move this weekend. I've found a girl who very closely resembles the hooker you did, and I've got an appointment to meet her at seven-thirty tonight.

"If she actually does resemble the pictures and the description she posted on the web, and if the conditions are otherwise right, I'll grab her and get her to the garage. I'll get her secured there and then, after I get off work tomorrow, we can meet, and I'll drive you over to the garage, that is if you can get away without arousing any suspicion on Aunt Martha's part. Otherwise, you could wait until Friday and tell her that you have to run some errands that afternoon."

His uncle simply laughed. "Bullshit, nephew. If you're going to grab her tonight, then I want to see her tonight. I don't want to wait until tomorrow night and I'm sure as hell not going to wait until Friday."

Jason shook his head. "Jesus, Uncle Fred, I keep reminding you that we have to be careful here. We don't want to screw ourselves over just because we were too anxious to wait a day or two."

"Right. So, what this amounts to is that you want to have the woman for a day or two all to yourself and once you've worked her over and used her up, you'll let me have the leftovers? No way, Jason. You call me as soon as you've got her and don't worry about your Aunt Martha; she won't be a problem."

Again, Jason shook his head. "Okay, Uncle Fred. I'm trusting you on this, but you'd better be goddamned careful."

"Don't worry. You're forgetting that I have more experience at this than you do. Give me the address of the garage. You can call my cell once you've got the girl and I'll meet you there."

"No, that I will not do. Having your car anywhere around that garage is just begging for trouble. Once I've got the woman secured there, I'll call you. We can meet at a place that's between here and the garage and I'll drive you over in my car. That way nothing will look out of place at the garage."

The elder Turner reached across the table and grabbed his nephew's arm. "What did I tell you the other day about giving me orders, boy?"

Jason jerked his arm away and said, "Fine. If you won't at least allow me to be reasonably sensible about all of this, then we're done. You can go back to abducting your own women."

His uncle looked away for a long moment, watching the traffic out on the street. Then he turned back. "Okay. Jesus, Jason, I'm sorry. I don't mean to be a pain in the ass, but it's been a long time for me, and the pressure's building. Certainly, you of all people should be able to understand that. But we'll do it your way."

Now Jason reached across the table and touched his hand to his uncle's arm. "I do understand, Uncle Fred. And I hope you know that I'm not trying to be a pain in the ass about this, either. I just want both of us to be able to enjoy this together without having to worry about getting caught. I should have the girl under control and safely in the garage by eight-fifteen or so. Once I do, I'll call you. And if it makes you feel better, I promise that I won't touch her until you get there. You can have the first crack at her."

Jason reached into his pocket and pulled out a slip of paper. "This is the address of the place where we can meet. It's a large building that's up for sale on Indian School Road about ten minutes from here. Pull around and park at the back of the building. We can leave your car there and it won't attract any attention at all. If you get there ahead of me, pull your car in close to the dumpsters and wait for me. I'll pick you up and take you to the garage and then I can take you back when you're ready to go home."

His uncle nodded and slipped the address into his own pocket. "I appreciate that, Jason. I'll be waiting anxiously for your call."

***

A little after eight-thirty that evening, Jason punched in the number of his uncle's cell phone. His uncle answered on the first ring, and Jason said, "Hi, Uncle Fred. I just wanted to let you know that the package we were expecting has arrived and is in very good shape. I'll meet you now, if you want to come take a look at it."

"I'm on my way."

Thirteen minutes later, Uncle Fred pulled into the parking lot of the building on Indian School Road. He saw that Jason had not yet arrived, and so, as per his nephew's instructions, he parked up close to the building, next to a row of dumpsters. He shifted into "Park," but left the engine on to keep the air conditioner running. Thirty seconds later, Jason stepped out from behind the dumpsters, walked up to the driver's side door and tapped on the window. Momentarily startled, his uncle rolled the window down and said, "You surprised me, Jason. Where's your car?"

"I thought I'd borrow yours," Jason said, raising a gun in his right hand.

"What the fuck?" was all his uncle could think of to say.

"Sorry, Uncle Fred, but I really don't want to share."

Jason fired three shots into his uncle's head at point-blank range. The .22 made three little popping sounds and Uncle Fred slumped back into the car. Moving quickly, Jason opened the door, yanked his uncle out of the car and onto the asphalt parking lot. He stripped the watch off his uncle's left wrist, then pushed him over on his right side and slipped his wallet out of his back pocket.

He checked to make sure that the rest of his uncle's pockets were empty, noting that his uncle's cell phone was lying on the passenger's seat. Then he stepped over the body, settled into the driver's seat, and backed out of the parking spot, in the process, running over what had been his uncle's last good leg.

Two miles down the road, Jason drove through a McDonald's and ordered a Big Mac and a Diet Coke. He ate his dinner in the parking lot and when he was finished, he dropped the .22 into the empty bag along with the wrapper from his burger. He broke open the burner phone that he'd used to call his uncle and put the phone's battery and the SIM card into the bag as well. Then he crumpled up the bag and dumped it into a trash can.

Ten minutes later, he parked his uncle's car at the curb in front of rundown apartment complex on Greenfield Road that catered mainly to people who were either living on welfare or off the books completely. He removed a little over two hundred dollars from his uncle's wallet and dropped the wallet next to his uncle's cell phone and watch on the passenger's seat. Then he got out of the car, leaving the keys in the ignition and the doors unlocked. He pitched the remains of the burner phone under a car that was parked in front of him. Then he walked half a block up the street and breathed a sigh of relief upon finding that his own car was still where he had left it and all in one piece.

Once in the car, he fired up the engine, stripped off the latex gloves he'd been wearing for the last forty-five minutes, and stuffed them into his pocket. That done, he drove slowly and safely home, fantasizing about his date with "Melanie," which was less than forty-eight hours away.

42.

For nearly a week, we'd been spinning our wheels, re-interviewing the families and friends of Allie Martin and Corrine Ray, and re-evaluating the little hard evidence we had, without making any new progress and all the while dreading the fact that our killer might well be preparing to strike again. It was all depressing and frustrating as hell, and I'd spent most of another night tossing and turning, trying to imagine what else I could be doing to catch this bastard before another poor woman fell into his hands.

On Friday morning, I grabbed a large cup of coffee on the way into work, hoping that the caffeine would compensate at least a little for the lack of sleep. I walked into the headquarters building a little after eight o'clock and, as was my habit, took a quick glance at the homicide board on the way to my office. I noticed that one new name had been added to the board overnight and stopped dead in my tracks when I saw that the victim was Frederick Turner.

I was still standing there, staring at the name a minute or so later, when Maggie walked up the stairs and stopped beside me. "What?" she asked.

"That," I said, pointing at the last name on the board. "How many Frederick Turners do you suppose there are in the metro area, and what are the chances that one of them would turn up on the board only two weeks after we interviewed a guy by that name?"

"I haven't a clue."

I saw that the case had fallen to the team that included Bob Morris. Maggie and I walked down the hall and found him in his office, talking with Valerie Roberts, another member of Bob's team. Morris was a veteran homicide guy who was a year away from retirement. Balding and a bit overweight, he had a face that inspired empathy and had an aw-shucks manner that had fooled more than one suspect into underestimating his intelligence and confessing to a crime before the suspect even realized that he or she had been played. Roberts was considerably younger, a petite Chicana who'd married a sergeant in the drug enforcement unit, and who had a reputation for not taking crap from anybody. "You guys caught one overnight," I said. "A guy named Frederick Turner?"

Valerie nodded, and I said, "Do you have an address yet?"

Bob checked his notes, looked up and said, "East Highland Avenue, why?"

"We just interviewed the guy two weeks ago, for one of our cases. So, where and how did he get it?"

"Behind an empty building on East Indian School," Bob said, "sometime late Wednesday night or early Thursday morning. We're waiting for the M.E. to give us a closer estimate on the time. He was shot three times in the head with a small caliber weapon.

"A garbage man coming to empty the dumpsters found the body lying in the parking lot at six thirty-seven Thursday morning. He called 9-1-1, and we responded. The victim's pockets were turned inside out and whatever he might have had on him—watch, wallet, phone, keys, whatever—were missing. His left leg was also missing, and we made the ID from the serial number on his prosthesis.

"Turner's wife told us that he left the house around eight-thirty Wednesday night, telling her that he had to run an errand. He didn't tell her what sort of errand, only that he might be late, and that she shouldn't wait up. They have separate bedrooms. She went to sleep about ten o'clock and never even realized that he hadn't ever come home. She got up around eight o'clock Thursday morning, and when he wasn't there, she figured that he'd just gotten up and run off to do another errand. Then we showed up at ten-thirty to tell her that he'd been killed."

"So, what are you guys thinking at this point?" Maggie asked.

"We don't know what to think," Roberts said. "According to the wife, he was retired and beloved by all who knew him. They had a relatively small circle of friends; he'd not had any recent beefs with anyone and wasn't in any sort of trouble, at least not that she knew of. It was hard for him to get around because of the leg, and so he stayed pretty close to home most of the time. She hasn't a clue about where he might have been going Wednesday night and couldn't think of a single time when he'd ever done anything like that before."

"She did say that he seemed a little anxious about something that night," Bob said. "He picked at his dinner and didn't make much conversation. But when she asked him why he was so distracted, he insisted that he wasn't—only that he was tired and not much in the mood to talk."

"Did he get a phone call or anything before he left?" I asked.

"She's not sure," Valerie said. "She was in the kitchen and he was in the living room. He always had his cell phone next to him and he could have gotten a call without her knowing it."

"So, you have no idea what he might have been doing over there?" Maggie asked.

Bob tilted back in his chair and shook his head. "None. The wife didn't recognize the names of any of the businesses along that portion of the street and couldn't imagine why he would have gone down there, especially at that time of night."

"Do you suppose someone got into the car somewhere else and made him drive over there, then shot him, stole his wallet and whatever else he might have had on him, and made off with his car?" I asked.

Again, Bob shook his head. "At this point, anything's possible. We've got a bulletin out, looking for the car. We're expecting the guy's cell phone records this morning, and once we've got them, the techs will try to track the phone. Maybe we'll get lucky and find it in the pocket of the mope who shot him."

"Why were you guys talking to him?" Valerie asked.

I explained Turner's connection to our case, and Valerie said, "You're right. It is pretty fuckin' weird that he'd get killed that soon after you interviewed him. Do you have any ideas to contribute?"

"Not at the moment," I said, "but keep us posted and, in particular, let us see a copy of Turner's phone records when you get them, will you?"

***

Bob and Valerie promised to keep us up to date on their case and Maggie and I promised to do the same. We then rounded up Pierce and Chickris and headed for the conference room. "It's just too much of a coincidence that Joseph Turner's brother gets shot to death three weeks after our killer grabs Allie Martin and two weeks after Sean and I interviewed him," Maggie said. "What's the connection here?"

"Well, for starters," I said, "Is it possible that Frederick Turner rather than his brother could have been the original killer? Jack Oliva said that they never had any reason to look at him, but we know that he did volunteer at his brother's soup kitchen, at least occasionally. He told Maggie and me that he didn't know if he'd ever met Ellen Friedman or not, but he could have been lying about that. And being down in the Deuce, even if not all that often, he could have had contact with the other victims.

"The guy lost his left leg in a traffic accident. He told us that he was in his late thirties when it happened, and it never occurred to us to confirm that. Nobody's ever been able to figure out why the original killer stopped after the fourth victim. But what if Turner lost the leg much earlier, say just after Rasmussen was killed? With only one good leg, it would have been difficult if not impossible for him to continue with the killings."

"But he saved his souvenirs," Elaine said, "and our guy found them somehow. So, who is our guy and how does Turner wind up dead in addition to Martin and Ray?"

"All good questions," I said, "but let's not get the cart too far ahead of the horse. We need to dig into the records and see when Turner actually had the accident that cost him his leg. And let's also find out if he ever owned a tan '72 Jimmy.

Greg volunteered to start checking the records, and I went back to my office to do some paperwork. Thirty minutes later, someone tapped on my door, and I looked up to see Greg standing there with his notebook in his hand. "Frederick Turner was broadsided by a guy driving a Ford pickup on January 17, 1977," he said. "Turner was driving a 1972 GMC Suburban."

43.

Thirty minutes later, it was all hands-on deck in the larger conference room, with Morris, Roberts, the sergeant, and the lieutenant joining the members of our team. I began by reviewing the case to date, pointing out that Frederick Turner had lost his left leg only a few weeks after Karen Rasmussen, the last victim in the original series, had been killed, and that he'd been driving a vehicle the same year and make as the one in which Nancy Petrovitch had last been seen. The lieutenant said, "So what are the possibilities here?"

"Well," I said, "assuming that Frederick Turner was the original killer and that he'd been holding on to his souvenirs for the last forty years, two ideas occur to me. First, Turner decided to go back into business. Obviously, he couldn't do it alone, and so he recruited a partner. The two of them did Martin and Ray together and then had a falling out for some reason. Maybe one of them got scared and decided he wanted to quit. Or maybe the partner wanted to go on alone without sharing the women anymore. So, he kills Turner, ending the arrangement, and making sure that Turner couldn't rat him out.

"As another alternative, without Turner realizing what had happened, someone found the souvenirs and decided to replicate the killings. Maggie and I then told Turner that personal possessions belonging to Friedman had been found with Martin. At that point, he realized what had happened and somehow figured out who had gotten the souvenirs. He confronted whoever it was, maybe tried to blackmail him or something, and the guy killed him."

No one raised an objection to the theories or had any other to add, and so the lieutenant looked at me and said, "How do you think we should proceed?"

"For the moment, under the radar as much as possible. We need to go through Turner's life with the proverbial fine-tooth comb to see if we can find any evidence to support either theory and if so, who he might have been working with or who he might have confronted over the souvenirs. The last thing we want to do is tip our hand and let our killer know that we might be on to him.

"We should be able to work quietly, at least for the moment, under the cover of investigating Turner's murder. We need to find every person that's had any contact with Turner over the last few months and we need to get a warrant and go through his house from top to bottom, in case the remaining souvenirs are still there." Turning to the sergeant, I said, "Why don't we get the warrant and then Maggie and I can team up with Valerie and Bob to go over there, interview the widow, and go through the house? Meanwhile, Greg and Elaine can be digging into the records."

Bob looked to Valerie and said, "Fine with us."

"Okay, then," the lieutenant said, getting up from the table. "We keep a very tight lid on this, people. As far as anyone outside this room is concerned, the only thing we're investigating for the moment is the murder of Frederick Turner." Turning to the sergeant, he said, "Have Media Relations issue a standard, low-key press release saying we think that Turner was carjacked and robbed. We don't know where he might have been going Wednesday night, but would appreciate hearing from anyone who might've seen or heard from him or who might have any helpful information, etc., etc., etc."

***

Ninety minutes later, McClinton, Morris, Roberts, and I were walking up the sidewalk toward Turner's house. "The widow's in her early seventies," Valerie said, "but she seems older and frailer than you'd expect for a person of that age. When we talked to her earlier, she was a little vague and uncertain about even some basic things, and we're wondering if maybe she's got a touch of dementia or some shit like that. It might be more productive for Maggie and me to talk to her while you guys go through the house."

The woman who opened the door was exactly as Valerie had described. To me, she looked more like a woman in her early eighties than her early seventies, with tightly curled short grey hair, blue eyes that appeared a bit clouded, and a very pale complexion. She was wearing the sort of housedress that my grandmother might have worn fifty years ago.

Bob introduced Maggie and me and explained that we needed to talk to her about her husband's activities and that we needed to go through the house to see if we could find any evidence that might help us identify his killer. Mrs. Turner simply nodded vaguely and led us into the living room where Maggie and I had interviewed her husband two weeks earlier.

Valerie guided the woman over to the couch and explained that she and Detective McClinton would be asking her some questions while detectives Morris and Richardson looked through the house. Bob and I left them there and went down a hallway to begin our search. We discovered that Turner had converted a small bedroom into a home office and decided to start there.

An HP laptop was centered on the desk, running in sleep mode, and a daily planner was sitting next to it. Turner apparently still kept his schedule on paper, rather than on the computer, and during the last week of his life, he'd scheduled appointments with both his dentist and his ophthalmologist. On the day before his death he'd scheduled a lunch with a couple of guys named Tom and Joe, but there was nothing at all on the calendar for the day he died.

I moved the mouse to wake up the computer and took a cursory look through the folders. I saw nothing that jumped out at me, so I shut down the computer and wrapped it up so that the tech people could check it thoroughly. Bob and I went carefully through the desk and the rest of the room but found nothing that appeared to have any bearing on either of our cases. The same was true of the other two bedrooms, the closets, and the remaining rooms in the house. We found no secret hidey-holes, and nothing that either of us wouldn't have expected to find in a house belonging to a couple of elderly people.

While working our way through the kitchen, we noticed a storage shed in the back yard. Bob got the key from Mrs. Turner and we unlocked the small building to find a collection of lawn and garden tools along with all the other crap that would have normally been in the garage if the Turners had possessed one.

On the back wall of the garage were some shelves, and on the shelves, were paint cans, tools, and several boxes, most of which looked like they'd been sitting undisturbed for a good long time. We dutifully opened and went through all the boxes, but again found nothing related to our investigations.

While searching the house, we'd noticed a panel in the ceiling of the powder room that allowed access to the attic. I had a hard time imagining that Turner would have been able to get up into the attic, but we borrowed a ladder from the storage shed and set it up in the powder room. I climbed the ladder and found that the last person to paint the room had apparently painted the panel and the trim around it without removing the panel. As a result, the paint had dried, binding the panel to the frame. I moved clockwise around the panel, punching each corner with my fist, breaking the panel free. Pushing it aside, I was immediately showered with tufts of insulation that had been blown into the attic.

Cursing, I brushed the crap off my face and out of my hair. Laughing, Bob handed me a flashlight and said, "Better you than me, pal."

I responded in an appropriate fashion, then climbed two more steps up the ladder until my shoulders were just above the level of the opening into the attic. I turned on the flashlight and carefully swept it over the space, but saw nothing, save for the insulation, which appeared to have been undisturbed since the day it had been blown into the attic.

I backed a couple of steps down the ladder and fitted the access panel back into place. Then I stepped down to the floor and brushed as much of the insulation as I could off my clothes. While I took the ladder back out to the storage shed, Bob found a broom and a dustpan and swept up the mess we'd made in the powder room.

That done, we returned to the living room and told Mrs. Turner that we'd be taking her husband's planner and his computer and that we'd return the computer once we'd finished examining it. "That's quite all right, officer," she said, "It belonged to Fred and I don't know how to use it anyhow."

"I noticed on the calendar, Ma'am, that the day before he died, your husband had an appointment for lunch with some people named Tom and Joe. Do you know who they might be?"

"Tom and Joe Howard. They were all friends from when they used to work together, and they go out to lunch at Dave & Buster's about once a month, except when Joe's out of town or can't afford to go, and then Fred and Tom just go by themselves."

I checked the address book in the back of the planner and found phone numbers and addresses for both the brothers. Looking up, I said, "Did you or your husband ever store anything in the attic, Mrs. Turner?"

She shook her head. "No. I've never been up there and, what with his leg, it would have been impossible for Fred to get up there."

"We saw the storage shed in the back; do you and Mr. Turner have any other place where you stored things—a storage unit that you rented someplace, maybe?"

"No, officer. Fred always insisted that we had to be good about getting rid of things we didn't need or use anymore. All the things we ever stored were in the closets here in the house or out in the shed in back. Old clothes and other things like that went to the Goodwill."

"One last thing. You haven't, by any chance, been burglarized in the last year or so? In particular, I was wondering if someone might have broken into your shed out back."

The question clearly startled the woman, but she shook her head and said, "No, Officer. We haven't had any problem like that and no one other than us has been in the shed for years, at least that I know of."

I looked to Maggie and Valerie, who shook their heads, indicating that they had nothing more to ask, so we thanked Mrs. Turner for her help and promised to be in touch as soon as we learned anything.

On the way back to headquarters, Bob and I explained that we'd found nothing helpful, and could only hope that something would pop up on the computer. "We didn't get anything, either," Valerie said. "Clearly there's a wire or two that have come loose upstairs with the widow. She didn't seem to know much about what was going on in her husband's life, nor did she seem to have much interest in it. She seems vaguely detached from just about everything and didn't even seem particularly upset about the fact that he was dead."

"We know there's a nephew," I said. "What other family is there?"

"That's about it," Maggie replied. "They had no kids themselves, and Jason, the nephew was an only child. Turner had no other siblings. Mrs. Turner has a younger sister in Kansas City, and she's on the way to help out with the funeral."

"How close were Turner and the nephew?" Bob asked.

Valerie shook her head. "Not at all. They maybe saw each other once a year, if that. There's apparently been a little more contact in the last few months since Joseph Turner died, mostly sorting out what family matters had to be taken care of. She said that right after the brother died, Jason, the nephew, was over a couple of times to talk with his uncle about funeral arrangements and his father's estate. But she says that he hasn't been here in the last several weeks, at least not that she knew of. When Maggie asked about the nephew, it suddenly occurred to Mrs. Turner that she should call him and let him know that his uncle was dead."

"What about visitors and other people who came to the house?" I asked.

"They had a few friends that they saw occasionally," Maggie said. "Sometimes at their house for dinner or drinks. Mostly people their own age that they've known for years. She has a few female friends who occasionally come over to the house, and he had a few male friends that he'd sometimes go out to have a beer with. Otherwise, the occasional service people—cable, pest control, that sort of thing. Didn't sound like anyone who'd be a logical candidate for our killer."

"It does sound, though, like Turner kept a good portion of his life to himself," I said. "Let's just hope that something will pop up out of his computer or daily planner that will point us along a path that the widow didn't know about. God help us if somebody like the fuckin' pest control guy was poking around in that shed, found the souvenirs, and went into business for himself, leaving us with no connection that we can follow from Turner to him."

44.

The garage was on the back of a large lot in an older neighborhood in south-central Phoenix, two and a half miles from Central Park. The owner, who lived in the house at the front of the lot, was a seventy-six-year-old widow who was increasingly hard of hearing and who thus no longer drove. Upon surrendering her driver's license, she no longer needed the Buick that her late husband had left her, and in consequence, she no longer needed the garage that he'd left her either. She'd sold the Buick and advertised the garage for rent three months earlier, and Jason Turner had been more than happy to pay the hundred dollars a month she was asking for it.

He told her that his name was Philip Dawson and that he needed a place where he could store some extra furniture and where he could occasionally park his van when his mother-in-law drove down to visit and parked her car in the extra space in his garage at home.

The widow accepted his story without question and said that no, she wouldn't mind at all if he wanted to redo the large attic above the garage so that he'd have a nice clean space to store his extra furniture. Turner appeared at her door promptly on the first of every month and paid her the hundred dollars in cash. And after showing him the garage that first afternoon, the widow had left him completely alone out there.

Which was a very good thing.

Turner had first reinforced the doors in the garage and installed a new set of locks that were much more secure than the ones he'd removed. Then he boarded up the windows. He was prepared to tell the widow that he was simply trying to make the garage more secure and to make it impossible for any thieves to look in through the windows and see his furniture. But she never asked and, for all he knew, she'd never even noticed the changes.

He cleaned the place thoroughly and for the next few weekends spent all his spare time redoing the loft in the garage. He ripped up the old plywood flooring, exposing the joists, and then installed two new layers of plywood, one above and the other below the joists with soundproofing insulation stuffed in between the two layers. The walls of the loft sloped up to a peak, eight feet above the floor, and these too he insulated to soak up virtually any sound that originated in the room. A set of folding steps that collapsed up into the ceiling provided access to the loft, and Turner put a good lock on that as well.

When the job was finished, he was left with about three hundred square feet of usable space in the loft, which was more than enough to suit his purposes. He rewired the garage, putting in some lights and a few additional electrical outlets. He went to OfficeMax and bought a tiny, office-sized refrigerator that would hold a little bit of food and a few bottles of water. At most, he'd only need to use the electricity for a few hours a month and he hoped that the widow wouldn't notice the spike in her utility bills. If she did, he hoped that she'd have the good sense to blame those greedy, money-hungry cocksuckers at the power company.

Someone had run cold-water service to a utility sink in the garage. Turner reworked the plumbing, leaving a tap on the lower level and running a pipe up to the room above. There he split the pipe, running water to a small sink that he hung on the wall and to a toilet that he bought on sale at Lowe's and installed in the corner of the room. He then ran a drainpipe to carry the waste from the sink and the toilet down to a ten-gallon bucket on the garage floor that he could seal and dispose of as necessary.

That done, he went to a livestock supply store and bought a galvanized tank that would hold fifty gallons of water. He set the tank against the wall on the concrete floor of the garage and bought a hose that he could connect to the tap a few feet away and use to fill the tank.

He furnished the loft with a table, a simple straight-back chair, and a metal cabinet in which he could keep his supplies. In the center of the room he built a platform, eighty inches long by sixty inches wide and thirty-six inches high. On the platform, he put a queen-sized mattress that he'd wrestled up through the joists before laying the new flooring. At the four corners of the bed, he bolted heavy iron rings into the floor.

By the end of May, he'd been ready to entertain his first guest, Allie Martin, and on a Friday night, a little more than a month later, Turner pulled his van into a parking place directly in front of the office of "Anderson Consulting," noting that, as had been the case on each of his scouting runs, virtually all the other offices in the building appeared to be closed by that time. He saw only two other vehicles parked in front of the building, a red Ford Focus that was parked facing the street, and a tan Lexus that was parked facing a darkened office at the other end of the building.

He'd made an appointment with "Melanie" for seven thirty that evening, and through the window at the front of the office he could see the woman standing near the desk in the reception area, looking expectantly at his van. She was wearing tan shorts and a light blue top, and at first glance appeared to be exactly as advertised.

As Turner approached the office, the woman moved to meet him. She twisted a knob to unlock the door, and Turner pulled it open. "Hi, I'm Chris," he said. "Thanks for staying a little late to see me."

The woman smiled, held out her hand and said, "Hi, Chris, I'm Melanie." Turner took her hand briefly, and then she said, "Why don't we go back this way?"

She locked the door again, then led him down a narrow hallway to a small room with a massage table positioned in the middle of the room. A few candles and a small lamp provided the only illumination in the room, and smooth jazz was playing on a phone docked in a speaker sitting on a shelf next to some lotions.

Standing at the door, "Melanie" said, "Why don't you get comfortable, Hon? You can hang your clothes on the hook on the back of the door, then lie down on the table facing the other way and I'll be back in a jiff."

Turner made a show of looking around the room, then said, "This is fine, Melanie, but I'd really feel more comfortable back at my condo. It's very nice and I'd pay you an extra hundred if we could go over there. It's only about fifteen minutes from here."

The woman smiled. "Sorry, Sweetie. Once I get to know you better, maybe we could do that. But for our first appointment, we need to stay here."

Turner paused a moment, then shook his head. "Well, I'm sorry, Sweetie, but I really must insist."

Grabbing her arm, he pulled the woman into the small room, clamped his left hand over her mouth, and pushed the door closed with his right. As Jackson struggled against him, he reached into his pocket and pulled out a small Taser. He held it in front of her face to let her get a good look at it, then jammed it against the rib cage on her right side. "Now listen to me, Honey. You need to follow my instructions exactly or I'm going to give you a taste of this. Believe me when I say that it hurts like hell and will leave you completely immobilized. Now you can either walk out of here with me or I can carry you out, but either way you're going."

Jackson began sobbing. "Please," she whimpered, "Please don't do this."

"It's okay, Baby," Turner said in a soothing voice. "I'm not going to hurt you; I just want to play with you for a couple of hours or so. I'm not going to ask you to do anything you haven't done plenty of times before, and if you cooperate, everything will be fine. When we're done, I'll drive you back here and I'll still pay you the money I promised."

Still crying, Jackson said, "You promise that you won't hurt me?"

"I promise," Turner replied. He moved his left hand to cup Jackson's right breast. "I just want to have some fun with you. Who knows, you might even enjoy it too."

Jackson sniffled and nodded her head. "Okay, I'll cooperate and give you what you want, as long as you keep your promise. But we don't have to leave. There's a bedroom in the next room; we could stay here and play in there."

Fondling her breast, Turner said, "No, Baby, I don't want to run the risk that someone might come along and interrupt us. I'd really be more comfortable back at my place. Where's your purse?"

"In the bedroom."

Turner turned her in the direction of the shelf with the supplies stacked on it. "Grab your phone," he said, "and then let's get your purse."

Now trembling, Jackson slipped the phone out of the docking station, then led him into the next room while Turner kept the Taser pressed hard against her ribs. She opened a drawer in the dresser and removed a large bag. "Open it and show me what's there."

Jackson set the bag on the dresser and opened it so that her assailant could see inside. Turner noted a billfold, some cosmetics, a set of keys and an iPad. He instructed her to drop the phone into the bag and then said, "Okay, let's go. We'll just walk nice and slow out to the parking lot and into my van."

Again, Jackson began crying, "Please, no."

Turner grabbed her left arm, squeezing hard while still pressing the Taser against her. "Move."

He walked the woman slowly back toward the front of the building. At the end of the short hallway, he paused to look out through the front windows. Seeing no activity outside, he walked her to the door and then snapped off the lights. "Okay." he said, "We wait for these cars to pass on the street, then we walk quickly outside, and you get into the van. If you try to get away or make even the slightest sound, I'll shoot you with the stun gun and dump you into the van. And then I'll make you pay for disobeying me."

Thirty seconds later, there was a break in the traffic on Greenway Road, and Turner could see no activity outside of the building.

Fiercely gripping Jackson's left arm, he pushed her through the door and marched her quickly to the van. "Open the door," he said.

Jackson pulled the door open and he pushed her up and into the passenger's seat. Then he slammed the door and, holding the Taser at his side, walked quickly around the front of the vehicle and got in on the driver's side. In the few seconds that it took him to do so, Jackson had leaped out of her seat into the back of the van and was attempting to push the rear doors open. As Turner got in and closed the door behind him, the woman began screaming and pounding at the rear doors, which refused to open.

Turner pointed the Taser at her and pulled the trigger. In a split second, the twin wires traveled the seven feet between Turner and the woman and the probes hit Jackson in the back. She spasmed and immediately dropped to the floor of the van, whimpering, and shaking violently. Turner quickly climbed between the seats into the back of the van, stripped a piece of duct tape from a roll and bound her wrists together. He stripped off another piece, bound her legs together and slapped a third piece of tape over her mouth. Then he grabbed a tarp from behind the passenger's seat, unfolded it, and draped it over her.

Moving back to the driver's seat, he took a quick look in every direction, but the activity seemed to have attracted no attention. He cranked the engine, backed slowly out of the parking space, and headed east out of the parking lot. At Greenway Road, he stopped and looked in both directions. Then he signaled a left turn and headed back in the direction of his rented garage. Fifteen minutes later, he opened the back doors of the van and grabbed Jackson by the ankles. Already hard with anticipation, he pulled the woman toward him, threw her over his shoulder in a fireman's carry, and turned eagerly toward the stairs leading up to the loft.

45.

Although several of us had regularly scheduled days off coming, we all worked through the weekend, praying for a break that would lead us to our killer. Everyone was running on adrenaline and caffeine, hoping desperately that he had not yet grabbed another woman, and running repeatedly through the pathetically small trove of evidence we'd collected in the hope that some clue or connection would finally leap out and allow us to catch his sorry ass before he *could* abduct and kill someone else.

Unhappily, though, nothing panned out. At mid-afternoon on Saturday, I got a call from Rick Muhlstein in the computer lab with a preliminary report on Frederick Turner's computer. "We're not finding anything that looks suspicious in his e-mails," Rick said, "but this damned thing is filled with porn, and most of it's pretty sick— lots of women in restraints, being abused in about every way you can think of and probably some that you can't. I feel like I need to go home and take a long hot shower after looking at this crap."

"But you haven't found any messages to or from someone who might be a running buddy or another enthusiast?"

"No, at least not yet. But we're still looking."

***

Later that afternoon, the service provider sent over the records for Turner's cell phone. The final call, which he received at eight thirty-four on the night of his death, lasted less than a minute and came from a prepaid cell phone that had been purchased for cash at a convenience store. The call to Turner was the last one made from the phone, and the techs were unable to pinpoint its location.

The techs were able to give us a current location for Turner's phone, which they narrowed down to a shabby apartment complex in central Phoenix. They weren't able to get us any closer than the building itself, but then, mid-day Sunday, a teenager named Marcus

Clay was arrested attempting to use Turner's Visa card in a shopping mall. We'd put an alert on the card, and when the kid attempted to use it at a sporting goods store, a store security guard detained him until a couple of patrolmen arrived to take Clay into custody.

When arrested, the kid was wearing a watch that Mrs. Turner identified as belonging to her late husband. In his pockets, the arresting officers found a couple of Turner's other credit cards, his phone, and his car keys. The car itself was out in the mall parking lot where Clay had left it while doing his shopping.

Bob and I interviewed Clay together. The boy lived with his mother in the apartment complex to which the techs had traced Turner's phone. He claimed that he had seen the car on the street late Wednesday night and noticed that it was unlocked with the keys in the ignition. The watch, wallet and phone were sitting on the passenger's seat, and Clay apparently decided that the setup was a gift from the gods. He grabbed everything up, locked the car, and then checked again the next morning to see if it was still there. When he found that it was, he assumed that it was now his new ride by default. He fired it up, moved it to a different parking spot, and then on Sunday, he decided to go shopping.

The kid insisted that he'd never heard of Frederick Turner and that he'd never been anywhere near the building where Turner's body had been found. More to the point, he had several witnesses, including a couple of adults, who confirmed the fact that at eight-thirty on the night that Turner was murdered, Clay had been at a cousin's birthday party, miles away from the scene. He hadn't left the party until well after eleven that night, and so we were left to conclude that someone else had killed Turner and had then left his car in front of the apartment building.

"It seems pretty clear that whoever did it was intentionally setting up some stooge like Clay as a diversion," Bob said. "Otherwise, why leave the car unlocked with the keys and the other stuff right there as a temptation for the first shithead to come along?"

"That seems right," I said. "But that pretty much shoots down the notion that Turner was killed in a robbery, assuming that he wasn't carrying a huge roll of cash that the killer kept for himself."

"Which gets us back to the question of why he left the house so quickly after getting that call Wednesday night. He must've been waiting for the call; who in the hell was he expecting to hear from?"

"Damned if I know. But the fact that the call came from a burner that we can't find, makes the whole thing more than a little suspicious. The bastard was up to something and wound up getting called out to his death. Clearly the widow isn't going to be a lot of help, but I'm thinking that I might talk to the nephew again. Even though they weren't very close, maybe he can shed some light on this that his aunt can't."

***

I dug out Jason Turner's number and called him, only to discover, of course, that his office was closed on Sundays. I got no answer when I tried his home phone, and I didn't have a number for his cell phone. On my way home, I swung by his house and rang the bell, but I got no answer and so decided to try to catch him first thing Monday. But then, just after six o'clock on Monday morning, still lying in bed with Sara, I got the call we'd all been dreading for the last several days.

46.

This time around, the killer had left the body in the same vacant lot where he had left Corrine Ray two weeks earlier. Through the familiar plastic sheeting, I could see that the victim was a brunette who appeared to be in her middle twenties and who, superficially at least, closely resembled the description in the files of Nancy Petrovitch.

Unlike Allie Martin and Corrine Ray, however, this victim had not been left naked. Instead, the killer had dressed the woman in a purple bra. A tag like the one we had found attached to Laura Garcia's rosary was pinned to the bra, and pressing the plastic sheeting against the tag, I could see that printed on the tag in blue ink was the name "Nancy."

I rose to my feet cursing the bastard who'd used this poor woman so badly and cursing myself for not having caught him before he had the chance to do so. We were now four weeks into this killing spree and no closer to catching the person responsible than we'd been on the morning when I stood over the body of Allie Martin. Clearly, the man we were chasing was very intelligent and extremely careful. But he'd also been very lucky, and looking down at the woman on the ground before me, feeling powerless and totally inadequate, I found myself reduced to praying that, if nothing else, at least his luck might finally run out.

Again, a close examination of the site where the body had been left revealed no useful evidence and neither did Sara's examination of the body itself. Like Allie Martin, this woman had eaten a pizza with sausage and green peppers within hours of her death, but as in the Martin case, this didn't get us any closer to the asshole who had killed her. Again, we turned up no witnesses who were able to provide any information about the person who had dumped the body.

No woman matching the victim's description had been reported missing and a check of the woman's fingerprints failed to get a result. I assumed that the murderer was still following the pattern set by the original killer, and thus also assumed that, like Nancy Petrovitch, the victim had probably been working in the sex trades.

It was possible that, like Petrovitch, this woman had been abducted while walking the streets soliciting business, but at first glance, she didn't look like someone who would have been reduced to that point in her career yet. Based on her initial examination, Sara reported that the woman did not appear to have been using drugs, which reinforced the conclusion that she had not been a streetwalker. Working from that assumption, I went online and called up several websites where local sex workers advertised their services, looking for brunettes who matched the description of the victim, and hoping that the woman might have posted a picture with her ad.

I struck out on the first three sites and then found a site called Fantacieland.com. I opened the site, clicked on "Massages," and found the photos of about thirty women who were seeking customers.

The seventh photo I selected advertised "a sexy, voluptuous, twenty-five-year-old, blue-eyed brunette" named Melanie. In the photo, the woman was posed in a skimpy red bikini. The woman's face was blurred, but by the general shape of her body, she was a very close match to our victim.

I assumed that a woman posting such an ad was not likely to answer her phone when the caller ID showed the Phoenix P.D., and so picked up my own phone and dialed the number included in the ad. The phone at the other end rang four times and then defaulted to voicemail. A woman who sounded like she might have been the right age and who definitely had a very sexy voice, said "Hi, you've reached Melanie. It's Friday the twenty-fourth and I'll be taking appointments today until six p.m. If you'd like to schedule an appointment, please leave your name and number and I'll get back to you as soon as I can. Thanks, and have a great day!"

I waited for the beep and then said, "Hi Melanie, my name is Jack. I saw your ad on Fantacieland.com and was hoping to make an appointment for late this afternoon. Will you please call me when you get this message and let me know if that would work for you? Thanks a lot."

I ended the call and put the phone back on my desk, pretty sure that I was never going to get a call back from "Melanie." Turning again to my computer, I looked more closely at the photo the woman had posted and noticed a small blemish on the woman's left buttock, just below the bikini bottom she was wearing.

I saved the picture to my computer, then opened and enlarged the photo. I could now clearly see a small red scar that somewhat resembled a fishhook. Picking up my phone again, I hit the button to speed-dial Sara and found her at her desk. She answered by saying, "I hope you're calling to say that you want to take me somewhere wonderful for dinner tonight. If that's the case, I can absolutely promise that you'll be very well-rewarded for doing so."

Laughing, I said, "You have no idea how much I'd love to do exactly that. It's possible that I might be able to take you to dinner somewhere later tonight, but it really depends on how the rest of the day goes and what we turn up with this investigation. But if you can be flexible, we can probably work something out."

"Well, as you know better than anyone," she said in a low, seductive voice, "I'm nothing, if not flexible."

"Indeed, I do know that, but for the moment I have an entirely different sort of question for you."

"Which is?"

"When you examined our Jane Doe from this morning, did you notice a small scar on her left buttock that looked something like a fishhook?"

"Yes; I have no idea what might have caused the scar, and whatever it was obviously happened several years ago, but it does slightly resemble a fishhook. How did you come up with that?"

I explained the process that had led me to the woman's picture and said, "So there's a very good chance that the victim might be this 'Melanie.'" I said. What I need to do now is figure out who 'Melanie' is, or rather was."

"Good luck. I know that this might keep you too busy to see me tonight, but I really would like to get together, even if we can't manage dinner and no matter how late it might get."

"I would too. I promise to keep you posted as the day goes along."

**

I gathered up Maggie and we walked down to the sergeant's office to tell him that we had a possible ID on this morning's victim, then I started preparing the paperwork so that we could serve a warrant on the website and make them produce the number of the credit card to which "Melanie" had charged the cost of her ad. At best, we wouldn't get the number for twenty-four to forty-eight hours and so once the paperwork was filed, Maggie and I set out for a belated discussion with Jason Turner.

47.

"I was stunned when Aunt Martha called me," Jason Turner said. "Why in the world would anybody want to kill Uncle Fred?"

Maggie and I had found Turner at his office in the early afternoon, and he explained that he'd spent much of the weekend attempting to comfort his aunt. "Aunt Martha said that somebody had robbed him and stolen his car. Do you have any idea who it was yet?"

"Not yet, Mr. Turner," I said. "As your aunt may have told you, we have recovered your uncle's car, but it's still very early in the investigation and I'm sorry to say that we don't have a suspect or any strong leads at this point."

Turner shook his head and Maggie said, "Were you and your uncle close, Mr. Turner?"

Again, he shook his head. "No, not at all. Uncle Fred was eight years younger than my father and they were never really all that close as kids. That carried over into their adult years, and our two families rarely ever saw each other—the occasional birthday or some other holiday, but that was about it. It's not that they didn't like each other or that they didn't get along, but Dad and Uncle Fred just didn't have all that much in common.

"Once I left home and started college, I probably didn't see Uncle Fred even once a year. Naturally, I've seen a bit more of him and Aunt Martha since my father died, but that was mostly to sort things out in the wake of my father's death. With that out of the way, I didn't expect to see much more of them at all."

"When was the last time you talked to your uncle?" I asked.

Turner scrunched up his face in apparent concentration. "Three weeks ago, maybe four? He called and asked me to drop by the house. He'd been cleaning out some things and found a couple of pictures of my father that he thought I might like to have. I dropped by to pick them up and stayed long enough to have a beer with him. Aunt Martha was out at a book club meeting or something."

"May I ask what you talked about over your beer?" Maggie asked.

Turner shrugged. "Mostly about my father. Seeing the pictures apparently stirred some memories in Uncle Fred. He talked a bit about when he and my dad were kids and said he was sorry that they hadn't been closer. He seemed a bit sentimental about it all, and I basically just sat there and listened."

"He didn't seem troubled about anything?" I asked.

"Only the passage of time. I think that maybe my father dying might have led Uncle Fred to begin thinking about his own mortality."

"And you have no idea if he might have had any trouble with anyone—any enemies?"

"I'm sorry, Detective Richardson, but the truth is that I really didn't know the man well enough to know any of his friends, let alone any enemies or problems that he might have had. Aunt Martha would be the logical person to talk to about that."

"Just to shift gears for a minute," I said, "Do you have any memories of your uncle from back when you were a boy?"

"That seems an odd question, Detective, and I can't imagine how that might help you find whoever who killed him."

"I know, Mr. Turner, but humor me. I'm just trying to get a sense of the man. Your aunt suggested that he pretty much stayed to himself around the house; I'm just wondering what he was like earlier in his life."

"Well, not surprisingly, I suppose, the defining moment of his life was probably when he lost his leg. I was still only a kid at the time, and I really have no memory of Uncle Fred before that. But based on what my father said, Uncle Fred had been a very active guy before the accident and naturally, his life changed pretty dramatically as a result."

"How long were he and your aunt married?" Maggie asked.

"Something like forty-eight years, I think."

"And they were happy?" I asked.

Turner threw up his hands. "I assume so, Detective, but I have absolutely no way of knowing. They did stay married for almost fifty years, and to all outward appearances they seemed content enough, at least on the few occasions I saw them." He gave a slight smile and said, "Surely you're not thinking that Aunt Martha finally got tired of the guy and hired someone to get rid of him"

"No, of course not. Again, I'm just trying to get a sense of your uncle and what might have been going on in his life. To be honest, your aunt really didn't seem to know much about how he spent his time when he was away from the house."

"Well, I'm sorry to say that I don't either. And I certainly have no idea what he might have been doing or where he might have been going on the night he was killed. The papers said that the police were proceeding under the assumption that he was carjacked and killed by someone he didn't even know, and that's the explanation that makes the most sense to me. I can't imagine who might have wanted to kill him for any other reason."

48.

Two hours after his conversation with the detectives, Jason Turner took an isolated table against the wall in a Paradise Bakery cafe. He set his tuna salad sandwich and a soft drink on the table next to his small laptop computer and connected to the store's wi-fi. Once online, he logged on to the Channel 2 news site to look again at the photo and basic information that the site provided for Ellie Davis.

As was the case with the other members of the channel's news team, there was a professionally-taken headshot of Davis that had been airbrushed and otherwise manipulated to make her look as attractive as possible—not that the woman needed any help. In the photo, Davis was turned slightly to her left and was looking back toward the camera. Her hair fell just below her shoulders and she was wearing a red dress, the color of which complimented her dark blond hair and hazel eyes. The dress had a small "V" in the front and the photo had been cropped to the point where it was just beginning to capture the swell of the woman's breasts. Turner found the picture sexy as hell and assumed that the combination of the dress, the pose, and the cropping of the photo had not been remotely accidental in that regard.

According to her station bio, Davis had graduated nine years earlier from the University of Minnesota with a degree in Communications. She then landed a job as a weather person for a station in a small town in Nebraska. After two years there, she moved up to a station in Albuquerque where she switched from the weather to the news, and after two years in New Mexico, she made the jump to Channel 2 in Phoenix.

The biography noted several of the major stories that Davis had reported, including her award-winning coverage of a wildfire tragedy in which several smokejumpers had lost their lives. According to the bio, the thing that Davis most enjoyed about her job was "interviewing and getting to know the wonderful people of this fabulous state and helping to keep the residents of Arizona better informed about the conditions that affect their lives."

Unlike several other of the news team's biographies, Davis's entry made no mention of a spouse or significant other. It indicated that in her off-duty hours, "Ellie enjoys watching the Suns, Cardinals and Diamondbacks. She loves yoga and snowboarding in Flagstaff during the winter and can often be found in the early morning hiking the fantastic local trails. She also volunteers at a local no-kill animal shelter."

The photo on Davis's Twitter feed was another headshot. In this case, she was wearing a black dress, and her hair was a bit lighter and considerably shorter. The same photo appeared on her Facebook page, and on each site, she posted a combination of news and other, more personal, items. Turner assumed that the latter were intended to humanize Davis and help connect her with her fan base.

Thirteen hundred people were following Davis on Facebook and ninety-eight hundred were following her Twitter feed, but none of them was Jason Turner. While he periodically checked the woman's posts, he didn't want to leave even the faintest of trails that might lead back to him when Ellie Davis and her career suddenly came to a very bad end.

A simple Google search of Davis's name and her Channel 2 affiliation produced scores of hits, most of which involved stories that she had covered. There were other tidbits of information scattered here and there, including photos of Davis at various charitable and other social functions. Turner had reviewed almost all the material over the last few weeks but kept coming back to see if anything new might have popped up. Plus, he simply liked looking at the woman and stoking his fantasies.

Not surprisingly, Davis's home address and personal phone numbers were unlisted, but that had turned out not to be much of a problem. Two weeks earlier, the station's website had indicated that Davis would be covering an event at a senior citizens' center in

Ahwatukee, early in the afternoon. Turner positioned himself outside the center thirty minutes before the event was to start and watched as a Channel 2 News van parked in front of the complex. A couple of minutes later, Ellie Davis arrived, driving what was apparently her own car, a red Honda Accord.

Davis conferred briefly with the cameraman while standing on the sidewalk and then the two of them entered the building. Forty minutes later, they completed the process in reverse, got back into their respective vehicles and drove away. Turner followed at a discrete distance as the two drove back to the Channel 2 building in downtown Phoenix, and he watched as they entered the station's employee parking lot. The lot could only be accessed by a key card which raised a barrier arm just long enough to allow a single vehicle to pass through. Turner was not surprised to discover this, but the obstacle was really of no consequence since he had no intention of entering the lot, which he assumed was probably monitored by security cameras.

Turner knew that Davis would almost certainly appear live on both the six and ten o'clock editions of the news that night and thus that she would not be heading home until at least ten forty-five or so. By ten-thirty, he was parked on the street with a good view of the exit from the Channel 2 parking lot. Like his van, the windows of his car were heavily tinted and, wearing a black stocking cap and slumped down behind the steering wheel, Turner assumed that he was basically invisible.

At five minutes after eleven, he watched as Davis's Honda pulled out of the parking lot. With no trouble at all, he followed the car to the 51 Freeway and from there north to the exit for Shea Boulevard. Davis turned east on Shea and drove another twelve blocks before turning into the driveway of an apartment complex. She waited for the barrier gate to roll open and Turner watched the car pass through the gate. He was relieved to see that, like the gate at the complex where Allie Martin had lived, this one remained open long enough for three or four vehicles to pass through before it rolled closed again.

Two nights later, Turner watched Davis make a report on the ten o'clock newscast, and once the report was over, he got into his car and drove to her apartment complex. He waited only a minute before the gate rolled open, allowing a Jeep to exit. Turner drove through the gate and made a loop through the complex, which consisted of several two-story buildings, each of which apparently contained six apartments arranged back-to-back. In the middle of the complex was a large area reserved for an attractive pool and clubhouse, and from what Turner could see in the available light, the buildings and the grounds appeared to be very well maintained. Looking over the complex, he assumed that the rents were probably fairly steep.

Back-to-back rows of covered parking places separated the rows of apartment buildings. Each of the spaces was numbered, with one covered space apparently reserved for each apartment unit. Scattered around the grounds were a fair number of uncovered parking places that were apparently designed for visitors or for second vehicles. At ten forty-five at night, virtually every parking space in the complex was taken, and anyone arriving that late would have been hard pressed to find a spot to park. Fortunately, just as Turner completed his reconnaissance and arrived back at the gate, a man got into his car and drove out of the complex, leaving open, at least for the moment, a covered parking spot with a good view of the entrance. Turner backed his car into the spot and slumped down in his seat to wait.

Not quite an hour later, Davis's Honda pulled to a stop in front of the gate and paused long enough for the gate to retreat. Turner started his engine and waited for Davis to pass his position. Once she did, he waited a few seconds, then pulled out and followed the Honda at a distance. Four buildings into the complex, the Honda pulled into a covered parking spot that was apparently reserved for Davis's unit. Turner pulled into an empty spot several spaces down, shut off his engine and watched as Davis got out of the car.

The parking lot was only dimly illuminated, and Turner could not see anyone else moving about at this time of night. The windows in several of the units overlooking the parking lot were dark. In a few others, light leaked out around the edges of drapes or blinds that the residents had closed against the night. But no one seemed to be taking any notice of what might be happening outside.

After closing the driver's door, Davis opened the rear door of the Honda, reached in for a moment, and then hooked a brief bag over her shoulder. She turned for a moment to lock the car with her key fob, then headed for the building behind her, in the process walking past three uncovered parking places, all of which were currently taken.

Turner watched as Davis climbed a set of stairs to the second floor and then walked along an exposed walkway to a unit overlooking the parking lot. She opened the screen/security door and then unlocked and opened the door to the apartment. She paused for a moment, apparently locking the screen door, then closed the apartment door behind her. A second later a light appeared in the window next to the door. Turner sat and watched the window for another minute or two, contemplating the situation, and then, satisfied, cranked his engine, and headed home.

49.

Early Tuesday morning, we received a response from Fantacieland.com indicating that the fee for "Melanie's" massage listing had been billed to a credit card belonging to a woman named Mary Jo Jackson. The records of the credit card company in turn, gave us Jackson's home address in a condo complex in central Phoenix.

Maggie and I had secured a warrant to search the unit, and a little after eleven o'clock, we were knocking on the door. We really didn't expect that anyone would answer and so, after waiting a minute or so, I nodded at the building manager who used a passkey to let us in. Even standing at the open door, the place had a stale smell and gave the impression that it hadn't been occupied at least for the last few days. In a loud voice, I announced myself as a police officer and asked if anyone was home. When no one answered, Maggie and I stepped into the unit, instructing the manager to wait outside.

It was a small, one-bedroom unit, maybe nine hundred square feet. But the floor plan was well designed, and the place was very neat and clean. Jackson had only a few pieces of furniture, but they were well chosen and, on the whole, the place had a very comfortable feel to it.

Friday morning's *Arizona Republic* was sitting on the coffee table in the living room and there were no later editions in evidence, suggesting that, like our two previous victims, Jackson had been abducted on a Friday night and held over the weekend before being abandoned sometime early Monday morning. Otherwise, the apartment offered no evidence to suggest what might have befallen her. There was no sign of any sort of struggle or violence, but that was hardly surprising. We assumed that, as in the cases of Allie Martin and Corrine Ray, the killer had taken the victim from someplace outside of her home.

As we walked into the bedroom, a small gray kitten looked up at me apprehensively from under the bed. With only his head sticking out, he appeared uncertain as to whether he could trust us enough to come all the way out or whether, in the alternative, he should retreat to a safer position. I went down on a knee and reached a hand out in his direction. "Hey, bud," I said, "have you been all by yourself here since Friday?"

By way of an answer, he scooted a couple of inches in my direction and tentatively butted my fingers with his head. I scratched his ears for a minute, which set him to purring, then carefully reached my other hand behind him, and scooped him up into my arms. As I continued to scratch his head, he peeked up over my shoulder as if expecting his mistress to come walking into the room behind us. Petting him, I said, "I'm really sorry, pal, but she won't be coming back."

Still holding the kitten, I walked into the bathroom. On the floor were two bowls, one of which was apparently for wet food and the other for dry. Both were licked clean, and the water bowl next to them was nearly empty. The litter box, which was sitting next to the tub, obviously hadn't been cleaned for several days.

While I continued to comfort the little guy, Maggie went in search of food and returned from the kitchen pantry with a bag of dry food and a can of tuna mixed with shrimp. The latter seemed like an odd combination to me, but as Maggie pulled the tab on the can and began spooning it into one of the bowls, the kitten began squirming in anticipation. I waited until Maggie had poured some of the dried food in the second bowl, then set him on the floor and stepped out of the way.

The kitten went after the food like he hadn't been fed in several days, which was, sadly, probably the case. I filled the water bowl and set it beside the food bowls. Then I closed the door to the bathroom, leaving the kitten to enjoy his lunch while Maggie and I went through the rest of the apartment.

Back in the bedroom, we found a metal box on a shelf in the closet, and in it we found a copy of Jackson's birth certificate, her high school diploma, and a few other personal items. A drawer in the kitchen contained a few bills, bank and credit card statements, a checkbook, and a few other financial items, all neatly organized. There was a copy of the lease for Jackson's apartment and another for an office space she had leased on Greenway Road. But we found no computer, phone or other electronic device, and no calendar or address book.

In the kitchen drawer, we also found a file folder labeled "Zane," which contained the veterinary records for the kitten whose full name was apparently Zane Grey. According to the records, he was seven months old and in excellent health at six and a half pounds.

Just as we were completing our search, the manager returned with a copy of the application that Jackson had completed for the purpose of renting the condo. On the form, she had listed her mother, Theresa Jackson of Emporia, Kansas, as the person to contact in case of an emergency. Using her cell phone, Maggie called the police department in Emporia, gave them Mrs. Jackson's address, and asked them to deliver the bad news. They would also interview the mother, but we weren't holding out any hope that she would be of much assistance in helping to find her daughter's killer. As we were preparing to leave, I turned to Maggie and said, "So what do we do with the kitten? We can't just leave him here."

Shaking her head, she said, "Don't look at me, Kemo Sabe, I'm allergic to the little beasts."

After considering the relatively few alternatives, I said, "Okay, I'll take him for the time being. Then we can pass him off to Jackson's next of kin. If they don't want him, I'll take him to the no-kill shelter so that someone can adopt him."

Back in the bedroom closet, I retrieved the small cat carrier that I'd noticed there. I zipped Zane Grey into the carrier and then emptied the litter box into a garbage bag and gathered up his food, the bowls, and a bag of litter. When we were good to go, I picked up the carrier and said, "Come on, bud, let's go for a ride."

Once in the car, Zane curled up in his carrier and displayed no concern at all. On the way back to the office, we swung by my house and I set him up in the laundry room with fresh food, water, and litter. I put the carrier on the floor, leaving the front flap unzipped so that he could use it as a bed if he wanted. He took a minute or so, carefully checking out the washer, the dryer, and the laundry basket. Then he wandered into his carrier, settled in, and looked up at me as if to say, "What now?"

I stooped down and scratched his ears for a minute, then said, "Don't get *too* comfortable, Zane; this is only temporary until we can figure out where you really belong."

I closed the door, thinking it was probably better to confine him to the laundry room, at least for the moment, and then Maggie and I got back to work.

***

An hour and a half later, we met the manager of the small office complex where Jackson had rented space. The adobe-colored building was just deep enough to accommodate a single row of offices and ran about three-quarters of a block in length. A driveway fronted the building, dividing a single row of parking spaces that faced the street from another that faced the building itself. Entrances on both ends of the driveway allowed access from either the east or west.

Jackson's unit was on the corner at the east end of the building, and virtually all the spaces, save for the one next to Jackson's, appeared to be rented. I noted a couple of insurance agents, an accountant, and a computer programming company among the tenants. The lettering on the door of the space that Jackson had leased indicated that the office was occupied by "Anderson Consulting," and that they were available by appointment only. The lights inside the space were off and it appeared to be unoccupied.

While the manager, a guy named Brian Babcock, stood by with his passkey, I rapped on the door before realizing that it was unlocked. I pushed it open, again announced myself as a police officer, and, as at Jackson's apartment, received no response. Not wanting to take any chances, Maggie and I instructed the manager to wait outside. Then we drew our weapons and slowly worked our way through the space to ensure that it really was empty.

Once we knew that the office was secure and unoccupied, we brought the manager in. The space had been subdivided into three separate areas with a small reception area at the front. A desk and chair faced the front door, as though they might have been reserved for a secretary or receptionist. A narrow hallway ran down the right side of the rest of the unit and the first door off the hallway opened into a small room with a massage table placed in the middle of the room. A short bench sat against one wall and on the other wall a unit with several shelves held towels, a variety of oils and lotions, wet wipes, and a small speaker into which one might have docked a phone or an iPod.

The second door down the hallway opened into a much larger room with a double bed, a dresser, and an upholstered chair. I flipped the light switch, which turned on two lamps on the end tables at either side of the bed. The lamps were set to a low, intimate setting, revealing pale blue walls that were coordinated with the duvet and pillowcases on the bed. A thick beige carpet covered the floor, and the dresser held another speaker unit, slightly larger than the one in the first room.

The dresser drawers contained several pieces of lingerie. There were also a few cosmetics, and in the nightstands, we found more oils and lotions and three different boxes of condoms in various colors and sizes. A dark blue wrap was carefully folded and draped over the arm of the chair, while a white blouse and a skin-colored bra lay on the bed, looking like they had simply been tossed in that general direction.

Finally, beyond the bedroom at the back of the unit, was a bathroom with a small shower stall and a rack containing several towels. As was the case at Jackson's apartment, there was no sign of violence in the unit, and the only thing to raise any suspicion was the fact that the door had been unlocked. Again, we found no purse or phone or any other electronic device.

As we walked the manager through the unit, he appeared to grow increasingly uncomfortable, and when we stepped into the bedroom he looked at me and shook his head. "I want you guys to know that I had no idea what was going on in here. The woman told me that she was an interior designer, and I haven't been in the place since the day she signed the lease."

I gave him a skeptical look. "When was the last time you saw her, Mr. Babcock?"

"Maybe three months ago. She came into my office on the day the rent was due and paid me in person. She said she'd written the check and then forgotten to mail it and didn't want to be late."

"And you're sure you had no inkling of what was going on in here?" Maggie asked.

"I swear, Detective. My office is a couple of miles from here and the only time I ever come over is to show a space to a prospective tenant or if somebody has a problem or is late with the rent. Ms. Jackson always paid on time and never had any complaints, and so I never had any reason to pay any attention to this unit."

I nodded and said, "Is this the way the space was arranged when you leased it to her, or did she modify it?"

"No, this is the way it was. There was a tax service in here before. They had a secretary in the front; the manager's office was in the second room, and they had a couple of desks in the larger room where they met with clients. Ms. Jackson painted the place, but she didn't make any structural changes."

"I notice that the space next door is empty at the moment; are all of the other units occupied?" I asked.

"Yeah, we've been luckier than some other places of this size. With the exception of the place next door, we've been full up for over a year."

Maggie looked out the window and said, "How much activity is there around here in the evening?"

Babcock shrugged. "Not much. As you can see, these are basically all office spaces and after six o'clock on most nights, most everybody's cleared out and gone home."

"Is there any video surveillance of the parking area outside?" I asked.

"Not by the owners. The office on the other side of the vacant space is leased by some computer consultants. They put a camera on a light pole facing the door at the back of their unit and another on a light pole facing the front. But I have no idea how much either camera shows."

***

Babcock had nothing else to offer and we sent him on his way after placing a police sticker across the door and telling him that the unit was to be strictly off-limits until our techs could go through it. Two doors down, Jeff Fisher, the manager of the computer consulting firm, told us that the camera mounted at the front of the building covered only his office and did not record video of anything as far away as Jackson's.

He did agree to show us the video from Friday evening, beginning at six o'clock. "I left the office at six that night," he said, "and I distinctly remember that the lights were still on in the office at the end of the complex."

He called up the video on his computer and turned the monitor so that we could see it. He found the six o'clock time stamp on the video and at a couple of minutes after six, we watched as he turned off the lights, came out of the door, locked it behind him, and then walked out of the frame.

Fisher then began fast forwarding through the recording, which showed nothing but the darkened front of his office until the time stamp hit seven twenty-seven and a dark-colored vehicle blew past the camera. The manager rewound the recording and then the three of us watched at regular speed as a van that Maggie and I knew all too well slowly rolled through the parking area, passing the camera, and then disappearing from view.

We fast-forwarded through the next ninety minutes of the recording, but the van never appeared again, suggesting that it had exited the parking area at the east end of the building. I asked Fisher if he had ever met the woman who rented the space at the end of the building, and he shook his head. "I saw her going to and from the office several times, but never spoke to her. To be perfectly honest, I would have liked to. She was very attractive, but coming and going she always seemed to be in a very deliberate hurry—like she didn't want to connect with anyone, you know? I waved at her a couple of times, but either she didn't see me or just didn't want to acknowledge me."

"Do you know what she drove back and forth to the office?" Maggie asked.

Fisher pointed at a red Ford Focus that was parked facing the street in front of Jackson's office space. "That's her car there. I was sort of wondering if everything was okay because I don't think the car has moved from that spot since Friday afternoon."

***

Fisher gave us a copy of the video showing the van moving past his surveillance camera, and we thanked him for his time. Jackson's Ford was locked, and peering through the windows, we saw no sign of a purse or a phone. Standing back, Maggie swore. "God damnit, Sean. The woman was advertising on the Net. She *had* to have a computer in order to place the ads. Where in the hell is it?"

I shook my head. "She must have had it with her in the studio and the killer grabbed it up, along with her phone, her purse, and whatever other personal items she might have had. I doubt that we'll ever see it until we finally put the cuffs on this asshole."

50.

There was little more we could do, at least until the crime scene techs had a chance to go through Mary Jo Jackson's office. Gary Barnett promised to get a crew out there first thing in the morning, and once we got back to the station, Maggie indicated that she had a date and was heading out for the evening. I gave her a look and said, "Is this the personal trainer again?"

"Yup."

"And what's on tap for the evening?"

"We're going to see the Bad Sneakers Band at the Rhythm Room."

"Sounds like fun, but don't stay out too late; we've got a full day tomorrow."

She flashed me a particularly wicked smile. "Oh, don't worry, Mom; I plan to have the kid tucked safely into bed practically the moment the band leaves the stage."

"Well, don't wear him out; he may have a big day himself to get through tomorrow in the personal training business."

"Your concern is touching, Partner, but he's had a full week to rest up since our last date and I plan to take full advantage of that pent-up energy. I expect to be in tip-top shape by the time I see you in the morning. Whatever shape he'll be in by then hardly matters at all."

***

With that, we said goodnight and Maggie headed out to her car. I sat at my desk for an hour or so, doing some paperwork, and then called Ellie Davis. The call went to voicemail, and so I left her a message. Fifteen minutes later, she called back and said, "It's nice to hear the sound of your voice, Sean; to what do I owe the pleasure?"

"Hey, Ellie, I just wanted to check in and see what kind of security arrangements the station has made for you."

She paused for a moment, then said, "None, I'm sorry to say. My boss says that there isn't enough money in the budget."

"You did make it clear to that idiot that you're at some considerable risk here?"

"I tried to, but he's not as convinced of that as you are. He says that even if the killer were to target a TV newswoman, there are tons of them here in the Valley and that he might pick any one of them. He also suggested that I shouldn't flatter myself by thinking that I was so special and said that if he started providing bodyguards for me, every reporter on the staff would be demanding the same protection. Sadly, he's probably right about that."

"Jesus, Ellie, I can't emphasize enough how wrong the bastard is. Sure, it's technically possible that the killer might target someone else, but there are just too many overwhelming reasons why he would most likely pick you. And, as you've reported, the guy's already killed his third victim.

"Like the third woman in the original series, this last one worked in the sex trades. The asshole is going right down the list and some TV newswoman is going to be next in line. *You* are going to be next in line, and at the speed this guy is moving, it won't be long before he makes a move to grab you."

"For what it's worth, I have been watching closely, but I haven't seen anyone paying undue attention to me."

"And you won't. Not until the son-of-a-bitch has his arm around your neck and is throwing you into the back of his van. Believe me when I say that the first three victims never saw him coming either."

"You're scaring the hell out of me."

"Good, because that's exactly what I'm trying to do. God knows I hope I'm wrong; the last thing I would ever want is for this sick bastard to have you in his sights. But I'm not wrong, Ellie. He's out there, and every instinct I have is screaming that he's coming after you."

I waited for a moment and when she made no response, I said, "What time do you finish tonight?"

"I have a piece on the ten o'clock edition, then I should be out of here at ten forty-five or so."

"Okay. I'll plan to swing by there around ten. I'm going to have a little chat with your boss, and then I'll see you safely home."

"No, Sean, you can't go after him. I'm a big girl and I don't need you to fight my battles for me, even one as important as this. Besides, I can tell you that it wouldn't do any good. He's made up his mind and he's never going to back down and admit that he could have been wrong."

My turn to wait for a few seconds, trying to contain my anger. "Okay," I finally said. "I won't go after him, at least not yet. But I am going to see you safely home, and tomorrow I'll talk to my sergeant and see if we can free up some people to watch you. I'll be at the station by ten thirty; do not leave that building for any reason until I get there."

***

I called Sara and told her that I wouldn't be able to see her tonight, without explaining the reason why. At ten-fifteen, I parked on the street outside of the Channel 2 building, locked my car, and rang the after-hours buzzer at the station door. My mood had not improved over the last couple of hours and more than anything I wanted to corral Ellie's boss and talk—or beat—some sense into the stupid bastard.

He was responsible for placing Ellie at risk by continuing to assign her to cover this story, and if, God forbid, she went missing, I knew that the asshole would exploit the story of the "Missing Channel 2 Newswoman" for every ratings point he could possibly squeeze out of it. I also knew that if that happened, I'd kick the living shit out of him.

A security guard appeared at the door and let me in after I flashed him my badge. I told him I was there to meet Ellie Davis, and he walked me through the bowels of the building and left me in a waiting room. I watched the end of the newscast on a monitor hanging from the wall, and twenty minutes later, Ellie appeared at the door. She gave me a quick hug and told me she was ready to go.

I walked her out of the building to her car in the employee parking lot. She drove us out of the lot, dropped me at my car, and I followed her home. She pulled into the parking space provided for her unit and I snagged a visitor's spot right behind her. Ellie got out of the car, grabbed her brief bag from the back seat, then locked the car and walked over to where I was standing.

Surveying the scene, I said, "I know I'm scaring the daylights out of you, Ellie, and I certainly don't want to. But I am really worried about you and I'd much rather have you scared than in the clutches of this bastard. In each case, he's abducted the victim from just outside her home or office, and looking at the setup here, I can see exactly how he'd do it."

Pointing back at her car, I said, "This is where you're most vulnerable—right where you're standing now. You've got to park over there and then walk right past these three visitors' spaces to get to the stairs going up to your apartment. The killer would park right here and grab you as you walked by. There's very little light here and at this time of night, none of your neighbors is paying any attention. It would be a miracle if anyone saw him take you."

Ellie crossed her arms and looked nervously around the scene. I touched her arm and she looked up at me. "We believe that in each case the killer has used a dark blue van to abduct his victims. If you pull in here some night and see a van like that parked anywhere around here, but especially in one of these slots between your car and the sidewalk, don't stop even for a second. Make sure your doors are locked, drive right back out to the street, and call my cell. The same applies if you're leaving for work in the morning and see a van like that parked here. Go straight back to your apartment, lock yourself in and call me."

She nodded her understanding, clearly unsettled. I walked her up the stairs to her apartment and waited while she unlocked the door.

She turned, laid a hand on my arm, and said, "Come in for a drink? I really don't feel like being left alone just yet."

"Sure."

I followed her into the unit, thinking about the times I had done so under much happier circumstances. The apartment was decorated with contemporary furniture and art, and she'd added a new painting to the collection on the walls in her living room. I stood looking at it while Ellie dropped her brief bag on a chair and then went into the kitchen. Without having to ask, she poured me a tumbler of Jameson, neat. She returned with the whiskey and a glass of wine for herself and we sat down on the couch.

I took a sip of the drink, set the glass on the table, and turned to face her. "Look Ellie, I'm really sorry about all of this. More than anything, I want to be wrong. Actually, more than anything, what I'd really like is to catch this asshole first thing in the morning so that neither you nor any other woman would ever be endangered because of him again. But that's not going to happen, and until we do get him, the most important thing to me is that you stay safe. As I told you when we had lunch, it would kill me if this guy got to you because I wasn't able to catch him first."

She nodded and touched my arm. "Again, thank you for that."

I took another sip of the Jameson and said, "I gather that you haven't had second thoughts about the fishing job up in Alaska."

For the first time all evening she finally smiled. "I confess that it is starting to sound a lot more appealing, but I really don't think it's in the cards. Besides," she said, turning serious once more, "assume that you're right—and I trust you enough to believe that you are. If this bastard *is* coming after me, and if I were to simply run away, he wouldn't just stop and give up this insane plan of recreating the original killings, would he?"

"No, almost certainly not."

"I don't think so either, in which case, I'd just be leaving him to fixate on some other poor woman. It seems like that would be a pretty shitty thing for me to do."

"Maybe, but as lousy a thing as it is for me to say, I'd much rather that he be fixated on someone else."

I finished the last of the whiskey and set my glass on the table. "What time are you planning to leave for work in the morning?"

"About eight-thirty. I have an interview to do in the station at ten o'clock."

"Okay. I'll be back a little before eight-thirty. I'll walk you to your car and follow you to the station to make sure that you get there safely. Then I'll talk to my sergeant and see if we can't detail some people to cover you while you're out and exposed."

"Thanks, Sean. Again, it means a lot to me that you still care so much."

The silence stretched for a few moments and then, taking my hand, she looked into my eyes. In a soft voice, she said, "You don't have to go home, you know; you could just stay here tonight."

I waited a moment, then shook my head. "No, Ellie, I'm sorry, but I just can't, even though there's a part of me that would very much like to."

She nodded her understanding and we sat there for another thirty seconds or so as she continued to hold my hand. Then, saying nothing more, I stood, and she walked me to the door. Once there, she put her arms around my neck and gave me a long, soft kiss. Then she laid her head on my shoulder and said, "I hope you know that I still really care for you."

"I do. And I hope you understand that you will always be very special to me."

We continued to hold each other for another few seconds, then finally I broke the embrace and twisted the knob to unlock the deadbolt on her front door. Ellie reached around and unlocked the security door and I stepped out into the night. She gave me another quick peck on the cheek and said, "Good night, Sean. And thank you."

I waited as she closed and locked the doors behind me, then turned and walked down the stairs and back to my car, shaking my head at the thought of how close I had come to not leaving at all.

51.
A little after one o'clock in the morning, I opened the door from the garage into the laundry room, so tired and so concerned about Ellie, that I totally forgot that I'd left a kitten in there. Zane Grey was sitting in the middle of the small room, looking up at me as I walked through the door. He watched as I punched in the alarm code, then walked over and brushed up against my legs. Both of his food dishes were empty again, and so I gave him a little more to eat. He settled into his late-night dinner, and I left the door to the laundry room open while I walked out into the great room and poured myself another short glass of whiskey.

I settled onto the couch and punched up the CD player on the audio system. I'd last turned it off in the middle of a Dawes album, "All Your Favorite Bands," and as I took a sip of the whiskey, the elegiac title track began playing softly. A couple of minutes later, Zane Grey walked into the room and spent a couple of minutes moving carefully around, checking things out. Then he sat on the floor in front of the couch and looked up at me very tentatively.

We watched each other for thirty seconds or so as the music continued to play, then the kitten jumped up on the couch, settled in next to me, and immediately dropped off to sleep. We sat like that for the next twenty minutes while I finished my drink, then I picked up the remote and turned off the audio system. The clicking sounds of the units powering down woke Zane Grey and he watched as I got up and headed off in the direction of the bedroom. When I reached the hallway, I looked over to see that he'd already fallen back to sleep.

**

Seven hours later, I watched Ellie walk into the Channel 2 building after making her promise me that she would not leave the building without an extra-large camera person or some other suitable escort.

263

Fifteen minutes later, I walked into the sergeant's office and dropped into the chair in front of his desk. I brought him up to date on the status of the investigation and then told him I was convinced that the killer would be targeting Ellie Davis next.

He sat there, thinking about it for a minute or so, then said, "I don't know, Sean. It seems to me that there are at least a couple of other female TV reporters who have been working this story pretty hard. Why would he necessarily pick on Davis rather than one of the others?"

"For openers, Davis was the only female TV reporter at the scene when Allison Martin's body was found, and so she's been on the story from the jump. This is a guy who went to all the trouble of dumping Martin's body on anniversary of the discovery of her grandmother's body, and on the exact same spot where her grandmother's body was found. He also left us the grandmother's DL so that we couldn't miss making the link. He's been playing us from the beginning, and you've got to believe that he's been closely watching the coverage of his exploits. Davis was the first reporter he saw.

"Beyond that, Davis is frankly much more attractive than the other women who've been covering the story. In addition, she also works for Channel 2, which is the same station where Karen Rasmussen worked. I know with every fiber of my being that this asshole is going after her."

Callahan said nothing, obviously still unconvinced.

"Look," I said, "if I'm right, protecting Davis could give us our best chance to finally catch this guy. She's probably safe enough while she's at home or in the Channel 2 building. We'd only have to cover her when she's out, and I know she'd agree to keep that to a minimum. Instead of giving her an obvious escort that the guy would spot immediately, we could put a loose net around her while she's out on the streets. That way, we'd be right there when the guy makes a play for her and we could grab him up. Otherwise, at least at the moment, we haven't got a lead worth squat."

"So how would you propose we do it?"

"Our one advantage is that we know that the killer is using a dark blue van to abduct these women. We have him on video both at Allie Martin's complex and at Mary Jo Jackson's office. I assume that he used the same vehicle to grab Corrine Ray, and that he would use it to go after Davis.

"It's possible that he might attempt to grab her while she's out on assignment for the station or while she's out running errands, but that's too iffy; the guy is too organized for that. I'm sure that he's been scouting these women, getting to know their routines, and picking the safest place for him to overpower them and get them into his van. In Davis's case, the likeliest spot would be at her apartment complex, possibly when she's leaving for work in the morning or, most likely, when she's coming home at night.

"I'm thinking that we can have her stick to a very strict schedule, leaving home to go to work and leaving the station to go back home at pretty much the same times every day. In each case, we could position a couple of people in an undercover van, staking out Davis's assigned parking spot at the apartment complex. If they should see our suspect van waiting at the time when Davis is either supposed to be leaving for or arriving home from work, they can call in reinforcements and we take the son of a bitch down. Otherwise, we shadow Davis as she drives to and from work or if she's out and about, in case he should attempt to grab her somewhere else."

Callahan shook his head. "And how long do you propose we should do this?"

"I doubt that it will be that long at all, Sarge. He only waited one week between Martin and Ray, and only two weeks between Ray and Jackson. I'm betting that he's jonesing pretty hard and that he's likely to make a play for Davis sooner rather than later, perhaps as early as this Friday night."

Callahan grunted and again shook his head. "You know that we're going to look pretty goddamned stupid if we assign all this manpower to Davis and then this asshole then turns around and grabs the woman from Channel 5."

"We would, Sarge, but trust me; that's not going to happen."

***

The sergeant told me that he'd buck my request up to the lieutenant. If the lieutenant bought the plan, he'd talk to the head of the Special Assignments Unit to see if they could spare some people to shadow Ellie. While he tried to work out the arrangements, I gathered Maggie, Elaine, and Greg in the conference room to lay out the plan. "We're still missing something here," I said. "We know that Fred Turner could not have abducted and killed Mary Jo Jackson, given that he'd been dead for at least thirty-six hours before she was taken. Assuming that he was the original killer, how did our guy come up with his souvenirs?"

"Damned if I know," Maggie said. "Logically, he wouldn't have left them around someplace where the wife might have stumbled onto them, like in the bedroom closet, for example. It's also not the sort of thing you'd leave in your safe deposit box at the bank for your heirs and the tax man to discover once you croaked. You guys ruled out the attic, and Mrs. Turner insisted that they did not have a rented storage unit anywhere. We found no evidence that Turner might have rented a space without telling her, and there's no paperwork for anything like that and no spare keys that we haven't been able to identify.

"The most logical place for him to have kept them would have been hidden well out of the way in that storage building in the back yard. But you and Bob didn't find anything like that there, and remember that when we asked about the shed, the widow told us that they hadn't been burglarized and that no one else had been in the shed in months."

I nodded, spinning the tumblers around in my mind when a new combination clicked into place. Looking to Maggie, I said, "As I recall, she said that 'No one but us' had been in the shed. I wonder if 'us' might possibly have included the nephew."

266

Maggie looked at me for a long moment, then said, "One way to find out."

***

Maggie and I walked down to Bob Morris's office. He looked up to see us standing in the door and I said, "So how are you coming with the Turner investigation?"

He dropped the folder he was reading onto his desk. "We're not. It's pretty clear that Clay, the kid we found with Turner's car and credit cards, can't be the killer. We've found a couple of other witnesses who swear that the car was parked there overnight, just the way the kid said, and given the witnesses who put him at the birthday party that night, there's no way he could have been the one who parked it there originally. Somebody else killed Turner, then drove his car to Clay's apartment complex and left it on the street outside, with the watch, wallet, and keys in it for someone like Clay to find. But so far, we don't have a clue as to who that might have been or why they might have done it."

"Anything new from the widow?" Maggie asked.

"Nope. She seems genuinely befuddled about the whole situation. She swears that her husband had no enemies and no problems, and she still doesn't have a clue as to where he might have been going that night."

"Did you get Turner's phone records?"

"Yeah, finally. Valerie is going through them now, trying to match the numbers of the calls he made and received with the names of the people at the other end. As soon as she's finished, I'll run you a copy."

I nodded my thanks. "We have a question for the widow. Would you mind running over there with us for a couple of minutes? It would probably be lot better if she saw a more familiar face."

***

Thirty minutes later, we rang the bell at Turner's house and the door was answered by a blonde woman who was maybe ten years younger than Martha Turner. She was stylishly dressed and obviously paid a great deal of attention to her hair and makeup. She introduced herself as Martha Turner's sister, Susan Devoe, and invited us in.

We found Mrs. Turner sitting on the couch in the living room, looking much the same as the day Bob and I had searched her house. Again, we expressed our condolences, and I apologized for interrupting her day. "We just have one quick question for you, Mrs. Turner, and then we'll get out of your hair. When we talked to you earlier, we asked about the shed in back and you told us that no one other than family had been out there for several months. Was there any family member other than you or your husband who was out there?"

She hesitated for a moment, as though searching her memory, then looked up at me and shook her head. "No, Detective, except for Jason."

I scrunched down in front of her so that my eyes were level with hers. "Jason was in the shed, Mrs. Turner?"

She simply nodded.

"And when was that,"

"I don't remember exactly now, but it was right after Joseph died. Jason was looking for some family pictures to display at the memorial service and I told him to look in the shed."

"I see. Do you remember if he found any pictures, Mrs. Turner? Did he take anything with him when he left?"

Again, she paused for a long moment, looking not at me but rather off into the distance somewhere. Finally, she turned back to me and said, "I don't think so, but to be honest, I really can't remember."

52.

"Son of a bitch," I said, getting into the car. "Fifty to one that Jason Turner is our guy. His father dies, and he goes out to that goddamned shed looking for old family pictures. Instead, he opens a box and finds Uncle Fred's souvenirs. He gets all turned on by the discovery and decides to go into business for himself."

"And then what?" Maggie asked. "We interview the uncle and tell him that items belonging to Friedman were discovered with Martin's body. He realizes what must have happened and confronts the nephew. He threatens to turn him in or something, so the nephew lures him out and kills him, trying to make it look like a carjacking?"

"I'm betting on the 'or something. The uncle can hardly threaten to turn Jason in; he'd only wind up exposing himself for the original killings. More likely, he tried to blackmail Jason somehow and wound up getting killed for his efforts."

From the back seat, Bob said, "I'll buy the theory, but how are you going to prove it? You haven't got nearly enough to get a warrant, and from what you've said, this is a killer who's covered his ass six ways from Sunday. Even if you could find a judge who was willing to sign off on a search of Turner's home or office, it's hard to imagine that you'd find anything lying around to incriminate him. You've got no DNA or any other physical evidence that you can use to check against him, so what do you do? Do you dare even question the guy? I mean, the second he thinks you're on to him, he'll pull in his horns and leave you dangling out there with no way to prove a case against him."

"Well, for starters," I said, "we'll very quietly tear his life apart. We've talked to the guy a couple of times without even getting a hint that there was anything hinky about him. If he is our guy, he's one very cool customer. We don't really know much about him at all, save for the fact that he was Joseph Turner's son and Fred Turner's nephew. Hell, we don't even know if he's married or not."

"The times we talked to him, he wasn't wearing a ring," Maggie said. "And you notice there were no pictures in his office of a wife or kids. Usually an insurance guy plays up the family angle, so I'm betting he's not married, which means that he wouldn't have to be explaining to the wife how he was spending his time on the weekends when the killer was holding Martin, Ray and Jackson."

***

Back at the station, the sergeant was tied up in a meeting, and so we'd have to wait until he was finished to run our thoughts past him. I was shuffling some papers at my desk and checking my watch every two minutes, when Bob walked in the door and handed me a couple of pieces of paper that had been stapled together.

"The records from Fred Turner's cell phone," he said. "The last call he received on the night that he died came from a burner. The techs can't trace it. It's apparently dead, which suggests almost certainly that the killer used it to lure Turner out to a meeting and then destroyed the phone after killing him. On a more encouraging note, the afternoon before Turner was killed, he called his nephew's office phone and talked for a little over two minutes."

"No shit? When Maggie and I interviewed Turner on Monday, I asked him when he last talked to his uncle. He made a great show of searching his memory and then told me he hadn't talked to him for three or four weeks."

"So, you're thinking that the uncle calls, gives him an ultimatum of some sort, and Jason stalls him for a day or so. Then he buys a burner, uses it to call the uncle out for meeting, and kills him?"

"It fits the facts as we know them so far, and I gather that you and Roberts have no other suspects?"

"Not even a whiff of one. So, I'm certainly on board with your idea, but again, how the hell do we prove it? We got nothing out of the uncle's car that would tie the nephew to it, and even if we did, he'd doubtless suddenly remember the afternoon when Uncle Fred

picked him up and took him out for a Dairy Queen or some fuckin'
thing."

***

The administrative assistant finally buzzed me to say that the
sergeant was out of his meeting, and Bob and I walked down to his
office and gave him the news. He listened without interrupting, then
said, "You make it all sound very plausible, Sean, but you're hanging
this entire argument on a couple of very thin threads. First off, you're
betting that Fred Turner was the original killer based solely on the
fact that the killings stopped shortly after he lost his leg and on the
fact that he happened to own a 1972 Jimmy, which may or may not
have been the type of vehicle the killer was driving the night Nancy
Petrovitch went missing.

"You're further assuming that just because Jason Turner was
apparently in the uncle's shed, he must have found the souvenirs and
decided to take over the uncle's franchise. But there isn't a shred of
physical evidence to link the older Turner with the original killings
or the younger Turner to the new ones or to link the younger Turner
to the murder of his uncle, right?"

"Right," I said, "at least for the moment. Pierce and Chickris are
digging into the details of Jason Turner's life so that we can get a
better handle on him. The problem, as Bob pointed out, is that we
don't dare let Turner know that we're investigating him. If he
realizes that we've got him in our sights, he'll just go to ground and
leave us standing here with our thumbs up our butts."

"So, what do you propose to do?"

"Frankly, I don't know, at least not yet. Let's see what we can dig
out about him and them maybe an approach will suggest itself."

53.

Jason Turner sat at a table in a restaurant down the street from his office, watching a YouTube video of Ellie Davis interviewing the detective, Sean Richardson, about the murder of Mary Jo Jackson, whom Turner had known only as "Melanie." Richardson was tall and thin, built like a long-distance runner. His dark hair was fashionably cut by someone who obviously knew what he or she was doing, and, as Turner had noticed when Richardson had visited his office, he dressed well in what looked to be very expensive suits. All in all, Richardson was a good-looking guy and watching him on the screen with Davis, Turner picked up a definite vibe between the two. Clearly there was an attraction there, and Turner wondered if the detective had ever made a move on the reporter. If he hadn't, Turner knew, his chances of having the opportunity to do so were dwindling rapidly.

Richardson was telling the reporter that they had a few leads in the Jackson case but that he wasn't at liberty to discuss them, which, of course, was pure bullshit. The police had no more leads in the Jackson case than they'd had in the earlier two, and Turner relished the fact that he had left Richardson and the other cops twisting in the wind without a single piece of evidence that could possibly lead back to him.

"Melanie" had proven to be a very satisfactory playmate, although contrary to what Turner had promised while abducting her, she clearly had not enjoyed the experience at all. Once stripped and tied to the bed, she had continued to plead with Turner, as had Allison Martin and Corrine Ray, but she seemed to understand from the outset, as had Martin and Ray, that she almost certainly would not leave the garage alive.

The knowledge produced a response that was all over the map. At times desperate, she promised to do anything that Turner demanded and gave in to the most degrading actions imaginable. At others, certain that she was going to die anyway, she struggled as best she could, attempting to hold him off and protect what little was left of her dignity. Either way, Turner enjoyed the experience immensely, right up until the last moment when he slipped the wire around the woman's neck and strangled her as he reached his final orgasm of the weekend.

Sadly, though, the satisfaction had begun to fade even as he bathed the woman's body, dressed her in Nancy Petrovitch's bra, and wrapped her in the plastic sheeting. By the time he dumped Jackson's body an hour later, the need was already beginning to surge again, and looking at the video of Ellie Davis, he wondered how he could possibly wait even a few days to grab her.

Turner was certain that Davis would be a very special treat—a bit older than the others, clearly smarter, and much, much sexier. And the thought of having her naked, helpless, and completely under his control gave him a rush that was totally off the chart.

54.

A search of the public records indicated that Jason Turner was forty-seven years old. He had a degree in business administration from the University of Arizona and had worked for seven years in the office of an independent insurance company before leaving to open his own agency. He'd owned a home in northwest Phoenix for nine years and had an excellent credit rating. He leased an Audi sedan as well as the space where his office was located, and he paid his credit card bills in full every month. His only significant financial obligation appeared to be the mortgage on his home.

He'd never married and appeared not to be involved in an ongoing relationship. He had a minimal presence on social media, which seemed mostly aimed at building his business. The records did not indicate that he owned a van, but I really wasn't surprised to discover that. I assumed that anyone who'd paid cash for a van to abduct women probably wasn't going to enter the sale in any public records.

While the rest of the team continued to dig into Turner's life, I put together another six-pack of photos, this time including Turner, and took them out to Hank McKinley, the guy who had sold the van. He patiently sorted through the pictures, looking at each of them a couple of times, and then tapped a finger on the photo of Jason Turner. "This looks more like the guy than any of the others you've showed me. But it's been so long now, that I really can't be sure. Maybe if he was wearing the hat…"

***

Back in my office, I checked with Dan Collier, the head of the Special Assignments Unit, which had been charged with the task of protecting Ellie Davis. "Davis is scheduled to call us each afternoon with the time she's planning to leave the station that evening," he said. "Each evening, she'll call to let us know what time she's leaving for the station the next morning.

"We've put a barricade in one of the three visitor's parking spots between her assigned place and the sidewalk leading to her apartment. An hour before she's scheduled to leave for home or for work, two guys in an undercover van will set the barricade aside and take the spot so that they can watch her in and out of the apartment. Before they do, they'll cruise through the entire complex, looking for a dark blue van with a dent like the one in the picture you gave us. If they see one, they'll block it in and brace the driver. If not, they'll simply park and watch to see that Davis makes it safely between her car and the apartment. Meanwhile, another team will shadow Davis while she drives between the TV station and the apartment. They'll pick her up and drop her when she leaves and enters the gates at either end. During the day, she's on her own, but she knows not to leave the station without an escort."

I listened to his description of the coverage, then said, "Okay, Dan; sounds like you've got it covered. In each of the first three cases, the guy made his move on a Friday night, so you should tell your people to be especially vigilant tomorrow."

"Will do. If this asshole shows up, he's not going to get by us."

55.

From the time he got into the office on Thursday morning, Jason Turner checked his watch about every five minutes, unable to believe how slowly the time was passing. The wait since he'd finished with "Melanie" had been excruciating, and he realized that he had now moved into extremely dangerous territory.

When he'd first found the box of souvenirs and decided to pick up where his uncle had left off, he'd been very calm and rational about the project. He was determined to move slowly and to act intelligently. But looking at the souvenirs was one thing; looking at Allie Martin, naked and spread-eagled on the bed in his rented garage, had been another thing altogether. The sexual rush he had gotten from looking at Ellen Friedman's purse, Laura Garcia's rosary and the other items in the box, paled in comparison to the stimulation he experienced once he had control of his first victim. And from that moment on, the more rational side of his being was fairly quickly overwhelmed.

It was much like being in the grip of a fantastic drug, Turner imagined, even though he'd never done any real drugs. Each experience hooked him more deeply and demanded that he satisfy his growing need more quickly than the time before. The two weeks between Corrine Ray and "Melanie" had almost been unbearable, but the need he had experienced over that two weeks was dwarfed by the pressure that was driving him now. He realized, intellectually, that he was moving much too quickly and that his compulsion might well cause him to make a mistake that could bring him down. But he had passed the point where he could listen to reason, even his own.

As with the case of Corrine Ray, Turner had decided to make a first attempt at Ellie Davis on a Thursday night, with Friday as his fallback position. He'd spent a couple of hours at the garage last night, making sure that everything was ready for the woman's

276

arrival, and afterwards, he'd found it virtually impossible to sleep as the anticipation continued to build. He'd been sleepwalking through the day at work, delegating everything he could to his office manager and her assistant while he sat in his office with the door closed, going over his plan and letting his imagination run free.

He finally left the office a little before five and drove home. At six, he turned on the Channel 2 news and was relieved to see that Ellie Davis was on the set, reporting a story. He assumed that she would update the report at ten and thus would probably not arrive back at her apartment much before eleven.

At seven-thirty, he went into the bedroom and changed into a pair of dark jeans, a long-sleeved black tee shirt, and a pair of black running shoes. At eight o'clock, he parked his car on the concrete pad next to his rented garage, and at ten minutes after eight, he was in the van, headed toward Ellie Davis's apartment complex.

56.

By late afternoon on Thursday, we'd uncovered little more about Jason Turner and still had nothing to suggest that he was our killer, save for my gut instinct, which was screaming that he had to be the guy. I knew that the Special Assignments Unit had Ellie covered, and so I decided to spend the evening keeping tabs on Turner.

The detectives that you see on TV can follow someone single-handedly without even breaking a sweat. But for the rest of us, it's pretty much impossible, unless you stick so close to the target that he can't miss you, which sort of defeats the purpose. Accordingly, I decided to give myself an edge. At four o'clock, I called Turner's office, using a burner phone. Claiming to be interested in a home insurance policy, I asked the woman who answered the phone if I could make an appointment to see Turner at four-thirty. She put me on hold for a moment, then came back on the line to say that four-thirty would be fine.

I left the office, again taking my own car, and drove over to the strip mall on Bell where Turner had his office. Cruising through the lot, I spotted his Audi parked a couple of rows away from his office and grabbed a spot four cars farther down. Walking in the general direction of a McDonald's at the end of the row, I stopped behind Turner's car and made a pretense of kneeling to tie my shoe. Checking to make sure that no one was looking, I slipped a small GPS tracking device under the bumper of the Audi, then straightened up, walked into the McDonald's, and bought a Coke.

Back in my car, I moved to a spot well out of the way and tested the receiver to ensure that the tracking device was working. The signal was strong, and so I dropped the receiver into a spare cup holder and settled in with my Coke, listening to a Fred Eaglesmith playlist on Spotify while I watched Turner's car.

Just before five, he walked out of the office and got into the car, apparently having concluded that his four-thirty appointment had stiffed him. I let him get a good head start, and then drifted out onto Bell, letting the tracking device do the work of keeping Turner in "sight." He drove directly home, and the tracking device indicated that the car had stopped moving. I took a chance and closed the gap, just in time to see Turner's garage door roll slowly down. I cruised past the house and then pulled to the curb at a spot where I could keep an eye on the house from a distance.

***

For a little over two hours, nothing happened, and I wondered if Turner was in for the night. Then, at seven-forty, the garage door rolled up again and the Audi backed out into the street and headed away from me. Again, I let the tracking device guide me and stayed well behind Turner's car. He led me south down the 51 and into the heart of the city, finally turning onto West Willetta Street. I made the turn a minute or so later, and just as I did, the tracking device indicated that Turner's Audi had come to a stop somewhere in the 400 block of the street. Not wanting to come up on top of him, I made a quick turn onto a side street and pulled to the curb, waiting for Turner to start moving again.

He didn't.

I sat there for several minutes, watching the static signal on the GPS, and concluded that Turner must have been visiting a friend or was perhaps making an evening call on a client. I put my car in gear again, circled around, and drove slowly through the 400 block. The street was framed by rows of tall palm trees that lined each side of the street, and there was very limited parking on the street. All of the spaces within view were filled with vehicles. Turner's Audi was not among them, but as I passed a large house on the east side of the street, the tracking device indicated that I was passing the car. The sun had set, but a light shining out of the window of the house illuminated the rear of the Audi, which was parked on a driveway just behind the house.

I needed to make sure that Turner didn't get a look at my car when he left, and given that I had no idea which way he might go, there was no safe place for me to park on either side of Willetta. With no other choice, I pulled onto a side street out of sight of the house and waited for him to start moving again.

57.

At eight-forty, having applied his disguise, Jason Turner followed a Jeep Cherokee through the gate of Ellie Davis's apartment complex. He rolled the van slowly past Davis's building and noted that two of the three visitors' slots between Davis's assigned parking place and her building were taken. Someone had placed a barricade blocking the third space. Turner was tempted to simply move the barricade out of the way and take the spot, but it occurred to him that if he did, he might attract the attention of the building manager or whoever else had put the barricade in place. The last thing he needed was a confrontation with some angry asshole who was attempting to reserve the spot, and so he decided to move along.

About seventy-five yards deeper into the complex there was a similar set of visitor's parking spaces, and the one closest to Davis's building was open. Turner backed into the spot and killed the engine. Fortunately for his purposes, a light above the parking spaces was burned out. The sun had set a little over an hour ago, and the three spaces were shrouded in darkness. Thus, rather than having to move into the rear of the van in order to remain out of sight, Turner was able to stay slouched down in the driver's seat, protected both by the night and by the plastic window tint in the driver's and passenger's windows. With any luck, one of the three spots in front of Davis's building would come open before she arrived home, in which case, he could move his position.

It would not be a comfortable wait. Just before nine o'clock in the evening, the temperature outside remained in the low nineties. Inside the van, it was like a sauna. Turner didn't dare let the engine run to keep the air conditioner on, and he couldn't roll down a window, which would leave the inside of the van open to any passer-by who might glance in. After only ten minutes, he was dripping with sweat and dreading the thought that he might likely be stuck in the van for another couple of hours.

At nine-thirty, he took a long sip of water and watched as a pair of headlights passed through the gate and moved slowly down the next parking aisle to the north. As the vehicle pulled even with his parking place, he saw that it was a gas company van and he watched as it moved about twenty yards beyond his position. Then the brake lights flashed, and the van came to a stop.

There were two rows of covered parking spaces between Turner's position and the next aisle over, and looking between the parked cars, he could see that the gas company van had stopped behind a dark-colored van about the vintage of his own that was parked nose first into the space.

A minute or so later two men got out of the gas company van and slowly approached the other vehicle from either side. Both appeared to be relatively young and athletic, and Turner noticed that they were dressed in jeans and light jackets rather than in the standard gas company uniform. Two lights illuminated the area, and Turner could also see that both men had their hair cut very close to the scalp in a military style. Everything about the two screamed Jarhead.

Or cop.

As the two men approached the other vehicle, they slipped their right hands inside their jackets, resting them on their right hips, as if on the butt of a gun, and at that point, Turner had seen enough.

While the attention of the two men was focused on the van in front of them, Turner quietly started his engine, pulled out of the parking spot, and drove slowly back in the direction of the gate. He waited a moment for the gate to roll open. Then he turned on his headlights, turned right onto Shea, and drove away as quickly and as carefully as he could.

What the fuck was going on here? Why would a couple of cops appear in Davis's apartment complex, driving what was obviously an undercover vehicle of some sort? And what in the hell were they doing checking out a van that so closely resembled his own?

The only logical answer was that his van had showed up on video someplace, most likely at Allie Martin's condo complex, and that the cops thus knew what sort of vehicle the killer was driving. Turner was suddenly very grateful for the fact that he'd been sensible enough to use stolen license plates, to put the tint in the windows, and to thoroughly disguise himself going in and out of Martin's complex.

But had they also deduced that he was likely to target Ellie Davis? They knew, of course, that he was following the pattern established by his uncle and that the fourth target was almost certainly going to be a TV newswoman. But why would they assume he had settled on Davis—or had they? Did the actions of the two cops in the gas company van mean that they were watching her, or did it mean that they were simply on the lookout for dark-colored vans of a certain vintage?

Five blocks away from the apartment complex, Turner swung through the driveway of a convenience store and circled back out onto Shea, this time heading back toward Davis's apartment complex. Two blocks before reaching the apartments, he pulled into a small shopping mall and parked the van in a spot behind one of the buildings, out of sight of the street.

In the back of the van, he slipped out of his jeans and into a pair of running shorts that he'd intended to leave at the garage. He stripped off his socks and put the running shoes back on over his bare feet. Looking carefully to ensure that no one was watching, he slipped out of the van, locked the door, and began jogging back toward Davis's apartment.

Timing his speed, he reached the gate just as a car was pulling out. He jogged through the gate and set a pace down the row of vehicles where he had first seen the gas company van, just another guy out for his late-evening exercise, trying to take advantage of the slightly cooler temperatures.

As he pulled even with Davis's building, he looked across the two rows of cars and saw that the gas company van was now parked in the spot where the barricade had been, and he realized that, almost certainly, the police were watching Davis's building and hoping to grab anyone who might attempt to abduct her.

Two buildings deeper into the complex was a large open area with a pool, some benches and a couple of gas barbecue grills. Even at ten-fifteen, the pool was still open, and several people were outside enjoying the slightly cooler evening temperatures. Turner dropped onto a bench that gave him a view back toward Davis's building and settled in to watch for a while.

Roughly thirty minutes later, a pair of headlights rolled through the gate, and Turner watched as Ellie Davis parked her Honda in the space reserved for her unit. She snapped off the lights, retrieved her brief bag from the back seat, and locked the car. Then she walked over to her building, paying no apparent attention to the gas company van as she passed it.

Turner watched as the woman walked up the stairs to the second level and then stopped and pulled open the screen door that fronted the building's middle apartment. She unlocked the apartment door, took half a step into the apartment, and flipped on the lights. Then she turned and locked the screen door. A moment later, she closed the apartment door behind her and disappeared from view.

Ten minutes after that, the gas company van backed out of the parking space. One of the men got out of the van, picked up the barricade which had been set off to the side, and put it back in place in front of the parking space. Then he climbed back into the van and the vehicle slowly drove down the aisle, through the gate, and disappeared down the boulevard.

Turner sat watching for another few minutes, staring up at the lights in Davis's apartment. Then he finally got up and jogged back to his van, on the one hand cursing his luck, but on the other, being very grateful to the driver, whoever he or she might have been, who had left the other dark-colored van for the cops to discover before they would have rolled right up to his.

58.

At eleven o'clock, I was still waiting for Turner to make a move. An hour earlier, I'd made another trip past the house where his car was parked and noticed that all the lights in the house were now off. It struck me that Turner could be spending the night with a girlfriend and that he might not be leaving again until morning.

Ellie had agreed to call me once she was safely tucked in for the night, and at eleven-fifteen she did so. We talked for a couple of minutes and she promised to call me again once she had safely reached the station in the morning. Then we wished each other a good night and I decided that there was no need to keep tabs on Jason Turner for the rest of the night.

I was heading north up the 51 when I looked at the monitor and realized that he was finally moving again. He too was headed back north on the 51, about seven miles behind me, and I concluded he was probably going home for the night. I continued to watch his progress, and twenty minutes later the tracking device indicated that he was indeed back at his house.

What with the hectic pace of the investigation, Sara and I had seen almost nothing of each other over the last few days, and so I'd promised to see her tonight, no matter the time I was finally able to call it a day. Just before midnight, I parked in front of her condo building, climbed the stairs, and rang the bell.

She answered the door wearing a Sweet Remains tee shirt over a pair of running shorts and came immediately into my arms. She kissed me eagerly and said, "I've really missed you, Babe."

"And I've missed you. It's been a helluva week."

I returned her kiss and, with the conversation out of the way, led her into the bedroom.

An hour later, we were lying in the dark under the ceiling fan that was rotating slowly above, both of us thoroughly spent. Sara was lying in the crook of my arm, tracing her fingers lightly over my chest, and said, "What kept you out so late tonight? Is there some break in the case, I hope?"

"I'm not sure. I've convinced myself that I know who the killer is, and I'm also confident that I know who his next target is going to be. I've convinced my boss that there's enough merit to the idea that he's going along with me, at least for the moment. We've got a protective net thrown over the woman that I believe the killer is going after next, but if he doesn't make a move pretty quickly, I'm not sure that the bosses will be willing to maintain the protection for much longer."

Sara propped herself up on an elbow and said, "So who do you think is the killer, and who's the next victim?"

I explained the deductions that had led me to believe that Jason Turner was the killer and that Ellie Davis was his next intended victim. I described the steps we were taking to protect Ellie and told her that I had spent the evening shadowing Jason Turner in the event that he might make a move against her or, for that matter, against some other woman. I explained that I'd finally been able to break off my surveillance once I knew that Ellie was safely home for the night and that Turner was back in his own home.

"Do you think he'll try to abduct her soon?"

"I don't know. But he's grabbed each of the first three victims on a Friday night, so I'm thinking that he may make a move tomorrow. But I wanted to keep an eye on him tonight just in case."

She nodded and nestled back up against me. I lay there for a couple of minutes, thinking things through and then said, "There is something I should probably tell you."

Sara propped herself up on an elbow and looked down at me. "It's almost always a bad sign when your boyfriend decides that he needs to make a confession at one thirty in the morning."

Shaking my head, I pulled her back down to me. "It's not really a confession, Hon, and it's something I've never mentioned up until now, simply because it wasn't relevant to anything. But a year and a half ago, Ellie Davis and I were involved for a couple of months. It was over long before I met you, and we've seen each other only rarely since then, mostly when she's been interviewing me about a case that I've been working. But naturally, now that she's become the center of this investigation, I've been seeing more of her the last week or so."

Sara took a minute or so to assimilate that. Then, without looking at me, she opened a little space between us and said, "Do you still care for her?"

"We're friends, and I'd be lying if I said that there wasn't any residual affection. We once cared for each other a lot and we parted on good terms. There's no romantic attraction any longer, certainly not since I met you. I can't help but be very worried about her, though, and I need to do everything I can to make sure that she doesn't fall into this killer's hands. But that's only because we were once close and certainly not because I wish we still were. Emotionally, I'm right where I want to be—and need to be—here with you."

We lay there, saying nothing, for another couple of minutes. Finally, Sara closed the space between us again and whispered, "I Love you, Sean." Then she kissed me lightly on the cheek, settled back into my arms, and eventually we dropped off to sleep.

59.

At five-thirty Friday morning, Jason Turner dressed in a nylon track suit and a pair of tennis shoes, then grabbed a stocking cap on the way out the door. The sun was just rising, and traffic was still relatively light, and so he made excellent time back to the garage.

Wearing the stocking cap and a pair of latex gloves, he spent an hour going over the interior of the van with a heavy-duty cleanser. Then he backed the van out of the garage and drove twelve blocks to a car wash where the automatic brushes made short work of the outside of the vehicle. That done, he drove a couple of miles south into one of the city's seedier neighborhoods, parked the van on a side street, and removed the stolen license plate. Then he walked away from the van, leaving the key in the ignition.

He hoofed it five blocks to a convenience store and used a burner phone to call a cab. The driver dropped him at another convenience store seven blocks from his Audi and at eight forty-five he walked into the house, called his office manager, and told her that he was feeling sick and would be taking the day off.

He spent a half an hour on Craigslist, then made a couple of phone calls, again using the burner phone. He walked nine blocks to another convenience store and then called for another cab, which drove him to a corner two blocks away from the address of a guy who had advertised for sale a green '97 Ford Ranger pickup with a camper shell.

The truck had plenty of dings and scratches, but it seemed to run well, and the seller pretty quickly agreed to take nine hundred cash on the spot, rather than the nine-fifty he'd been asking. The guy signed over the title, wrote a bill of sale, and removed his license plate. Just before eleven, Turner drove the pickup into his rented garage and attached the license plate he had removed from the van. Then he collected his Audi and drove home.

***

Five years earlier, Turner had written a fire insurance policy on a small apartment complex on the west side of the city. The property manager was a friend, and Turner had amply rewarded him for throwing the business his way. Three and a half years later, a fire had seriously damaged several of the units when a tenant attempting to fry chicken had started a grease fire which quickly ran out of control.

On the afternoon that Turner was to inspect the damage, the property manager was unable to accompany him because of some problem that suddenly came up at another complex the guy managed. In his office, he handed Turner a ring containing several master keys and said, "The locks on these units are pretty standard for a complex like this. One of these keys should open any of the units you need to get into. Once you're finished, you can drop them back. If I'm not here, just leave them with my girl."

The keys had allowed Turner access to the several units he needed to inspect, and driving back to the property manager's office, it occurred to him that having a set of keys like that might be very useful at some point. Accordingly, he detoured by a home improvement store where a kid who seemed totally clueless ground duplicates of each of the keys.

At one thirty on Friday afternoon, now dressed in a golf shirt and a pair of casual slacks, Turner stopped by his agency and assured the staff that he was on the mend. He explained that he wanted to pick up some files that he could work on over the weekend and disappeared into his office. He pulled a few files for the sake of show and then grabbed the ring of master keys from his desk drawer. Twenty minutes after arriving, he was out the door again, after wishing the staff a good weekend.

60.

A little after seven on Friday morning, I said goodbye to Sara, then drove home and showered, shaved, and dressed for the day. On the way out the door, I cleaned Zane's litter box and gave him fresh food and water. He sat on the floor in the laundry room, waiting patiently while I got things arranged for him and then settled into his breakfast. I watched him for a minute or so and then reminded him that this was not a permanent arrangement. But he simply shot me a look that seemed to say, "That's what you think, pal."

I got into the office at eight thirty, and at nine, Ellie called to say that she had arrived at the station and was planning to be there until after the ten o'clock newscast. She promised to call again once she was home for the night and we wished each other a good day.

An hour later, our team met in the conference room, joined by Morris, Roberts, and the sergeant. We reviewed the investigation to date, but no one had anything new of any consequence to add to the discussion. Bob and Valerie were continuing to pursue their separate investigation into the murder of Fred Turner, but they'd come up with absolutely nothing and were hoping, along with the rest of us, that Jason Turner would soon make a mistake that would allow us to take him into custody and resolve all the investigations currently on the table in front of us.

Given that it was a Friday and that our killer had abducted each of his previous three victims on a Friday night, we were all a bit on edge. I'd reminded Dan Collier that the Special Assignments team should be especially vigilant tonight, not that he really needed the reminder. He assured me that once Ellie got off work tonight, one of his teams would shadow her from the station to her apartment complex and that another would be positioned near her parking place well ahead of the time she got there.

Listening to the recap, the sergeant looked to me and said, "I still don't know, Sean. You've got an awful lot of resources tied up in what could still best be described as only a hunch. From what I'm hearing here, you guys still don't have a shred of real evidence to tie Jason Turner either to the murder of any of these women or to that of his uncle. And you have no concrete reason to believe that the killer, whether it's Turner or some other asshole, will be going after Davis next."

"I understand that the tie to Turner is thin, Sarge, but it's the only one that makes any sense. If he isn't the guy, then where in the hell did the killer get the souvenirs from the earlier killings? Not to mention the fact that we've got absolutely nothing to point us in the direction of anyone other than Turner.

"As for Davis, I still think it *is* logical to assume that she's going to be the next target, even on the remote chance that the killer should turn out to be someone other than Turner. As I've said repeatedly, she's been much more prominent in the coverage of this investigation than any other female reporter. If our guy were to pick another TV newswoman, it would run counter to the pattern established by the first killer."

"But," he said, "you still can't even be completely sure that the first killer and the current killer are not one and the same person, which would easily answer your question about how he got the souvenirs. I know it seems unlikely that the guy would take forty years off and then begin a new spree, but it seems to me that it's just as likely as the scenario you've woven around Turner."

He took off his glasses, set them on the table and rubbed his eyes for a moment. Then he looked around the room and said, "If Sean's right, I hope for your all sake's that Turner makes his move within the next few days. The lieutenant's giving me grief already and we simply can't afford to continue allocating all the resources we're devoting to this one theory of the case. If nothing happens over the weekend, we're going to have to pull the Special Assignments Unit off Davis, and you guys are going to come up with some new approach to these cases."

With nothing more to be said, and with nothing more that we could think of to do regarding Jason Turner, Morris, Roberts, Pierce and Chickris all followed the sergeant out of the room, indicating that they were going to get back to work on some of their other open and unsolved cases. Maggie and I remained at the table, and once the others were gone, she said, "The boss kind of left you hanging out there. What are you going to do if he pulls the protection from Davis and points us in another direction?"

"I have no idea. I guess I'll worry about that once we get through the weekend."

She nodded. "I just wish we had one tangible piece of evidence against Turner."

I smiled and shook my head. "Are you doubting me too?"

"No; I think your theory makes more sense than any other that we've got; I just wish the bastard hadn't been so careful and so lucky, leaving us without anything more to go on than a hunch. So how do you plan to spend the day?"

"To be honest, I'm too fuckin' wired to focus on anything else. I'm going to sit very loosely on Jason Turner this afternoon and tonight to see what he's up to, while I monitor the coverage of Davis."

"Want some company?"

"No, thanks Maggie. There's no point in both of us sitting on him, especially if he just goes home and stays there all night. If he should make a move, the Special Assignments Unit will be close at hand, and that should be more than enough muscle to bring him down."

"Okay," she said, finally getting up from the table. "But if you change your mind, just let me know."

***

I left Maggie in her office and walked down the stairs to my BMW. In truth, I could have used the help and would have enjoyed the company, but in its infinite wisdom, the Supreme Court had ruled that a law enforcement officer cannot put a tracking device on a suspect's vehicle without a warrant. As the sergeant continued to remind me, we didn't have nearly enough evidence against Jason Turner to get such a warrant, and I wasn't about to make Maggie complicit in my violation of the law. If Turner did turn out to be the killer, my conscience really wouldn't bother me all that much. If he didn't, I'd quietly remove the device and say a couple of Hail Marys as my penance for having wrongly suspected him and for having violated his civil rights.

In the meantime, I intended to stick to the son of a bitch as close as I possibly could.

61.

Anxious as he was, Jason Turner actually managed to take a nap late on Friday afternoon. He was up again at six and made himself a roast beef sandwich for dinner. After eating the sandwich, he dressed again in his dark blue nylon track suit. Earlier in the day, he'd put his black running shoes through the washer and left them to dry in the laundry room. Satisfied that the shoes were squeaky clean, he pulled them on and went out into the garage.

In the garage, he dug his oversized golf travel bag out of a cabinet and emptied all the crap out of it onto the floor. Then he dropped the backpack containing his supplies into the travel bag, dumped the bag into the trunk of his Audi, and headed down to his rented garage. Once there, he popped open the camper shell on his new pickup and transferred the travel bag to the truck. At seven forty-five, he backed the pickup out of the garage and headed toward Ellie Davis's apartment complex.

When he rolled through the gate, the sun had just finished setting, and he was pleased to discover that the visitors' parking space closest to Davis's building was open. The middle of the three spaces was occupied by an older Toyota, and the third was blocked off again by the police barricade. Turner backed into the open spot and shut off the ignition. Seeing no one moving about, he quickly got out of the truck, retrieved the travel bag from the back, and walked up the stairs to the second level.

He set the travel bag down in front of Davis's door, pulled open the screen door, and knocked three times. He waited for an interminable thirty seconds, and when no one responded to his knock, he reached into his pocket, and came out with the ring of master keys. His hands trembled as he nervously tried to fit the first key into the lock without success. The second key also failed to work, but the third turned smoothly and the lock clicked open. Turner opened the door, carried the travel bag into the apartment, and locked the door behind him.

Once inside, he pulled on a pair of latex gloves and then put on a plastic shower cap and pulled it down low over his ears. The cap would prevent him from dropping any loose hairs in the apartment and the track suit would shed no fibers that some CSI asshole might trace back to him. Anything that he might have tracked into the apartment on his shoes would lead the cops only as far as the apartment complex's parking lot.

Certain that he would leave no trace of his presence in the apartment, Turner stepped over to the living room window and cracked the blinds just long enough to look down into the parking lot. Satisfied that no one had apparently paid any attention to him entering the apartment, he closed the blinds again and made a quick trip through the empty unit.

He concluded his tour in the master bedroom, which was down a short hallway just off the living room. The blinds over the two windows in the room were closed, and Turner carried the travel bag into the room and shut the door behind him.

He removed his backpack from the travel bag and picked a small flashlight out of the backpack. Moving the light carefully, he searched through the bedroom closet and the dresser. In the dresser, he discovered several very sexy bra and panty combinations in various colors. Smiling, he stuffed the lingerie into a pocket of the travel bag. In the bathroom, he scooped up some cosmetics and a bottle of Gucci Guilty perfume. He added those to the pocket in the travel bag, and zipped it shut. Then he turned off the flashlight, sat down on the carpet in the bedroom and settled in to wait.

Sitting there, he realized that he was taking a huge and very idiotic risk. He should have just walked away, regrouped, and waited six months or so to come after Davis when she would have dropped her guard and when the police would have stopped paying such close attention to her.

The fact that he hadn't done so was, at least in part, a matter of pride. The cops had stepped up their game and he was determined to demonstrate that he could answer in kind. And, while they might have identified the van, he knew there was no way that they might have identified him. But above all that, he had built up such an enormous need for the woman that he simply couldn't back away without having her now, regardless of the risk. He would take special care to enjoy their time together, and he knew that the chances he was taking to possess her would significantly heighten the rush when he finally claimed her for his own.

Sitting there, he promised himself that once he was through with Davis, he would pull back and take a good, long break, leaving the cops to stand around with their dicks in their hands, wondering how the killer had outsmarted them and where he had gone. But for now, he could think of nothing beyond getting the woman back to the garage, strapping her down, and relishing what he was sure would be the best weekend of his entire life.

***

There was a small television set on the dresser in the bedroom, and just before ten o'clock, Turner tuned it to Channel 2, quickly muting the sound. He watched as Ellie Davis silently reported the third story on the newscast, wearing a bright red blouse that clung to her breasts and showed just the tiniest hint of cleavage. The story apparently had something to do with a murder-suicide earlier in the day, and following Davis's piece, the anchor segued to the weather report.

His heart pounding, Turner clicked off the television set and walked over to the living room window. He very carefully peeked around the edge of the blinds and saw that the "gas company" van from last night was back in position in the parking space that had been protected by the barricade. Knowing the score, he returned to the bedroom and settled down on the floor.

Forty minutes later, he heard the screen door open and slowly rose to his feet. Someone, presumably Ellie Davis, unlocked and opened the door and then turned on a light in the living room. Turner listened as Davis first locked the screen door behind her, then closed and locked the door to the apartment itself. He waited for a brief moment and then stepped out into the living room.

Still wearing the red blouse, Davis was digging into her brief bag. She pulled her cell phone out of the bag and suddenly looked up to see Turner standing eight feet in front of her. She had only a split second to begin drawing in the breath that would have enabled her to scream out before the twin darts from the Taser ripped into her chest.

62.

I knew that Ellie would be safely tucked away at the TV station until she left for the night, and so I waited until just after six o'clock before picking up Turner's trail again. The tracking device indicated that his Audi was at his home, and so I drove into his neighborhood and parked one street over from his house.

Just after seven, the tracking device indicated that Turner was on the move and I trailed him back south to the house on West Willetta. Again, he had parked the Audi at the rear of the house and again, there was nowhere to park on Willetta within three blocks of the house. With no other choice, I took up a position on the side street where I had parked last night, well out of sight of the house.

I sat there for the next couple of hours, channeling music from the Spotify app on my phone through the car's stereo speakers. Finally, to relieve the boredom as much as anything else, I circled the block at nine-thirty, noting that the Audi was still parked in back but that all the lights in the house were off.

By eleven o'clock, I was staring at the phone, expecting Ellie to call at any moment to tell me that she was safely home, and watching my carefully constructed hypothesis collapsing around me. I'd convinced myself that Jason Turner was the killer responsible for the deaths of Allie Martin, Corrine Ray, and Mary Jo Jackson, and that he would be going after Ellie next. I was also certain that he would be making a move against Ellie sooner rather than later, given the haste with which he had taken his first three victims. But it seemed clear that he wasn't going to do so tonight.

I was, frankly, disappointed. God knows, I didn't want Ellie to be at risk, but if Turner was going to make a move against her, I desperately wanted it to be at a time when I had an eye on him and when the Special Assignments Unit was guarding Ellie closely. I hated the thought that, come Monday, the bosses would likely pull

Ellie's protection and she would be left on her own if and when Turner did decide to strike.

By eleven-thirty, I still hadn't heard from her and I was beginning to get a bit worried. She'd told me that she was going home right after her report on the ten o'clock newscast and certainly she should have been there by now. I grabbed my phone, speed-dialed her number, and listened to her phone ring four times before defaulting to voice mail. "Hey, Ellie," I said, "I'm still waiting to hear from you. I assume you've been delayed leaving for home, so please call and let me know what's up. Thanks."

I broke the connection, getting a decidedly uneasy feeling, so I called headquarters and had them patch me through to the team from the unit that was assigned to watch Ellie's apartment. The team leader came on the phone and I asked if they were still on the stakeout. "Nope," he said. "She got home at about eleven and we watched her all the way into the apartment. She locked both of the doors behind her and we gave it another ten minutes or so and then pulled the plug for the night."

"I don't know what the hell's going on, then," I said. "She didn't call me to tell me that she was safely home and when I just tried to call her, I got no answer."

"Well, shit. I don't know what to tell you, man. She got home and into the apartment safely. There was no dark-colored van anywhere around and no one paid the slightest bit of attention to her while she was walking from her car to the apartment."

I thanked the guy and then called Ellie's phone again. But again, I got no answer. Something was definitely wrong, and so I fired up the engine, circled the block and checked to ensure that Turner's car was still parked where I had last seen it. Turning the corner, I raced three blocks to the I-10 Freeway and shot out of the entrance ramp at a hundred and ten miles per hour. Fortunately, traffic was light, and ninety seconds later I veered onto the 51 and raced the nine and a half miles up to the Shea exit, blowing by the handful of vehicles that were on the freeway at that time of night. Ten minutes after leaving

Willetta Street, I braked to a stop in the middle of the parking aisle of Ellie's apartment complex, right behind her Honda, and raced up the stairs to her door.

There were no lights showing from the unit. I pulled the screen door open and banged on the door but got no response. I waited a few moments and then banged again. A light came on in the unit next door, and a large guy in a butt-ugly bathrobe stuck his head out the door and said, "Knock it off, asshole. People are trying to sleep in here."

I stepped over to the door, stuck my badge in his face, and said, "Have you seen or heard anything from the apartment next door tonight?"

Now a bit flustered, the guy shook his head and said, "No, nothing."

"Then shut the fuck up; get back inside and mind your own business."

The guy retreated, slamming his door behind him, and I returned to Ellie's door. I tried the door, but it was locked. The blinds were tightly closed, and I could see nothing inside the apartment, which appeared to be empty and dark.

I knew that if Ellie were inside, she would have locked the screen/security door behind her. The fact that it was unlocked suggested that she wasn't inside, but where in the hell could she be, especially when her car was in its assigned space?

I tried calling her again and pressed my ear against the door to see if I could hear the phone ringing but heard no sound at all.

The guy from Special Assignments had said that they had watched her lock the doors, plural, behind her. Had she gotten home and then stepped out to visit a neighbor? But why hadn't she called me? Was it possible that she had inadvertently left her phone at the TV station?

There seemed no good explanation, and the more time passed, the more worried I became. It was now eleven forty-five. Not knowing what else to do, I called Greg Chickris who was at home and just getting into bed. I explained the situation, telling him that I'd trailed

Turner to a house on Willetta and without mentioning the fact that I'd put a tracer on the car.

"I'm going to go back over there and keep an eye on him," I told Greg. "I'd like you to come over here and keep an eye on Davis's apartment while we figure out what the fuck is going on. I'll keep trying her phone."

Greg promised to be there as quickly as he could, and I pointed my car back in the direction of the house on Willetta.

63.

Ellie Davis collapsed on the floor, convulsing, and in an instant, Turner was on top of her. He flipped her over, stripped a piece of duct tape off a roll and bound her hands behind her. He wrapped her ankles as well, then turned her over again so that she was lying on her back, still gasping for breath. He ripped another piece of tape off the roll and showed it to her. "I'll give you a couple of minutes to catch your breath," he said. "But if you try to scream, I'll slap this tape over your mouth and you'll most likely suffocate."

For several more minutes, Davis continued to shake violently while Turner straddled her waist. He removed the probes from her chest, running his hands over her breasts as he did so. Gradually, the shaking was reduced to a slight tremble, and then Davis was finally calm again. Turner taped her mouth, being careful to make sure that she could still breathe through her nose. Then he picked her up, carried her into the bedroom, and set her on the bed. "Don't you dare move," he said. "I'll be back in a second."

Back in the living room, he snapped off the light, then stepped over to the window. Peeking around the edge of the blinds, he watched as the "gas company" van backed out of the parking place, leaving the barricade again blocking the spot. He gave the cops a minute to get clear, then opened the door just wide enough to unlock the screen door. In the event that anyone should come checking on Davis, he didn't want them to know for certain that she had to be in the apartment.

That done, he picked Davis's phone and brief bag off the floor. He returned to the bedroom and sat on the bed next to Davis who was obviously petrified. Reaching out a hand, he began caressing her leg, gradually moving his hand up under her skirt. "It's very nice to finally meet you in person, Ellie. I've been looking forward to this ever since I saw your first report on the murder of poor Allison

Martin. You and I are going to have a lot of fun together this weekend."

Davis shook her head and tried to slide away from him, but Turner simply laughed, gripped her leg, and pulled her back. She was clearly scared to death, and for a moment, Turner considered the prospect of pushing her skirt up and taking her right then and there. But he didn't want to take the chance of leaving any trace evidence on her bed, and he knew that the longer he waited to have her for the first time, the sweeter it would be.

Taking his hand from under her skirt, he patted her on the leg and said, "We're going to wait a bit for things to quiet down around here and then we'll go for a little ride."

With that, he dumped the contents of her brief bag out on to the bed next to the phone. He found an iPad, a couple of notebooks, and various other things that Davis obviously used on the job. There was also a small clutch, and opening it, he found her billfold and some cosmetics.

He snapped the clutch closed again and as he did, Davis's phone began ringing. The screen displayed the caller's name as "S.M.R.," and Turner held it up so that Davis could see it. "The boyfriend?" he asked. "Did you have plans for the evening, Babe? If so, I guess they just got cancelled."

The phone defaulted to voice mail and then rang again about five minutes later. Again, the screen indicated that "S.M.R." was calling, and Turner said, "Persistent son of a bitch, isn't he?" Reaching over, he fondled her right breast. "Of course, I can't really blame him. If I was looking forward to a taste of this, I'd be pretty fuckin' persistent myself."

Turner removed his hand and sat silently for the next several minutes, thinking through his plan. He was about to go check the scene outside again when someone began pounding on the apartment door. Turner grabbed a pistol from his backpack and moved silently into the living room. Whoever it was banged on the door again, and then somebody opened the door of the apartment next door and laid into the guy. Could it be "S.M.R." outside, wondering what had happened to his date?

Turner listened as the guy next door went back inside, and a moment later he heard Davis's phone ring again in the bedroom. The sound was faint, and Turner was sure that "S.M.R.," or whoever the hell it was, would never be able to hear it outside. He waited with his ear pressed to the door, and then heard footsteps walking away.

After a minute, Turner peeked around the blinds again to see a guy walking in the direction of a BMW that had been left parked right in the middle of the aisle. It was dark enough that, from this distance, Turner couldn't get a good look at the man, but he watched as the guy sat in his car for a few minutes before finally driving off and disappearing out onto Shea.

Turner dropped the blinds back into place and returned to the bedroom. "Time to move now, Sweetheart."

He unzipped the travel bag and stretched it out to its full length on the floor. The soft-sided bag was long and wide enough to accommodate a professional golf bag with a full set of clubs plus shoes, and other essential paraphernalia. He turned, lifted Davis off the bed and set her feet first into the bag. She struggled desperately against the tape that bound her hands and feet and moaned as loudly as she could through the gag over her mouth.

Now sobbing violently, she was clearly begging him not to hurt her. For a moment, Turner almost felt a twinge of pity for the woman, but that ship had sailed. He scrunched her down into the bag, bending her a bit at the knees and at the neck. Then he set her clutch into the bag with her, leaving the phone on the bed so that anyone attempting to trace it would track it to her apartment.

Davis began struggling violently and Turner grabbed her by the face and said, "Knock that shit off, bitch. You need to stay calm and quiet in there and if you start struggling once we get outside, I'll give you another taste of this taser."

Still crying, Davis became still. Turner pulled the sides of the bag together, zipped it closed, and then stood it up on its wheels. He pulled it out into the living room, then again looked out through the blinds. No one seemed to be moving about outside, and so he took a deep breath, opened the door, and pulled the bag out onto the walkway.

He took a moment to lock the door behind him and then pulled the bag to the stairs. There, he slipped the carry strap over his shoulder and walked the bag down the steps. At the bottom, he set the bag on its wheels once again and pulled it over to the pickup.

Setting the bag carefully on the ground, he popped the access door on the camper shell and lowered the tailgate of the truck bed. He picked up the travel bag, slid it into the bed, and then closed the tailgate and the shell again.

A minute and a half later, he was rolling down Shea, headed back to the garage, with a hard-on the strength of which could have put him in the Guinness Book of World Records.

64.

Twenty minutes after leaving Ellie's apartment, I was back at the house on Willetta. Turner's Audi was still parked at the back of the house, and for the first time it struck me that he might have driven to the house and swapped vehicles. Cursing myself for being so fuckin' stupid, I grabbed a flashlight, got out of the car and ran up to the porch of the house.

The house was still as dark as it had been two hours ago. I punched the doorbell and stepped away from the door. Thirty seconds later, nothing had happened, and so I knocked loudly on the door. Finally, a light came on inside the house and a minute later, an elderly woman came to the door, clutching her arms over a faded blue bathrobe. She flipped on the porch light, and I put my badge wallet up against the window in the door so that she could read it.

She studied the badge for a moment, then unlocked and opened the door. Looking up at me she said, "Is there a problem, officer?"

I stuck the badge wallet back into my pocket and said, "I'm sorry to disturb you so late, Ma'am, but I'm looking for the man whose car is parked behind your house."

Trembling slightly, she said, "You mean, Mr. Dawson?"

"Mr. Dawson drives the grey Audi that's parked in back?"

"Yes, officer. He rents my garage and sometimes leaves his car parked in the driveway when he's out there or when he's driving his other car."

"What other car does he have, Ma'am?"

"It's a blue van. I'm sorry, but I don't know the make."

"And how long has Mr. Dawson been renting your garage?"

"About four months now."

"Okay, Ma'am. I'm going to go back outside and wait for Mr. Dawson to return. I may call some other police officers to help me, but if you hear any noise out here, I want you to stay in the house with all the doors and windows locked until I come and tell you it's safe again."

***

The woman was clearly frightened and told me that she would do exactly as I asked, without even asking why the police might be looking for the man who had rented her garage. I ran back to my car and moved it a block down the street so that it wouldn't be conspicuous when Turner returned. Then I raced back up the street and made a quick circuit around the garage. There was a window on either side of the large building, but both had been boarded over on the inside. There was a heavy door on the north side of the building, secured by what looked like a very good deadbolt lock. A heavy-duty paddle lock protected the main garage door at the front of the building.

Given the way that the building was secured, there was no chance that any light would leak out, and I had no way of knowing whether Turner was inside or not. The fact that the main garage door was locked from the outside suggested that he was not there, but I realized that he could have driven into the garage, then come out the side door, locked the main door, then retreated inside, locking the smaller door behind him.

I ran over to his Audi, retrieved the tracking device, and stuck it into my pocket. Then I called Greg who said that he was parked outside of Ellie's apartment. "Any sign of life?" I asked.

"None. It's dead quiet here."

"All right. I've tracked Turner to a garage that he rented on West Willetta." I gave him the address and said, "His car is here and the woman who rented the garage to him tells me that he's storing a blue van in it. He doesn't appear to be here now, and so I'm thinking that he somehow managed to get Davis out of her apartment after the Special Assignments team left there for the night. If so, he's probably bringing her back here.

"I want you to raise a swat team and rendezvous here as quickly as you can. Have them park discretely a couple of blocks away and wait for my call. You wait a block or so down the street where you can keep an eye on the driveway. If you see Turner pull in, give him enough time to get into the garage, then pull up and block the driveway so he can't get away."

"Will do. I'll get back to you as people move into place."

***

I ended the call, switched my phone to "vibrate," and headed back to the side door of the garage. It was possible that, having grabbed Ellie, Turner was on his way here, but it was also possible that they were already here in the garage.

I shuddered at the thought of what might be happening to her, should that be the case, and realized that I couldn't wait for the rest of the team to get into place. Standing in front of the door, I checked my gun, then took a deep breath and kicked the door as hard as I could, right at the spot where the deadbolt joined the door frame.

It gave a fraction of an inch, but that was all. Still, it was enough for me to realize that while the door itself was new and solid, the frame around it was not. I stepped back and threw my foot into the door again, putting as much weight behind it as I could. This time, the frame splintered and the door flew open.

It was totally dark inside, but I realized that if he was in there, Turner might have turned off the lights when I first hit the door. Standing up against the outside wall, I held the flashlight at arm's length and shined it into the garage, waiting in case Turner took a shot at it. When nothing happened, I dropped to the ground with my gun in one hand and the flashlight in the other. Still holding the light away from my body, I played it around inside the garage, which was clearly empty.

I got to my feet, closed the door, and pressed the piece of wood that had broken away from the frame back into place. It wouldn't stand a close inspection, but from a distance, no one would notice the damage. Looking around, I saw only a large galvanized tub which sat against the far wall, with a hose curled up next to it. At the back of the garage, a set of folding steps led up to a loft or attic.

Still holding both the gun and the flashlight at the ready, I moved over to the steps and slowly climbed up to a point where I could peek into the loft. Again, holding the flashlight away from me, I played it around the space and realized that no one was there.

I climbed up and stepped into the loft, which appeared to be about fifteen feet by twenty-five. The walls and ceiling had been layered with insulation, presumably to soak up any sound. A queen-sized Mattress covered by a fitted grey sheet lay on a platform up against the far wall of the loft. Another sheet and a blanket were folded neatly on the mattress.

Large iron rings had been bolted into each corner of the platform, and a length of thin rope was neatly coiled up next to each of the rings. A vibrator and a few other sex toys were arranged on a table next to the bed. A chair, a toilet and a small sink completed the furnishings.

I was standing there contemplating the horrors that must have occurred in the small space, when I heard the sound of an engine pulling up the driveway. I snapped off the flashlight, drew my gun, and dropped to the floor near the stairs, positioned so that anyone coming up the stairs would have his back to me.

A few moments later, the large garage door slid back, and a vehicle pulled into the space below me. The driver shut off the engine and quickly closed the garage door behind him. Then he flipped a switch that turned on lights both in the loft and the space below. I heard a squeaking sound followed by a louder clunk. Then a voice I recognized as Jason Turner's said, "We're finally home, sweetheart."

The next sound was that of something being dragged across a metal surface of some sort and shortly after came the sound of a long zipper being opened. "Okay, baby," the voice said, "up we go."

I slid back another couple of feet as someone started carefully up the steps. Turner slowly rose into view, one step at a time. He had Ellie over his left shoulder in a fireman's carry. Her head was hanging just below his waist, and his left arm was wrapped around her knees, securing her in place. As his head cleared the opening, he turned, saw me lying on the floor behind him, and said, "Ah, fuck!"

"Ah, fuck is right, asshole." Aiming the gun right at the back of his head, I said, "Step very slowly and carefully up into the room and set the woman on the floor. Then step away."

He held his place, thinking for a moment, and then said, "No, I don't think so."

"You don't have a choice Turner. In another sixty seconds, this place is going to be swarming with cops. It's over; don't make it any harder on yourself than it already is."

"That's a good one, but here's the thing. The truth is that I'd rather just die right here and now, as opposed to spending the rest of my life wasting away in some goddamned prison, so you've got no leverage."

Looking at me with no apparent fear, he said, "It's about eight feet from here down to the concrete floor below. If I just let go of the bitch's knees, she'll drop straight down and land on her head. Twenty to one, she breaks her neck; if not, her brain will be scrambled into mush. So, here's what we'll do. You leave the gun right here and then back away into the far corner. I'll take the gun and back down the stairs. I'll leave the woman down there and take my chances against the cops outside. Your choice, Detective."

"No deal, Turner. You climb up here and set the woman down just like I told you. I'll place you under arrest and maybe a good lawyer can get you off on grounds of insanity or some bullshit like that. If you drop her, I won't shoot you in the head and let you take the easy way out. I'll put a bullet in each elbow and another in each of your knees, and you can spend the rest of your life gimping around prison in searing pain every single goddamn minute."

"I'll bet your Internal Affairs guys wouldn't like that very much."

"You think I give a fuck? Trust me, I don't. You are not going to leave this garage dead, asshole. How healthy you are otherwise is completely up to you."

He stood there for another minute, staring me down and turning over his options. Finally, he sighed and said, "Ah, shit. Okay, you win."

He took another couple of steps up into the loft but appeared to be having trouble squeezing both himself and Ellie through the opening. "Could you give me a hand, at least?" he asked.

I moved around to the wider side of the opening and positioned myself on Turner's left. "Here," he said. "Put your arm around her and help me lift her up."

Still holding my weapon in my right hand, I turned and slipped my left arm between Ellie and Turner's left shoulder, wrapping my arm around her waist. Through the entire ordeal thus far, she had remained completely limp and quiet, but now she moaned, turned her head to the side and looked at me with sheer desperation in her eyes. I got a good grip on her and began lifting her off Turner's shoulder. As I did, Turner dropped down the ladder, leaving me holding Ellie over the open space.

I set the gun aside, wrapped both arms around her, and lifted her into the attic. Then I rolled over, setting her on the floor behind me, and as I did, the garage went dark again. From below, Turner fired two shots wildly in our direction, then the larger garage door slid open. A moment later, it closed again, and I heard the sound of the heavy paddle lock being dropped into the hasp.

Leaving Ellie, I grabbed my gun, slid down the stairs and found my way to the side door. As I opened the door, I heard the sound of Turner's Audi revving up. I ran through the door and pressed up against the side of the building at the front of the garage. Looking down the driveway, I saw Greg just stepping out of his Mustang, which was now blocking the entrance to the driveway.

I watched as Turner threw the Audi into reverse and raced backwards down the drive, slamming into Greg's car. The Mustang was thrown maybe a foot back into the street, but that was all. Two large palm trees guarded either side of the driveway at that point, leaving no way for the Audi to pivot and escape.

It took an eternity for the next five seconds to pass. As Turner sat in the Audi, revving the engine, I lifted my gun into the combat position and began walking slowly down the driveway with the gun trained on the Audi's windshield. I was about ten feet away from the garage when Turner dropped the car into gear and slammed the accelerator to the floor.

I had only a second to fire off a shot and then dive out of the way. The Audi brushed past me and an instant later, slammed through the garage door and shuddered to a violent stop after crashing into the pickup truck that Turner had apparently substituted for his van.

Greg came running up the driveway, his weapon drawn, and we slowly approached the car from either side. I wrenched the driver's door open and saw that the airbag had exploded with the impact. Turner had not taken time to put on his seatbelt, and his head was flopped over, lying at an impossible angle. The bullet hole in his neck probably hadn't helped matters much either.

***

Greg and I holstered our weapons and I said, "Davis is inside. Call for backup and a couple of ambulances."

With that, I ran back into the garage, found the light switch, and flipped it on. I raced up the steps and found Ellie weeping quietly. I sat down on the floor and rolled her into my lap. As gently as I could, I peeled the tape away from her mouth. "Oh, God, Sean," she cried. "Oh, Jesus."

I used my pocketknife to cut away the tape binding her ankles and then cut her wrists free. She threw her arms around my neck and pressed into me, weeping uncontrollably. For the next few minutes, I held her as tightly as I possibly could, while I listened to the sounds of the approaching sirens. They died at the foot of the driveway and a couple of minutes later, a medic climbed the stairs into the attic. "Okay, Miss," he said. "Let's get you out of here and into the ambulance."

He reached a hand out to touch Ellie's arm, and she recoiled, screaming, "No!" and clinging to me even tighter. The medic looked up to me and said, "She's in shock; I'll get a sedative."

I assured Ellie that everything was going to be okay and a minute later, the medic returned. I held her tightly and pressed her head against my chest, soothing her and telling her that she was safe now. The medic gently rolled up her sleeve and administered the sedative. A moment later, she went quiet in my arms and we gently maneuvered her down the stairs and laid her on a stretcher.

Two medics wheeled the stretcher out of the garage into a sea of lights flashing red and blue. I walked the stretcher to a waiting ambulance and asked the medic how long she would be under. "Long enough to get her to the hospital so that the doctors can examine her. They'll give her another sedative that should let her sleep through the rest of the night."

I told the medic to tell the doctor that I'd be checking in on Ellie first thing in the morning and watched as the ambulance carried her away. Then I walked back up the driveway to join Greg.

As the activity swirled around us, he looked first at Jason Turner, lifeless and still in the Audi, waiting for the M. E. and the crime scene techs to arrive. Then he looked back down the drive at the remains of his six-month-old Mustang. Looking back at Turner, he shook his head and said, "Jesus Christ, I hope that son of a bitch had good insurance."

65.

At nine-thirty Saturday morning, I met with Ellie's doctor who told me that while Ellie had been roughly handled and terribly frightened, she had not otherwise been assaulted or injured. "At this point, I can't judge how much psychological damage she might have suffered," the doctor said, "and I'm sure she may need to spend some time talking to a good counselor, but physically, she should be recovered in no time."

Five minutes later, I walked into Ellie's room with a huge bouquet of flowers. She was sitting up in bed and when she turned to see me, tears flooded into her eyes. I set the flowers down on the dresser, then went over and sat on the bed beside her. Crying harder now, she pulled me close. Through the tears, she finally managed to say, "Oh Jesus, Sean; I was so scared."

Holding her as tightly as I could, I whispered, "I'm so, so sorry Ellie, but it's over now and that bastard will never hurt you or anyone else ever again."

Through her sobs, she said, "I can't imagine how he got into my apartment. The police were downstairs, right where they were supposed to be, and the front door was locked just the way I left it. I had just locked both doors and was reaching for my phone to call you, when he was right in front of me and shot me with a stun gun.

"I couldn't do anything before he had me bound and gagged. He showed me the phone, and I saw your initials in the caller I.D., so I knew you were calling, and then I heard you at the door. But I had no way of letting you know what was happening. He kept me there forever, telling me all the things he was going to do to me once he got me back to that garage. When we got there, and he lifted me out of the bag and began carrying me up those stairs, I was sure that you weren't going to get there in time. I wanted to die right then and there, rather than let him have me. And then you were there, and I'll never be able to tell you how grateful I am for that."

I leaned back and dried her tears. "I'm just so thankful that we did get there, Ellie, but I'll never forgive myself for the fact that we didn't catch him before you had to endure that."

***

We sat there for another twenty minutes or so, holding each other and apologizing, until the doctor came in and insisted that it was time for Ellie to get some rest. As the shock of the experience wore off, she recovered fairly quickly and left the hospital late Sunday afternoon. Through it all, Channel 2 News maintained a constant presence outside of the hospital, giving frequent updates on her condition and suggesting, not very subtly, that the abduction of their fearless reporter had been the key to stopping Turner's killing spree. On Tuesday night, Ellie was back on the job with a special report, detailing her experiences and profusely thanking the Phoenix P.D. for her timely rescue.

In the meantime, a search of the attic in Jason Turner's rented garage revealed virtually no end of revolting evidence, including the remaining souvenirs from his uncle's killing spree and the collection that he had begun building of his own. The sick bastard had recorded much of the horror he had inflicted on Allie Martin, Corrine Ray, and Mary Jo Jackson. The recordings left no doubt that Turner, acting alone, was guilty of all three crimes, and watching the video, several seasoned homicide detectives were reduced to tears.

With a couple of days off to rest and relax, I finally had time to call the no-kill animal shelter to see about making arrangements for Zane Grey. The woman who answered the phone told me that I could drop him off on any weekday between the hours of nine and five, and I promised to get him over there within the next couple of days. But one thing or another kept getting in the way, and a week and a half after I'd found him, he was still sleeping on my couch and generally making himself at home.

On the Friday of that week, I invited Ellie to join Sara and me for dinner at Zinc Bistro. It was an experience I didn't particularly want to have, but the two women were extremely curious about each other and I needed to assure Sara that the traumatic experience that Ellie and I had shared was in no way a threat to our relationship.

Dinner seemed to go quite well, at least for the two of them, and they spent much of the evening dissecting my qualities as a boyfriend. They both seemed to get a kick out of my obvious discomfort, and by the end of the dinner, there seemed to be a real chance that the two women might become friends. I wasn't at all sure how I felt about that.

***

The following afternoon found me sitting with a pale ale in my hand out on the covered patio at Jack Oliva's house. The Monsoon Season had begun, and earlier in the afternoon a storm had swept through the Valley, dropping an inch of rain on Oliva's neighborhood and lowering the temperature by about fifteen degrees.

Dressed in a crisp white shirt over jeans and a pair of boots, Oliva appeared to be nearly recovered from his wound and looked to be back in fine form. He took a pull on the beer, looked up at the clouds scudding across the sky, and said, "Fred Turner. How could I possibly have missed that son of a bitch?"

"Shit, Jack, don't be silly. How could you have ever tipped to him? The only reason you had for looking at the soup kitchen was because of Joseph Turner. Once you realized he wasn't the guy, there was no reason to go back looking at the other people who volunteered there, certainly not at somebody who was only there a handful of times.

"I mean, Jesus, when you stop to think about it, there were hundreds of guys who moved through the Deuce at least occasionally, and who would have been suspects just as legitimate as Turner. It would have been different if he'd had left you any real evidence, but he didn't. He was a needle in a fuckin' haystack, Jack.

Nobody would have caught the bastard on the basis of what you had."

Oliva cracked open a couple more beers and handed me one. "I know you're trying to make me feel better, Sean, and I really do appreciate the fact that you caught the asshole for me. I have to tell you, it's a huge load off my mind, knowing that case is finally put to rest."

"Well, I certainly didn't do it alone. And if you want to be strictly fair about it, it was really the goddamn nephew who stumbled onto Turner and then gave him his just desserts. Beyond that, you were a huge help yourself. I wasn't kidding when I said that if it hadn't been for you, my team and I would still be buried up to our asses in those old files, without having the slightest idea who or what we were looking for."

He saluted me with the beer. "You know that I don't believe that either, but I appreciate the fact that you said it."

We sat quietly for a few minutes, watching the remnants of the storm play out around us and then Oliva looked surreptitiously at his watch. "Am I keeping you from something?" I asked.

"No, no. I've got a date tonight and just wondered how late it was getting to be."

Smiling, I said, "You've got a date? Do you mind if I ask who the lucky girl is?"

He took another sip of the beer and said, "One of the nurses from the hospital."

"Not the shapely brunette?"

He nodded, and I said, "Jesus, Jack, you stud. I'm seriously impressed. What is she, about forty-five?"

"Fifty-two, actually. And I know what you're gonna say—that she's too goddamned old for me. But I tell you, Sean, the woman's got a helluva lot of energy for being fifty-two."

I laughed and said, "So where are you taking her?"

"I've got tickets for the Jason Isbell concert at the MIM and then I thought we'd grab dinner at the Mission after."

"You asshole. I really wanted to see that concert but when I went on line twenty-five minutes after ticket sales opened, they were already sold out. How in the hell did you manage that?"

Smiling, he shrugged and said, "I know a guy...."

We sat for another couple of minutes finishing our beers, then I set down my bottle and stuck out my hand. "Thanks for all your help, Jack. I really enjoyed working with you, and I mean that sincerely."

Shaking my hand, he said, "Back at you, Sean; I enjoyed the hell out of it myself. You made an old man very happy."

He walked me back through the house and stood on the porch, leaning against a post as I walked out to my car. I was nearly there when he called out after me, "Hey, Kid..."

I turned, and he saluted me with the beer bottle. "We would have made a helluva team," he said.

"That we would," I replied. "Don't be a stranger, Jack."

He nodded and watched me into the car as I headed off to dinner with Sara.

He was still standing there when I made the turn at the corner and he disappeared from the rearview mirror.

ACKNOWLEDGMENTS

As ever, I'm indebted to several people who generously helped bring this novel to fruition. In particular, I'm grateful to Barbara Peters, owner of the Poisoned Pen Bookstore in Scottsdale, for inspiring the title of the book in an off-hand remark that she made a number of years ago, and I'm especially thankful for the fact that she has created my favorite of all bookstores. Through the years, I've attended scores of events at the Pen and have had the opportunity to meet there virtually all of my favorite crime fiction authors. The store is a fantastic destination for readers and writers alike.

Again, retired homicide detective Tim Moore graciously answered my questions and provided valuable insights into the way the Phoenix Police Department functions and about the mechanics of a homicide investigation. I've taken what I hope are some minor liberties with the information he provided me, but the responsibility for any mistakes I might have made certainly rests with me and not with him.

Special thanks to my friend, Ellie Davis, who has allowed me to use her name for the character of Ellie in this and in previous Sean Richardson novels.

This is my third novel with Moonshine Cove, and I greatly appreciate the care they have taken with my books and the advice, editorial and otherwise, that they have offered along the way. Again, thanks especially to Gene Robinson.

As always, I'd like to thank the readers who have supported my earlier books, and I'm particularly grateful to those who have posted reviews of those books to sites like Amazon, Goodreads and others. On-line reviews, even if they only amount to a couple of sentences or so, are now hugely important to a book's chances of success, and I'm grateful to those who took the time to do so.

Again, thanks to my wife Victoria who has been a constant source of inspiration and support on my journey as a writer and through the years of our life together. As for my cat, Zane Grey, sadly he has not been nearly as consistent in his affection, but all in all, he's still a pretty decent companion. Finally, I owe a huge debt of gratitude to my teacher in the second grade at St. Anthony's in Missoula, Miss Grace Flynn, who impressed upon me at a very early age the importance of good penmanship.

CPSIA information can be obtained
at www.ICGtesting.com
Printed in the USA
LVHW090921051120
670788LV00007BB/617